D0260196

Caroline England was born and brought up in Yorkshire and studied Law at the University of Manchester. She was a divorce and professional indemnity lawyer before leaving the law to bring up her three daughters and turning her hand to writing. Caroline is the author of *The Wife's Secret* (previously called *Beneath the Skin*), the top-ten ebook bestseller *My Husband's Lies*, *Betray Her* and *Truth Games*. She lives in Manchester with her family.

To find out more about Caroline, visit her website
www.carolineenglandauthor.co.uk
or follow her on social media:

Twitter: @CazEngland
Facebook: www.facebook.com/CazEngland1
Instagram: www.instagram.com/cazengland1

Also by Caroline England

The Wife's Secret (previously Beneath the Skin)
My Husband's Lies
Betray Her
Truth Games

The Sinner

Caroline England

PIATKUS

PIATKUS

First published in Great Britain in 2022 by Piatkus

1 3 5 7 9 10 8 6 4 2

Copyright © Caroline England 2022

The moral right of the author has been asserted.

*All characters and events in this publication, other than those
clearly in the public domain, are fictitious and any resemblance
to real persons, living or dead, is purely coincidental.*

All rights reserved.
No part of this publication may be reproduced, stored in a
retrieval system, or transmitted, in any form or by any means, without
the prior permission in writing of the publisher, nor be otherwise circulated
in any form of binding or cover other than that in which it is published
and without a similar condition including this condition being
imposed on the subsequent purchaser.

A CIP catalogue record for this book is available from the British Library.

ISBN 978-0-349-43148-2

Typeset in Garamond by M Rules
Printed and bound in Great Britain by Clays Ltd, Elcograf S.p.A.

Papers used by Piatkus are from well-managed forests
and other responsible sources.

MIX
Paper from
responsible sources
FSC
www.fsc.org
FSC® C104740

Piatkus
An imprint of
Little, Brown Book Group
Carmelite House
50 Victoria Embankment
London EC4Y 0DZ

An Hachette UK Company
www.hachette.co.uk

www.littlebrown.co.uk

To my husband Jonathan – 'I think you can rely on me!'

The Manchester Crematorium

Another coffin; another crematorium, another grieving crowd.

Sometimes it feels as though I'm surrounded by death. But aren't we all? Industrial accidents, car crashes, drownings; ill health, old age. Earthquakes, ethnic cleansing, executions, tsunamis. They buzz all around us on the radio, in newspapers, on the internet and TV. Background noise.

Faces here are like that. Listening to the grief in the air, but not really hearing. Paying their respects but not engaging in sorrow. Friends of friends, neighbours, work colleagues, hangers-on. It's not personal for them. Or maybe they're bewildered first-timers who haven't been here before, haven't felt that slam of gutting emotion we try to keep hidden. Because we're in a public place and we're too bloody scared or embarrassed to let it all out.

But when you've already been there, it brings it all back. The real thing.

God, I hate funerals. A stupid thing to say; who doesn't? Yet it is cathartic on many levels: respect for the dead; a final goodbye; continuity and hope for the living; an acknowledgement that one's relative was loved; a celebration of their life.

Or maybe just the nailed-down confirmation that the bastard is dead.

1

New Year's Eve

Cordelia

Perched in my usual pew, I watch the tall, handsome and impressive vicar move to his lectern, smooth back his shock of thick hair and take a deep breath before speaking.

'Sisters, brothers, family,' he begins, his voice echoey in the red sandstone church. He gestures to the forty or so parishioners who comprise his regular flock. 'Thank you all for joining me tonight. Admittedly it's late for the little ones, but what better reason than to welcome in a brand new year.'

He smiles at the line of his front-row ladies. 'And to kneel in prayer, joining in unity to celebrate the glory of the Lord. To catch God's heart and ask him that the New Year will be one of opportunity and transformation for ourselves and our community. To mend broken lives and work together for each other. To say thank you to God for all our blessings, the many good things he has offered us this year – the friendship, the healing, the fraternity, the love.'

His expression more grave, he lifts his arms to the

nineteenth-century stained-glass window above him. 'To confess our sins in penitence and faith.'

Though Abbey is squashed between us, I hear Harriet's intake of air. My mother-in-law has never committed a sin – unless one counts gluttony, greed and sloth.

Berating myself for such an unkind thought, I revert to my husband's eloquent tones.

'In the name of the Father and of the Son and of the Holy Spirit . . . '

'Amen.'

'The Lord Jesus Christ be with you.'

'And also with you.'

'Let us pray.'

Mindful of the disabled and the elderly, Vincent doesn't insist on actual kneeling, but out of habit I do, and I drift as the prayers waft over me.

I'm eventually brought back by my daughter's elbow. 'Mum,' she hisses. 'Don't be embarrassing, it's nearly time.'

'Sorry,' I reply, quickly scrabbling to my feet at her usual reprimand.

The six bellringers head for the tower door. Tonight they are here to chime in 'new beginnings'. Thirteen years ago, I was one of them, fervent and joyous, my eyes on my heavily pregnant stomach and thanking the Lord for his blessings.

Blinking the memory away, I smile as Vincent approaches. He cups Abbey in one arm and me in the other, then pecks the tops of our heads. 'My family,' he says. 'I am one blessed man.' He bends to Harriet's powdery cheek and plants a kiss. 'Made complete by my dearest mother.'

He reverts to his congregation and grins. 'I hope you are all wearing your hats, gloves and scarves. It's somewhat nippy outside, but once we're accustomed to the chill, we'll breathe in the night air, watch the bells as they peal out their joyful chimes from the tower and pray.'

His elderly ladies pull up their collars and nod enthusiastically, and though the younger generation look a little dubious, as ever Vincent's persuasion and enthusiasm are hard to deny.

'A few words before we brave the weather,' he says. He glances at me with the secret smile he gave to me in this very spot two decades ago. 'On New Year's Eve groups of church bellringers gather all over the world to pray, reflect and ring in the New Year, so we are participating in a long tradition. At the great turning point of "In Memoriam" – Tennyson's wonderful exploration of time and eternity, mortality and resurrection, doubt and faith – come his famous and beautiful lines which begin . . .'

He clears his throat. '"Ring out, wild bells, to the wild sky." It concludes – and do forgive me if I misremember a line – "Ring in the valiant man and free, / The larger heart, the kindlier hand; / Ring out the darkness of the land, / Ring in the Christ that is to be."'

As Harriet leads the enthusiastic clapping, her latest best chum whispers loudly in her ear. 'Your son is a marvellous orator, isn't he? How he finds the time to write such exquisite, meaningful sermons and speeches, I'll never know.'

He takes a theatrical bow. 'Thank you, Monica. Your appreciation makes it all the more worthwhile.' He signals to the arched doorway. 'Onward to our local benefactor's resting place in the graveyard!'

I rotate to take Abbey's arm, but she's already slotted it through her daddy's. Feeling the usual tiny stab at their two-person club,

I smile at the mostly female throng and motion for them to go ahead. Bringing up the rear, I wonder what my prayers – or perhaps my contemplation or wishes or hopes – might be this year; there's no point asking for what has already been firmly declined – both by God and my husband.

'Dee!'

Hearing my big sister's voice, I stop and turn. She slides to a standstill on the icy path. 'Bloody hell, I thought I'd missed it!' Looking edgy and alternative despite the bobble hat, she catches her breath. 'Happy New Year, Dee Dee. Well, almost.'

'And to you!' I look over her shoulder. 'No Britt?'

'She's fast asleep.'

'Oh, of course. There was no need to trek out into the cold this year.'

Mari raises her dark eyebrows. 'And miss all the fun.' She squints at the parish ladies circling Vincent. 'Warmed by purple-perm adoration, eh? Now I know why our debonaire rector doesn't need a coat.'

I chuckle despite myself. 'Mari—'

'Anyhow . . . ' she quickly continues before I can admonish her. 'It's nearly time to call our little bro.'

It is the one time we're guaranteed Ed will answer his mobile. Wherever he happens to be, he'll always pick up to wish me and Mari a happy New Year just after UK midnight.

The thought of my beach-bum brother brings a genuine grin. 'All for one and one for all!'

Mari wraps her arms around me. 'Always. Even if the silly sod is on the other side of the world.'

As the bells start their knell, I sniff. Ed is the one musketeer who managed to escape.

2

New Year's Day

Cordelia

Though Harriet hasn't yet lifted a finger to help, I've been putting out food and replacing platters, filling glasses and flushing the downstairs loo since three o'clock.

'So sorry, like everything else in this cherished vicarage, it's as old as the hills,' Vincent says to Mrs Craven this time. Slipping his arm around my waist, he kisses my forehead. 'Would you do the honours, darling? I know it's a chore, but we will get it fixed, I promise.'

He reverts to his audience. 'I've no idea how my beautiful wife does it, but she has the technique. It must be her fair hands.'

Mrs Craven pats my arm. 'Thank you, dear. I did close the lid.'

'No worries at all.'

Although Vincent only invited the ministry team and their partners, it feels as if all the congregation are stuffed in my kitchen, celebrating and taking turns to espouse their New

Year's resolutions. What are mine? Communicating with my daughter would be a start.

'I'll sort out the toilet then look in on Abbey,' I say to no one in particular.

When I reach her bedroom, I take a breath before knocking. 'How's tricks?' I ask.

Her laptop open, she's lying on the new furry throw I bought her for Christmas. She mildly frowns. 'I'm just watching a prog, so . . . '

'Oh, OK. Can I fetch you something to eat?'

She nods to the plate on her side table. 'Dad brought me up some stuff earlier, so . . . '

I withdraw at the loaded '*So* . . . ' I know teenage years can be a challenge, but it feels as though I've been the recipient of that word ever since she could talk. I make my way to the stairs, but instead of going down to the clamour below, I climb up to my attic sitting room, step to the mirror and study my reflection. Am I still 'beautiful' as Vincent described? Is the feisty Dee Dee Stephens still somewhere behind the sensible haircut and clothes? Or am I simply the servile, toilet-flushing vicar's wife?

'You're only thirty-five; you're only flaming thirty-five,' I say to the pale woman staring back. And though I'm fully aware it was me who wilfully chose this life fifteen years ago, I'm suddenly overwhelmed by a need to escape, so I grapple with a hoodie and my trainers, grab my mobile and hurry down to the hallway.

I pause at the door. Should I take keys? Nope; this sprawling old house isn't just mine and Vincent's; it's everybody's, portals and rooms open to all and sundry, whatever the weather. As *if she's listening to my thoughts, Harriet's deep chortle echoes* through. Yes, it's her home too, the controller and warder, ever bustling and busy and loud.

Feeling a spike of guilt for my unkindness, I look at the sky and blow out my hot agitation. The rain has stopped, so that's something. I'll walk until the desire to bolt has receded; walk until they've noticed I've gone. Then I'll retrace my steps and retreat, climb from my angry body and morph back to what I signed up for.

I glance up to my sitting-room window and wryly smile. Yes, 'the woman in the attic', as Mari calls me.

Wishing I'd brought gloves, I set a brisk pace and listen to my feet smack the suburban pavements. Save for the flash and twinkle of Christmas lights, the dusky streets are still, the handsome Victorian houses seemingly empty and quiet.

'If only mine was too . . .' I mutter out loud.

Yet I know that isn't fair: a vocation's a vocation. Even at the tender age of twenty I knew that. And I really have nothing to complain about; I'm married to a good man who looks after me, a husband who went beyond the call of duty when I desperately needed him to.

Pushing *that* thought away, I hunker against the fine drizzle, shove my hands in my pockets and continue to tromp. Will either Vincent or Abbey have noticed my absence? And why do I have the paradoxical need for them to? I chuckle to myself. Mari would have a theory. My psychologist big sister always does, even if at times she gets too close to the bone with her analysis of the relationship between me and our dad. Not that there is or has been a bond between us for many years.

The rainfall abruptly full pelt, I take in my bearings and spot a covered bus shelter opposite. Though a car is approaching, there's time to sprint over, so I splash through the puddles. But when I reach the other side, I realise my mobile has fallen from my pocket. Snapping around, I scan the tarmac and see it glint in the path of the oncoming vehicle. My phone is the one thing that only I have sole access to – including my kitchen, my lounge, my bedroom, my books, even the flaming bathroom, not to mention my husband – so I lift my palm in a 'halt' sign and step onto the road. Surely the motorist will see me and slow down? But the blinding full beam and shrill blare of a horn tell me otherwise, and before I can react, my feet have gone from beneath me and I'm thudding heavily to the ground.

Winded and shocked, I stay frozen for moments, but when I finally glance around there's no vehicle and no one else, just the steady rain, still lashing down. Good God, the driver didn't stop. Sure, I was at fault, yet it wasn't as though he or she didn't notice me, the ringing in my ears and flashing shapes in my vision are evidence of that.

I slowly hitch to the kerb and test fingers and toes. Though my pulse is galloping, I'm actually OK; the bonnet caught my side and nothing feels broken; I'll have a bruised buttock and grazed palms, but I'll live. I rock forwards to stand, but my legs refuse to comply, then my heart follows suit, thrashing as if to burst through my chest, so I lower my head and gently talk to myself like I used to: breathe, Dee, just focus on breathing, in and out, in and out.

A shadow then a voice penetrates my nauseous fug. 'Hello? Are you OK?' A man's Mancunian twang. 'Are you injured? Do you need any help?'

'No, I'm fine.' I briefly look up, but I can't quite focus. 'Thank you. I just need a moment.'

The figure doesn't move. 'You don't look it. What happened?'

'No, I'm good.' Feeling self-conscious and stupid, I will him to leave. 'A car was approaching and in my haste I slipped, that's all. I'm just catching my breath.'

'Can I help you up?'

'No, thanks. I'll do it in a minute.'

I suck in air. Thank goodness I didn't puke; that would be mortifying. It's still teeming though, the rain like small spikes on my skin. 'You'll get wet,' I manage. 'I'm really OK. Don't let me stop you going on your way.'

Sound filters through – the hum of a stationary car, presumably this man's. But when I squint through the squall, I see he's parked on the very spot where my phone fell.

He follows my gaze. 'What's the matter?'

I sniff back the need to cry. 'I think you've just run over my mobile.'

'Have I?'

Squatting on his haunches, he peers beneath his vehicle and pulls out my treasure which he rubs on his jeans. 'You're lucky, it looks fine. Nothing appears broken.' Handing it over, he frowns. 'How about you?'

I awkwardly laugh. *Lucky*, I'm not; I ran out of that several years ago. 'All good, thanks. Well, except my pride.'

He eyes me a little strangely. 'Pride. Yes, that can take a while to heal. If ever.' Seeming to notice the downpour, he gestures to his car. 'Do you want a lift home?'

I do, preferably one that transports me directly from here into the privacy of my sitting room, but this man is a stranger and it'd be too, too embarrassing to ask for a ride to the vicarage, of all places. Should I call Vincent and ask him to fetch me?

11

No, I can't risk a throwback to those days when he thought I'd completely 'lost it'. Though in truth, I had. Besides, he's been drinking all day.

'Or you can borrow a brolly.' The man's voice breaks into my thoughts. He looks vaguely familiar; do I know him from somewhere?

'Thank you . . .' I quickly consider what to do. The rain has seeped through to my skin and my hot flush has been replaced by icy shivering. This thirty-something guy seems OK. 'Thank you, that's kind of you. If you don't mind your car seat getting wet . . .' Then picturing the millions of carriers in the boot of Vincent's Volvo, 'If you have a plastic bag, I could sit on it . . .'

He laughs. 'We're cool.'

He offers his palm. Though taking it feels strangely intimate, my limbs have solidified and a dull ache has set in. 'Thanks,' I say, as he hefts me towards him.

For a beat and another, he observes me intently, then releases my hand and climbs into his car. When I've done the same, he tosses me a towel from a kitbag behind him. 'So where are we going?'

Distracted by my mobile, I don't reply. There's no message or text from either Vincent or Abbey. 'Sorry, what was that?'

'Do you want to go straight home or have a quick drink to dry off?' His chiselled features are softened by an easy, white grin. 'The Horse and Jockey has an open fire.'

I go back to the blank screen. So much for 'family'. But in all honesty, I've been invisible for years.

Disgruntlement flaring, I study my saviour. His shoulders are wet and his cropped hair's sparkling with raindrops because he had the kindness to stop. Goodness knows how I appear, but right now I don't care. 'We're both pretty drenched. Do you think they'll let us in?' I ask with a shaky chuckle.

He sheds his jacket and puts the car into gear. 'There's only one way to find out,' he replies.

3

Cordelia

The haunting sound of Chopin's Nocturnes in the background, my new friend doesn't speak as he drives. Although accepting a lift from a stranger – let alone going to a pub – is a surreal and dangerous thing to do, there's a tight knot of rebellion lodged in my chest, so I blot out my jangling nerves and keep a careful eye on the landmarks we pass. I soon gather we're on our way to Chorlton, and if the guy is abducting me, I reason there are cameras everywhere these days. No one gets away with an illicit kiss, a red light, a drunken moment or crime without the incriminating photograph popping up on Facebook or Twitter. Except invisible me, in all probability.

I inwardly sigh. Vincent will twig I've disappeared eventually. Won't he?

Still astonished that I said yes, I glance at my Good Samaritan and take in his sculpted profile. My eyes slide to his muscled forearms and I smile at the image of Guido Reni's torso-toned Archangel Michael defeating Satan. Maybe he is a Malakim, one of Harriet's human-like messengers of God, swooping down in my hour of need. *Did I really believe in all that biblical baloney once* upon a time? Yes, pretty fervently. Or was the delirium simply my huge and obvious crush on the charismatic man who later became my husband? The one I couldn't get enough of back then.

When I focus again, heat shoots to my cheeks. As though he's been reading my carnal thoughts, my chauffeur has parked on a residential side street and he's studying me through the glow of streetlight.

'What is it?' I ask, quickly averting my gaze to my sensible trousers. Though still damp, patches of dirt have started to dry. Oh God, what a stupid idiot I was; irresponsible too; I might have injured myself badly and I have Abbey to think of.

'You've bled. You must have hit your head . . .' Taking the towel from my lap, he pads my forehead, then he moves to my hair and explores my scalp with expert fingers.

Detecting a musky aroma of deodorant or shampoo, I hold my breath and try not to flinch, not just from the tiny stab of pain but from this man's proximity and the startling stir of attraction in the pit of my belly.

'Yeah, there's a small laceration from your fall. Grit probably, but it looks clean. It's stopped bleeding but it had seeped . . .' He demonstrates with his own temple and smiles. 'Well, it wouldn't be a particularly good look. Maybe for Halloween, but not New Year's . . .' He abruptly turns away and climbs out. 'It's stopped raining. Come on then, let's go.'

'Right – OK.' Shaking myself back from the ridiculously sensual moment, I open the door and swing out my stiff legs. I'm achy all over, particularly my ribs, and I wonder if I have damaged them, but the thought is fleeting; stupid though it is in the context of the shocking incident, the need for a mirror to inspect my appearance feels more imperative just now.

Not quite rubbing shoulders, we stride to the Tudor-style building. Once inside, I gesture to the sign for the toilets. 'I just need to—'

'Are you all right? Do you feel nauseous?'

'No, I just . . . ' I feel my deep blush. 'I just need the loo.'

'Ah. OK. What are you drinking?'

'A glass of wine would be great, thanks.'

His brief friendliness from earlier appears to have disappeared. 'Anything specific?'

'No, just house plonk will be lovely but red would be preferable.'

'Of course; like Holy Communion. I'll find a table . . . '

The ladies is empty, thank goodness. I take a much-needed pee, then turn to my injuries. My right buttock feels tender but my whole left side positively sizzles. I drag off the soaked hoodie, and pull up the sleeve of my vicar's-wife blouse. My elbow and upper arm are grazed, and when I smooth fingers over my ribs, it's sore beneath my bra line. But both are manageable, so now it's just a question of my face . . .

Smiling wryly to myself for caring so much, I step to the sink and examine my reflection. It's not a pretty picture: any trace of blood has gone, but my usually neat bob is half frizzy and half matted, and the 'small laceration' has stained it on one side. I'm perfectly aware a hit-and-run isn't something to laugh at, yet a peculiar mirth bubbles up to my throat. This type of mishap doesn't happen to sensible, passive Cordelia Hardy. Nor does popping to the pub for a drink with a good-looking guy whose name I don't even know yet. I'm almost tempted to take a quick snap for Mari's amusement with the quip: **Pink streaks! Bet you a tenner you'll never guess what happened and where**

I am? But my saviour's comment from just now suddenly hits. What did he say about the wine? *Holy Communion.* What does that mean?

My heart races at the phrase as I wash my face. Has he attended St Andrew's at some point? Is that why he seems familiar? Please no; that would be too humiliating. I routinely make the effort to remember the features, name and backstory of every churchgoer, but if it was thirteen years ago . . .

Brought back down to earth, I take a steadying breath and enter the heaving front bar. Clearly a gastropub, the lounge is chock-a-block with diners, but there's no sign of him. Half-hoping he's gone, I thread through a line of people waiting for a table and find another room. Will I even recognise the guy? Well, yes. Fairly tall and lithe, dark hair and stubble. Striking green eyes and those muscled arms.

I spot him near the open fire as promised, but as I gaze another thought occurs. Was his 'Holy Communion' comment actually menacing? Should I bolt whilst his head is down to his mobile? As though reading my mind, he looks up and smiles that compelling white smile, so I make my way over and perch opposite him.

'All OK?' he asks. 'No headache or dizziness?'

'No.'

'No nausea or vomiting?'

'No, but . . .' I didn't intend to say anything but the question flies out. 'Do you know me?'

He eyes me a little too long for comfort. 'I was at Grasmere Road the same time as you,' he eventually says.

My primary school. That throws me. 'Oh, really?'

'You don't remember me.'

I was only there for one year before high school and no, I don't

17

recall him at all. My cheeks burn again. 'Sorry, I don't recollect your name.'

Frowning, he takes a swig of his honey-coloured drink. 'It's Calvin. Cal Rafferty.'

The hot flush spreads. 'Sorry, I have a dreadful memory. Please tell me you weren't in my class.'

He shakes his head.

'My brother, Ed's?'

'Yup.' He nods to the glass of wine on the table. 'It's Australian Shiraz. Hope that's all right.'

'Yes. Thank you.' Then, still needing to know, 'Do you go to our church? The Anglican church in Didsbury? St Andrew's?'

His demeanour relaxing, he throws back his small measure and grins. 'Religion? Hell, no.'

'I take it you're not a fan?'

'I'm not; you only have to glimpse the world news to see it does far more harm than good.'

Sipping my drink, I don't reply. Vincent would have a well-reasoned, equanimous and charming answer to that, but I gave up trying to defend God's actions long ago.

'On a personal level too,' he continues. 'The *helping* clergy, for example. Help isn't praying or asking some divine being to assist; it's hands-on doing it. Being practical, grounded, effective. And even those few do-gooders who don't have a less-than-devout agenda, they never stop to consider who they're "doing good" for.' He lifts his arms. 'It's for themselves. All altruism is. Which is fine to a point. But too many let it spill over into sanctimonious control. And the recipients have to be oh-so bloody grateful.' He peers at me then. 'Am I being offensive? In all likelihood you're one of them.'

Sanctimonious control. Yes, that's my mother-in-law to a T.

18

Picturing Harriet's sucked-in cheeks, I chuckle. 'A do-gooder? Me? Unlikely these days, and if I was one once, I failed miserably.'

'You don't look or sound like the failing type.'

'*Type?* Well, thanks for that.'

'So, I have offended you now.'

I consider asking what kind of person he assumes I am – or even letting out the old Dee Dee and *challenging* him – but he rubs his head.

'Sorry, rant over. Are you still feeling well? Not dazed or confused?'

In all honesty, I feel both, but from his soft gaze, I gather he's talking about the bump to my head.

'I think I'll live.'

'Glad to hear it.' He nods to my glass. 'Drink up and I'll drive you home.'

'Only if it's all right. I can always catch the—'

'I wouldn't offer if it wasn't.'

'OK, thanks. You could drop me at the Didsbury lights if it's no trouble. I can walk from there . . .'

4

Cordelia

Avoiding street lamps and pitted puddles, I grip the umbrella and yawn as I head for the park. The glass of wine has sapped me. And the accident, of course. A hit-and-run driver a mile or so away from my sheltered, middle-class village! It's shocking, but illusory. Despite my injuries, it seems dreamlike and long ago. Then there's my bizarre diversion home. That feels more tangible and real, slightly wild and exciting too, if I'm honest. Not that I am *honest*. Me and Vincent threw it out of the window long ago.

I pull my thoughts back to Calvin Rafferty, Cal.

'Didsbury lights if it's no trouble.'

I sigh at my own words. Why do I always do that? Humble, apologetic and hesitant, instead of just 'thanks'. He dropped me at the intersection as asked, but as I waited to cross, he wound down the window and called me. 'Dee Dee. It's raining. Take this,' he said.

It felt strange to hear my childhood name on his lips. Except for Mari and Ed, everyone calls me Cordelia these days. Shaking the spark of *something* away, I close the umbrella and turn into the driveway of the large, ramshackle vicarage, allegedly my home.

Taking a deep breath, I hop up the steps and reach for the handle. Has anyone noticed my absence? Or even locked me out? But as the door swings open, a cacophony of sounds and smells greet me – the roast we had yesterday, the mouldy, dank aroma I've never managed to vanquish, the heady smell of Harriet's hair lacquer *and* her shrill voice. Should I say hello? It might be fun to witness the shocked expressions of 'Team St Andrew's' . . . Yet outwardly I'm no longer deranged; I'm dry and the blood was erased by that impenetrable stranger who seemed to swing between indifference and anger and tenderness.

Deciding it best to show my face, I drag a brush through my hair and pop my head around the kitchen jamb. His flushed hairline a telltale sign that he has imbibed plenty, Vincent is surrounded by a fresh bunch of parishioners hanging on to his every word.

'Darling,' he says, calling me over. 'Have you met Jacqueline Carmichael? I'm persuading her to join us. A new year, a new church family. Convince her, Cordelia.'

Jacqueline titters. 'I think you've already done that, Reverend.' She offers me her hand. 'Lovely to meet you, Cordelia. What a thoroughly charming husband you have. He's been singing your praises and you are indeed very beautiful.'

A jolt of guilt hits my belly. 'That's very kind, thank you.'

I duly chat to Jacqueline about St Andrew's and Vincent's undoubted achievements over the years. Then he takes me to one side. 'Are you having a lovely time, darling? More party-goers, which is wonderful, but I think we're running short of nibbles and so on. Any more of where that delicious bruschetta came from?'

'I'll see what I can rustle up.'

'Marvellous. I'd be lost without you.'

'Are you coping, dear?' Her ears ever hound-like, Harriet has bustled forward to join us. 'If you need any help whatsoever, Cordelia, I'll just be over there, listening to poor Monica's woes.'

Vincent squeezes his mother's arm. 'A stalwart as always.' He pecks me on the forehead. 'Thank you, darling.' Then gesturing towards the hallway with a theatrical grimace, 'And when you have a moment, could you do the honours with the . . . '

'The downstairs loo.' Unsure if the image it invokes is hilarious or tragic, I swallow back my mixed emotions and nod. 'Of course, chopped tomatoes and nibbles first, then I'll get right to it.'

5

Calvin

Breathing in the chilly night, Cal hops up his front steps and glances at the moody sky. The heavy rain has stopped, but a smatter of wet splashes his cheeks. Fine hail? Even snow? Not the latter, he hopes. Too many painful memories from childhood come with a downfall. And on a more practical level, Mancunians can't cope with even a small covering – there'll be slips, falls and accidents, gridlock on the roads. He and his colleagues are busy enough as it is, so it won't be a good start to the month.

Cooking aromas from next door pierce the keen air. Tonight it's an intoxicating blend he can't quite grasp. The family are a recent addition to his long row of Victorian terraces; indeed, his neighbours in general change pretty frequently, but Cal likes the nomadic and eclectic mix in his street; he welcomes the privacy. Sure, he says hello and exchanges a few pleasantries when he sees any of them, but intimacy isn't required.

And that is just perfect.

Not bothering with lights, he saunters to the kitchen, sloshes an inch of brandy into a tumbler and ambles to the lounge.

He flops back on the settee and absently watches the sleet tap his bay window. What a night. The God squad, do-gooders, religion. And stunning Dee Dee Stephens. During that tumultuous year at school and beyond, she never gave him so much as a second glance.

He throws backs the sharp nectar and grimaces. Well, she has now.

6

Mariana

Mari is completely awake. Why she went to bed at eleven-thirty, she doesn't know. It isn't that early by most people's standards, but she's always been a night owl, which is why it's a bugger that her employment is mostly nine to five.

Watching the shadows on the ceiling, she tries a different mindset: *Come on, Mari, look at tonight's sleeplessness as a good thing. Clear your head and think of strategies for your patients.* With an effort she shifts her troublesome thoughts to her appointments next week. In fairness, she loves her job. The desire to interpret and study human behaviour was there from an early age – wanting to climb in other people's souls, see what makes them tick and ultimately help them from themselves. It's just a shame she's never quite understood her own feelings and failings, or been able to help herself. Especially now, with these churning, jumbling emotions which plague her every night.

She turns to her partner and softly combs the blonde hair from her forehead. Her skin is as smooth and shiny as an apple's. Then there's her perfect nose and those full, inviting lips. Bubbly and chatty when they get into bed, Britt always drops off the moment she pulls down her eye mask, gliding as effortlessly through sleep as she does sentience.

Mari sighs and rolls away. Her smiley, beautiful Britt. She felt a shocking thwack of attraction the moment she fell into her glorious wake over a year ago now. It's still there, each moment, every day. Is that why she feels so bloody insecure and jealous?

She puffs out a stream of trapped air. Yes, Mariana Stephens, the tenacious, confident woman who rarely worried about anything, is fearful now.

Starting at the sudden peal of her mobile, she snatches it up and peers at the screen. Abbey? Why on earth is her niece calling at this time?

'Abbey,' she says quietly, 'one minute.'

She slips from the mattress, heads to the bathroom and sits on the loo. 'Abbey, are you still there?' she asks, tugging on her robe.

'Yeah, I'm here.'

'Are you OK? Is your mum OK?'

'That's why I'm calling.'

Abbey's posh voice sounds thin and slightly whiny, but that's expected when one has just turned fifteen. Whilst Mari and her siblings didn't have the questionable benefits of a private education, she was pretty peevish herself at that age. That or bloody bolshie, and not just as a teenager.

'What's up?' she asks.

Her niece audibly takes a big breath. It isn't unusual for her to moan about her mum. On the one hand, Mari feels a little disloyal – Dee is her younger sister, after all – but on the other, Abbey needs to sound off from time to time, and that's far preferable to bottling it up. Which is precisely what Dee does; what she's always done. And whilst Abbey's complaints are mostly petty adolescent angst, they all arise from Dee's ridiculous down-trodden passivity. It drives Mari bonkers too.

'So I needed stuff from the bathroom and Mum was in there . . .' Abbey starts.

Mari cringes. Poor Dee Dee. Lack of privacy or what? That bloody vicarage doesn't even have a lock on the downstairs bog. '*Sorry, Mari. Health and safety, apparently,*' Dee explained when the bolt was removed, barely even rolling her eyes.

'She was having a bath and though the water was bubbly, she . . .'

Mari resists the urge to laugh. At least Dee wasn't mas-turbating. Though would she, anyway? Certainly not with a vibrator – where the hell would she stash it?

'She . . . ?' she prompts.

'Well, she tried to slip further down and conceal them, but she had these scratches on her shoulder and down her arm. I mean, that's weird, isn't it? All she does is hide away and read books in the loft. Where did they come from?'

Mari straightens. 'What kind of scratches?'

'Not cuts like that. I'd have said if they were.'

'OK, glad to hear it. What did they look like, then?'

'Grazes, I suppose.'

That does seem a little odd. 'Did you ask her?'

'Of course not! I just left the room. But I couldn't get to sleep for thinking about it.'

Mari snorts to herself. Communication, or rather lack of it. Same old story she hears every day. 'I'm sure she'd tell you if you asked.'

'No, she wouldn't. She'd just say it was nothing.' She mimics her mum's voice. '*Nothing for you to worry about, love.*' Her tone becomes derisory. 'Like terrorism, global warming, nits, bullying and the rest.'

'All the assurances mums give to protect their kids, to stop them from fretting—'

'Maybe when they're five, not fifteen.' The sulkiness goes up a notch. 'Why does she have to be that way? My friends' mums aren't. It's embarrassing, and I hardly need protecting; I'm almost an adult.'

'True. Perhaps you need to tell her that. Explain how you feel. One thing's for sure, it's born out of love . . . '

A dramatic, teenage groan. 'I knew you'd say that. But . . . '

'But?'

'Do you think she's OK?'

'I do, Abbey, honestly. And if I was worried, I'd tell you. OK?'

'OK. At least I'm tired now. Night night, Aunt Mariana.'

'Night, kiddo.'

Making her way to the bedroom, Mari smiles wryly. That child is far too like her – she called her 'Aunt Mariana' to wind her up. But she likes her vitality and humorous defiance; she wants her to be a strident and strong young woman like she was.

She abruptly stops at the door. A figure is sitting at the end of her bed. It's not Britt but Mari's mum, Felicity. Though dead fourteen years, she turns and smiles softly.

'You are brilliant, resourceful and brave, Mariana. And still so young. You can reach the very top. Don't let anyone or anything hold you back.'

Mari blinks her mother and the familiar words away. Yes, the spirited woman Mariana Stephens once *was*. Her eyes slide to her sleeping lover. Where the bloody hell has she gone?

7

Cordelia

'Hello, Vincent. You're looking particularly dapper today.'

'Thank you, Mariana. A compliment from you always brightens the hour. Cordelia is having a well-earned rest in her—'

'Padded cell?'

'Lovely sitting room, I feel, is a more apt description . . .'

'Right you are, Vinny.'

Mari's conversation with Vincent floats up to my attic snug. Moments later, she appears in person.

'Those flaming stairs creak more each time I come up.' She rakes back her tousled mass of dark hair. 'Tell me you have something to drink; I'm parched.'

Silently wincing, I stand from the sofa. The grazes have stopped stinging, but my top ribs seem to have worsened. When I peer in the mirror to examine them, I expect to see a massive bruise beneath my bra, but nothing has appeared. It's disappointing in a weird way, but good too. What on earth would I say to Vincent if he happened to notice before bed?

'I have red wine, tea or coffee. If you want white, you have to brave the kitchen.'

'Bloody hell, *hot* drinks?' Mari turns and squints at the sideboard. 'Praise be; it's a miracle! You've finally bought a kettle for up here.'

I chuckle. 'It was a Christmas present to myself. Just don't tell Harriet or any of—'

'Vinny's harem. Yes, team harem; it even rhymes. It looked as though there were half a dozen downstairs even now.' She glances at her watch. 'Don't they have homes to go to?'

'It seems not. What are you having?'

Mari flops down on the sofa. 'I'm tempted to go for the white wine just to ruffle a few feathers, but I can't be arsed to trek down again. Red. A large glass, please.'

I smile in anticipation. Red wine. Every time I feel a twinge of discomfort, it reminds me of my New Year's Day adventure. I swing from disbelief, guilt and embarrassment to a sense of danger, but there's excitement too, and in truth my dull daily routine has been lifted by the prospect of unravelling all these emotions with Mari, the one person I can confide in.

I pour us both a glass and take a big breath. 'Guess what happened—'

Mari speaks at the same time. 'Sorry I'm later than planned. Viola called and I couldn't get rid of her.'

Tensing at the mention of my half-sister's name, I fall quiet and sip my drink.

'She's trying to get Dad into a home, poor sod. Or rather, Gilly-witch is. One fall when he was a bit pissed and the bloody woman is determined to get him under lock and key. I already knew about it, though, as Dad got in first by ringing me.' She raises her eyebrows. 'You'll know what his first words were: *How sharper than a serpent's tooth it is to have a thankless child!*'

30

She pauses. 'Oh, come on, Dee. Even you can see the humour in that. Or satire, perhaps.'

I study my fingernails. There was nothing remotely funny about the shocking discovery that our father had a mistress and a baby on the way. Though years have slipped by, I haven't spoken to him since.

Mari peers at me. 'Come on, Dee, you're thirty-five. You can't just put your hands over your ears and not listen or pretend Dad and Gilly don't exist. And it isn't poor Viola's fault she was born.' Her features crease into the usual concern. 'Bottling it up isn't good for you; you know that.'

'I'm fine, thanks, Mariana.'

'Are you, though? Dad made a choice, a crappy one for all of us, but you've let it rule your life for too long now.'

Rule my life's a pretty strong statement. I'm happy; I have a daughter and a husband who's—'

'So busy selling God to his parishioners and showing off that he's never here for you.'

Heat spreading in my chest, I don't reply. Mari does this straight-talking analysis from time to time. I know she wants the best for me, but I wish she'd just stop.

'Look, I'm not saying Vincent is a bad guy, but let's face it, you were on the rebound when you met him.'

'Rebound? From what?'

'From Dad, of course.' Mari sighs and takes my hand. 'Look, I know you don't like to speak about it, but you'd been his special girl for fourteen years; you were certain of his adoration. You must have felt . . . well, dumped, I imagine.'

A memory flashes in of Dad cowering away from me. Needing to defuse the rising panic, I smooth the worn arm of the sofa. 'Very technically put. Can we talk about something else, please?'

'The discovery that he wasn't who you'd thought was debilitating. It left a gaping, confusing hole. So you went for the opposite – security, stability and control, the ready-made family of the Church. It was perfectly understandable, but you were . . . well, still pretty young when Vincent took you under his—'

'Enough, Mari! I don't know what's eating you today, but you have no idea how I feel – or felt – about anything so—'

'Tell me then, Dee. Perhaps it's time to talk properly about – well, everything.'

Though I grit my teeth, my anger flies out. 'It seems to me you're doing all the *talking*, and actually you're just being a bitch.'

Clearly surprised, Mari jolts back. 'Well, that's . . . silly. I'm simply endeavouring to—'

'Help?' Identifying a liberating fury, I stand. 'Let's try it on you then, shall we? After Mum protecting us from the truth for years, we discovered Dad had shagged anyone and everyone who wore a skirt. So what did you do?' I put a finger on my chin. 'Let's see. You went off to university and emulated him by shagging anyone and everyone who had a penis, then you moved on to the skirts.'

Mari stares coldly. 'There has only ever been one *skirt*, as you put it. You know that.'

Sighing, I flop down again. Where the hell did that tirade come from? And at my sister, of all people. 'Sorry, I know. Britt isn't a skirt, she's a person and a very lovely one too.' I reach out a hand. 'I was completely out of order there. Sorry.'

'You were.' The *icy gaze is splintered by Mari's infectious*

32

laugh. 'But go, Dee Dee Stephens! The legendary temper is back. Have you banged your head or something?'

Finally! Now's the moment to share. But Mari squints. 'You have; I can tell ...'

I frown. The *laceration,* as Cal put it, is hidden by my hair. None of my other injuries are visible. 'Ah, so you've been talking to Abbey.'

'She was worried about you.'

I know I sound childish, but I can't help myself. 'Yeah, so concerned that neither she nor Vincent noticed I was gone for, well, ages.'

'Gone where? When?'

'Nowhere important.' I try to push the hurt away; it isn't Mari's fault she and Abbey are close, far closer than I and my daughter are. 'I popped out for some fresh air a few days ago, slipped when it rained and fell. I had a few grazes but I didn't want Abbey to worry by mentioning it.'

'Maybe you could have just told her that? Stopped her from imagining it's worse. Because that's what kids do, don't they? Blow up a tiny unknown into something huge?' Her expression sympathetic, Mari rubs my arm. 'What about confiding in her more? In each other, in fact. Perhaps you'd both feel less ... pushed away.'

Surprised at the ease of my own lie of omission, I smile thinly. 'I expect you're right. But she's fifteen now and has been a daddy's girl since the day she was born. I think I've left it too late. Don't you?'

8

Epiphany

Mariana

Mari squints at the bedside clock. No, it can't be seven already. No, it can't be a whole new year of dragging herself out of the sack when she's only had six or so hours of sleep. But focusing on work will be a good thing, even better than the buzz she gets each time she says goodbye after the hour's session with a client. Well, mostly. Has she made a difference to this person's life? That's the test. However minute, has she made one?

After two weeks off, she has to shake herself down and get back in the zone. Her caseload is eclectic and she likes that – from severe anxiety to OCD, from eating disorders to postnatal depression. Sadly, paperwork is part of the job too. How nice would it be to dictate her sessions to a shorthand typist like her dad used to, rather than input it herself with two unwilling fingers.

She glances at the end of the bed. Her mum only 'visits' occasionally and always in the dead of night, but she still hears her eloquent tones: *'Having fun, darling? So proud of my brilliant girl!'*

A wave of sadness ripples through her. The shorthand typist was her mother, a woman she admired, respected, adored. They were so very close, Felicity gently pushing her eldest to take advantage of the opportunities that weren't available to her, to work hard and focus and strive for the top. Mari still misses her enormously; undoubtedly the reason why some part of her psyche 'sees' her. Isn't it?

Pushing that particular discomfort away, she drags her thoughts to her sister. Dee's relationship with Felicity was more distant, like the one she has with Abbey. Over the years she's tried to persuade her to talk to a therapist, but she has always politely declined, which is why Mari attempts to do it herself now and then. Of course, she's too close and Dee is too clamped, so they are generally bungled and angsty, but parental behavioural traits are a funny old quandary. The more one dislikes them, the more one seems to do them oneself. Felicity shielded all three of her kids from the bad things in life – including their father's regular liaisons with his students – and Dee is doing the same. Then there's the tight, all-consuming bond she had with Bill, their dad. Paradoxically, it has been replicated between Vincent and Abbey. Poor Dee Dee. No wonder she's so unhappy; not that she'd describe her busy-but-empty existence as that.

The tinsel on the Christmas tree twinkles through the gloom. Only Britt would decorate every room in the house with joyful trashy spangles and fairy lights, their downstairs toilet included. But today is Twelfth Night, so she has faithfully promised to take them down.

'Every single one, Mariana, I promise,' she sweetly said before bed last night.

Mari frowns at the thought. Why is it so important to pack

35

them away today? She doesn't believe in the spiritual, be it mystical, authoritarian or intellectual; there are no gods or higher deities. And yet she's superstitious. Very. It's just one of her many anomalies.

Propping her head on an elbow, she absorbs Britt's still face before it animates with her enthusiasm for *he, she or it*. Will she remember? Will she have time in her busy la-la day? The stomach-churning wave of anxiety hits again and makes her groan. Is this how her mum felt each waking morning? Did Felicity turn to Bill and feel overwhelmed by this crippling insecurity?

She pulls back the duvet and reprimands herself. These unhealthy thoughts have to stop. Mari Stephens is *the* she, the one Britt has chosen. And wasn't it her flirtatiousness, enthusiasm and vitality that knocked Mari off her feet in the first place? That and her eager plans for their future?

Ironically it was *Saint* bloody Vincent who brought them together. Though is he really so bad? She might even like Vinny in another life – if he wasn't her brother-in-law, if he didn't consume and control her sister's life, if he wasn't such a smug king in his castle with his 'team' minions buzzing around him like flies. Yet in fairness he excels as the village rector. In Church of England terms, he's incredibly progressive with diversity and inclusivity, including the lesbian and gay community, which is how she met the love of her life – another thing she didn't believe in before now.

As though reading her thoughts, Britt stirs. She pulls off her eye mask and squints. 'Oh, Mariana. You're back at work today – I'll miss you,' she mumbles. Then, when Mari doesn't reply, her tone a little sulky, 'You're meant to say you'll miss me too!'

Mari gazes for a beat. She wants to say: *'No, you won't! You'll be so busy and smiley and making everyone feel special, you won't give me a second's thought!'* But she isn't a psychologist for nothing, so instead she leans forward and pecks those lips lightly. 'Christmas decorations please; don't forget!'

'I won't. It's too cold to venture out anyway. Phone me at lunchtime? I might need a treat to make up for you abandoning me.'

'Hmm, maybe.'

Britt chuckles. 'You know you will.' Then, when Mari swings out her legs, 'Hey, don't go before I give you a . . .'

Catching Mari around the neck, she plants a lingering kiss on her lips. Though desire spreads through her body, Mari's mind is analytical. This woman is perfect; she doesn't even have morning breath. Or is it simply that she can't smell it? Made senseless by love, or desire, or by this . . .

She gently rests her head on her lover's huge, pregnant belly. Yes, this incredible but wholly confusing gift? A baby, *their* baby, due in a short, anxiety-inducing eleven weeks.

9

Cordelia

I scoop up the late-morning post from the doormat, move to the hall table and sort it into the usual piles – junk mail, private and confidential for Vincent, even though Harriet opens it more often than not – then the rest in a heap for me to sort out at my small desk in the attic room. I could do it down here in the 'office', but Harriet plants her ample behind on the leather chair and doesn't budge unless there are visitors, a team meeting or her stomach demands it. Still, upstairs means I can escape from the telephone and the inevitable sniping from parishioners for a while – if Harriet deigns to answer it.

The woman's deep tones now filter out from the kitchen. 'I don't think an *apology* is appropriate when no offence was intended, Naya . . . '

'The point is that I *feel* offended, which is why I'm here.'

The families team leader arrived ten minutes ago, and from what I have gleaned, discord is afoot within the hallows of the church squad. Per se, it's funny, something to quietly snigger about with Mari, but it'll come my way somehow, so it's best I go in and smooth the ruffled feathers.

Her arms folded and expression truculent, Harriet's sitting at the table, and an equally angry-looking young woman is perched opposite.

'Hi, Naya, how are you? Sorry to interrupt.' I make for the kettle. 'Can I get either of you ladies a tea or coffee?'

'Case in point, Naya. Cordelia did a similar thing only last night. Didn't you?'

Harriet has a rare talent for turning the tables rather than simply saying sorry. Wondering how she'll do it this time, I glance over my shoulder. 'Oh, really?'

'Yes, about seeking permission from the diocese before attaching a new roll of toilet paper.'

It's almost true – and loo-related again – but she's clearly been eavesdropping on my conversations with Mari. 'That was just a joke with my sister, Harriet.'

'Precisely!' With a triumphant look, she goes back to poor Naya. 'There we have it – a little jest with no offence intended. I'm sure neither of us will be asking the vicar's wife to phone the archbishop and *apologise.*'

Giving up the losing battle, Naya smiles thinly. 'No drink for me, thanks, Cordelia, I have a busy day.' She scrapes back her chair. 'I'll let myself out.'

When the front door slams, a sizzle of irritation flares up at Harriet's self-satisfied expression. 'Naya was obviously upset about something. Is it so hard just to say sorry?'

'Perhaps you should look at your own behaviour, Cordelia.'

'Sorry?'

'Mocking the Church—'

'That was a private call, Harriet.'

'And not pulling your weight on any level, especially as a . . .'

39

Blocking out the usual rant, I stare at her wagging chin. She does this occasionally, espousing her general dissatisfaction with me as a daughter-in-law, a mother, a wife. A human being too, or so it always feels, but only when her son is out of earshot. Even after all these years, it still hurts.

I puff through the astonishing urge to shout in her face. 'I take it Vincent is on visits this morning,' I say instead.

'Don't assume there's no gossip . . .'

'I beg your pardon?'

'People notice things and come to me.'

Oh God, New Year's Day. I hold my breath. 'Noticed what?'

'Your absence.'

'When?'

'At the team meetings, of course. The way you cherry-pick which you're apparently willing to attend. I'm there at every one, supporting my son.'

I let out the trapped air and pat her arm. There's no point saying that Vincent 'excused' me from the gatherings many moons ago. 'Well done, you. I'll let you know when lunch is on the table.'

A sense of freedom enveloping me, I climb the stairs to my sitting room with a smile. For a sheer moment of panic I thought I'd been seen in the car or the pub with my handsome archangel. Why the thought makes me feel exhilarated and alive, I really can't say.

10

Calvin

Cal throws down his house keys on the sideboard and rubs his face. God, he feels exhausted. The six-to-six daytime shift is usually OK, but he had a series of vivid sleep terrors last night, so he was knackered even before he began.

He loves his job, he even likes navigating the traffic jams when every second counts, and the life-and-death situations are invigorating and rewarding, but the downside is that folk don't always appreciate interference in their lives. He's had verbal and physical abuse many times, and despite being twice the size of the guy, a homeless man tried to land him one today.

Sighing, he stretches his stiff limbs. A shower, dinner or something more immediate to relax him? Should he, though? He's managed to hold off smoking for six months, and even before that it wasn't worth the grief Sadie gave him. But she is long gone and it would be good to escape the horrors of his nightmares which stayed with him all day.

He trots down to the cellar, flicks on the fan heater and spends several moments rolling a perfectly cylindrical joint. But when he puts it to his lips, he remembers a conversation he had with the psychiatric nurse who occasionally travels with him in the Rapid Response Vehicle.

'So does the "think of a happy place, memory or moment" help?' he asked her.

As though reading his mind, she looked at him curiously. 'Yeah, it does. Are you OK? Want to talk?'

He so wished he could. 'Me? Nah.'

Now closing his eyes, he pictures the 'happy memory' he's been mulling on for a month: the bustling school yard at break-time. Waves of kids parting like the Red Sea as the year sixes swish by. Just the usual until ... Wow, there she is – the new girl everyone's talking about. Tall, slim and with beach-blonde swinging hair, she sashays like a model. But the smile, what a smile, flashing directly at him.

He lights up and inhales deeply. He was deluded, of course. The stunning beam wasn't reserved for him. He was a good-looking boy, sure, but a little younger than her. And even if he wasn't, would a posh middle-class girl look at him twice? Nope; not even as teenagers when they rubbed shoulders at a party or passed on the street.

Hope, stupid hope, how he'd hated it. Still, she noticed him on New Year's Day. The question he's still debating is: should he do anything about it?

11

Cordelia

Though nearly two weeks to go until the fourteenth, I study the Valentine's display at Tesco with a strange sense of wistfulness and regret. Parish duties dictate that we rarely dine out, but Vincent always buys me an elaborate greeting card and a showy bunch of flowers for the hall table. And, if I'm lucky, one of the vicar's-wife blouses he's so keen on me wearing. He likes to make a fuss of the day at church too. How did his sermon go last year? It started with an interesting historical résumé about St Valentine, then continued along the lines of:

'*The Feast Day of St Valentine invites us to mark and acknowledge the all-loving God. He blesses those who love one another whatever their background, their sexuality, their culture or creed. Let us love one another, for love comes from God, love is the Lord.*'

I pick out two cards: an affectionate but spiritual one for Vincent and a silly one about the importance of hugging for Abbey. She'll probably deride it, but it's just a bit of fun and an oblique opportunity to tell her I love her. I sigh and amble on, dully throwing the usual toiletries in the trolley: own-label shampoo and conditioner, bars of unperfumed soap and whatever toothpaste and mouthwash is on offer. I choose a couple of actual brands for Abbey, then put them back; I'll get it wrong and anyway she buys her own from the generous allowance Vincent gives her.

At the sanitary protection shelving, I have to stop and breathe for a minute or two, but I shake myself down, retrace my steps and randomly select a pair of expensive skincare products, then move on with my list for the bi-weekly food shop.

Finally through the checkout, I politely thank the cashier and take the receipt, then smile at the security guard as I pass. The usual surge of relief hits when I inhale the fresh air. I've stolen two Olay facial items I'll probably never use. Why I occasionally do this, I don't really know. I sometimes bump into parishioners, and one or two of the staff recognise me as the vicar's wife. Is it simply for the tingling, heady taste of danger? Or does this need for a high go much deeper than that?

12

St Valentine's Day

Cordelia

It's a relatively balmy evening and the budding crocuses suggest early spring is on its way. I stretch my hamstrings and wonder how the flowers do it. Against the odds they manage to push through the hard, hostile soil, then appear so delicate, serene and sweet.

If only my existence with Harriet was that easy. But at least I resisted the urge to retaliate for another verbal attack this morning. Sticks and stones and all that. Yet the words 'ineffective', 'lacking', 'hopeless' do get to me, probably because they endorse how I feel about myself. Still, I'm trying to be positive. My New Year's expedition reminded me that getting out of the house makes a huge difference to my happiness. So I did make resolutions after all: a walk or a run every day is one; not belting down the stairs each time the phone rings is another.

Though the grazing is long gone, my top rib still feels uncomfortable at night. It's sort of pleasurable, if I'm honest, a small reminder that there's life beyond the four walls of the vicarage. I never did tell Mari about that surreal day. On reflection, even she wouldn't approve of my reckless disregard for my own safety, both in foolishly saving my phone and for accepting a lift from a stranger. But Cal isn't a stranger; he knows Ed. The next time my brother appears on the doorstep, I'll ask him. *If* he ever turns up again. Mari met him in Singapore two or three years ago, but I haven't seen him in person for five. We speak by FaceTime occasionally, yet my mental image of him is always at eighteen: handsome, lanky and saying goodbye to the UK with a grin and two raised fingers. Yes, Edmund Stephens did escape all those years ago, and pretty damned effectively.

Setting off at a slow pace, I jog towards the park, but rather than lapping it as usual, I take the gravelly 'Poppy Path' at the rear, heading up the slope towards the bridge. It's fairly dark but the track soon opens out to a dog walker and St Chad's beyond. Picturing my mother-in-law's sneer, I chuckle. Though they worship the same God, the local Catholic church is the enemy in her eyes, not a fight over the body and blood of Christ in this instance, but the number of 'bums on seats', as her son puts it. St Chad's outdoes St Andrew's on that front every time. But at least Vincent has played a master stroke with his diversity projects. His 'toleration, love and celebration' events have been well-deserved successes. He's very much welcomed the LGBT+ community and has instigated a feminist youth choir for both boys and girls. He might have hit fifty-two years of age, but he has his finger on the pulse and I admire him for that.

Admire him? A little shocked at my own choice of word, I

almost stop. What happened to love? At fifteen I was beyond besotted, keenly volunteering for local projects and thrilled to travel in the front seat of his car when he drove me home. Still a curate then, he was steady and kind and attentive. Extremely handsome too. Then at some point he said: 'We're passing my digs, Cordelia. Fancy coming in for a cuppa?'

Feeling myself flush, I ignore the steady stone gaze of Our Lady and trot past. Whatever Mari says, I was definitely sixteen before doing the full dirty deed. And if anyone pushed our relationship further, it was me with that mix of adolescent horniness and desperate need.

I pull down my cap and increase my speed as I run past the mix of shutters, blinds and curtains. I admit to myself that this is the route I took six weeks ago, but it isn't as though I haven't run this way before. It's my non-slushy route around the outskirts of the village, and though it isn't raining tonight, it's safer than the dense wooded paths in Fletcher Moss.

Safe. I was far from that the last time I ventured this way. My foolishness still invades my dreams, waking me with a jolt as I'm unexpectedly caught from behind. I did have a bruise on my bum, but Vincent didn't notice, which is hardly surprising; save from the rare occasions he forgets his caution, any intimacy between us passed long ago.

Clocking every vehicle driving past, I listen to my own steady respiration. Was the offending vehicle silver in real life? It is in the nightmares, but perhaps that isn't the car that I'm looking for . . .

I check myself short. Oh God, Dee Dee, *really*? Even admitting it to myself is embarrassing. Cal was my saviour, that's all. He was there when I needed someone, caring but not intrusive. He sweetly gave me his umbrella, now hidden at the very back of my wardrobe. An excuse to get in touch and say thanks? But I don't have his number; he didn't offer it.

Suddenly deflated, I halt and take in my surroundings. Hurling myself forward with some kind of vague optimism is one thing, but I have to schlep back. I tighten my hair elastic, replace the cap and set off at a desultory jog the way I came. As I approach the bus shelter, I glance over the road. Almost past it I look again, pull up to a stop and turn.

What the ... ? Breathless, I stare for several moments. His fingers laced between his spread knees, a man is gazing back at me. He doesn't move, or smile, or lift a hand in greeting. Is it really him?

That tingling sense of riskiness rising, I deeply inhale. Carry on towards home, or cross the road and say hi? But suppose it isn't him? Or what if he blanks me? But if I'm honest, very honest, this is exactly what I hoped for after today's debacle with Harriet. Escape, excitement. And I'm bloody fed up of playing *safe*.

Attempting to hide my nervous smile, I stride over. 'Cal, right?'

'Yup.' He hitches along the bench. Taking that as an invitation to sit, I squeeze into the small space beside him, then find myself prattling to fill the silence. 'No rain or speeding car today, thank goodness.' God, why did that sound so plummy? 'It's really silly, but since then I feel nervous near roads. It's as though ... '

He turns and studies me. 'As though, what?'

'As though my body might hurl itself in front of a car. You know, against my will.' I laugh thinly. 'Sorry, I told you it was silly.'

'Nope. Not silly at all. It's a weird but fairly common experience after a scare like that. It's trauma. Even if your physical injuries aren't life-threatening, emotional and mental anguish happens.'

Trauma, deep paralysing trauma, I know about that. Needing to cry out of nowhere, I lower my head. 'Like post-traumatic stress disorder?'

'Yes, exactly like that.'

Floating above thoughts of my precious boy, I stare at Cal's feet. What did my mum always say about men and first impressions? That one could assess them by their teeth and their shoes. This guy has a lovely white smile. As for footwear, do designer trainers count? Too used to Hush Puppies, I'm not in a position to judge. Vincent wears commando soles at gravesides to avoid slipping, and disrespectful though it is, the incongruous sight always makes me want to chortle, a surge of hilarity I have to quickly swallow.

Cal bumps my shoulder with his. 'Interesting cap . . .'

Self-consciously, I touch it. 'Yes, stolen from some poor soul who left it at the vicarage. It's so no one recognises me – you know – from the parish. Otherwise I'll get stopped by the purple-perm brigade and assailed with the usual gripes, ailments or . . .' God, that sounds disloyal. And horribly judgemental. I try for a quip. 'But I'm probably safe from them here. You know, over the Didsbury border.'

'In lowly Burnage, you mean?'

'No, not at all. I meant that . . .' I glance at his set jaw; oh God, he comes from here, doesn't he? It's just an 'in' joke at the vicarage, but yes, a snobbish, insular one. 'Sorry, a bad . . . I'm just nervous and talking too much.' Feeling foolish and chastened, I stand. 'I'd better get off, anyway.'

I begin to move away, but Cal catches my hand and gently tugs me towards him. 'I'm parked just up there. Do you—?'

'You came in the car? Don't you live around here?'

'Nope. I was passing and . . . ' He shrugs. 'Do you fancy going for a ride?'

Surprised and conflicted, I don't reply for several seconds. What does 'go for a ride' mean? To talk or something more? I'm a married woman and to the local vicar, for goodness' sake! Yet I feel a stirring sensation deep in my belly, a surge of heat that I'd almost forgotten.

Freedom, *excitement*, pulses through my head. And yes, I am bloody fed up of playing *safe*.

13

Calvin

His gaze fixed on the road, Cal heads the car towards Stockport. Why he suggested a drive, he isn't sure. Taking Dee to a pub was spur of the moment, and if he saw anyone he knew, there was a perfectly good reason for it – he was keeping an eye on someone who'd had a head injury – and her appearance confirmed it. But his mind is now refusing to think; all he knows is that he wanted to keep her a little longer, so he had to do something to stop her leaving. So when his suggestion rushed out, he surprised himself.

Finally getting a grip, he indicates right and trundles down the hill. Though it's not far from his childhood home, he's never been down this road before, but he guesses it leads to the River Mersey. When he reaches a farm gate, he turns the car around and pulls up against the trees.

Once the headlights dim, he turns to his companion. 'Why were you out on New Year's Day?' he asks, breaking the silence.

Surrounded by the woods, her face is all shadows. She studies her entwined fingers, then quickly glances at him before looking away. 'Escape, I suppose.'

Though she's even more beautiful than she was years ago, he

struggles to reconcile this cowed woman with the girl he remembers. 'I assume there's a path nearby. Shall we walk?'

'Sure.'

He spots a fenced track, lit by the slice of moon. 'Looks like this is the way down to the bank.'

'OK.'

They reach the dark riverside. 'Right or left?' he asks.

'I don't mind.'

Their knuckles touching, they amble and hesitantly chat for a while.

A scurrying sound filters up from the reeds. Dee chuckles. 'Is that a duck or a rat, do you think?'

'Or a European otter, a water vole, an American mink, a beaver.'

She smiles. 'A river mammal specialist, eh?'

'That's me. Not just a pretty face.'

'What do you do job-wise?'

'Tending to head and other injuries, as it happens.'

'Ah, I should have known. So . . .'

She takes a breath to ask more, but he speaks at the same time. 'Why did you need to escape?'

'How long have you got?' Then she frowns and presses her palm to her chest. 'From this, actually.'

Her heart? Wondering what she means, he looks at her quizzically, then realises she's shivering. It's a bloody cold night and she's only wearing her running kit, so he unzips his puffer jacket and opens it. 'Climb in,' he says, and she does, slipping her arms inside and reaching them around his back.

He rests his chin on her silky hair and gazes at the glinting, winking ripples. She's so slim, so docile, so needy somehow.

'Thank you. It's just what I needed to warm me up.'

'I'm glad to oblige.' He finds himself planting a kiss on her head. 'No cuts you need me to check out today?'

Looking up, she smiles that stunning smile, and before he can stop himself, he leans in for a kiss. She pauses, wide-eyed, and just at the moment when he thinks he's made a humiliating mistake, her lips are on his and they're soft and pliant, yet energising too. Then he's pulling her in, drawing her so close that it feels like they're one, deeply kissing and kissing and lost.

Sheer desire pulses through him, burning his whole body. Christ, he's aroused and so hard, made all the more exquisite by her hand on his jeans, gently pressing his groin. But reality snaps in. He's told a barefaced lie and she's another man's wife. What the hell is he doing? Really, what the hell?

14

Mariana

So pleased it's Friday evening at last, Mari strolls up Clothorn Road and stops outside her handsome Edwardian home. Save for a crack of light through the window, it's in darkness. Drapes are a fairly new addition, chosen by Britt.

Though she was only a few weeks into her pregnancy at the time, she'd pressed Mari's hand against her belly. 'Curtains will be much more cosy for this one. Prettier too. We'll choose together.'

They hadn't, of course. Mari returned home from work one day and found the fabric, swags and pelmets in situ. But that's more her fault than Britt's. Rather than fight any losing battle, it's easier to step away. Not that there's ever a set-to; any conflict is entirely in Mari's head. Like now. Like the past several months. She has to rid herself of the turmoil. And soon.

Pulling out her mobile, she nods to herself. There's no time like the present. She types:

Just remembered I need to drop off something at Dee's.

Will Britt have cooked dinner? Even a basic salad, waiting in the fridge? She doubts it, but still.

Hope dinner can wait! See you in half an hour.

Mari taps at the back door of the vicarage and waits. Harriet has already seen her through the kitchen window, so she must have failed the admission criteria. Nothing new there. She raps a little louder. Her cheeks predictably sucked in, the dragon opens up and peers over her glasses. 'Evening, Harriet. Can I come in?'

'We're about to sit down.'

'I'll be as quiet as a—'

'Mariana!' Vincent appears, towering above his mother's shoulder. 'How lovely to see you. Come in and join us for supper.' His eyes sparkling, he gestures to a dish on the table. 'We're sampling Mrs Rankin's . . . ah, casserole. It smells delicious.'

Mari looks too. Unless the steam is coming from Harriet's nostrils, the grey-looking dish is definitely hot. Other than that she has no idea what she's agreeing to. But Vincent is already pulling out the chair next to Dee's.

'Do sit next to my beautiful wife, Mariana. Can I tempt you to a glass of wine? I've opened a rather nice Malbec.'

'You can indeed. Thank you.'

Good old Vinny. He's passable really. Offerings from his parishioners are a regular occurrence and not everyone would attack each and every 'delicacy' with such gusto. Yes, in fairness to him, being the satisfied emperor of his domain can't always be fun. But on closer inspection, his hair's looking a bit too russet today. Oh, heck, that's funny. He *has* taken to dyeing it.

55

She high-fives Abbey. 'Loving the edgy off-the-shoulder look. I might have to borrow it.'

'I'll trade you for that leather jacket.'

'You'll be the first to hear when I'm bored of it.' Mari raises her glass. She plans to drag Dee upstairs to talk, but a minute or two here will be fun. 'Cheers, everyone . . .'

Harriet ladles lumps of *something* into bowls.

'Turnip dumplings, apparently,' Vincent comments.

Dee smiles at Abbey. 'Perfect for you, love.'

'There's nothing wrong with being vegetarian, Mum.'

'I know. I didn't say there was.'

'You don't need to *say* anything, it's obvious from your—'

Quickly interrupting Abbey's swipe, Mari turns to Harriet. 'It looks very tasty and thank you for offering, but not for me. Britt's cooking tonight.'

Dee's eyebrows rise sceptically, but Vincent puts a hand to his chest. 'Ah, our beautiful Britt-Marie. Such a talented young lady.'

Gritting her teeth at the man's usual 'our', Mari helps herself to crusty bread and dunks it into his bowl. 'Just testing.' She takes a bite. 'Actually, it's not bad.' She gives him a friendly tap on the shoulder. 'You're looking even more dashing than usual, Vinny. I can't put my finger on it. Ah, your hair . . .' She cocks her head and pauses dramatically. 'Got it! I know what's different; you've had it cut.'

Finally upstairs in the snug, Mari flops down in the old armchair. Dee curls up on her sofa and throws a cushion. 'You are rotten to Vincent, you know. He's very proud of his hair.'

'Precisely.'

'And whatever you think, he doesn't dye it.'

'If you say so.' She chuckles. 'It's so thick and luscious, I can't resist teasing him. Thing is . . .'

She pauses. Why does she take such pleasure in goading the poor man? Is *pleasure* even the word? Certainly not when he tries to claim Britt as his in that avuncular way. Though he does it to everyone in his congregation – 'our' Matthew or Peter or Gaynor – as though he's God, rather than just working for him. But she won't say that to poor Dee. She has to live with it.

'He takes it so well, too well. Maybe I'm looking for the chink in his smarm . . .' Clapping a hand to her mouth, she guffaws. 'Sorry, charm.'

Dee doesn't smile. 'Too far, Mari. You always go too far. He's my husband, the father of my child; his job is full on and he helps people in all sorts of ways. Not everyone is willing to work six until ten, pretty much seven days a week. It doesn't hurt to be kind every now and then.'

Mari reaches out. 'Sorry, you're right.' She studies her sister's flushed cheeks. Dee hasn't been this defensive of Vincent for a long time, and she isn't quite meeting her eyes. 'Are you OK?'

'Yeah, fine.'

'The New Year's bump to your head?'

The blush seems to deepen. 'Something like that.'

Though Dee always struggles to share what's really going on behind her pretty features, Mari sips her wine, hoping for more. When nothing comes, she puts down her glass and takes a deep breath. She just has to say it, let the ugliness out. 'I wanted to talk to you, actually. More like needed to, I guess.'

Concern flooding her face, Dee pulls down her long legs and leans forward. 'Oh, Mari. Are you all right?' She peers for a second. 'Is it Britt? Or the baby?'

It's both of those things, plus panic, paranoia, anxiety, stress. Shame too; she's ashamed about her jealousy. Bloody terrified about how it might affect her when the baby is born.

She rubs her hands. 'So, you know Britt and I discovered we both wanted kids, talked about it more seriously and decided to . . .'

Was it really that way, though? Mari thinks back. For her it began with a drunken conversation very early in her and Britt's relationship, one that planted a seed she couldn't quite let go of.

'*So you never fancied having kids, Mariana?*'

'*Quite the opposite, but I . . . I think I've missed that particular boat.*'

'*Oh, sweetheart, don't look so sad! We could have a baby, you and me . . . In fact, oh wow, wouldn't it be amazing?*'

She goes back to her sister, patiently waiting.

'Well, it was fun, exciting.' She searches for an analogy. 'I don't know; like planning the best Christmas ever. Going to the clinic and talking through donor options – tall, short, fat, thin; black, white or blue. British or Swedish. In truth I didn't care about any of it so long as the sperm was screened and healthy, you know?'

'Of course.'

'So then there was the discussion about which of us would go first. Britt was the obvious choice. You know, younger, prettier, *kinder* than me . . .' Dee squeezes her hand but says nothing. 'More fertile, in all likelihood. In the end we agreed we'd both do it. Sort of involve chance, fate, Vinny's God or whatever. If we both got pregnant, we'd cope with double trouble. But . . .'

Hoarse from the effort of finally spitting them out, the words emerge splintered and cracked. She takes a gulp of air. 'But Britt, but she . . .'

Hot tears soon follow. Oh God, is she really crying?

Dee passes her a tissue, then speaks. 'But Britt got there first? And now you're beating yourself up because you feel envious when you're supposed to be the proud parent-in-waiting?'

Wiping her nose, Mari nods. Cordelia, dear Dee Dee. The only person in the world who instinctively knows how she feels. Inhaling deeply, she tries to breathe through her clash of emotions. 'I love Britt and any decent person would tell me to get a grip. "Next time will be your turn," they'd say. "And you have a baby on the way; you are incredibly lucky." And they'd be right. But . . .'

She meets her sister's soft gaze. It's a classic case of '*Physician, heal thyself*'. More than anyone, she knew there could be issues of non-biological mother identity, or feeling ostracised from in-utero bonding, but as much as she's tried to look at the situation objectively, she can't stand back from her own terror.

She takes another shuddery breath. 'But suppose I don't bond with this baby? What if I feel totally detached? Even worse, suppose this, this horrible, dreadful . . .' She gropes for the word. '*Resentment* is still here when he or she is born? Is this what the future holds? Feeling completely set apart from Britt and *her* baby?'

Dee holds out her arms and folds Mari in. When she kneels back, she smiles thinly. 'Maybe men go through this. We never stop to ask, do we?'

'That's true.' The wave of worry hits again. 'But what if the baby senses all this? And who will I be? Mari, Mariana?' She sighs. 'Let's face it, I won't be "Mummy".'

Dee's smooth forehead creases. 'Oh, Mari, I don't know the answer. Life can be so unpredictable, uncertain, cruel. But my gut feeling? You'll both be great parents but I don't think either of you will get to decide.' Her gaze slides away. 'The child does that.'

Acknowledging her sister's own struggles, Mari doesn't speak for a while. A burst of shouting and a slammed door eventually splinters the silence. Dee abruptly laughs. 'Oops. And it wasn't even my fault.' She lifts her pale eyebrows. 'Not yet, anyway.'

Mari returns the smile. Glimpses of the old Dee Dee are so lovely to see. She inhales the lemony smell she's always associated with her sister. 'Why didn't you try for another baby?' she asks quietly.

It never felt appropriate to ask before now. There's no reply for several seconds. Has Mari gone too far?

But finally Dee speaks. 'After Luke's ... death, Vincent wouldn't allow it,' she replies.

15

Calvin

The gym air feels solid and smells of sour sweat. Cal strides to the treadmill and programmes in a ten-minute blast.

The guy leaving the next one dips his head. 'Not seen you in a fair while, mate.' He winks. 'Best take it easy, eh.'

Cal doesn't bother to reply. He hasn't fancied schlepping here of late, but that doesn't mean he's neglected his body. He's done his HIIT at home – squats, lunges, push-ups – and a skipping rope is all that he's needed.

He sets to work, running fast. Fat-burning, muscle-building high-intensity interval training can work miracles, but you have to do it right. Less is more, which suits him and his long shifts. But if intensity training's going to work, then it needs to be, well, intense.

When he's finished, he heads to the barbells. He'll do lunges, then squats before moving on to the dumb-bells. Then finish off with two sets of fifteen dips, a total of thirty minutes without thought, job done.

Only today isn't *without thought*, is it? His mind has been buzzing since Monday evening. No, since the bloody New

Year. And not just his head either. He's tried to focus on the dismissive, flaxen-haired girl from school, but the real woman has plagued him. What happened to the confidence which shone from her eyes? Even in the pub she only met his fleetingly before looking away.

Though determined to block her out, he still kicked himself for being . . . well, himself, he supposes. Not revealing too much. He should have asked for her number or put his in her phone. Finally, he gave in to temptation and drove home the same route he took that day. Trundled up Parrs Wood Road, trying not to look too bloody obvious. No luck until Monday. Her short ponytail peeping out from the back of her cap, he might not have recognised her, but the long, slim limbs he did. So he turned back, parked up and waited at the bus stop. Would she look over and see him when she passed? She did. And that smile, especially for him. He had to remind himself of that old stupid hope, the disappointment and anger. But later they kissed, really kissed, and he ached with pulsing desire. He's thought of nothing else since.

He throws down the barbell and groans out loud. What the fuck is he doing?

Cordelia

It's Monday, so I dutifully scroll through the church Facebook page liking posts and comments from the weekend and adding suitably upbeat, sympathetic or joyful replies.

I stare at the yellowing water stain on the ceiling. What inspiring quote or helpful link can I post today? It was biodegradable refuse bags last week, a Venn diagram of 'belief' the week before.

Despite my alleged failures, Harriet graciously nominated me to be the group administrator several years ago. Though she knows nothing about IT, she still inspects my efforts from time to time, complaining that I'm not sufficiently selective when allowing people to join.

I wryly chuckle. As ever, Harriet hasn't quite grasped the meaning of 'inclusivity', even though the page banner sports that very word. And it isn't as though the world and his wife want to connect, anyway. Four poor souls this week. Secretly hoping one has scandalous news or murderous intent, I've clicked 'accept' for each one.

Goodness, is this little spurt of defiant pleasure the best I can do to lift my day? I touch my lips. Actually, no, not by a long chalk, but I'm trying very hard not to think about *that*.

Reverting to the screen, I open a fresh document then sit back to think of ideas for this Sunday's sermon. I've been writing them for Vincent for the past ten years. Each week I compose a thousand considered, all-embracing, thoughtful – and duly 'sandwiched' – words, then collude in his pretence that they're just 'concepts' he'll develop. He doesn't. Nor does he disclose my speech-writing role to Harriet. 'Our little secret,' as he says.

I shudder. And not the only one.

Matthew 5: 7. Sermon on the Mount, I type. *Not everyone entering heaven . . .*

My heart races again. However much I try to distract my febrile mind, it comes back full circle to *him*, Calvin Rafferty and our fervid kiss. Yet something went wrong. One minute we were kissing and it was as if we *fitted*, not just our lips, but our bodies too. Like a form of CPR, it felt as though he was breathing in life from my head to my toes and the tips of my fingers. Then he abruptly pulled back, shoved his hands in his pockets and stalked away so quickly it was hard to keep up.

What happened? Do I have bad breath? Am I a crap kisser? Did I say something to offend him? A loop back to our earlier conversation at the bus stop, perhaps?

Or was it because I slid my hand to his groin? Oh God; did I really do that?

I blow out long and hard. I hate uncertainty, dread feeling in the wrong. Loathe that old replaying of events frame by frame, desperately trying to work out where life went awry, what I could and should have done differently. Of course, some things one can't change – like my boy's death which is horribly, *irreversibly* set in stone for ever – but this escapade with Cal . . . It's preferable just to know, surely?

Once we'd returned to his car, he drove back to the village in silence and pulled up outside the cricket club. I duly tugged the door handle to get out, but he muttered, 'Hold on,' rummaged in the glove compartment and found a broken biro. Then he handed me a business card and said, 'Night, then.'

My fingers slightly trembling, I now extract it from my running jacket pocket. The familiar yellow logo of a taxi firm is on one side and a barely legible number on the other. I chuck it on the desk. So he gave me his mobile number, but what on earth does it *mean*? Save for snogging boys at teenage parties, I've been with Vincent for ever. I'm used to a dull but simple life; do I want to get caught up in the intricacies of this, whatever *this* is? No, it's crazy. I'm the vicar's wife, for goodness' sake. I've already been incredibly stupid, reckless, in fact. Climbing into his car. Walking into the black night. Quickly becoming intimate. Kissing and kissing and yearning for . . .

Cringing at the thought of my unexpected and heady surge of desire, I go back to my laptop. A new post has appeared on the Facebook page from Audrey Goodwin, a nice lady. A bishop prayed for her at a gathering, and her thyroid medication has since been decreased. Audrey is thankful to God for her healing. Praise the Lord!

I gasp at the sharp stab behind my eyes. It's a lovely contribution; the power of prayer has made Audrey a more contented person, a healthier one, in fact. But is this existence, this marriage, this life really for me? Mariana was right. When the rug was brutally pulled by my dad, I spiralled hopelessly in that huge black void. Then I discovered the fellowship and support of the Church, people who were smiling and supportive and offering their hands. But most of all I found the love of the Lord. God was constant; he wouldn't leave me. So I transferred my devotion from my father to *the* Father, healing that chasm overnight.

Heaven, dedication, conviction. Complete and utter faith. When Luke died, it fell away as quickly as it came. I so wish I could still sense it, but I can't feel anything these days. Yet that kiss? Yes, I felt that. And his erection against me, hard and urgent behind the denim.

Taking a deep breath of resolve, I pick up my mobile and punch in Cal's number. I quickly type and send:

Did I do something wrong?

I return to the sermon and delete my notes so far. *Corinthians 13*, I type instead. *God is faithful; he will not let you be tempted beyond what you can bear.*

A minute passes, then another. What have I done? Half-expecting the gratification of an instant reply, I scoop up my phone. Unlike when Luke died, the screen stays empty. I scoff at the memory of Vincent's hourly inquisitions back then:

How are you feeling?

Have you eaten?

Has anyone called?

What are you doing?

Where are you?

As though I'd be anywhere other than here.

Well, right now I need to get out. Somewhere far away would be infinitely preferable, but a quick run will have to do.

17

Mariana

Work is the best thing to distract her, but even so, Mari knows she isn't firing on all cylinders.

'Mari?' It takes a moment for Sanjay's voice to filter through. 'Mari, are you with us?'

She looks at her team leader. 'I am. Absolutely.'

'So, which do you want?' He wafts two buff folders. 'The PTSD or perinatal depression?'

Though the numbers are depleted, it's the usual staff meeting to start the day. With half the department off with flu, it's good of Sanjay to offer her the choice rather dump both on her desk. He briefly described each case, but the moment he said the words 'perinatal' and 'depression' in the same sentence, she felt breathlessly anxious.

Almost like having bloody PTSD, she grimaces to herself. A bad joke, of course, as both conditions are debilitating and ruin lives. She's just attempting to give her own self-indulgence an almighty shove by using humour. She does *not* have depression, perinatal or otherwise! She's just feeling the natural apprehension many people have when parenthood is impending. *Still, she isn't* in the right frame of mind to give that one her very best, so she opts for the other.

She thrums her fingers on the cover. 'So this is the dad who just flipped twenty-something years after failing to save his child from a house fire?'

Sanjay nods. 'Every parent's darkest nightmare. But at the time he just got on with life. Picked himself up and carried on as usual.'

'Until now.'

Mari sighs. Bottling it all up like her sister and brother. Like their mother. And herself; she shared part of it with Dee, but not everything. Her abortion, for example. Because in truth that's a vital ingredient of this whole jumbled bloody emotional angst. But when she took a big breath to spit it out to her sister, Luke and his tragic, dreadful cot death at only ten weeks loomed large. Though it was many moons earlier, she'd made a positive decision to 'terminate' her baby, but Dee devastatingly lost hers for no reason whatsoever, so it felt wholly wrong to snivel about it now. And in retrospect she feels rotten for raising it at all; issues of babies and bonding must feel horribly close to the bone.

Sanjay lifts his shaggy eyebrows. 'Yup. Delayed-onset PTSD. Delayed far longer than most, but it happens.'

'How did it finally emerge?'

'He freaked out in a restaurant. Badly. Threw plates, kicked chairs. It was his best mate's sixtieth birthday meal.' He smiles thinly. 'Baked Alaska for pud. Of all things, the flames brought it back.'

Mari's chest feels tight. 'Bloody hell, poor guy. Just goes to show how we never really escape the past.'

'And it's all the worse for not having dealt with it at the time.'

He sucks in air. 'As we always say, there's no scot-free. People kid themselves they've got away with it, but no one ever does.'

'True, very true.'

She swallows. Trauma, shame, sin, guilt, grief. And yes, regret or making the wrong call. When they're not eating you from inside, they're waiting around the corner, ready to make a tumultuous comeback.

18

Cordelia

'Cordelia! Hello, I didn't know you liked jogging.' 'Goodness me, you're all skin and bone as it is, Cordelia. Don't wear yourself away completely!' 'Cordelia. Glad I've bumped into you. Could you give our dear rector a little nudge?' 'I still haven't had a reply about my addition to the agenda . . .'

And the rest. As I head for Fletcher Moss, I tut to myself. A run is hardly a run when I'm stopped every two minutes. My own fault, though; I usually choose the least busy times to deal with the office mail, but I found myself stuck in a long queue at the post office with no means of escape.

The breeze buffeting my cheeks, I lope through the gates and pace past the tennis courts, pulling to a stop at the rockery to absorb the marching army of snowdrops. The sight usually brings a smattering of pleasure, but my stomach is churning. Why did I send Cal the flaming text? And why so direct? It didn't leave much scope for an equally pointed and possibly hurtful reply. Though he hasn't responded at all. Which is preferable – 'ghosting', as Abbey calls it, or honesty? One thing's for sure, neither feels good.

I set off again, trotting past the Alpine Tea Room and down the cobbled slope, taking care not to slip. Another fall won't look good; it'll have Mari peering at me in that mind-reading way again. But at least it isn't raining, and the plethora of winter grooves in the bushy path have been filled with sand, so that's good as well.

Continuing my search for positives, I cross the boardwalk, its smooth decking a far cry from the previous rotten and rickety affair. When life was teenage-perfect, me and my school mates came down here on summer evenings, the boys mucking around and making to push the girls in the swamp either side, but once my dad left, a towering version became part of my dreams. With his arms outstretched, he'd be at the far side, encouraging me over, yet when I reached the middle, the slats were missing and I'd jolt back to consciousness as I plunged.

Passing a man with three dachshunds on their leads, I scramble up the slope, then puff along the worn path through the woods. I eye a huge upturned tree trunk, its viper's nest rhizomes slithering out, and wonder how something so firmly rooted can topple over. From being rotten, I suppose, but what damage it could do to innocent passers-by.

A single magpie lands on the track, so I salute it, a habit passed on by my sister. I spot another and another, all alone. Why don't they clump together to give someone joy, a girl or a boy? The puddle ahead looks fairly shallow so I splash on through it, but the freezing water soaks my trainers and saturates my socks. Typical; it was much deeper than I'd thought.

My optimism completely annihilated by the plethora of allegories, or whatever the portents are, I hobble past the poplars and trudge back up the hill. Unsafe bridges, uprooted great oaks, profound pools and sole magpies pretty much sum up my life. Still, they'll be useful parables for Vincent to eloquently elucidate at some point. And in truth, Cal's ghosting is probably for the best. No good will come of taking the fledgling ... well, *thing*, with him any further.

Quickly bypassing the church, I cut through Parsonage Gardens. More snowdrops and crocuses wave, so I sit on a bench to admire them. Yes, accepting my lot and getting on with life is the way forward. And it's probably time to start preparing dinner.

As though reading my thoughts, my phone rings. Harriet, of course, probably to complain I didn't fill out the form for day release from prison. With a sigh, I make to answer it, but a message flashes up on the screen. Oh Lord ... I didn't link his name to his number, but I'm sure that it's him. Breath stuck in my chest, I glance around. Only trees are leaning over my shoulder today. Well, I wanted to know and now here it is.

Half-squinting, I poke the icon and read the short message.

Nothing. Walk again soon?

19

Mariana

Mari isn't sure which she hates most, the bus or the tram. Right now the carriage is packed so full that she can count the nostril hairs of the man to her left. The one to her right with over-gelled hair is composing a text with the little room he has. Two thumbs, of course, unlike her with a long index finger.

If your thr b4 me ...

'It's *you're*, as in *you are*,' she wants to correct him, grammar police like her mum. She peers again. Now her teeth are on edge:

If your thr b4 me, grab a seat. Cant w8!

The bus tomorrow, she promises herself. It takes far too long, but in general she finds somewhere to sit, even if it does involve squeezing between shopping-trolleyed pensioners, whose dull stares challenge her not to.

The thought of oldies reminds her of her dad. Though the stylish charmer won't ever fit into the tartan-bag category – and would stand to offer his seat – aided and abetted by his wife-witch Gilly, he seems more fragile each time she sees him. The 'aiding' is precisely the trouble, in her view. Insisting on a stick and treating him like an invalid creates the very monster the woman wants gone. Or perhaps that's the plan. As he put it himself: '*Though this be madness, yet there is method in't.*' He's probably right, the poor bugger.

She wishes she could persuade Dee to see him. Even now her sister is the first thing he enquires about. How is his little princess? Is she still with that insufferable prick?

'Dee Dee' has always been their father's undisguised favourite. From time to time Mari examines her own soul and asks herself if she was or even *is* jealous. Of course, Bill has Viola these days, but when he had only three kids, he never bothered to hide his adoration of one in particular. But that's just the way it was; she and Ed were close to their mum, so life evened out. Besides, examining her own soul is something she tries hard to avoid. Except when she's visited in the still, black night by her mother; it's inescapable then.

A memory flashes in of her and Ed at sixteen and twelve, Ed splitting away from his mates and finally acknowledging his eldest sister on the last stretch of Clothorn Road. Ribbing each other about hair – his fringe was so long he couldn't see where he was going; she'd gone for the opposite, having her long, dark locks cropped short, a reminder whenever she looked in the mirror that the next two years were for study, to get into Cambridge, and not for frivolous fun. But as the house came into sight, they stopped. Even though their dad had been banned from visiting their home, his vintage Mercedes was on the driveway and he was opening it up to leave. But something was off ... Why was his navy shirt stuck to his chest? And why were his forearms wrapped in towels? By the time they reached the door, he'd gone, but sudden panic consumed Mari. Felicity, her mother, was she OK? Had he hurt her? Terror pumping through her veins, she tumbled to the kitchen, but her mum was turned away, slotting the carver back in the knife block.

Ed collided behind her. 'What's going on? God, it reeks of disinfectant in here.'

Their mother spun round, her startled expression replaced by a smile. 'I've just washed the floor so don't come in, it's slippy.'

Even then on some level Mari knew her dad's top had been sticky with blood and that the coverings hid 'defensive' injuries. But she didn't want to imagine, let alone know, what had gone on between her parents. And right then it felt more important to make Ed promise not to say anything to Dee Dee when she came home.

Blinking away her father's shattered look, she replaces it with a more recent image of him. Though an easygoing liberal, she thought it best to tell him in person about her relationship with Britt. 'Darling girl!' he said when the telltale Viola had finally allowed her into his too-hot front parlour. 'I hear you've become a lesbian. Good on you.'

His phrasing made her smile, but is that what she is? Or bisexual? Pansexual? Fluid. Or any other sexual orientation? A colleague at work welcomed her to the 'Dinah club' the other week. The woman laughed at her obviously bemused expression.

'Get with it, Mariana. Be prepared for the questions,' she advised. 'They'll come whether you like them or not. You'll find the number one spot belongs to, "Which of you is the guy?"

76

"Neither," is how I usually reply. "We're both girls, which is kind of the point ... "'

In truth, she doesn't identify with any *label* she's found; it's a question of love and ... need, she supposes. Apparently, the number two hot hit is: 'Have you always been a lesbian?' Her colleague's answer: 'I was straight until I wasn't.' Well, she was die-hard *straight* until she met Britt.

Tuning in to the rain-stained world outside, she notices with a jerk that the tram has almost reached her stop. She has a last peep at gel-boy's phone to see if his lover has replied and corrected his syntax, then she steps to the doors, homeward bound.

When she reaches her sodden street, a sigh treacherously escapes. She had to look up what 'the Dinah' was. Back at university, she was the life and soul of any gathering or party, and she still likes a laugh, a drink or a bop with Abbey, but the largest lesbian event in the world would not be her thing. Nor are festivals or raves, excess alcohol or drugs any more. But that's one layer of her complicated feelings – she knows someone whose scene it is.

20

Calvin

His heart clattering against his ribcage, Cal forces himself to consciousness. Bloody hell, the shrill siren from his dream is actually his mobile alarm. How can it be four-thirty already? Cutting the noise, he falls back against the pillow and catches his breath. As usual he's drenched with sweat from the terror, probably one of the million reasons Sadie moved out.

It's a February Wednesday, a six-to-six shift. Though solitary at times, he likes handling the fast response vehicle and being the first at the scene of an emergency. The need to drive carefully at speed, then immediately put lifesaving skills into action, gives him an adrenaline high which leaves little room for other thoughts. He likes his job, and more importantly, he's bloody good at it.

Inhaling sharply, he throws off the duvet and feels the perspiration turn to ice. Right; shower, eat breakfast, make a sandwich for lunch and iron his uniform. Then drive to work, bag his favourite RRV and check it has the LUCAS machine, defibrillator, gas and drug bag. He likes the systematic start to a working day; it suits his 'robotic' personality, as *Sadie* so kindly described it. But like the chicken and the egg, which came first, his work or the detachment? Because one has to be professionally distanced to do a good job, right? And doing his best is hugely important to him.

'You're like a flaming robot, you don't feel anything,' Sadie complained regularly before the final time.

The criticism hurt – not the machine-like part so much as not feeling anything. It showed she didn't know him at all.

21

Cordelia

Thumping awake, I jerk upright and turn to Vincent's side of the bed. It's empty already; the poor man seems to rise earlier each season that passes by. I nod in an acknowledgement: a labour of love, a vocation and *meaning*.

The dream rushes in. It was so very vivid, the tears which pushed through to reality are still blinding my eyes. A speeding car and a thud yet again, but this time the victim was Abbey and I was the driver. Culpability swamps my chest at the tangible memory. Why is my subconscious taking me to such an awful place? Mari would have a theory, but I won't mention it to her; her interpretations are never uplifting, and besides, I feel too culpable; it's as though I've deliberately harmed my own daughter.

Deeply sighing, I fall back against the mattress. I can't pretend I don't have a difficult relationship with Abbey – not even difficult, more distant – nit-picking and angsty on Abbey's part and passive on mine. Like me and Mum, if I'm honest. Can a child be blamed, though? I was a wilful adolescent and that's what kids do. It's what I've always inwardly said to assuage feelings of guilt, but in truth there were times I callously pushed *my mum* away or belittled her attempts to show love. And that's precisely my relationship with Abbey.

I picture my graceful mother. Her behaviour with Mariana and Edmund was so smooth, so natural, so instinctive. Maybe a little dominating too? Yet with me it felt as though she was acting. If I sat opposite her now, what would I say to improve our relationship?

'Don't make such a fuss about peripheries that don't matter, Mum,' I say out loud. 'Be chilled, let things be. Don't allow your face to reveal your true feelings. The worry, the concern, the alarm.' I frown in thought. 'But don't let me get away with being rude or disrespectful to you, either. Be more assertive and show me your hurt . . .'

I look at the bedside clock. That's actually a good idea; I can catch Abbey before she flounces off without breakfast.

Harriet's at the kitchen table, but she doesn't bother lifting her head from the newspaper.

'You're up early,' she comments.

'No earlier than usual,' I lightly reply. 'I've come down to make Abbey something to eat before school.' And though evidence of Harriet's usual fry-up still pervades the air, 'I'm toasting her a bagel. Can I get you one or anything else?'

The woman's saggy chin wags. 'She's not a morning person. I think you'll find it'll go to waste . . .'

'That's fine; I'll eat it if she doesn't.'

'Hmm . . .' she replies, scraping back her chair and making a loud show of clearing her son's dishes.

I go about my business with a wry smile. Harriet professes to be 'ninety-nine per cent vegetarian'. A large portion of Danish bacon and several Cumberland sausages each morning clearly don't count. Nor do the lashings of roast beef she piles on her plate every Sunday lunch. But when Abbey mentioned her vegetarian-free breakfasts, Harriet replied with a sigh, as though it was her penance. 'Somebody has to be up, look after Daddy and keep him company. It wouldn't do for him to waste away, now would it?'

Heroically ignoring her raised eyebrows as I sprinkle on seeds, I finish my chore, then climb the stairs with a tray. I almost knock on Abbey's door, but catch myself just in time.

'Morning, love,' I say, striding in. I yank open the curtains and sit in the wicker chair. 'Tea and Marmite on bagels for two.'

She looks mildly surprised, then narrows her eyes. 'It had better not be that disgusting margarine.'

I take a bite. 'I guess you'll soon find out.'

Apparently accepting defeat, Abbey hitches up and tucks into her food. No 'thank you', of course, but that's fine, it's just nice to have companionable silence with her. But after a couple of minutes, she swings out her legs. 'Oh God, just remembered! It's music today; I need to straighten my hair.'

I wipe the butter from my fingers. 'It'll be quicker if I do it.' Then nodding to the raindrops patting the widow, 'And if you're a good girl, I'll give you a lift to school.'

Smiling to myself, I amble to the hallway for the key to my car. I've had a really pleasant half-hour, finishing the pot of tea over a leisurely chat about algebra and equations, then tending to my daughter's thick copper hair. Until recently Abbey loathed being 'a ginger' and frequently demanded she be allowed to dye it, but I suspect *the light-bulb moment has finally sparked – so* many of her friends are pretty too, but Abbey's vibrant locks stand her out from the pack. It's a nice feeling I can remember myself – in my case it was height. I'd hated it for years, then realised its benefits when I joined Grasmere Road School in Year Six. Strange now it seems, I turned heads. The attention was a new and exciting experience. It was addictive too; not always a good thing.

Lifting today's pile of post to search for my fob, a thought abruptly hits. Music and straightened hair ... My heart sinks. Could she have a crush on a teacher? But I blow out my alarm. Infatuations are normal, part of growing up, and besides, times have changed in the last twenty years. If an older man is the object of Abbey's affections, it'll hardly be reciprocated. She's smart and savvy, alert to male privilege and power, interested in the #MeToo movement as much as anyone. And today's a good day; I have to trust my daughter's judgement and stop this constant worry.

Vincent's eloquent tones filter out as I near the kitchen. Hearing the word 'Mum', I stop in my tracks.

'It's kind of Mum to help, but we can always get you a tutor. I'm sure there'll be a couple of parishioners with maths degrees, or even a teaching qualification. I know Mum means well, but even she will admit she's no academic, so she isn't really ... well, an expert, is she? And if one doesn't know the methods or—'

He looks up when I enter. 'Hello darling, you look bright and bushy-tailed this morning.' Then following my scan of the dresser, 'Are you after something?'

'My car key. I'm sure it was in the drawer yesterday ... '

He digs in his pocket and holds it aloft. 'Sorry, darling, I didn't expect you to be down so early.' He chuckles. 'You and your parking. Thought it would be easier to borrow the Polo, rather than squeeze by in mine and risk a scratch.'

He looks from me to Abbey, then up at the clock. 'Ah, I see; you're giving our clever girl a lift to school.' He takes the violin case from her hand. 'Don't worry, I've got it covered. I'm still wearing my coat, so it'll save you the bother. Might as well make a few more house calls while I'm out.' He kisses my cheek. 'I should be back for lunch, if not sooner, but make one of your delicacies that keeps, just in case, eh?'

Deflated, I take off my jacket. 'Righto.' I try for a smile. 'Your hair looks beautiful, love. Enjoy music.'

'Will do.'

As the rain spats in, I watch my husband and daughter climb into my car. It's a good job I don't need it this morning. Is it *mine* anyway, though? Do I own anything surrounding me? The house, the furniture, the garden, the plants? Nope. Not even my daughter. But the passenger door flings open and Abbey tumbles out. 'Did you forget something, love?' I ask her.

'Yes; this.' She gives me a hug, and though only fleeting, she casts a smile over her shoulder. 'And thanks for the hairdo. Love you,' she adds.

22

Mariana

Mari glances at the dashboard. It's four o'clock but her mind is still wired from her last appointment and she doesn't fancy going back to Clothorn Road just yet, so she indicates right and heads along the tree-lined lane towards Cheshire. It's 'cutting off her nose to spite her face', as her mum would say, but since the onset of this stupid paranoia, she's spent more time out and about than at home. More hours worrying about the whole damn thing with Britt rather than enjoying her company.

The Christmas break was wonderful, though. They pretty much spent the whole holiday glued to each other. Did she feel insecure during that period? Not particularly, but when they had visitors, mostly Britt's fans from the parish, yes, it did needle then.

She groans to herself. Britt is a flirt, she has to accept that. No, 'flirt' isn't fair, she just likes to be the centre of attention, particularly with men. The good-looking new curate, the charming Church architect guy, the personal trainer who lives next door, even bloody Vincent, polishing his ego and making it shine even brighter than before.

St Vincent ... Remembering Dee's reprimand, she mentally admonishes herself. There's no doubt he works extremely hard. She has to be *kinder* both to and about him. He is ridiculously bountiful in his ways, but overall he's a good man. From dawn to dusk, his energy knows no bounds. Who can blame him for loving the praise and adoration of his minions? Sure, he's horrendously vain – he catches himself in every mirror with a satisfied smile and he forbade the whole family to even mouth the word 'fifty' when it happened, let alone say it out loud (oops, she had, of course) – but many people are like that, it doesn't make them a bad person.

A signpost welcomes her to 'historic' Knutsford, but she absently drives past the attractive medieval buildings today. Is Britt a *bad person*? Absolutely not. Quite the opposite, in fact. This obsessive anxiety is just down to her. So what has she done about it? She's evaded and avoided, distanced herself. Bloody classic case of dealing with worry. She talked to Dee, and that helped a little, but she only confessed part of the fear, which is why she found herself heading here.

Finally arriving at her dad's, she peers at his pretty eighteenth-century cottage. The thatched roof, picket fence and garden are as pristine as always. Though half the size of her home, it's worth a bloody fortune, so it's no wonder Gilly-witch is trying to farm the poor bugger out. A thought occurs: this visit is on the spur of the moment. Will the coven be in, casting spells? Will he?

Hoping for the best, she slams the car door and takes a minute to work out the flaming gate latch. When she looks up, Bill's already at the porch-covered door, his eyebrows raised inquisitively.

He chuckles and kisses her cheek. 'No, you're safe. College and

God knows where. This is a nice surprise. Come on through and I'll make us a drink.'

Following him in, she notes he's not using a walking stick, so that's a good start, and though a little stooped these days, he reassuringly still has to dip his head to avoid bumping the kitchen doorframe.

'Will this muck do?' he asks, lifting a jar of instant coffee.

'I'm parched, so yes.'

He spoons granules into teacups, places a selection of short-bread on a china plate and heads for the front parlour. 'Let's sit by the fire and risk wrath via crumbs.' When they're settled, he studies her. 'How's life? Is all well with Britt and the bump?' he asks, his hand a little shaky as he takes a biscuit.

Mari tries not to stare. It has only been a couple of months since she last saw him, but he suddenly looks older, his taut skin glued to his angular face. But his eyes are still twinkly and blue, and somehow his flowing hair still looks blond.

'Busy,' she answers, sidestepping the Britt question. 'I've just visited a client in Wythenshawe, so thought I'd drive on and skive an hour to see you.'

He nods, so she continues to speak and evade his query a little longer. 'I'm glad to see you're still here and not in the stifling front room of some care home or other.'

'I'm made of sterner stuff. Besides, have you seen the cost of those places? It'd be cheaper to live at the Ritz.' He cocks an eyebrow and rakes a hand through his fringe. 'Rather think that would suit me, though. Live out my final years in a hotel room where I can read books in peace and raid the minibar without censure.'

'Hmm, like *Lady* Thatcher.'

His lips twitch. 'Perhaps not the best example. But there's a long tradition woven from the glamorous and distinguished.'

'Then it's clearly a must for you.'

'Tennessee Williams, Richard Harris, Omar Sharif. Then there's Coco Chanel who moved into the Paris Ritz during the war, along with several Nazi officers.'

She smiles. 'Maybe stick to hiding your favourite tipple in your old penny-loafer shoebox, then.'

'Did I tell you about my secret stash?'

'You did, but don't worry, my lips are sealed.'

Bill leans to a wicker basket, selects a chunk of wood and throws it on the grate. He spends a few moments settling it in with a poker, then he turns, his eyes piercing. 'Why are you here, Mariana?' he asks. 'What's troubling you, love?'

She rubs the polished arm of the chair, then laughs. 'Was I always so transparent?'

'Yes. But that's a good thing, isn't it? What you see is what you get with my eldest.'

Bloody hell; she hopes that isn't entirely true. Then a thought hits: oh God, is she being 'see-through' with Britt? Is that the real reason she's keeping her distance? Fear of being caught out?

'Jealousy,' she states. Then after a sharp breath, 'How did Mum cope with it?'

He looks at the flames. 'As you know, Felicity didn't.'

'No, before that. When we were still a family. She must have known about your . . . your flirtatiousness.'

He smiles thinly. 'The euphemism is appreciated. But the answer . . . I don't know; she never challenged me.' He frowns thoughtfully. 'A pathetic explanation, of course, but that made it easy to be the man I was. I could get away with the occasional dalliance, so I did. If she'd told me to stop then I—'

'That's a lousy excuse, Dad.'

'I know, and it shames me.' He tilts his head. 'You want honesty, don't you?'

'Yes. Yes, I do. So, why did you do it in the first place?'

'Immaturity? Insecurity? Selfishness? Simple lust? I've never quite worked it out. Your mother was the one woman I truly loved. When she finally stood up to me, it was all too late.' He sighs. '"Better three hours too soon than a minute too late." I still miss her very much.'

Mari watches her father blow his nose. He has been punished in a way, she supposes, but that doesn't justify the swathe of damage he's caused. To Felicity, Ed and Dee. But also to her, more than anyone knows.

Why didn't you save me, Mari?

Pushing those familiar words away, she stands. 'The teatime traffic will be dreadful; I'd best get off.'

'Righto.' Bill catches her hand. 'But before you go, tell me about Dee Dee. How is my little princess? Is she still with that insufferable prick?'

23

Shrove Tuesday

Cordelia

Hoping I'm behaving as I normally do on Shrove Tuesday, I mingle in the lounge with Vincent's 'minions', as Mari calls them, offering the finger foods I've been preparing all day from the silver platters which came with the house.

'A spiced chorizo pastry slice or a date, blue cheese and pancetta polenta stack?' I ask Monica.

Harriet's bestie looks a little crestfallen today, and if my mother-in-law's earlier diatribe was anything to go by, I suspect the poor lady has been demoted from the top spot. Still, it's a comfort of sorts – it seems I'm not the only one who gets caught in the slipstream of Harriet's strong opinions.

The woman herself elbows in, and though she puts two 'stacks' on her plate, she takes me to one side. 'Not everyone is a fan of Danish blue, Cordelia.'

'That's why I'm mentioning it. There's more food coming, so eating one isn't compulsory,' I reply.

I move away, offering the day-before-Lent delicacies to the

other members of the church team who're both appreciative and a little tipsy.

When I return to the kitchen, I switch off the oven and carefully pick the mini carbonara quiches from the tray.

'Shall I carry those through?'

Rotating to my daughter, I take in her usual crop top and extremely short skirt. Fashion is understandable, but this house is so cold. I manage to bite back any comment. 'Yes, please, love.'

She lifts the tray. 'God, this is heavy.'

'I know. I think they're solid silver.' I raise my eyebrows. 'Good job Mrs Fairclough's handbag isn't big enough to half-inch one.'

Abbey laughs. 'That's actually LOL.'

I follow her through with another platter. Catching Vincent's smooth voice from the back of the room, I make my way over and proffer the food. Simon, Gaynor and Matthew help themselves, but Abbey tugs her father to the window.

'Did you have a think about it? Please, Dad. Everyone else is allowed out until ten-thirty. I *am* fifteen, not a kid.'

I gather they're discussing Abbey's curfew. I consider butting in and saying that despite it being half-term, a later time isn't appropriate as the evenings are so dark, but would that appear odd when I hope to go out in the inky night too?

Feeling torn, I take a breath, but Vincent replies. 'We'll compromise at ten o'clock, but you're not to wear that skimpy outfit, Abbey. It isn't midsummer. Trousers, a jumper and a coat are in order. It's non-negotiable. Yes?'

A groan and a sigh, but she eventually replies, 'Thanks, Dad.'

'My kitchen queen!' Slipping an arm around my waist, Vincent peers at my offering. 'What have we got here?'

'Halloumi and courgette kebabs or smoked salmon pancake rolls.'

He pops one in his mouth. 'I'm detecting a smattering of crème fraîche. Delicious; cooking is most definitely your forte.' Then, when he's swallowed and padded his mouth with a serviette, 'Our little girl is fast growing up, eh? You don't mind her having an extra half-hour, do you, darling?'

Trying to cover the usual prickle of alienation, I begin to shape a reply, but he kisses my forehead. 'Of course you don't mind, we discussed it, didn't we?'

'I don't think we—'

'You and your terrible memory. But never fear, the forecast is mild with no rain, so all is well.'

Relieved of the opening, I ignore his usual comment about my poor concentration. 'Mild with no rain? That's good. It sounds like a perfect evening for an energetic run.'

24

Calvin

His whole being clenched from a blend of excitement and agitation, Cal sits in his car and stares at the dusky sky through the windscreen. It's gone seven o'clock, where's Dee? All day at work his mind oscillated between: 'Trouble, trouble; why are you even thinking about it?' to: 'Don't be soft, man, what's the harm?'

In the end he thought, 'Sod it.' The guys on his team were rushing home to eat pancakes with their loved ones. Why the hell shouldn't he have fun? Smiling, he closes his eyes. His last meeting with Dee wasn't just fun, it was erotic, arousing – her sweetness, her smell, her eager soft lips. And her hand on his erection, that knowing firm pressure . . .

He feels himself stir. Christ, she is coming, isn't she? He's waiting just over 'the border', so she has quite a way to walk. Or run. He didn't know where else to suggest. He can hardly pick her up outside the vicarage, wherever it is, and he knows her situation is difficult. He'd like to take her somewhere nice and show her off, but is that feasible for either of them? She's a married woman with a kid, the bloody vicar's wife. And he . . . Well, he wouldn't want to be spotted either.

Turning on the radio, he flicks through the frequencies, listening for only a moment before moving on to the next. He likes classical to relax, but he's selective, so generally not the populist stuff they play on Radio 3. But today, he stops there and lets the exquisite strings swamp him. God, he loves and hates this composition in equal measures. But emotions are a good thing, aren't they? Not fucking *robotic* at all.

The opening passenger door interrupts his contemplation.

'Hi,' Dee says, climbing in.

'Sorry,' he says, shaking himself back. 'I was miles away, listening to—'

'Adagio for Strings.'

He can't quite interpret her expression; it's sad, almost broken. 'You know it?'

'Yes, it's beautiful, but it's often chosen for . . . They played it at Grace Kelly's funeral, apparently.'

He mutes the sound. 'Yeah, I heard that.'

Her chin is down and she's wearing the cap, so it's difficult to make out her countenance, but he instinctively reaches for her hand. 'Hey, are you OK?' Then, trying for humour, 'Traumatised to be over the border and into the dreaded Burnage?'

She lifts her head and smiles. 'Not funny!' Then, 'I'm just a bit nervous.'

A rush of warmth hits his groin, then spreads to his chest. Lust and anticipation, of course, but there's more. It takes a moment to identify the sensation. For fuck's sake, is it really *happiness*?

'What do you fancy doing? We could find a pub but . . . '

'I don't know . . . ' Dee bites her lip. 'And I'm on a "run", so time is fairly short.'

94

He turns on the ignition. 'Same again, then? Walk along the riverbank and see where it takes us?'

'Yes, please.' A bashful flash of white again. 'That sounds really nice.'

25

Cordelia

Breath caught in my chest, I stare through Cal's windscreen as we trundle down the hill towards the Mersey again. What on earth am I doing? It feels as though I've gone through a gamut of sensations already this evening. There was worry, of course – the pre-fasting gathering was still in full swing so I couldn't leave the vicarage as early as I'd hoped, so I trotted through the dark Poppy Path route to save time. What if I was too late? Suppose I was mugged? Would Cal even be there? Then there was relief – his car was parked in the same place as before. But when I opened the door, he was clearly far away, his expression so melancholic or moody that the whole thing felt wrong. Yet seconds later his look turned to concern, and in all honesty I wanted to kiss him. Then he laughed and I thought, Yes, he does have lovely teeth.

I glance at him now. It's our third . . . meeting . . . but I still haven't looked at him as closely as I'd like to. Those cheekbones and full lips. His muscular arms, let alone what's hidden beneath his hoodie and jeans. Yes, I'd like to see him naked. And if I'm truly honest, I'd like him to undress me and . . .

Embarrassed by my explicit thoughts, I shift in my seat. What the heck is wrong with me? The sound of his voice brings me back to reality. 'Someone has parked in our place,' he says, gesturing ahead. 'Where now?' he asks, almost to himself. 'Yeah, we can park further up and walk on the riverbank there.'

Though I'm terrified of being spotted, I pull my cap towards my nose, hunker down in my seat and squeeze out an 'OK'.

After a few minutes more, he swings the car to the left, so I peer through the window to get my bearings. There's a high wall on one side and housing on the other, but as we approach the bottom of the residential street, it becomes an unlit lane, thank God. Cal follows an inky track, pulls into a potholed area, cuts the headlights and turns.

'I'm guessing this is by the river. I'll check ... '

'OK.'

When the interior lamp dims, I puff out a nervy wheeze and glance around. Surrounded by looming trees, the space is isolated and empty. And it's very, very black; the moon's barely a slice and I can't see any stars. So silent, I jump when Cal opens the door.

'Typical Manchester,' he says, climbing in. 'It's just started to drizzle.'

'Oh, OK,' I reply, rubbing the chill from my arms.

'You're cold,' he says. He drags his jacket from the back seat, tucks it around me and pecks my lips. But instead of a proper kiss, he observes me through the gloom, then pulls off my cap. 'That's better, I couldn't see you properly. And you're very, very beautiful.'

They're the words that often slide off my husband's tongue, but the intensity of Cal's gaze makes me believe them right now.

'That's very ... ' I begin, but the rest of my sentence is stifled by his mouth, and the hot kisses I remembered and bottled from the last time are here for real, delicious, insistent, urgent. After a few minutes, so are his hands, unzipping my hoodie, sweeping over my vest and down to my waist. Oh God, they find my bare midriff, slide into my leggings and slip into my knickers.

His touch is so exquisite that for moments I'm lost, then I remember my manners and reach for his belt to reciprocate. He leans back with a smile, but when I move to his flies, he abruptly stills. 'Shit, did you hear that?' he asks.

Alarm immediately hitting, I drag on my cap. 'What was it?' I whisper.

'The crunch of footsteps.'

Both sitting back, we stare out of the windscreen. Then Cal shakes his head and laughs. 'Can't see anything. It's just a dog walker minding his own business, I expect.' He tugs me towards him with a grin. 'Do you still fancy that walk or . . . '

Quite honestly, I'd like to finish off what we started. I'm all tingly with desire and a little frustrated, but I have to be sensible. How long does my usual run take? Knowing my luck, tonight my family will be watching the clock.

I give him a final soft kiss, then peel myself away with a rueful smile. 'Much as I'd like to stay, it's probably best I get back.'

Wiping off the inane grin, I fix my face into a neutral expression and enter the vicarage. Sound filters through from the lounge. Should I go in or escape upstairs for a bath?

As though answering my thoughts, Vincent's voice echoes through, shortly followed by a wave of laughter and . . . *clapping*? Really? I suspect my husband and his henchmen are now the worse for wear. A somewhat different evening from mine. I still feel hot and musty and *touched* inside, a sensation I haven't experienced since ... Well, since I was one of those adorers in there. I have no idea who that besotted girl was, but at some point the glow finally and truly rubbed off.

Shrove Tuesday; a day to 'shrive' or confess, an occasion for self-examination, penitence, self-denial and preparation for Easter, and yet here am I ...

I briefly close my eyes. Calvin Rafferty. His smell, his lips and his skin are still there. And that thoughtful frown. 'One more cuddle before we go,' he said. 'We can start where we leave off the next time. Yeah?'

26

Mariana

Hearing the rattle of keys, Mari snaps shut her laptop and takes off her glasses. She has nothing to hide, but Britt's been nagging her about spending too much time on work-related stuff: Mariana slogs ridiculously hard as it is, she shouldn't bring it home with her, weekends are for relaxation, having time together, and so on.

'I'm in here! Have you had fun?' she calls from the kitchen table.

Britt has been to a church event, a 'St Andrew's Got Talent' fundraiser, but Mari declined the invitation, saying she fancied staying in to read, which isn't a word of a lie. She *has* been reading, not the fluffy romances Britt devours, but research papers and a dissertation she foolishly promised to look over for a friend's son, Rohan. Well, sort of a friend. Konnie is actually an embryologist at their fertility centre in Wilmslow. At their first consultation, Mari realised she knew Konnie from rubbing shoulders down hospital corridors, as well as through a mutual pal, so when Mari duly attended the clinic on ovulation day, Konnie did the 'procedure' herself rather than pass it over to a nurse. On any other occasion, Mari would have pleaded lack of time to peruse a 20,000- word thesis, but the request was made halfway through insemination itself. With her legs akimbo as precious semen was inserted – well, it was hard to refuse.

She now sighs. Flaming typical. She's spending her leisure hours as an unpaid PhD supervisor and the four goes at speculum-and-catheter conception haven't bloody worked. Konnie even had the gall to chase her dissertation feedback under the guise of a **When are you and Britt next coming in for treatment?** text. If she'd bothered to look at Britt's notes, she'd have known the answer is not any time soon. Still, her son's writing and analysis are pretty damned good, and the mention of her own name from a long-ago research paper is a surprising and pleasurable boost.

The door finally opens and her fresh-faced partner appears. 'I can't believe that it's March. It's freezing out there.' Bringing in a waft of cold air, she eases herself down on the couch and rubs her stomach. 'I don't mind the cold, but none of my coats button or zip up over this.' She groans. 'I'm bored of it now. When's it coming out?'

'Believe me, three weeks isn't long. It'll fly by.'

Britt's moaning about her third trimester seems to increase every day. That – and all her other pregnancy-related complaints – Mari usually finds irksome, but the tip of her nose is sweetly pink. As are her apple cheeks. True, she has a huge bump, but pregnancy suits her – she looks as pretty as ever.

Rearranging the bright cushions, Mari squeezes beside her and leans in for a kiss. The smell of alcohol breathes back. 'Have you been drinking?'

Britt rolls her eyes. 'Three sips of Guinness won't hurt the baby, Mariana. On the contrary, he said it was full of vitamins. And as you know, I've been low on iron.'

Mari finds herself nodding when she wants to protest. This isn't the first time Britt has had 'three sips', undoubtedly more during the first trimester. Doesn't she realise how bloody lucky she is to be pregnant? What about the baby's development? And though Mari knows it's a stretch, how about foetal alcohol spectrum disorder, or any other condition the experts haven't discovered yet?

Another thought hits, but this one pops out. 'Who is *he*?'

Britt lifts her shoulders. 'An Irish guy with curls called Maher. He said his mum was prescribed it back in the day. Guinness, that is. You know, when she was "with child".'

Mari pictures the pile of Green & Black's in the cupboard. 'Dark chocolate contains iron ...'

'Yeah, thanks for buying those, but it's revolting, so I'm not wasting calories.'

'More revolting than Guinness?'

But Britt doesn't reply as she's already chortling. 'The event was such fun. You should have come. Vincent was brilliant. He *became* Simon Cowell. Even Cordelia looked happy for once. Well, when she wasn't checking her phone—'

Mari frowns; though she and Britt natter about everything, she's always been careful to avoid discussing Dee. 'Who said she isn't happy?'

Britt raises her fair eyebrows. 'You mainly, but she was smiling and chuckling today. Anyhow, Maher did five minutes' hilarious stand-up, and did you know Matthew could sing?' She laughs. 'Well, maybe it is a requisite for a curate, but he was Robbie incarnate. Then Simon played jazz, if you can believe that. Oh, and did I mention that Steve's a member of the Magic Circle?'

'Wow, really? Sounds great.'

Mari snorts to herself. Of course St Vincent *became* Simon Cowell, who else? And Matthew or Mark and the rest of his apostles are all inevitably fabulous. But that's fine, absolutely. Britt has had fun and Dee is contented; her dad's eyes still sparkle with mischief and Ed has promised to visit before long. Family is what matters and very soon there'll be a brand new addition.

27

Mothering Sunday

Calvin

Cal hoofs the ball from beneath the striker's feet. It's a perfectly clean tackle, but he still lifts his arms and looks at the referee. He gives a corner kick, so that's fine. Today, at least. The other team's number seven has always been a diver, but some refs are just blind and see what they want to. Like some people.

In fairness, the guys are pleased to have him back. They know his five-days-on, five-days-off shifts mean he can't always play anyway, but for the past few Sundays he hasn't had the . . . the what? The energy, the inclination, the fire? Yeah, all those things. Still, this morning he feels great and it's nice to shine. A big fish in a small pond rather than his Academy days when everyone was bloody brilliant. Not that he wasn't pretty damned hot. Life just went to shit. As Brando's Terry Malloy says: '*I coulda been a contender.*' But he doesn't want to think about that – today's a good day – tonight he has a date!

Hearing the final whistle, he stops running and shakes hands with the opposition players. Then chuckling wryly at the misplaced word 'date', he heads towards the showers. Walk, drive, assignation, sex? Because that's where it's going, isn't it? Sex, sweet bloody sex. The thought makes him stir. Well, that's already a result! After months of zero interest, the anticipation, the build-up and excitement are more than just brilliant; they're a fucking relief too.

Last night he struggled to chill after a full-on shift, so he went down to the cellar and rolled a joint. But instead of smoking it, he sat in his battered chair and listened to Debussy. Then he picked up his phone and fired off a text:

Thinking about you.

For minutes Dee didn't reply. It wasn't surprising with a husband and daughter; presumably Dee was doing all the churchy stuff that churchy people did on a Saturday night. But still he kicked himself and played a round of self-flagellation in his head. Then his mobile beeped.

Snatching it up, he peered at the screen.

Oh yes?

Only two words but somehow they said everything. He had to adjust his boxers, and though tempted to satisfy himself right then, he wanted to hold back. After all, he'd waited for ... how long? Perhaps his thoughts weren't quite so specific at ten years of age, but definitely later when he saw her with a group of laughing girls in the village, or at a teenage party and surrounded by boys like ants around sugar. Dee Dee Stephens: the pulsing heart of the room, seeming to say hi and hug everyone except him. Then she all but disappeared until someone mentioned she'd got pregnant by a middle-class, older man. The only real shock was that he turned out to be Reverend Vincent, the smarmy 'do-gooder' curate from his mum's Burnage church days.

28

Mariana

Cuisine has never been Mari's strong point, but there's no doubt she's become more experimental the last year, mostly because Britt likes to be cooked for. She doesn't mind, though; Britt isn't demanding or exacting. Her pleas are more sweet and charming: 'Mariana, darling, I'm peckish. What delicacy can you rustle up for us?'

'Us' being Britt and the baby. *Her* baby too.

Mari sighs. OK, maybe her partner can be a little guileful, but some people are talented at getting their own way by being super nice. And if both parties to the relationship are into that arrangement, all is good. Isn't it?

She studies today's creation. Two halves of a panini layered with home-made guacamole, streaky bacon and fried eggs, Britt's current preferred breakfast. Though it's actually brunch, if not lunch. Still, that's fine. Britt needs her sleep and she's had an enjoyable Sunday morning mooching around the house, tidying up and enjoying the quietness.

Opening the door with an elbow, she backs into the dark bedroom.

'Happy Mother's Day! Breakfast is served.' She puts down her offering on the chest of drawers. 'It's noon. Time to wake up.'

She turns, but immediately stops in her tracks. Oh God, the form in the bed is rigid, too stiff and still for life or the living. Her whole being icy, she listens for sound, any sound. Nothing is there, no puffs of sleep, no snuffles, no respiration, no movement at all. And is that a stench, a clash of fetid smells?

With a huge effort she blows out the flash of sheer terror. No, Mari, no. This is Britt, this is *Britt*; it's not her dead mother. But her legs are insubstantial and the walls are looming in. Christ, is she really about to pass out? Inhale and exhale, Mari; hold on to reality and slowly breathe.

Quickly falling to her knees, she lowers her head and drags in some air. When the dizziness finally passes, Britt is sitting up, her eye mask on her forehead.

'Mari? What are you doing on the carpet? Are you OK?' she says loudly.

Swallowing hard, Mari scrabbles for her normal voice. 'Yup, I just felt faint for a second.'

Britt takes out her earplugs. 'That's better. What did you say?'

'Nothing. I'm fine. I've brought up your breakfast.'

A small frown mars Bitt's smooth, shiny forehead. 'It doesn't look like nothing; you're as white as a sheet.' She claps a hand to her mouth. 'Oh my God! You couldn't be—'

'No, of course not.' Insemination or not, Mari's pretty sure she won't ever get pregnant. She forces a sardonic chuckle. 'White as a sheet is not a good look with hair as dark as mine. I was just dizzy for a second. Low blood pressure, probably.' She struggles to her feet. 'All good now.'

'Are you sure?'

Endeavouring to hide her tremulousness, she places the food on Britt's lap. 'Absolutely. Come on, eat up. Cold fried eggs aren't nice.' Then, with a reassuring smile, 'I'm sure, but I've forgotten your juice. I'll be back in a mo.'

Taking care to grip the banister, she makes her way down the stairs. Finally safe on a kitchen chair, she covers her face. She isn't 'fine' or 'sure'. She's freaked out, in fact. What the hell just happened? Where did the vivid flashback come from? She knows perfectly well that Britt wears an eye mask and earplugs, that she's dead to the world most mornings.

Dead but not dead like her mum.

Her heart thrashes. Why has she gone back to that day of horror and panic and fear right now? It's fourteen years since Felicity died in that very bed; fourteen years since she made a decision to hide the horrible truth about their mum's suicide from her siblings.

Wiping tears from her cheeks, she hears Sanjay's words.

'There's no scot-free. People kid themselves they've got away with it, but no one ever does.'

Nodding in acknowledgement, she puts a hand to her stomach. Yes, regret, making the wrong call. And trauma, shame, guilt and grief, making their tumultuous comeback.

29

Calvin

Cal stuffs his damp towel in his kitbag and heads for the car. He inwardly groans at the prospect of today's diversion from home. His Sadie visits aren't easy at the best of times, but her mum doesn't work at a weekend, so she's always the first to the door, hand on hip and ready to give him the third degree before allowing him safe passage inside.

The glow of his 'date' anticipation wearing a little thinner, he pulls onto the motorway and sighs. The cohabiting wasn't his choice – neither Sadie's moving in, nor her walking out. Or the rest, for that matter. Of course he's a robot and devoid of human emotion, but that wasn't the reason for Sadie returning to Bolton and her mum's house. Not the main one, anyway. But Erica still gives him at least ten minutes of grief before settling down and reluctantly nodding to the stairs.

Eventually indicating left, he drives past the row of identical new-builds. But as he nears Erica's semi, the tension eases from his shoulders. There's no car in the driveway, so she is out. Is that an entirely good sign, though? Painful as she can be, she's a barrier of sorts. When her mum's around, *Sadie seems to hold* back from the fraught angst, heavy tears, shrill arguments and all the other emotional stuff he's crap at. And more recently her unsubtle moves to get their relationship back on track: 'I think it's time I came home again, don't you, hon?'

What can he say when he's trapped by her question? But when Erica is there, she answers for him: 'It's too soon, love. Too soon.'

He raps the knocker and folds his arms as he waits. Dull nothing spreads in the cavity of his chest. Perhaps Sadie is right. Even the excitement of tonight's tryst has clean gone now. He stares at the shiny new letterbox. He so wants to feel something; he's tried his damnedest to find love, even a spark of affection, but bugger all is there.

'Is that you, hon? Come in this way; I can't find the keys.'

Shaking himself back to Sadie's husky tones, he strides around the side path. Wearing fluffy slippers and an oversized jumper, she gestures him in the back door. 'Hurry up. I don't want to let in the cold.'

The wall of heat hits him. The 'cold' wouldn't stand a chance in this house. It has always felt like entering a huge ball of wool, but these days it seems even more tangled and suffocating. Psychological, undoubtedly; he knows that.

Clearing his throat, he finds his voice. 'No car on the drive. Your mum not around today?'

Sadie smiles. 'You're in luck; she's gone to the Trafford Centre with a friend.' She lifts her eyebrows. 'Which leaves just you and me ...' She holds out her arm. 'Come on then, hon. Let's go upstairs.'

The pleasure, the excitement, the eagerness on her undoubtedly attractive face. Oh God. What can he do, but take her proffered hand?

111

As she pulls him behind her, he watches the sway of her ample, firm bum. On the landing she grins, opens the door and tugs him playfully towards the bed.

Praying that today will be different, he closes his eyes before focusing again. Enveloped in a white blanket, the baby is asleep in his cot. Not a baby, but *his* baby, his four-month-old son and the reason why Sadie left him. Though he transferred to a permanent daytime six-to-six shift when she became pregnant, it didn't satisfy either her or her mum. They still complained that the new working arrangements meant he left the house at an 'ungodly hour' and wouldn't be there to help in the morning. So Sadie moved back here to her mum's before he was born.

Would it have made a difference if she'd stayed in Whalley Range? He truly doesn't know, and though he's digging deep to feel *something*, only emptiness is there.

He tunes in to Sadie's voice. 'Sorry, what was that?'

Her cheeks glow with pride. 'I said, "Isn't he perfect?"'

'Yes, yes, he is.'

She motions with her hands. 'Shall I pass him over? Would you like to give him a cuddle?'

Cal shakes his head. 'No, it'll wake him.' Then, avoiding her eyes, 'Really, it's fine. He looks so peaceful, let him sleep.'

30

Cordelia

Inwardly fuming, I sit at the oak dining table and take in the Sunday lunch leftovers.

'Oh dear. Rather badly judged, Cordelia. You need to remember you're not feeding the five thousand, dear,' Harriet commented when she'd polished off her second helping of the treacle sponge pudding I'd made especially for her.

No flaming '*Thank you for making the huge effort for me for Mother's Day*' or '*I know it's hard to anticipate quantities when the meal could be for four or four hundred.*'

After slaving in the kitchen all morning, I was tempted to fire out a curt reply, but Vincent glanced at me with his 'Darling, you're too sensitive' look.

'Don't worry. Nothing will go to waste,' I said instead, as lightly as I could muster.

Still, it's better than not preparing enough. It happened only the once, but the humiliation of having to resort to bread and butter to feed the extra surprise visitors has stayed with me ever since.

Following his mother out, Vincent patted my shoulder. 'Better luck next time, darling. You know I'd help with the dishes, but it's time for me to get off.' He studied me for a moment, then pecked my lips. 'Beautiful. Very beautiful. I knew a lighter shade of lipstick would suit you better.'

The slab of glistening beef evokes a childhood memory of my dad. As though he's sitting there now, I listen to him eloquently tell the story:

'*So, dearest children, you will all be shocked to learn I wasn't always a debonair and erudite university don. I was actually a cosseted young innocent, brought up in a village in the sticks called—*'

'*We know, Dad. Called Netherthong.*'

'*And at eighteen I left with my knapsack to discover the world. On my first foray to an inn, I was offered a "joint". Naturally, I assumed it was a chunk of knock-off meat rather than a spliff, so I readily accepted . . .*'

He related the tale so often the three of us groaned and rolled our eyes, but he'd add a little embellishment each time to make us laugh.

I shake the affectionate picture away. An *innocent*. Well, Bill certainly made up for lost time. As a handsome and charismatic professor of English Literature, he had a pop-star type of fame and behaved accordingly – drugs, partying, student groupies and affairs – until he got Gilly pregnant. Of course, I only found this out later, when my mum expelled him from Clothorn Road and angrily spilled the beans of his double life to her astonished children.

My charming father, the man who pulled out my very heart and chucked it away. Before then he'd been the love of my life.

Though Felicity's decision to oust him was unswerving, it didn't stop him turning up at our house from time to time, generally late at night, blind drunk and blathering his pitiful apologies to us all. On one occasion he stumbled into me and Vincent in a clinch outside the front door. His face a livid red, he pointed at his future son-in-law. 'You sick, sick bastard,' he mumbled, then he threw an ineffectual punch.

I rub the pitted tabletop thoughtfully. At the time I was astonished at my father's temerity, his sheer bloody hypocrisy. The two men were chalk and cheese, I thought. Vincent was solid, stable, a rock; my dad was a two-timing, flaky bastard who had betrayed not just his wife, but me. And yet as the years have gone by, I've discovered they aren't so very different. Vincent has celebrity in his own realm too; he revels in his christening, wedding or funeral 'parties' and he sure has his adoring followers. Was their similarity the real reason I fell so deeply in love with him? Do I still *love* him now?

Winded by my own thoughts, I remind myself that Vincent has never let me down. Quite the opposite, in fact. He did something for me well beyond the call of duty. Whenever I feel unappreciated, I need to focus on that.

I methodically gather the plates and dishes, but when it comes to the knives, I study the carver thoughtfully. After Luke's death Vincent locked sharp implements away in a cupboard. Cleavers, scissors, pruning shears. Even his box of tools. To protect himself, Abbey or me, I'm not sure. In my zombified, compliant and grief-stricken state, it didn't matter. I just drew breath and obeyed until my existence became a crack more bearable. But it took far, far too long, and by then I'd lost Abbey completely.

Abbey, my adorable baby girl. She's almost a woman, the same age as me when I first met the tall, handsome curate and developed an infatuation so huge that it hurt. A *crush*. Metaphorically, physically. Disabling me, paralysing me, somehow. So fearful of losing him and the certainty I craved, I abandoned my friends and my plans for university. I stayed here and got stuck.

How I wish I could be more effective as a mother and say to Abbey, 'Don't make the same mistakes as me!' But we don't have that intimacy. Occasionally I glimpse connection, even affection in her eyes, but it always dissolves like a mirage. Same as today – not acknowledging that Harriet wasn't the only 'mother' around the table when Vincent gushingly toasted her, then pushing away the remains of her nut roast without a hint of gratitude, and eventually stalking from her chair. Did Vincent reprimand her for her surliness? Of course not.

Puffing the dull angst away, I cut a slice of beef into the tiniest of cubes, add a small blob of gravy and make my way to the back door. A dog would be lovely company, but Harriet is allergic to pet hairs, so I've adopted a cat or two. Clearly anticipating their lunchtime call, the moggies dart in.

When I knelt for prayers at this morning's service, I mulled over tonight's assignation and firmly decided against it. There were so many people in hardship at our church alone – physically, financially, mentally, emotionally – whereas I had health, a roof over my head, a husband and child. As the vicar's wife, I should be setting standards; betrayal and disloyalty were wrong on every level; so were lust and greed. And I was being greedy, wasn't I – another sin of desire – wanting to acquire or possess more than one needs; what on earth was I thinking by even contemplating it?

I watch the cats purr their appreciation. But right now I don't give a damn.

31

Calvin

His heart pumping with exertion, Cal stops at the bus shelter and bends over to catch his breath. He's pretty much sprinted the whole way from his home, so that's something. He's managed to squeeze a positive out of the dark gloom he's felt all afternoon.

He so wanted to feel a sense of love for the baby, hoped this time would be different. Zachary. Zach. A bit biblical, but a good name. A nice child too, he can see that – button nose, dark eyes and glowing skin. But today was no better than before – it was like peeping into a stranger's pram and going through the polite, meaningless motions: isn't he cute; he's grown in just a week; how's he sleeping, is he feeding OK?

Slipping her arm through his, Sadie kissed his cheek. 'Weren't we clever to create something so amazing?' she said, and he knew the next comment was on her lips even then: *I think me and Zach should come home now. Don't you?*

He swerved it like he'd swerved it the last time. 'Is your dad awake?' he quickly asked. 'I'm on call later, so can't stay that long. It would be good to say hello.'

He now falls back against the bench. So much better with the dying than the living, he stayed 'chatting' with Sadie's terminally ill father for some time. About football and cricket; the weather, his job, the usual bloody politics at work. He was mostly talking to himself, but he knew the poor sod was listening from the weak squeeze of his hand, the almost imperceptible nod.

'*I'm so sorry,*' Cal wanted to say to him, '*but I don't love your daughter or your grandchild as I should. I promise I'll provide in any way I can, but I don't want them to move into my home. We won't be happy. I'm unable to do contentment, even for myself. What good would I be to them? You do understand, don't you?*'

He sighs and wipes the perspiration from his brow. That elusive *joie de vivre*. Catching glimpses here and there only makes it worse. Indeed, he felt so negative that he composed a message to Dee:

Sorry, can't come tonight . . .

But instead of sending it, he found himself changing into his running gear. Not to meet her for sex or any physical contact – that desire had vanished – but to see her and talk, tell her about Zach and how the feelings he should have for his son are simply missing.

He looks down at his mobile to check the time. She's late. He snorts at the irony. Maybe he's pelted three and a half miles for nothing; perhaps she's stood him up. But when he lifts his head, there she is, looking left and right, then crossing the road at the very spot the car hit her.

'Hello.' She's smiling that smile, bashful and sweet beneath her cap. Then it falters as she nears him. '*Oh, have you been* running?' Her eyes widen. 'Are *we* going for a run? I don't think I could possibly keep up with you . . . '

His own despondency slaps him. The sweat is now icy on his skin. He probably looks like shit. 'No, sorry. I felt a bit . . . flat, so I thought some exercise would shake me up and I didn't want to let you down by not coming . . . '

True words. That's exactly how he feels. And so refreshing just to say it out loud.

She sits next to him and stretches out her long limbs. 'Same here after lunch today. Well, not just today. Flat. It's a good word. So very flat, I'm invisible. But this time I decided to be . . . ' She seems to search for a word. 'Rebellious.'

He turns to study her face. Though the peak partly hides it, she's lifted her chin in a defiant type of way. It reminds him of the girl from primary school, someone he's almost lost sight of.

'*Invisible?* Golden girl Dee Dee Stephens? Hardly.' It comes out more harshly than he intends.

'Yes, invisible, every single day.' Then she frowns and stands up. 'Anyway, what would you know about it? You don't live my life.'

Why her flash of anger turns him on, he can't say, but he reaches for her hand to stop her leaving. 'Sorry, don't go. I'm just in a shit frame of—'

'Fine, but don't take it out on me.'

'I came because I wanted to see you, to talk—'

'Talking involves *listening* too, Calvin. I have enough self-absorbed people in my life without you adding to their number.'

He finds himself smiling. 'Bloody hell, self-absorbed. That's telling me.' He tugs her back to his knees. 'So cruel when all I want is a kiss.'

She looks at him pointedly. 'Well, that's not going to happen.'

He laughs. 'Liar.'

'Hmm, at a bus stop in *Burnage*? I'm not twelve.'

'My place, in the morning then?' The words are out before he can stop them. But why the hell not? 'I'm not working tomorrow, so you could come round during the day. Say you're out shopping. I'll make lunch and I promise to listen.'

'I'll think about it.' And with that she pulls back her hand and paces away.

32

Cordelia

My chest tight and stomach churning, I indicate left and drive past the long row of three-storey terraced properties. **Number eleven**, Cal said in last night's text, but there's no space to park outside his house or his neighbours' either side, so I continue to the end of the street. Stopping at the junction, I expel my snared breath. Am I going to do this? Because coming to Cal's house is huge, isn't it? It's far more than a walk or a smooch in his car. Should I just drive on to the big Asda and actually *shop* as per my muttered excuse when I bumped shoulders with Harriet at the door?

An old memory flashes in. 'My son was married to God,' she once said. 'You pushed him to break his vows; you deliberately forced his hand and made him an adulterer.'

I straighten my shoulders at the thought. Does she really think that? Vincent isn't a Catholic, let alone a Catholic priest, and even she must be aware of his penchant for female adoration of any shape, age or size. What did Mari say in her usual sardonic tone when I told her our marriage plans? 'Uh-oh, the ladies' fave eligible bachelor bites the dust. Watch your back, Dee Dee. There'll be tears, tantrums and hat pins at Evensong.'

Adulterer. Is that why I'm here? Is it some sort of symbolic revenge on the woman? No, more likely the desire to be appreciated, wanted, cared for, even simply noticed. Or perhaps it's more carnal than that. Cal has aroused sensations which have hibernated for years. Do I simply want sex?

My legs fizz with anxiety. I should stop this, shouldn't I? I should give myself a good talking-to and just say no. Sure, his mother is a nightmare, but I'm married to a good, compassionate and loyal man. What *am* I doing here?

I glance at my bright eyes and pink cheeks in the mirror. I'll turn the car around, park up and find out.

The doorbell is covered by ivy, but I eventually locate it and nervously push. Wearing my cap would be a little OTT, but I'm conscious of Cal's neighbours as I wait. Will anyone think it odd that some random woman is on his doorstep? Well, no, why would they? I could be an old friend, a district nurse or here to tend to his spiritual well-being. Though I wasn't good on that score yesterday, was I?

Ring again or just bolt? I'm on the point of retreating when the door blasts open. 'Dee!' Cal looks genuinely surprised. 'I was upstairs in the ...' His face breaks into a grin. 'Come in, come in.'

He's wearing grey joggers and his slightly damp T-shirt is moulded to his chest. He must have been in the shower. And yes, his torso *is* toned if the outline is anything to go by.

'Wow, you're here,' he says.

'Only for the promised lunch,' I reply. Though I try for a sardonic tone, I can't help smiling back, and pleasure fizzes in my belly at his obvious delight in seeing me.

He rubs his head. 'Lunch, ah.'

'You forgot about feeding me?'

'Well . . . ' He laughs. 'As it happens, I have secret skills. Give me three ingredients, any ingredients, and it'll be the best food you've tasted.' He gestures to his front room. 'Go on through. What can I get you? Tea, coffee, juice?' He doesn't wait for an answer. 'I honestly didn't think you'd come.'

I perch on the leather sofa and take a breath. I was thinking about this last night, analysing it I suppose, and I've spent too long keeping everything buttoned up, being compliant instead of saying what I feel. For so many reasons I know that's my lot at the vicarage, but it's important to be different with this man – actually open and honest.

'I'm sorry about yesterday. I shouldn't have been so snappy but . . . ' I feel myself flush. 'I'd been uncertain about it, but I made a decision to come. I wanted to see you; I was looking forward to it; the last time we'd met was so nice. Then when I got there . . . '

Cal sits next to me. 'I was self-absorbed *and* sweaty. Not a good combo.' He softly kisses me. 'You wanted to see me, eh?'

'Yes.'

He moves his lips to my ear and works down my neck to my shoulder blade. 'You were looking forward to it?'

'Yes.'

'*Really* looking forward to it?'

I laugh. 'Don't push your luck.'

A little giddy and smiley, we kiss for a while, but when it becomes more intense, Cal pulls away and looks at me earnestly. 'It *was* so nice. Incredibly nice. Shall we go upstairs?'

Oh God, this is the moment. This is the second I make a

choice. But in truth I've already made it, haven't I? Or at least my yearning body has, so I nod.

My heart hammering in my chest, I take his proffered hand and follow him up the stairs to the first landing. As though making a decision he pauses, but he points to the left. 'That's the bathroom and the bedroom is—'

'I'll just pop in there now, if that's OK.'

'Sure.' He gestures towards the room at the front. 'I'll be in there. See you in a minute?'

'Yes.' My voice is stuck in my throat. This is too, too surreal. In the early days of passion with Vincent, he stripped off my clothes and consumed me the moment we were alone. He couldn't get enough of my limbs, my flesh, my bum and my boobs. Afterwards he lavished me with kisses, compliments and delirious thanks, but this whole experience feels different. Unbelievably arousing, yes, but tentative and tender too.

Just needing a few moments, I sit on the loo without lifting the lid. I couldn't force out a wee even if I tried. Speaking, swallowing, even respiring is a struggle right now. After a minute I stand on shaky legs, move to the sink and wash my hands. But I can't look in the mirror; seeing my own reflection would make it more real.

I softly push open Cal's bedroom door. Offering an arm, he hitches to one side of the mattress.

'All good?' he asks.

'Yes.' I glance at my boots. It seems wrong to lie on a bed with them on, but Cal is still dressed, so removing them seems suggestive.

'You're so pretty,' he says, tracing a finger down my nose. 'Even more pretty than I remembered.'

My breath is trapped in my lungs; I need to exhale. 'It was only yesterday,' I manage to croak.

'Yeah, I'm sorry about my moodiness. I don't always sleep that well.'

'Oh no, why not?'

'Oh, just overthinking stuff.'

'What type of stuff?'

He laughs. 'Self-absorbed stuff you don't want to hear.'

I give his chest a little shove. 'I do, actually. Try me.'

'Sometimes I have . . .' His eyes flickering, he pauses then he grins. 'Well, last night was pretty bad.'

'Bad, how?'

'I was thinking about this.' He pecks my lips, then kisses me more deeply. 'Tormented, plagued by it all night, in fact.' As he moves to my throat, he smooths a hand over my clothed body, my breasts, my stomach, my thighs. 'And by this, and this.'

My belly flips. 'Funnily enough, me too. This plague must be contagious.'

He stops and studies me. 'You know what?'

'No . . .'

'I know I shouldn't, I really shouldn't. But I do like you.'

33

Mariana

'Have you managed to get out at all this week?' Mari asks her client.

Her eyes huge with concern, his wife Amancia answers for him. 'We did, didn't we, love? We had a little walk on Friday, but out of nowhere he saw another house on fire. Of course, I looked too, but . . . ' She shakes her head. 'So now he doesn't want to leave here at all.'

Mari nods. 'How did the incident affect you, Seamus?'

'I was terrified.'

'You were afraid. Did you want to run away?'

'Yes.'

'And how did that make you feel?'

'Guilty.' He covers his face with trembling hands. 'Guilty, guilty, guilty.'

Mari glances at the large crucifix adorning one wall. 'OK. Let's go a little deeper. Just focusing on Friday, try and describe what you could see and hear, what you could smell or taste . . . '

She carefully listens to his reply. Of course, objectivity is the key. As well as empathy, impartiality and communication;

honesty and integrity. But it isn't always easy. Her work covers a whole gamut of problems, but some cases affect her more than others. Though she'd deny it if asked, she knows which common denominator brings the burn to her nose – guilt, loathsome guilt. Every bloody time, the ravages of remorse catch her short.

Today is no exception. Right now she's gazing at the fragments of a man. Though tall and broad, he's withered. Physically, mentally, emotionally. He's undoubtedly suffering from late-onset post-traumatic stress, but it's his failure to save his child which has crippled him. After blocking the truth out for so long, he's finally blamed himself and wants nothing other than to stop living. Having buried it so deeply, the pain is too much to bear.

It's not for everyone, but the team have decided on trauma-focused CBT to help him process it. The plan is to gradually expose him to thoughts, memories and feelings relating to it so he can learn to deal with them rather than avoid them.

Avoidance. Blocking. Culpability. Guilt. Mari inwardly sighs. *'Physician, heal thyself.'* She's fed up of thinking it.

Mari carefully closes the door behind her. She prefers to call those she helps 'clients' rather than 'patients', but she's increasingly calling them 'people' to reduce the power differential. The people in this case are both Seamus and Amancia. The poor woman's terror was etched on her face as she saw Mari out, so she didn't need to say, 'Do you think my husband will kill himself?' but the hushed words bubbled out in the porch.

Is Seamus a suicide risk? He denies having those thoughts, but Mari will have to carefully monitor it and develop a crisis plan if necessary. She makes a mental note to talk it through with Sanjay.

Waving in case anyone is watching from the window, she walks down the flagged path towards her car. Her limbs feel as leaden as her head. She pulls the door to and yawns so widely that her cheeks seem to crack. Quite honestly, she could sleep at the wheel from lack of shut-eye and particularly anxiety; constant mental thrashing makes her tired, it always has.

She turns on the ignition and shakes herself down. Only last week she read an article which stated that 46 per cent of National Health psychologists suffer or have suffered with depression themselves. Perhaps with their day job it isn't surprising, but right now her trembling fingers are not from work stress – she's still winded from her panic attack yesterday. What brought it on? And more to the point, will it happen again?

Fighting another yawn, she stares through the window. If she shared her 'episode' with Sanjay, she knows perfectly well what he'd say – that new trauma often has a snowball effect; it rolls along, dragging up old stones and historical dirt as it spins. And he'd be right. So it's down to her to stop overthinking and douse it with salt. Not just the past, but the present too. Swill the stupid paranoia and apprehension away. There's no time to dwell now anyway. Though she could steal a short break for a sandwich, it'll take her more than half an hour to get back to the clinic, and she has, what? Another three or four patients to see this afternoon? God, she'd better get a move on.

Putting the car into gear, she navigates the warren of identical council houses, clocking several youths who should be at school. One of them makes to step out in her path with a grin. She blares the horn. Stupid bugger. Like Ed when he was that age – reckless almost to the point of a death-wish. She misses the *silly sod*.

'When are you visiting us?' she demanded when she last spoke to him. 'I need to pin you down.'

He laughed. 'At some point during the first six months of the baby's life.'

Which, by her brother's terms, is pretty damn soon.

The thought of Britt and the baby reminds her that her phone is on silent, so she pulls up on the pavement and peers at the screen. Oh hell. Missed calls from Britt followed by several messages. Her heart thumping, she scans them.

The first:

Just called you. Think labour has started. Can you turn back right away?

Followed by:

Where are you? Call me!
Why aren't you answering?

I'm in pain, Mariana. Where are you?

Are you on your way?
Bloody call me.

Then the last:

I think my waters have broken. Can't believe you're not here. I'm calling a taxi.

34

Calvin

'I do like you.'

Cal's own words jangle in his head. Shit, why did he say that? But Dee leans forward, puts her lips to his and kisses him so tenderly it's hard not to squeeze her tightly and crush the aching sweetness out of them both. And though his penis, his body, his whole bloody psyche longs to explode, he can't quite read Dee, their relationship or this situation. All he knows is that he does like her, that everything about her arouses him, that somehow she makes his negativity turn on a sixpence. That he wants to punch the bloody air from her being here in his arms.

He strokes a strand of hair from her cheek. 'I was wondering ...'

'Yes?'

'Whether you might take your boots off at some point?'

She chuckles. 'Are they dirtying the duvet?'

'Well, I didn't like to say ...'

'In that case ...' Swinging her feet to the floor, she bends to unzip her knee-high boots. *Her slim back turned away, she pulls* off her tights. Then she stands and peels off her jumper dress. She rotates and smiles. 'Your go.'

For a pulse he's frozen as he stares. Christ, a black silky camisole and matching briefs. And clearly no bra. His erection urging him on, he quickly rallies, standing from the bed and shedding his clothes.

Aching with desire, he meets her toe to toe. Then taking a heady breath, he slides down the thin straps of her slip.

35

Mariana

Finally in the maternity car park, Mari shoots into a corner space and grabs her bag with fumbling hands. How she's arrived here in one piece, she doesn't know, but she jumped a fair few amber-to-red lights. Tumbling out of the car, she rushes past the ticket machine and hurtles down the steps as fast as her heels will allow.

Bloody hell; Britt's first message was not long after she'd left for the first home visit. It's professional practice to put a phone on silent for consultations, but three hours have gone by. While she was more than empathising with feelings of self-recrimination, Britt was in labour. Fucking ironic or what? What must Britt have thought when no reply to her calls or messages came? Mari is her labour partner; she's been with her to all the NCT classes. Broken waters aren't just flaming theory; what if she's missed the actual birth?

Almost skidding to a stop at the reception, she has to take a moment before speaking.

'Hi,' she says when her panting is under control. 'I'm here for—'

But a familiar deep timbre is echoing her way. Frowning, she turns to look. Bloody hell, it's Vincent. What the . . . ? His back turned, he's on his mobile and strolling away. What the hell is *he* doing here?

Hot annoyance strikes her chest, swiftly followed by another choking thought. Oh God, he's a vicar. How does he laughingly describe his job? *Hatch, match, dispatch.* Has something dreadful happened? To Britt or the baby?

Her limbs tingling with fear, she inches down the corridor towards him. When she's almost at his shoulder, he suddenly spins round.

He jumps, but not half as much as she does. 'Mariana! There you are at last.'

The air squeezes from her lungs. Even Vincent wouldn't look so jolly in the face of a tragedy, but still she needs to know. 'My mobile was on silent. How's Britt? Is everything OK?'

He gestures to an open door. 'Ask her yourself.'

Almost sick with apprehension, Mari walks towards it and peeps around the jamb. A monitor around her huge belly, Britt is propped up on the bed. Her arms are folded, her expression closed and surly.

'Finally,' she snaps. 'I heard you out there. Why didn't you check your phone? We're about to have a bloody baby!'

Both the relief and the 'we're' feels like a pleasurable ache in Mari's chest. She steps towards her irascible lover. 'I know and I'm so, so sorry. I turned it to silent for the home visits but I still should have checked.'

Vincent's aftershave wafts in behind her, so she turns, trying to control her irritation. Civil but firm is the approach. 'Thank you, Vincent. I think I can take it from here.'

Almost tapping his heels, he gives a little bow. 'Any time, Mariana. Always glad to be of assistance, especially for family.'

'Right. Thanks again.'

Britt shakes her head when he's gone. 'What was I supposed to do, Mariana? I phoned you a million times, then I tried Cordelia. Neither of you answered. Vincent was the next best thing and he was able to bring me here straight away.' She raises her eyebrows. 'He's not very pleased with Cordelia going AWOL. He's been calling everyone, trying to track her down.'

Mari absently nods. Bloody St Vincent. It's no surprise taxi-cum-ambulance driving is part of his skill-set. But in fairness, he's done them both a massive favour. He's good like that; heroically hurtling from A to D in someone's hour of need; she's heard it often enough from his fans. Pity she can't say the same for when his wife was in desperate straits. Talking of which, where on earth *is* Dee?

She comes back to Britt, sits on the chair and takes her hand. 'Sorry again. How are you doing?'

Her face is cloudy; she isn't yet for relenting. 'How do you think?'

Shaping a suitably worded grovel, Mari takes a breath, but her ears finally tune into the sound from the monitor. Despite the sheer terror, she finds herself laughing. Britt is understandably angry, but she's still beautifully pregnant and the sound of *their* baby's heartbeat is the sweetest background music.

36

Cordelia

Sweaty and wilted, I fall back against the pillow and close my eyes. I'm tingling and satiated and spent. How the heck did that happen? Any orgasms in the past were entirely self-induced once Vincent fell asleep.

'Hey.'

I flip my head to Cal. Propped on one arm, he's observing me with a gentle frown. Oh boy, he's handsome, his face so lean and angular, and those burning teal-coloured eyes, which seem to be asking a question. Vincent never enquired about my 'satisfaction', but there's something in Cal's gaze that wants to be sure.

'That was exceptionally nice,' I say with a smile. 'Thank you.'

'No, thank *you*.'

He pecks my lips, then flops against the mattress, his glossy chest heaving. When his breathing becomes slower and lighter, I gather he's asleep, but after a minute or two, he rocks back to me.

'I promised you lunch. Bet you're hungry. I am,' he says. 'But you've devastated me. Just give me five minutes and I'll get on the job . . .'

Still euphoric and relaxed, I stretch and smile. Should I nap

135

too? Could I in some stranger's bed? Well, that's a silly question, and anyway I need a wash. Careful not to wake him, I hitch up and take in my surroundings. Plain, pale grey-painted walls. A tall Ikea bookcase against one, a chest of drawers and a slim wardrobe on another. Not much to go on. Would my bedroom tell someone looking through the keyhole more? Probably not; double bed, double wardrobes, double married lives. My personality is reserved for my attic sitting room; Vincent's is locked in his 'corner of peace' study. Neither room has an actual lock and key, but each of us respects the other's private space.

Feeling a little intrusive, I step over the discarded condom and peep at the contents of the bookcase. A few of the usual thriller suspects, but the shelves are mainly stacked with CDs. I tilt my head to read the spines. Classical, mostly. That's interesting.

Scooping up my clothes en route, I tiptoe to the bathroom and take it in properly this time. Compared with the minimalist front room, it's a bright, warm surprise. Renovated with Victorian fixtures and fittings, the white replicas are shiny, clean and draped with colourful floor mats and towels.

I move to the sink and peer at my reflection this time. My cheeks are flushed and my hair needs a good brush, but do I look any different? I have just lost my virtue, after all. And not only that; I've broken my marriage vows, I've committed adultery and betrayed Vincent. But sensations of culpability are noticeable by their absence. True, I've now crossed a huge line, but I'm not sensing the weight of it. On the contrary, I feel light, almost glib.

A shower seems overly familiar, so I rinse my body with soap and pad myself dry. Once dressed, I glance down the stairs. Cal was right; I am starving, but a cuppa will be a start. Surely he won't mind if I make us one?

Curiosity defeating my nerves, I pad down and check around the banister. The kitchen door is ajar, so that's OK, and though the blinds are half down, it's friendly inside. Mismatched china mugs on a tree, decaf and regular coffee, a terracotta pot stuffed with teabags and a wooden tray slid to the side. I fill the kettle and flick it on, then I look at the fridge. Opening it feels more invasive, but with a quick breath I do. Apart from milk, there are bottles of beer, half a dozen eggs and a packet of bacon, one piece of steak, butter and cheese, half a quiche. It's clearly a single man's; nothing like the packed one at the vicarage.

My lips twitch. Cal wasn't joking about the three ingredients. He'd clearly forgotten about his lunch promise, but that's fine. I feel so calm and carefree when so much could have gone wrong. The sex might have been stilted or strange or disappointing. Suppose I'd freaked out or asked him to stop halfway? And what if he hadn't or became aggressive? I'd willingly come here and put myself in possible danger. But it was so flaming nice, his kisses silky in all the right places, his fingers gentle but knowing. And I responded in kind, exploring his beautiful body with eager lips and hands. It was fun and natural, passionate and romantic. And as for that intense, heady ending . . .

Good God; the vicar's wife has a lover! Feeling myself flush, I squeeze out the teabags and add a dash of milk. Does Cal take sugar? I chuckle to myself; I know he has a tender spot just below both his ears, that kissing his inner thighs makes him groan, but I don't know something as simple as that. Placing it on the tray with the drinks, I retrace my steps to the bedroom and peep in. Other than his light snoring, Cal is motionless. So what now? There's nowhere to sit, so the lounge is the best place to go. My handbag's in there too. I can check the time on my mobile and drink my tea; if he isn't up in ten minutes, I'll slip away and drive on to Asda as planned.

Mug in hand, I amble away. But instead of going down, I look up to the next floor. Cal's fast asleep. Why not have a quick look?

Hoping the distinct creak won't give me away, I climb to the top landing. There are two doors again. Spare rooms or maybe a study? I turn the first porcelain knob, glance in, then stare in surprise. Covered with bright scatter cushions, a king-sized bed fills the cosy, carpeted room. Smart fitted wardrobes and a dressing table adorn the far wall and expensive-looking drapes frame the window. Goodness, it's a very nice guest room if it is one.

A thought suddenly hits; perhaps Cal has a tenant.

Feeling bad for violating someone's privacy, I quickly pull away. I intend to retreat, but I catch the decorative plate on the other door. I step closer and read it. Zachary. Who's he? Surely not another lodger?

Placing my drink on the floor, I lightly push the pine panel and the portal sways open. Realisation hits like a sharp slap. A box room. What else do people use them for? For a cot, of course. One with blue bedding, soft bolsters and toys. And though I don't need to confirm what's blindingly obvious, I find myself crossing the supple carpet to the framed photograph on the wall. Zachary, presumably, with his smiling mum and dad.

Sick with shock, I spin around and clatter down the stairs to my handbag. This man has a wife or partner, but more importantly a baby son. The old grief grips my throat. Luke, my lost boy. I have to get away; I have to leave before panic consumes me completely.

Almost at the front entrance, I look down to my toes. My

boots; they're still upstairs. Feet barely touching, I dart back up to the dusky bedroom and reach for my footwear.

'Where were you?'

The sudden roar takes my breath. His features distorted and eyes almost bulging, Cal is sitting upright and glaring.

'I was just—'

'Get out!' he yells. 'Get out, get out. Get out right now.'

37

Mariana

Though a good twenty minutes have passed, Britt remains sullen. A trainee appeared in lieu of Vincent, chatted for a little too long about herself, but finally asked if Mari was OK and whether she'd like a cup of tea. That certainly hasn't helped Britt's mood, but Mari's struggling to maintain her apologetic face. She's just pleased to see her, so relieved nothing's amiss and that she hasn't missed the birth of their baby. Because he or she is *their* baby and being here at the start is the key.

Like Felicity at the other end of life.

'*Where are you, Mariana? I need you.*'

Blocking out her mum's plaintive voice, she inhales deeply to hide the discomfort. But the stab of grief is still there – if circumstances were different, her mother would be here, beautiful, contained and gentle, waiting patiently on the sidelines for her grandchild to appear. She was there for Dee Dee when Abbey was born, but not for long.

Although a huge effort, Mari holds out a metaphorical palm to stop the mental flagellation, to firmly halt the snowball's progress, and focuses on matters more imminent. Britt's still looking away, her expression stony.

'You know how sorry I am.' She squeezes her hand. 'But I'm here now and I'm so excited. What have they said so far?'

She thinks back to the NCT sessions. If she's honest, she isn't sure how much she took in; she was the passenger in the car, not the driver, and that stupid resentment was like constant road humps. But the jealousy has now gone, a miraculous blessing. All she can feel is intense love for this woman and their unborn child.

She briefly glances around the room. The classes included a quick tour of the delivery suites, but again she wasn't fully there. She does remember Britt looking pretty terrified at the sight of the birthing forceps and vacuum delivery kit, or 'instruments of torture', as she named them, and she complained about the 'stench'. But Mari works in a hospital clinic, she's used to looking at all sorts of strange implements, not to mention people, and if there's a smell, she no longer notices it.

She sighs inwardly. Oh, hell, she's been a crap birthing buddy so far, hasn't she? She needs to up her sensitivity and her game. She comes back to Britt, who hasn't replied. 'Any major contractions yet? They won't take you to the birthing pool until five or six centimetres, right?'

Britt rolls her eyes. 'You're not very observant, Mariana. Aren't you supposed to be a doctor?'

'Well, a doctor of . . . ' Mari peers more closely at the equipment attached to her partner. A blood pressure pad, cannula, intravenous liquids. 'Oh, right. You've had an epidural.'

'Yes, I have.'

'But I thought—'

'You're not the one giving birth, are you?' Britt's chin

wobbles. 'The contractions really hurt and you weren't here to talk it through. I was upset and they said it would help me get some rest.'

'OK.' Mari shakes the surprise from her head. It's fine, absolutely, but it was Britt who banged on about natural birth right from the start. She only agreed to a hospital because Mari persuaded her it would be a more sensible option for a first baby, and in case intervention was needed.

'Of course it's OK. Your choice absolutely.' She cups Britt's cheeks. 'Look, I am so sorry for not being here earlier, but now I am, can I get you anything?' She tries for humour. 'A box of chocs, scintillating conversation, Top Trumps or a stiff gin?'

Britt finally makes eye contact but doesn't smile. 'I'm tired, actually. I didn't sleep well last night.'

'Oh, right.' Mari wasn't aware of it. 'You should have woken me and said. But you were asleep this morning and I didn't want to disturb you, so . . . '

Britt yawns. 'The midwife said to relax while I can. There's a day room somewhere.'

'Right. Good.' Attempting to ride the ridiculous surge of rejection, Mari nods. 'So, where is the midwife?'

'A shift change, she said.'

'OK.' Mari studies the monitor and frowns. Is it OK just to nap when contractions are clearly going on? 'I'll go and see who's taking over. Back in a bit.'

Fighting a battle of emotions, she closes the door behind her and looks at her feet. Culpability fizzes. She should have known about Britt's sleepless night; she should have been more sympathetic about odours and instruments of torture; she should have been more attentive *all round. At the very least regularly checked* her mobile this morning, rather than focusing on work. Sighing deeply, she lifts her head.

'All well, Mariana?'

She stares. What the fuck? She all but told him to get lost half an hour ago. Bloody typical Vincent, wanting his finger in every pie. No doubt she didn't polish his halo quite as much as he desired.

She can't help snapping. 'There was no need to stay.'

He smiles benignly. 'It was only for a few minutes and I made some calls. Cordelia says I should delegate more, and so I have. Though where she is right now, I have no idea.'

That brings a small smile. Dee escaping from Vincent's radar can only be a good thing, but Mari wants him gone. 'Thanks for everything, but you can go now.'

'Right you are.' He lifts Britt's overnight bag. 'Though I think the new mummy will be needing this at some point, don't you? In our rush to get here, we forgot it. She asked me to pop back and fetch it. I would've brought it in earlier, but I thought the two of you might need a few moments ...' He pauses, lifts his eyebrows meaningfully, then adds another blasted strike. 'She was more than a little distressed earlier, not least because her birth plan is in here too.'

Bloody hell, five-nil to Vincent. But Mari has to be gracious; he's actually been a saviour; going to the hospital and back twice is beyond the call of duty. And she's desperate for a wee. 'You've been an absolute star, thank you, Vinny.' She nods to the valise. 'Can you hold on another minute while I pop to the ladies?'

Rearranging her expression from the one she's just seen in the mirror, Mari finally emerges from the toilets. The 'minute' has become five, perhaps more. She sat on the loo seat feeling fine, then moments later a wall of sweaty anxiety hit. Recognising the tingling in her hands and the onset of palpitations, she breathed deeply and waited for the bubbling panic to pass, but it's thrown her again, scared her, in fact.

Lifting her chin, she strides down the corridor and joins her brother-in-law. When she turns to Britt's door, a large lady emerges. She bustles towards them. 'Britt-Marie Nilsson?' she asks, addressing Vincent. 'I'm Jane, her midwife.'

The day really is not going well. Swallowing her exasperation, Mari steps forward. 'Hi, I'm Britt's partner, Mariana Stephens.'

'Sorry, Mariana, I've just started my shift. I understood from the handover that a man was . . . ' She glances at Vincent, then smiles. 'Ah, *Grandad*, of course. That's lovely; it's usually grannies who like to get involved in the . . . '

Mari heroically holds back the snigger, but the midwife's sentence trails away and the cheeriness drops from her peachy face. She taps the paperwork she's holding. 'Mum is fine, but I'm a little concerned that baby's heartbeat is dipping. This might simply be because of Mum's contractions or . . . ' She smiles thinly. 'It could be a sign of foetal distress.'

38

Cordelia

Sound finally seeps through, jolting me back from my zombie-like malaise. Feeling curious eyes on me, I look up to the till then down at my cup. That's right, I drove straight from Calvin's to here and ordered a hot drink. I pick it up, but my hands tremble so badly the liquid tips over the side. Spilled tea; flaming spilled tea. But my distress is so much bigger than that. My baby Luke. Just when I start to believe that the cavernous, huge hole in my heart has healed, out of the blue something happens, bringing it all back. Like now: the nursery, the happy family portrait; Cal's anger, the enormity of what I've done. The realisation slapped me as I hurtled away. Not only had I committed adultery, I'd betrayed the one man I could depend on, the person who was there when I needed him.

Trying to tame the rising panic, I focus on my surroundings. Asda café. The aroma of coffee and toast. Conversation buzzing around me. How long have I been sitting on this hard plastic seat? I glance down at my tea. Long enough for a milk skin to form.

Skin. Cal's skin and mine, so glued together it felt as though we shared the same one. How utterly misguided was I? Did I actually think *instinct* would suffice? Such a fool; a complete fool.

I take a deep breath to steady my nerves. Should I go home? No, not yet, and besides, my legs feel like jelly. What, exactly, is the time? I delve into my handbag. A purse and my folded shopper are in there, but no mobile.

The young girl at the counter has been joined by an older lady and they're both glancing my way. Are they talking about me? Do I look ill or even deranged? Possibly; probably. Oh God; I just need someone to tell me that everything is fine, perhaps even hold me, then I'll be on my way. But I can hardly do it with a stranger; I've already done that and look what has happened.

Mariana, call Mari. I know her work number. Yes, that's a plan, a good plan. Standing stiffly from the chair, I shuffle over to the customer services desk.

The assistant has kind eyes behind his glasses. 'Yes, love?' he asks.

'I seem to have lost my mobile.' I gesture to the telephone hung on the wall behind him. 'Would it be possible to make a call, please?'

He looks at me with a strange expression, but he nods and unhooks it. 'I can't let you come round here, I'm afraid, but if you stand to one side, you should have a bit of privacy. Dial nine for a line.'

'Thank you.'

Inhaling deeply, I press 9, but instead of Mari's number, I find myself punching other digits I know by heart.

It's answered after three rings. 'Knutsford six two seven five.'

146

It's how Dad always answers the phone. Paralysed, I listen to the beat of silence.

'Hello? Six two seven five.' Then after another second, 'Dee Dee, is that you?'

Tears prick my eyes. Is today going to be the day I finally reply?

'Cordelia, darling, please talk to me. Even better, come and see me. Or I'll come to you. Any time, any place, you know that.'

I so want to forgive my father; I so want him to forgive me. Pinching the top of my nose, I steel myself to speak. Say anything, say something, Dee. But as I draw breath, my step-mother's scornful voice filters through: 'Is that another cold caller? For goodness' sake, Bill, stop giving them the time of day. That's why they phone back so often.'

Though the line has been cut, I keep the receiver to my ear for several more moments. 'No answer,' I say when I finally hand it back. 'But thank you so much anyway. You've been a great help.'

I stare at the spattered windscreen and just breathe for several moments. I feel much calmer now. Whether it's from hearing my father's voice, finally lining my stomach or the shoplifting, I'm not sure. The theft is only a few bits and bobs today, but it gives me a buzz as always. It's not just the relief that I walked through the supermarket doors without feeling a hand on my shoulder, but the satisfaction of having *something* the Church hasn't paid for.

Slowing down behind a bus, I glance at the passenger seat. An argan oil shampoo, a shower gel and a deodorant – a spray one at that. God forgive me for using a non-ecological plastic container when a bar of soap will do – or damaging the ozone layer – but surely a few little luxuries are allowed? And besides, using the same roll-on antiperspirant that Vincent liberally applies every morning sets my teeth on edge.

I catch my clenched face in the mirror and blink. God, did I really just think that? It's mean-spirited, unfair and uncharitable; he doesn't deserve my loathing. He's a good man, my champion; today of all days is a reminder of that.

As I turn into my flagged driveway, I make a silent vow. I'll be kinder, more patient, more loving. Not just to Vincent, but his mother too. Difficult though she is at times, they come as a pair.

As though telepathic, she immediately appears at the front entrance with folded arms. Inwardly groaning, I climb from the car. So much for my pledge, but I have to try.

'Hello, Harriet.'

She looks pointedly at her watch. 'Where have you been?'

'To the supermarket. I did mention it.'

'For three and a half hours?'

Feeling myself flush, I open the boot and pull out the carriers. I was too distracted and despondent to think it through, but my meagre purchases hardly justify such a long absence.

'I had a drink in the café,' I say, having to push past Harriet's sturdy frame to enter the house.

Ignoring her steady stare and unnerving silence, I busy myself slotting milk, butter and cheese into the fridge. Though I know *something* is coming, it still makes me jump.

'Don't think I don't know exactly what you've been doing, Cordelia.'

I turn. 'I beg your pardon?'

Her face is puce. 'Not even an attempt to be subtle. And I don't suppose I'm the only one who knows.' She shudders theatrically. 'What will people think?' She puts a hand to her ruddy neck and her eyes moisten. 'What will my son think?'

I try not to gape. Then panic takes over. How the hell does she know? What should I do? What should I say? Flatly deny it? Or beg her to keep quiet? In truth, I *have* been indiscreet; I've brought this on myself. And if Vincent finds out, what then? He forgave me once, but this is wholly different.

Harriet's still glaring. 'You think I don't have evidence?'

What? 'No, I . . . Look, Harriet—'

But she scrambles from the room, so I lower my head and suck in some air.

'There!' Steadying myself, I peer at what my mother-in-law is thrusting at me. It's a box of PG Tips, but the smell . . . 'Go on, open it,' she commands.

Blowing out long and hard, I find myself chuckling. '*Evidence*, Harriet? What are you going to do? Have them tested for DNA?'

'I don't like your tone and it's not a laughing matter, Cordelia. We set an example here, for both adults and children.' Bustling to the worktop, she rummages in my remaining carrier bag. 'So they're not here. Where are they?' She sidles up to me, sniffing like a police dog. 'In the car? Or have you had a day's fill already?'

I struggle not to guffaw out loud. Her 'evidence' is a heap of cigarette stubs, clearly found outside and collected with forensic skill. And they're not mine but my husband's. It'd be liberating to tell his judgemental, pious mother that he isn't quite as

149

perfect as she thinks, but that works both ways, so instead I look her in the eye.

'I know this is important to you, so please believe me when I say that I don't smoke and never have. I expect it's the local kids or even nervous or upset parishioners. We deal with stressful situations, don't we? Illness and death; funerals and marriage. It's understandable, isn't it? We can forgive them for that, can't we?'

Deflating like a balloon, Harriet sniffles and nods.

'Good. OK, so . . .' I glance at the clock. 'Where's Vincent?'

'At the hospital.'

'Oh, right. Who is he visiting today?'

Back to indomitable, she straightens her shoulders. 'Well, if you answered your mobile, you'd know. He's been calling you since this morning.'

Alarm spreads through my chest. Irritation too. 'Just tell me, Harriet.'

'Your sister and . . .' She wafts an arm, the distaste clear on her face.

'Her name is Britt.'

'Yes. Her.' Harriet looks at her watch and jerks back in surprise. 'Oh, goodness, time has flown. I thought he'd be back long ago.' Her chins shake. 'I do hope everything's all right. I don't know the ins and outs, but the last I heard, she'd started in labour.'

I take a deep breath, but sheer anger overwhelms me. For Vincent's sake I try hard with this woman, I ignore or swallow back her put-downs, her criticisms, her sniping and swipes. But this is a step too far. Mari is my sister. Her partner is having their first child.

'So instead of simply telling me that Britt is in hospital, you spend half an hour challenging me, smelling me and searching my private belongings. Why is that, Harriet?'

Clearly shocked at my clipped tone, she steps back.

'Well, because we have standards, of course.'

I grab my car key and handbag. 'No, Harriet. It's because you're a spiteful, interfering old cow.'

39

Mariana

Mari softly strokes the hair from Britt's forehead. Only this woman could nap so soundly when her own heart is threatening to burst from her chest like the monster in *Alien*. But the thing inside her lover's womb isn't a fictional, threatening creature, it's a baby in distress, their baby.

She and Vincent watched the midwife hasten away with a ream of graph paper, talk at length with another woman, then nod and disappear. Long minutes later she returned with the sort of forced smile Mari sometimes has to use at work herself.

'The consultant is on his way,' she said. 'He's just attending another patient and won't be long. If you'd like to wait in the delivery suite, we'll come and find you there.'

As though she'd be anywhere else! But Vincent caught her arm. 'Are you all right? Would you like me to stay?'

So shaky and tremulous, she was tempted to say yes. But they were in a hospital with professionals, for God's sake. And Vincent, of all people?

'Thank you, but we'll be fine. You have your flock to look after.'

'She was quite distressed earlier.' He frowned as though searching for words. 'Not her usual sunny self.'

Mari now looks at Britt's smooth, sleeping face. Fuelled by frustration and impotence, her irritation is back. What does bloody Vincent know about anything? God, that man is a prick. And where the hell is the consultant?

She inhales slowly through her nose and breathes out through her mouth. She, of all people, understands that the National Health Service is brilliant, but that it goes at its own pace.

The door opens eventually, the room suddenly full. A suited man with a bow tie steps forward and introduces himself to Mari.

As though she's been feigning sleep, Britt snaps awake. 'What's going on?' she asks.

The consultant speaks to the ceiling. 'Jane asked me to look at your readings. Your contractions have stopped and the baby's heartbeat is dipping. This isn't unusual, and there's no need to panic, but I'm recommending an unplanned Caesarean section. I've discussed it with Jane, taken all the relevant factors into consideration and we agree this should ensure the best possible outcome for you and the baby.'

Wide-eyed, Britt simply stares.

'But the good news is . . .' Textbook speech done, he finally lowers his gaze. 'The good news is that you already have the anaesthesia in place, so it's just a case of topping it up and taking you in for surgery. Then you'll be awake and soon meet your newborn.'

'No!' Britt's yelp makes everyone start. 'No, no, no.' She jerks her head from side to side. 'You want to cut me open when I'm *awake*?'

Clearly surprised, the obstetrician steps back. 'It's very straightforward, it'll be over in minutes and you won't feel any pain. Ultimately it's your choice, of course, but a general anaesthetic will involve a complete loss of consciousness, then there's recovery time afterwards and the risks—'

'That's what I want.' Her eyes flicking wildly, she grabs Mari's arm. 'Tell them, Mariana. I don't want to see those things we saw ... not tools or knives or even the inside of an operating theatre. I don't want to be awake.' Her tone is shrill and pleading. 'Don't make me do it. Please. I want to be asleep. This is really, really important. Mariana?'

Stunned at Britt's terror, Mari takes a deep breath. 'I understand completely, I'd be scared too, but let's just take a moment to think what's best. You've already gone through the epidural, so there won't be any pain and you're halfway there—'

'No, I said no!' Britt glowers at her. 'This is your fault. Your fault!' She pushes Mari's shoulder. 'You made me do it.' Covering her face, she sobs. 'I want to get it out now. Just put me to sleep and get it out.'

Made her do it? Is that actually true when Britt was the first to raise the prospect of them having a baby? When she honed in on Mari's desperate desire? Dangled that tempting, compelling carrot? But now isn't the time to analyse their whole relationship.

She turns to the consultant. 'A general anaesthetic, please. I think Britt has made her decision.'

40

Cordelia

I lift my chin at the entrance to the maternity ward. I know that the distinct smells and sounds will bring back mixed memories, but I'm here for my sister. Trying to dispel the blend of anxiety and adrenaline, I pace the long corridor to find the right room.

Part of me feels strangely uplifted after my harsh words to Harriet; a little shocked at my own gall too. But I don't have the time to appraise it right now. I need to find Mari and check everything is all right. God, I pray that it is. When I asked for Britt-Marie Nilsson at the reception, 'She's been in theatre, but ... Yes, room twelve,' was the reply.

Finally at the doorway of the ward, I glance around. Four beds, three occupied, but no sign of a beaming blonde woman and her newborn. I almost turn away, then look again. My sister is in the corner, nursing a child.

Mari stirs as I quietly approach. Her smile rueful, she holds out her hand. 'A boy, Dee.'

Hiding the sharp slice of emotion, I pull up a chair, peer at the baby and speak in a low voice. 'Gosh, he's so beautiful.

Congratulations, Mari.' Then glancing at the sleeping figure, 'How's Britt? A tough labour?'

Mari kisses the tiny tot's brow. 'All's well that ends well, thank God, but pretty much everything that could go wrong did.' She snorts softly. 'Starting with me. I didn't even know she was here for hours. I was visiting clients, but I'd turned my mobile on silent and forgot to check it between appointments. Apparently she tried you, then resorted to St . . . ' She frowns and shakes her head. 'Sorry, that's unkind. Vincent was brilliant. He brought Britt to hospital, went back to fetch her bag, then hung around until I arrived.'

An image of Cal's face pops into my head. Not the contorted one when I left, but the one before that, soft with tenderness. I push it away and clear my throat. 'Mobiles, eh? I would have been here like a shot, but mine went missing.' I pull it from my handbag. 'I found it down the side of the driver's seat just now.' I actually did, but it sounds so feeble. 'I haven't had a chance to look at all the messages yet. Sorry.'

Mari cocks her head. 'Are you OK, Dee Dee?'

'Yes, of course.' Ignoring the heat which hits my cheeks, I take my sister's hand. 'I'm so thrilled for you. Really. Today is your big day. Britt's too, of course. How are *you* feeling?'

Tears swell in her eyes. 'Unimaginable, actually. They let me in the theatre as soon as the procedure was over and . . . ' She swallows. 'Everyone was so lovely. They all clapped and suggested I might like to do skin-to-skin with the baby, so I did. I never dreamed for a moment how completely awesome it would be. His perfection, his beauty, his smell . . . ' Her voice cracks, so she pauses for a few seconds. 'God, just listen to me! Who would have thought . . . '

156

Skin-to-skin and skin-to-skin. Pushing both memories away, I kiss the top of her head. 'I did. You were there for me and Ed. Always. You were our rock.' Needing to weep myself, I glance at Britt. 'So what happened?'

Mari snorts. 'Best-laid plans and all that. From a natural water birth to an emergency section.' She softly strokes the baby's cheek. 'I feel a bit guilty for having first dibs, but Britt ... Well, she pretty much insisted on a general anaesthetic, so ... She came round in the recovery room, but she's been sleeping on and off since. Would you like a cuddle?'

'Absolutely!' I hold out my arms, but Britt abruptly moves.

'Mariana?' she mumbles. She tries to sit up. 'Ouch. Oh my God, that hurts.'

Mari stands. 'Shall I raise the bed, then you can try holding him again?'

'Just give me a minute. Still feel so groggy.' She drifts away then pats her throat. 'Is there some water? My mouth's unbelievably dry.' Seeming to drift off, she falls silent, then her eyes flash open. 'Mariana,' she says, her voice tearful. 'I feel really sick.'

I shift position in the day-room chair. My hand a little shaky, I stare at the coffee from the vending machine. It smells pretty rank, but it's better than my first attempt with the tea. Batting *that* thought away, I focus on the joyous aspect of today. Who would believe it? Mariana Stephens has a child! What did she always say to me and Ed when we were growing up? *'I'll never have pesky kids. You two and all your whingeing have put me off for life. Anyway, I'd rather have a car.'*

Her obvious bonding with the little mite was wonderful to see, but Britt became quite tetchy.

'It's just the anaesthetic. It'll pass soon,' Mari said soothingly about her nausea.

'That's easy for you to say,' she replied. 'I feel as though I've been hit by a bloody bus.'

Poor Mari. I like Britt well enough, she's chatty, smiley and fun, but also a tad demanding. She's even . . . I think about that one. Surely not *controlling*? Mari has always been fiercely independent. And yet . . . Harriet calls Britt 'that manipulative young woman' with the usual frown of disapproval. Is she right? Could Britt really have the better of my sister? Leopards *can* change their spots and I'm a case in point; it's hard to believe I was once as feisty as Abbey.

Though the old Dee Dee made a spirited appearance with Harriet earlier, didn't she?

Lifting my hands to my nose, I inhale. While Mari attended to Britt, I held the baby. I put my face to his feathery hair and breathed in that heady, exquisite aroma of newborn innocence I remember so well. I was lost in the past when Britt snapped again. 'I'm tired now, Cordelia, can you go?'

But I don't blame her for her moodiness. Childbirth is tiring, painful and arduous, even without intervention, and her hormones will be overflowing for a while – just one of many new motherhood challenges nobody mentions. Yet the prize at the end is so, so worth it.

Looking out to the dusky evening, I sigh. Should I stay or go? I want to help and be useful somehow, but half an hour has now passed with no show from Mari, and thoughts about where I was earlier and *what* I was doing are now kicking in.

I picture the framed photograph in that box bedroom. Sure, I'm married and have a daughter, but *I've* never *hidden it*, whereas Calvin Rafferty has a girlfriend or wife and a beautiful baby he's conveniently forgotten to bring up in conversation. That isn't nice or normal, is it? Then his furious attack when I reached for my boots . . . He knew I'd been nosying and snapped. Anxiety sizzles in my chest. Such irrational rage out of nowhere . . .

41

Calvin

Though bleary-eyed and still yawning, Cal enters the staff car park. It's Tuesday and he's supposed to be off, but everyone is dropping like flies from flu. What will today bring? It's human nature to panic, but he wishes people would resist calling out emergency services for routine colds or aches and pains. How often does he have to grit his teeth and softly rebuke a worried relative or patient? *'For every person whose life is not threatened, I'm unable to support one whose life is.'*

Pleased to see his favourite RRV is there, he throws in his kitbag to nab it for his shift, then heads to the machine for a coffee. He's actually too early, but that's fine. Coming in on a non-working day is OK too. Better than sitting at home, his erratic thoughts prodding like a woodpecker. All afternoon yesterday, his mind was too active, swinging from regret to irritation to wistfulness: Dee Dee Stephens in his arms; holding, stroking, caressing, kissing, then invading her slim body. She was ... well, everything from shy and funny to so, so sexy and arousing, knowing exactly where to plant her lips and teasingly linger. He wanted to reach her physically, but also intuitively and quite honestly he thought he'd succeed on both scores. But he fucked it all up; like an idiot he gave in to the temptation of sleep.

He can't recall what happened before he heard the slamming front door, but he shouted at her, he knows that. The weight of despondency thumps like a wave again. Perhaps if he'd told her. Maybe if he'd warned her about the parasomnia, night terrors or whatever they are . . . And she did give him that opportunity. He could have told the horrible truth, let out all the angst, his guilt, his anger. But he's contained his emotions for so long, he doesn't know what damage the deluge will do.

He wrote several texts to explain, but none sounded right. Then, when he went upstairs to grab some clean clothes, he found a mug on its side, the brown liquid seeping into the box room's cream carpet. That threw him again. He should have told Dee about Zach, but what else might she have looked at or unearthed?

Cal stretches in his parked RRV. Starting with two falls by elderly patients, the morning has been slow. No trainee today, so he's working alone and in the long silences he's found his mind straying back to Dee. He didn't deliberately omit mentioning a son to her. It's intricate; his feelings – or lack of them – are bloody difficult to explain, even to himself. And if he opens that can of worms, so many more might wriggle out.

His mobile in his hand, he absently gazes at the rain spattering the windscreen. A simple text to explain that it's complicated? Or maybe ask to meet Dee and tell her in person? He spends a few moments composing another message, then deletes it and tries again, but his efforts are interrupted by an emergency call. A male in his thirties with a severe foot injury, fairly nearby.

Glad of something constructive to do, he belts up and pulls

out, negotiating the back streets and arriving at some electronic gates in an impressive three minutes. They duly slide apart, and when he reaches the front door with his kitbag, it swings open too and a man ushers him in.

The bloke smiles. 'Cheers for coming so quickly.'

'So, where am I going, mate?'

'In here will do,' he replies, gesturing to a glossy kitchen, then walking ahead with a limp.

The penny drops. 'You've called emergency services for yourself?'

'Yup.' The man rolls up his trouser leg. 'Hurts like buggery. Out drinking last night, managed to get home and sleep till lunchtime, but ... maybe it's broken?'

Hiding his frustration, Cal nods. 'I suggest you ring your GP or get yourself to a hospital for an X-ray.'

'How am I supposed to do that?'

'A taxi, a bus, a friend, a relative.'

'But you're here now. You can take me.'

'Sorry, emergencies only, mate.'

Cal turns to feed back to HQ, but his shoulder is grabbed. 'Firstly, I'm not your mate. Secondly, I pay more in tax than you earn, so I have a right to bloody treatment.'

Cal stares for a beat. It'd only take a couple of jabs, a cross and a hook to toy with him, and then ... But he'll save that for the gym. He steps away. 'Emergencies only, I'm afraid, sir. Good luck with the foot.'

Puffing out his hot irritation Cal manoeuvres the BMW around. What did his mum always say if he was left out or derided at school because he didn't have the branded trainers or latest cool clothes? 'Keep your head up, son. Remember, you are

162

as worthy as the next human being. Don't ever let yourself down by showing otherwise.'

His mum. Picturing her dancing to Whitney with her easy white smile, he breathes through the usual hurt. Her absence in his life is loyalty to his dad, that's all. Can he still blame her for it? Relationships are *complicated*, that's for sure. Perhaps it's time to get in touch and reconcile.

42

Mariana

Trying not to show her exasperation, Mari watches Astrid pad into the kitchen and yawn. She looks like her daughter but she's wholly different personality-wise. Unlike Britt, she doesn't smile and her whole demeanour is like a shrug of indifference, albeit a very graceful one.

Mari collected her from the airport yesterday and suggested they visit Britt and the baby en route home. 'What, today?' Astrid said, as though it was an off-the-wall suggestion.

'Well, yes, I thought you might like to see your new grandson straight away.'

She simply looked out of the passenger window, so Mari took that as a yes. Eventually she spoke. 'Does this baby have a name?'

A slightly contentious point. Until the birth, she and Britt had agreed on Oliver, but since 'meeting him' Britt declared he wasn't an Ollie and firmly suggested the name Cosmo, the Greek word for harmony and beauty. God knows where that idea had come from. As she said to Dee on the telephone, 'Can you imagine when I say, "Pass me Cosmo" . . . '

Still, Astrid saved the day. She took one dismissive look at the newborn and nodded. 'Isak. I-S-A-K. After your grandfather.'

'Thanks Mum, I like it,' Britt replied. 'Hello, little Isak.'

Mari clearly didn't warrant a role in the consultation, yet it was still a relief after seeing Britt's set-jaw determination over 'Cosmo'. And Isak is a good name. Though – as she also mentioned to Dee – the poor boy will have no end of trouble correcting the spelling. Her lips twitch at the thought. Bloody hell; she's sounding like a granny herself!

She now comes back to Britt's mother. Wearing a dressing gown remarkably like her own, she languidly brushes by and heads for the cupboards. Chatty, she's not. And now Mari looks properly, the internal light bulb flashes. It *is* her dressing gown. But she shouldn't be surprised; last night Astrid helped herself to her bedroom too. She threw her suitcase on the double bed and said, 'Night, then. I'm exhausted.'

Mari considered directing her to the pristine spare room, clean towels and bedding, but she chickened out and said, 'Just give me a sec,' while she quickly collected what she needed for the night. Pyjamas, toothpaste and face wipes. And clothes for today, though she forgot clean knickers and socks, so had to handwash the dirty pairs in the main bathroom sink and hang them overnight to dry. They're still a little damp even now.

She watches Astrid move on from the dry-food shelves to the fridge. She peers in, then closes it again.

Mari tries not to guffaw; clearly this hotel isn't up to scratch. 'Anything I can get you for breakfast?' she asks.

As well as cleaning the spare room and scrubbing the bathroom suite until it shone yesterday morning, she had belted around Tesco, bundling a whole host of delicacies in her trolley.

165

'We have eggs, cold meats and cereal. Then there's croissants, crumpets, pancakes and a seeded loaf in the bread bin.'

As though surprised she's there, Astrid's blonde barnet wafts around. 'Thank you, but I'll get brunch in town.'

'Oh, right. You're going into Manchester?'

'How could I not while I'm here?'

'Well, I thought you might—'

'A little shopping, a mooch around. It's a beautiful city.'

Shopping? Really? Mari tries not to gape. Astrid barely looked at Isak yesterday, but she put that down to travel tiredness. And she's hung around all this morning waiting for her to wake up. She'd stupidly assumed a new grandma would want to see as much of her grandson as she could. Her own mum would have. She'd have been joyous, generous, helpful and sweet. It's an uncomfortable thought that's been prodding since Isak was born.

Breathing away the emotion, she nods. 'OK. Then I'll get off to the hospital. Have you any idea what time you'll return? I can come back here to fetch you and save the cost of a taxi if you like.'

Astrid pulls a stray hair behind her delicate ear. 'Very kind, but let's see how it goes.' She leans forward confidentially and finally smiles her daughter's smile. 'Between you and me, Mariana, babies are a lovely novelty, but they're not terribly interesting.'

43

Cordelia

Pulling the front door quietly behind me, I step out to a new Thursday to buy flowers from the village. It's surprisingly balmy, and if I'm not mistaken, the aroma of spring flavours the air. Yes, I'll buy tulips as well as daffodils. The showy buds always give me hope and I very much need that today.

Wondering if I'll be too warm in this padded jacket, I glance back at the house and spot Harriet peering out of the lounge window. She hasn't spoken to me since my outburst, but I shrug the mild agitation away. Her cigarette challenge was a non-starter, and whatever madness happened with Cal won't be repeated, so the flaming woman can spy all she wants. Besides, Vincent hasn't said anything about my absence on Monday. He's as pleased as anyone that little Isak has arrived safely and that all is well.

We visited the hospital together on Tuesday. We clucked and cooed over the baby and Mari joined in. Looking back, we made a comical trio, each of us competing to admire the little man's beauty. His hands and tiny fingernails, his button nose and perfect toes.

But Britt clearly wasn't in the mood. 'If you're going to make

167

so much noise, take him into the day room,' she snapped. Though the rosy colour was back in her cheeks, she folded her arms. 'I can't move because I'm sore and I can't eat because I feel sick. I can hardly keep my eyes open and yet I'm expected to wake every two hours to feed a baby. But don't worry about me, you all have fun.'

Shamefaced, we put Isak back in his cot and all spoke at once. 'Poor you, but you'll feel better before you know it.' 'Is there anything I can get you from the canteen?' 'You've done brilliantly, and made us all very proud.'

In truth I wanted to say: *I know it's hard right now but you don't know how very, very lucky you are.*

I didn't, of course, but when we left, Mari ran after me. 'Britt's still getting over the anaesthetic, that's all,' she said with an apologetic smile. Then, offering her open arms, 'Thanks for being here for me, Dee Dee. I love you so much, you know that, don't you?'

When she pulled away, her face was so loaded with emotion, it was difficult to leave, but Vincent tugged me away.

'I know you'd have preferred to stay,' he said when we reached his Volvo. 'But it's best to leave them to it, Cordelia. A period of adjustment and trust on both sides.' He kissed my cheek. 'But we know that as much as anyone, don't we, darling?'

The flowers duly purchased and safely on the passenger seat, I drive towards Cheadle, taking a right turn before the village to the cemetery.

Clutching my blossoms, I weave through the neatly tended monuments and plaques, studying the tokens of memory, grief and love on each until I find the right one. Decorated with bright shrubs and bedding plants, there it is. Lovely Betty. She was the grown-up rock in my life from the moment I joined the church at fifteen. In her fifties then, she felt more like a genial granny, but as the years went by, she became a loyal and trusted friend. Though I knew it was coming, her death was still a dreadful shock. I was inconsolable, crying for days, unable to shake myself out of it. But I wasn't just mourning for Betty, it was for the loss of my mum too, something I didn't see until Mari talked me through it.

Whether it was personalities or simply being a wilful teenager, I now understand that there was a disconnection between me and Felicity. I still loved her enormously but struggled to show it because on some level I blamed her for letting Dad stray.

I shake my head. So unfair to my mum, and of course history has repeated itself with me and Abbey. Not because of anyone's infidelity – far from it – but from an emotional rupture none-theless. And yet I felt that tenuous connection, a beautiful spark over bagels and hair-straightening only a few weeks ago. And now she's back to cold and indifferent. Whatever that glint was, it has gone.

Saying a silent hello to Betty, I thread the daffodil stems through the grate at the foot of her grave. Mum often said they were her favourites. '*They don't last long, but how brightly they shine while they're here.*'

Nodding in acknowledgement, I tiptoe across the damp grass to a bench and sit down beside the tulips. Thirteen years ago, I came here every day, walking the mile or so from home until Betty or Mari fetched me back. Sometimes Vincent came for me, but with his eight-to-ten job, he didn't always have time.

The breeze gentle on my face, I close my eyes and drift until the beep of my phone brings me back. I idly look at the screen, then sit up in alarm. Oh my God, a text from *him*, the man I was with in the most intimate way one minute, but who shouted me out of his house the next. Trepidation clangs through me. What on earth does he want? I'd taken his silence as a good sign, that the dreadful thing I'd done could be hidden in a far recess of my mind and forgotten.

Eventually I sigh; I know I have to look.

Sorry about the sleep terror shouting. And I should have mentioned Zachary. He doesn't live here and it's complicated. Hopefully meet soon x.

I read it again. Sleep terrors. That makes sense – he was deeply unconscious one moment, then yelling the next. As for tangled relationships ... Dad, Mum, Abbey. Even Ed. I understand those. Feeling a spread of relief – and pleasure – I smile and consider how to reply.

Suddenly aware of a shadow, I flick up my head.

'Vincent!'

'Hello, darling,' he says, sitting down. 'Thought you might be here.'

I slip the mobile away. His spy and the flowers, no doubt. But it's nice he's here, good we both are.

Turning to the commemorative plaque between us, I lightly trace the etched dedication to our son. Little knowing she'd follow sooner than she'd like, Betty suggested this bench as a memorial for Lukie, and though the teak wood is becoming a little weathered, the brass sign is still as bright as the daffodils.

Vincent kisses my forehead. *'It's been quite a week, hasn't it?*

170

And you know, it isn't a sin to feel sorrow, bitterness, anger or even envy ...'

I nod. Mari and Calvin both have a living son, but my baby boy died, so yes, I felt all those emotions.

'But it's balanced out by love.' He smiles a sad smile. 'Isn't it? And that's what counts.'

The tears finally come, splashing down from my cheeks. Drawing me to him, Vincent's silent for a while, but he pulls away and peers into my eyes.

'It wasn't your fault.' Putting a hand either side of my shoulders, he looks at me steadily. 'You were not to blame,' he says, stretching out the words. 'Say it, Cordelia. Come on, say it.'

I wipe my face and take a shuddery breath. 'I wasn't to blame.'

Yet we both know I was.

44

Mariana

Her new son in her arms, Mari looks at the identical overnight cases and shakes her head. One is Britt's coming in, the other Astrid's going out. Her flight isn't until this evening, but she's been pacing like a caged panther all morning.

'Do you want to come with me to collect Britt and Isak from the hospital?' Mari asked her at breakfast.

'No, why?'

'*Well, you're leaving tonight and you've barely seen your grandson,*' she wanted to retort. Or perhaps: '*You have a perfect, gorgeous grandson. Aren't you the least bit thrilled? If not for yourself, for your daughter?*'

She managed to behave and simply reply with an 'OK', but Astrid's passivity, lack of interest even, makes her hopping mad. She's cross on Britt's behalf, little Isak's too. Astrid is the only grandma he has! But it goes deeper than that. Can't the bloody woman make an effort, perhaps act if she has to? Dee has. God knows how deeply the pregnancy, then the birth of a boy, has cut her, but she's been an absolute Trojan, visiting the hospital every day with an offering for both Britt and the baby. And more importantly than that, she's sported a warm, loving and enthusiastic smile.

Then there's her own mum. Though Felicity is always in her thoughts, her aching absence has gone up a notch. Mari so wants her back to share all the new-baby moments and listen to snippets about her own infanthood. And not least, have her pearls of wisdom about the million incidentals one needs to hear from a person who has experienced it themselves. She could ask Dee, but unless she offers, Mari can't do that. Though she's barely spoken about it over the years, the ramifications of a cot death run deep.

Sighing inwardly, she makes her way to the lounge and gently lowers Isak into his Moses basket. The thought of finding him limp and lifeless sends shivers down her spine. She feels guilty too. Her nephew would be thirteen now. Was she there enough for Dee when it happened? She'd finished her degree, but not her doctorate then. And though she'd done voluntary work, she hadn't had any one-to-one clinical experience. Like so many things in life, she could empathise and she certainly tried to, but real focus or clarity only comes when one is in the same position or has something to lose. She kisses Isak's tiny forehead. Like this little man.

She takes one last glance to ensure he's settled, then ambles to the kitchen. Has the frostiness thawed between mother and daughter yet? God, she hopes so; filling long silences is actually pretty damned hard. She found herself gushing about Beyoncé, the Kardashians, Taylor Swift and #harryandmeghan, just to generate a response from one of them. Britt replied from the couch but, perched on a high stool at the island, Astrid found her nails more interesting. Though in fairness, when it comes to the Kardashians et al, Mari's with her on that score.

Ready for more blather, she pushes at the door. Astrid's now standing by her daughter, hand on hip. Her usually pale cheeks are stained with two patches of bright pink.

Mari quietly steps back. Oh hell, they're arguing. Go in further or leave them to it?

Astrid's tight voice wafts through the crack. '*I'm* selfish?' She laughs without humour, her eloquent tones only betraying the hint of an accent. 'You have always done exactly what you want, regardless of anyone else, Britt-Marie. Picking up people, then discarding them as fast. Axel, Elias, Emil. And the rest of your nice friends. Half of them still live in our village. Then you come to the UK and suddenly change from chasing boys to girls. Where did that come from, your father and I ask. Did we miss something or do something wrong?' A long pause. 'Then Mariana comes along and once again you are smitten. But you can never just stop for a moment, can you? Stop and think of the consequences? You're greedy; you always want the next bigger and better thrill. But a baby . . .' She sighs deeply. 'A *bebis* isn't something you can toss to one side when you get bored. Did you stop for a moment to think about that?'

A sullen reply. 'I won't get bored.'

'Of course you will. You always do.'

'What little faith you have, Mamma.' Britt's voice is teary. 'Why did you bother coming?'

'Because you're my daughter and I love you.'

'What about Pappa?'

'He does too.'

'Then why didn't he visit with you?'

'You know the answer to that, Britt-Marie. In the Christian religion, children should be a product of love. Not some random donor and a turkey baster or—'

'It wasn't like that. You know nothing about it.'

Her heart pounding, Mari waits for Britt to say the words. Seconds pass. Then more. A sob bubbling up, she begins to turn away, but she finally, finally speaks.

'And anyway, Mamma. It was love.'

45

Calvin

The March Sunday morning has flown by with back-to-back call-outs. None of them life-threatening thankfully, but Cal and his trainee haven't even had time for a drink until now.

Glad he stuck just to coffee, Cal breathes in the fetid aroma of fried oil. He offered to buy Ali lunch for his birthday and he selected a McDonald's. It isn't Cal's first choice of cuisine, but at least the drive-through has the benefit of speed.

'So how's the big day going so far?' he asks.

Cal smiles at the sight of Ali's stuffed cheeks as he waits for a reply. He personally took a degree in Paramedic Science, but Ali was accepted by the ambulance service as a student paramedic and is learning on the job.

He swallows his mouthful and grins. 'Good. I mean, why would I want the pick of the chicks when I can spend the day with you?'

Cal laughs. 'Yeah, I get that all the time.'

'So, are you coming for a pint after work?'

Cal rubs his head. 'Yeah, if—'

A call crackles through, interrupting his reply. He listens

to the instructions about a male in his seventies with possible cardiac arrest, acknowledges the job and squashes his paper cup in the door pocket. 'Ready?' he asks, glancing at Ali. 'Category one; belt up.'

Feeling the usual surge of adrenaline, he programmes the satnav, applies the lights and siren, then negotiates the busy roads as fast as safety will allow.

'Can you see the house numbers?' he asks Ali once they hit the long street. But a white-faced young woman is at an open door, her arms above her head and waving madly. She rushes to the BMW as soon as they're parked.

'I was late, but it wasn't my fault,' she says with a noticeable East European accent. 'The previous client had lost her keys and I couldn't get in.'

Cal nods. 'OK. And you are?'

She pats her navy uniform. 'Cristina. His carer.'

'OK, Cristina. Try to relax, we're here now. Where is the patient?'

'In the kitchen.'

'His name?'

'William Watkins. Willy.' She claps her hand to her mouth. 'Oh God, oh God. If I'd been here earlier . . .'

Gesturing to Ali to take charge of the distressed woman, Cal grabs the kit and defibrillator and strides into the freezing house. A man is lying prone on the floor. He kneels by his side. 'Willy, can you hear me?'

As expected, there's no reply. Noting his pallid colour and feeble chest movement, Cal assesses him quickly. Possibly a stroke several hours ago with severe hypothermia is his guess; a rapid-response ambulance will need to take him to hospital as a matter

177

of urgency. But at least the old guy has a slow pulse. Trying to block out the carer's increasing hysteria from the hallway, he covers Willy with a blanket, applies oxygen to assist his breathing and calls for back-up.

'Fuck. Fuck!'

He turns to the sound. Cristina has appeared at the door, Ali behind her.

'He's dead, isn't he? Oh my God. Will I be in trouble?'

'No, he isn't, but he is very ill, so if you could—'

'I need this job!' Her voice shrill, she pushes at his shoulder. 'Do something then. You have to—'

'If you wouldn't mind stepping back and giving us some space.'

Catching Ali's helpless expression, Cal stands and lifts his hands in a conciliatory way. 'I'm here to help Willy. I won't be able to do that if you don't stand back.' When she doesn't move, he raises his eyebrows. 'Both carers and emergency services staff deserve to be treated with respect. Agreed?'

A sob escaping, she sinks to her knees. Moments later, two paramedics sweep through the front door. He helps his colleagues put Willy on a stretcher and load him into the van. When the doors finally close, he looks back to his trainee who's still struggling to settle the overwrought woman. Striding over to help, he smiles wryly. What a baptism of fire for a twenty-first birthday.

46

Cordelia

I finish scrubbing the fridge and stretch my back. That's the trouble with my kitchen being everybody's – people help themselves to milk, juice and often dishes or baking I've prepared for the family. I don't mind that so much as the furtive inspection: is it gleaming? Full of the right sort of food? Is the vicar's wife up to scratch? There was a time she wasn't so well, don't you know . . .

I turn to the chilled items and peer at the codes. The four-pack of Activia is three weeks out of date. Bin or keep them? Or rather, do I want to maintain the temporary truce with Harriet? After many days of stony silence, she sidled up to me during this morning's handshaking.

'Peace be with you,' she said.

My response was automatic: 'And also with you.'

But I'm glad we've made up. Perhaps Vincent was the instigator, but it lifts the tension in the house, even if all the adults are still tiptoeing around Abbey and her moods.

I slot the yogurts back on a shelf. The kitchen is as much Harriet's as mine, and if she's happy doing the 'sniff test' before eating, who am I to protest?

'We might get lucky and she'll poison herself,' Mari once said.

'You can't say that!' I replied.

'Well, I just did. If I'm struck down by lightning, you'll know why.'

My lips twitch at the memory. After a fraught few days one way or another, I feel lighter today, as though someone has lifted a weight off my shoulders. I adore baby Isak. I was so worried I wouldn't, that the old madness might consume me, that I'd shout or hit the walls or pull out my hair. All the things I did after Lukie died.

I shake the graphic images away. No good comes of going back to those days, but it was hard not to dwell on them during Britt's pregnancy and feel all the negative, painful emotions Vincent described. He was spot on about that and he knew to offer comfort just when I needed it. He's an excellent vicar and a good and wise man; I forget that too often.

Hearing a beep, I scoop up my mobile. It's another text from my big sis. Sitting down at the table, I smile in anticipation. Several photos of Isak arrive each day. I was fearful Mari would hold back from sharing her excitement and joy, but she gets it just right by involving me but not overstepping the mark. Whatever that is; it's new for us both.

My thumb hovers over the last message from Cal. I didn't reply after all. Vincent was so loving and understanding at the cemetery that I made a silent vow not to continue whatever we'd started. I should delete the message, but can't quite bring myself to. Then there's my treacherous mind which keeps drifting back to our lovemaking, that skin-to-skin intimacy and specifically the sensation of him sliding into my body with his lips hot on mine, then that intense, burning heat building and building. And when he moved to my neck . . . Oh God, that's when I—

'What's for tea, Mum? I'm starving. What can I have to eat while I wait?'

Almost jumping from my skin, I snap around to my daughter. 'Is it that time already?' I gesture to the fridge. 'Do out-of-date yogurts take your fancy?'

She flops down beside me. 'Haha,' she replies without humour. Then peering at my phone, 'More photos of Isak? The spelling's pretty stupid, don't you think?'

I'm glad of the question to recover myself. 'It's a bit different and that's a good thing, perhaps? Like you becoming an A-B-I on Facebook?'

Scowling, she scrapes back her chair. 'For God's sake, I was about eleven then,' she mutters. 'I've got homework to do. Can you make me some toast and bring it up?'

Settling down at my desk, I turn on my laptop and absently gaze at the screen as it loads. So much for feeling jolly – I've made yet another daughter *faux pas*. I duly prepared Abbey's snack and delivered it to her bedroom, but she merely glanced at it and went back to her schoolwork without speaking. But at least the *'Abi'* conversation has reminded me about the church Facebook group. So busy with other things, I haven't posted for at least a couple of weeks. No doubt the parishioners of St Andrew's are waiting with bated breath for my inspirational 'thought for the week'. Not. Still, some poor soul might be on the other side of the ether; it might make their day more bearable.

I peer at the screen. Goodness, not one but two people want to join. Hoping they'll be 'types' who *won't* pass Harriet's approbation, I blithely accept them, then scroll down to the last date I logged on to see what I've missed. Methodically working backwards, I mark everyone's contributions with likes or hugs and add upbeat comments where appropriate. As I scan a long article about air pollution, my eyes catch the next item on the page. I lean in closer. How strange. Someone has posted a picture of a car with the windows and the number plate blanked out in Tipp-Ex-like white.

Perplexed, I continue to move up the feed. There it is again, but if I'm not mistaken, the parts obliterated by marker pen are just a little less. Further up, there's another.

Comprehension hits like a punch to my stomach. The vehicle is silver, and though the photograph has obviously been taken at night, tall trees are apparent in the background. Oh my God, it can't be Cal's car, can it? My fingers trembling, I scroll on. What the . . . ? The top of the windscreen can be seen in the next photo. Almost faint, I rush through the following few posts. The final image appears to be the same as the last, but this time wording has been added:

'*Want to find out who's dogging in Didsbury? Watch this space for the big reveal!*'

My heart clatters with sheer panic. Bloody hell, bloody hell, what to do? Inhaling deeply, I make myself focus. I'm the administrator – get rid of them, of course. I spent minutes reading through the damned piece about Manchester smog when time was vital. Quickly clicking the ellipses, I delete each image, then snap the lid shut.

Bending double, I breathe through the frothing queasiness. What the hell is going on?

47

Calvin

Though Cal's avoiding eye contact with her, the woman opposite him lifts her arched eyebrows each time he glances up from his pint.

He hoped to slope off after work, but Ali was having none of it. 'After the day we've had, you're coming,' he said.

And it was quite an afternoon. Willy's ambulance started to pull away, then abruptly stopped. He'd gone into cardiac arrest, so Cal jumped in and helped his colleagues with the defibrillator and other treatments as they sped to the hospital.

Wondering what had become of Ali and the RRV, he hung around the Heart Centre with the other paramedics. Then a nurse collared him, saying Willy was conscious and asking for him, so with mixed feelings he went to search the man out.

Conversation billowing around him, he sips his beer contemplatively. Does he feel proud when he helps someone, possibly saves their life? Yes, absolutely; there's nothing quite like the satisfaction of fulfilling his duty, doing what he signed up for and honouring a faithful promise he made.

Tubed, wired and weak, Willy offered a frail hand and

thanked him. 'Living alone is a bugger,' he croaked. 'Three kids and a wife and they all left me.' He drifted, then spoke again. 'Probably deserved it. Liked my own company too much.' He observed Cal for a beat. 'Don't make that mistake, son.'

Cal snorts inwardly. Would Willy say that to anyone, or is there something that singles him out as a loner? Because a lone wolf he is. And yet ... Connection, attachment, feelings. Dee Stephens roused all three. It's a bugger she's married to someone else. Added to that, she hasn't been in touch.

A slap on the back makes him turn. It's Ali, the birthday boy. Bleary-eyed, he rolls back on his heels. 'Another pint, mate?'

'Nah, it's my round. What are you having?'

Cal asks who needs a drink. The numbers around the table have thinned, but the woman opposite thrusts out her glass.

'I need more wine,' she says bluntly. 'Whatever colour is going.'

What's her name again? Cristina 'without the h'. God knows how she managed to wangle her way into a work event, but Ali briefly gave him the lowdown earlier: once the ambulance had left Willy's house, her hysteria went up another notch and Ali ended up driving her home in the RRV. Still, she seems to have made a full recovery now. Or perhaps she's self-medicating with wine.

While he waits at the bar, he pulls out his phone. Still no reply from Dee. Yet he felt that *attachment*; deep in his chest, he's sure she felt the same.

'A woman, I'm guessing.' Appearing by his side, Cristina squints at the screen. 'Why don't you text her rather than waiting for the "taking turns" game?'

Her directness is refreshing or jarring; he can't decide which.

'So what do you suggest?'

184

She shrugs. 'Say what you want to say. If she doesn't reply, you won't have lost anything. If she does, then you'll know, either way.'

He smiles thinly. 'I might lose pride.'

'Male pride. Pah.' Snorting, she moves away and heads for the toilets.

He blankly stares at the array of bottles behind the bar, jolting in discomfort when the black-and-red label of Tia Maria comes into focus. Perhaps it is better to know, but in truth he wants to shake something nice from his mobile. Something affectionate, positive, hopeful, special. Because that's how Dee made him feel. He composes:

Hey. Are you OK? Can we meet? Collect you in the car? Go for a walk, or come to mine?

Does it sound too needy? *Will* his pride be irrevocably damaged?

But there isn't time to think about it more deeply; the barman's asking for his order and Cristina is back.

'A large glass of that Merlot,' she says. Then, 'For God's sake, press "send".'

Time has passed and Cal's senses are dulling. He lifts the glass and throws back the fiery liquid. Though a bad idea, he ended up ordering a large whisky for himself at the bar. Cristina helped him back with the drinks and slipped into the bench beside him.

'Mobile,' she said, taking it from him and placing it on the table. He didn't mind her playful game at first, but her tactile flirtatiousness is now getting on his pip. Or is it because Dee hasn't bloody replied?

He slips it in his pocket, but as though it was waiting for privacy, it immediately vibrates. His heart stupidly thrashing, he stands. 'Going for a piss,' he mumbles, heading for the gents, then diverting outside.

Though the night air is cold, he feels hot, almost breathless. Bloody hell, what's wrong with him? He doesn't need an excuse to leave the table and if this message is from *her*, she's a married woman, for God's sake. Yet still he leans against the damp wall for several moments before peeping at the screen. Fuck, it is from her. Inhaling quickly, he opens it.

Do not contact me. Please. Do not contact me again.

What the . . . ? His mind gluey, he tries to work out her knee-jerk response, but an arm is slotted through his.

'Smashed pride, eh?' Cristina says, pulling him away from the building. She stops and pecks his lips. 'Never mind, handsome man. I know just the thing to fix it.'

48

Mariana

Breathing in the spring air, Mari ambles home from the bus stop. Her gaze inescapably sweeps the large oak by the park. A solitary bird today.

She doffs an invisible cap. 'Morning, Magpie.'

It isn't morning though, it's Monday lunchtime. She's returned to work after her paternity leave, but for half a day only. Smiling wryly, she wonders how Britt has coped by herself. She's never been an early bird and for the past three weeks she's basically stayed in bed, watching daytime TV and flicking at magazines, interspersed with naps and feeding Isak. Mari has done the rest by preparing tasty snacks, changing nappies, washing, cleaning, nursing. Online food shopping, too, and thank God for that; with so few hours in the day, they might otherwise have starved.

A small voice in her head warned that it wasn't a good idea to wait on Britt hand and foot, but she reasoned that her section scar was still healing – which it still is – and besides, she loves her one-to-one time with Isak. When he's awake, she carries him around the house or garden chatting to him, showing him birds, the budding flowers and trees. He's a good baby and only cries when he's hungry, and then she hands him back to Britt and her plentiful supply of milk. She feels truly blessed.

Spotting a second magpie join the first, she smiles and waves. Two for joy. Sure, she doesn't believe in Vincent's God, but she's grateful to *something* for her happiness right now.

At her gate she stops and looks at her empty hands. Should she have bought lunch on the way through the village? No, there's plenty of food in the house and she asked her sister to pop by mid-morning on a 'I happened to be passing' basis to check all was well. Dee hasn't texted, so presumably it has been.

She hops up the step and pulls out her key, but the front door swings open.

'Oh, Dee Dee! You're still here—'

Dee puts a finger to her lips, then gestures to the lounge. Stepping over a pile of nappy bags, Mari follows her in. 'Is everything OK?' she whispers.

'Yes, of course.' Dee looks pale and purple shadows are smudged beneath her eyes. 'There's nothing to worry about. Britt's feeding Isak at the moment, but I wanted to give you the heads-up.' She flushes. 'It's just . . . just new-mum stuff, but Britt's been pretty fed up. You know, that she's tied to the house and feels like a milking cow.' She reaches for her jacket. 'Right, I'll get off and leave you to it.'

Mari walks her to the door. 'How about you? Are you OK?'

'Sure.' She rotates, then comes back, her cheeks pinking again. 'Any reason why I shouldn't be?'

'No, not at all.' Mari gives her a quick hug. 'Thanks, Dee. You're a star, as always. Can you still manage tomorrow? Ten minutes will do. You know, just to make sure Britt and Isak are—'

'Absolutely, *no problem. Any time.*'

Once the latch has clicked to, Mari climbs up to the bedroom. Though she's lying on her side, her partner's eyes are open. Once they meet hers, she turns away.

Inwardly sighing, Mari peeps into the Moses basket. Isak is clutching his blanket with tight little fists. All's well with him; so what about Britt?

She perches on the bed. 'Hey, what's up?'

'You have no idea.'

'No, I haven't, so tell me.'

Britt hitches herself up. 'I hate this.'

'Hate what?'

She gesticulates to her baggy T-shirt. 'Isn't it obvious? They leak constantly. Quite frankly, it's disgusting.'

Damp circles surround her nipples. 'If you wear the nursing bra you can . . . ' Mari glances around. 'I bought you breast pads. They were up here before.'

'I'm in bed. What's the point? Anyway, when I use them they're sopping wet in minutes. I have too much milk. I don't want to do this.'

Mari takes her hand. 'You're actually very lucky; some women can't get the baby latched, others struggle to feed them at all, so you're clearly a natural!'

Britt pulls away, so she tries another tack. 'What about expressing? That would be a win-win. I could help with the night feeds and you'd get more sleep.'

'Weren't you listening to anything at the NCT lessons, Mariana? It's a . . . a vicious circle. The more milk I squirt out, the more I produce.'

'Right.' Mari pauses to work it out. 'Well, if you express it instead of a feed, then I guess it would even out eventually?'

Britt plays with a strand of her hair. 'That's what she said,' she mutters.

'Who's "she"?'

'Cordelia.'

Goosebumps spread. 'What did you say to her?'

'Oh, nothing much.' Britt pecks Mari's lips. 'I'm so glad you're home; I've missed you and I'm starving. Please say you've brought me a nice lunchtime treat.'

49

Calvin

Hoping he's not over the limit, Cal keeps an eye on the speed signs. He's still kicking himself about last night. What was he thinking drinking whisky in the pub, then going back to Cristina's digs? Her place wasn't a 'flat' as she described it, but a dank-smelling box room in a grotty shared house. Thank God she was even more shedded than him, so despite her initial fumbling attempt to get him hard, nothing sexual happened, but later she woke him and offered him a joint. He was wired, but in a bad way, so he took a few drags to chill out and relax, but it was so strong that he felt his heart accelerate, then anxiety and paranoia set in. Only one thing was certain right then – he had to get the hell out.

Too fearful to call a taxi, he ended up walking home in the early hours. His keys were in his jacket which he'd grabbed with his mobile before bolting out, but even so he was soaked from the downpour, and so freezing that he had to warm up in the shower.

He rolls his shoulders. Wet, sodden, but particularly stupid. Sure, he was agitated about Dee – the sheer excitement that she'd made contact; the tumbling disappointment as he read her message – but hanging out with a woman he didn't know from Eve was a huge mistake. When they arrived in her room, Cristina held out her palm for his phone again.

'You're here. You pay attention to me now,' she said.

Like a sap he handed it over. When he finally arrived home he discovered she'd deleted Dee's number and messages. Still, it's probably just as well.

He yawns yet again. Thank God he booked today off in lieu. And life isn't all bad; he's had a long lie-in, and on finally waking he focused on Willy's words, forced himself out of the sack and called Sadie.

Preparing himself for an Erica grilling, he parks outside her semi and hops out of the car. The woman herself is lugging a bag from her boot so he takes it from her.

'What have you got in here? Gold bullion?' he asks.

She cracks a tiny smile. 'I wish.' Then, 'We don't often have the pleasure of your company on a Monday.'

'I was torn between Bolton and root-canal treatment, but when Sadie said you were doing *Bake Off* this afternoon, it was a no-brainer.'

'Cheeky sod. In you come and see your little smasher.' Turning, she raises an eyebrow. 'He's turning into a right handsome bugger. Looks more like you every day.'

Feeling a mix of emotions, Cal closes Erica's front door. He and Sadie walked Zachary in his pram to the park and stopped at the café. It was nice, but bloody difficult too. Despite Willy's warning about ending up alone, he knew then that the relationship had to be *the right one and this wasn't it. Several times it was on the* tip of his tongue just to say it, but Sadie was so proud to be out with her 'two boys' that the will withered and vanished.

'Hey, lover-boy, not so fast.'

He turns. Erica is holding out a tartan-patterned cake tin. 'Victoria sponge. I've made it with fresh cream, so it'll need eating by tomorrow.'

'For me?' It's the first cake he's been baked for nearly twenty-five years. 'Cheers, Erica. That's very kind of you. I'll bring back the container next time.'

She glances over her shoulder. 'Keep it; she's getting restless and Zachary's in a routine these days.' She smiles sadly. 'I'll miss the little chappie, but Sadie needs her own kitchen, her own home again. I know you'll look after them. You're a good man.'

He inhales deeply. He knows he has to act, that he's been a bloody coward for not doing it sooner. 'Actually, I'm coming back inside.'

Zach asleep in her arms, Sadie's still on the settee when he returns to the lounge. 'Hi, hon, I thought you'd gone.'

'I need to speak to you. Do you want to give Zach to your mum?'

'No, why?'

'I need to say something you might not want to hear.'

As though knowing what's afoot, Erica appears, takes the baby from her daughter and silently closes the door behind her.

Her face already crumpling, Sadie holds out a palm as though to stop him, but he has to spit it out.

'I'll always be here for you and Zachary.' He swallows. 'You know, financially and in a supportive, caring, parenting role, but you deserve someone far better than me.'

'You're dumping me?'

193

Christ, he feels like a shit. 'No, that's not the word.' He takes a big breath. 'We'd already broken up, drifted apart or whatever the phrase is.' He wills her to understand. 'We have Zach, and that will always be an amazing thing between us, but we haven't been a couple for a long, long time. If you're honest, you already know that.'

Tears seep from her eyes. 'But we could get back on track and be a family. Me and Zach could come home and—'

'I know that won't work and deep down I think you know it too. I'm sorry, Sadie, but the answer is no.'

50

Cordelia

It's Tuesday already. Keeping my hood up and head down, I hurry through the park towards Mari and Britt's house. I made them beef Bourguignon first thing, but it's heavy, the handles of my hessian bag roughly yanking my shoulder. I feel internally damaged too, like a punchbag. But feeling sorry for myself is silly; Britt is just Britt and the rest of the mental agony I've brought on myself.

So sick with nerves, I've struggled to eat since seeing the Facebook image. Who on earth posted it? What do they want? I've been too frightened to look again, and though I've tried to think logically, my mind has been sticky with panic. Delete every member? Shut the whole page down? No, I can't do anything extreme; Harriet would notice and think it was odd.

Over the last forty-eight hours I have tried to function normally, but I've swung from terror to strange calm: if the perpetrator posts it again, there's nothing to link a prank photograph to me; my mother-in-law clearly hasn't seen it; I would certainly know if she had.

But the downside is horrifying. Someone maliciously posted

that photograph; they know about me and Cal; they seem to be slowly exposing more of the windscreen and the people sitting behind it. Oh God; what can I do?

Then there was Cal's text on Sunday evening. It popped up when Vincent was in our en suite, noisily cleaning his teeth, and my heart almost burst from my chest as I fumbled to turn the phone off before he came back. I had to wait until his wheezing was deep and regular before slipping from the bed to check what it said. Like a burglar, I crept downstairs to the toilet, then huddled with my back to the door, as it loaded. The sheer, breathless panic increased when I read it. Oh God, Cal was asking to meet! I could never exchange texts, let alone see him again. So I had to quickly get that message across:

Do not contact me. Please. Do not contact me again.

Though I barely slept, I felt a little better on waking. My reply to Cal was clear and I'd sorted it, job done. When I eventually felt brave enough to turn on my mobile, a text from Mari appeared, asking me to bob in on Britt to check she and Isak were OK. It gave me a focus and it felt good to be needed. But the moment I let out a long sigh of relief, another message from Cal popped up. I forced myself to open it.

youll be so sorry cristin.

The alarm was immediate. Was he *threatening* me? I read it again. Christian. He'd made that comment about Holy Communion when we first met, then had that rant about religion. I pictured his burning eyes when he'd derided 'do-gooders' and said I was one. Was he unhinged after all? And what did he mean by I'd be *so sorry*?

My heart clattering again, I now look up to the cloudy sky. *Christian*. Am I still one? Do I believe in anything these days? But if there is a God I can hardly pray for salvation here. I've been unfaithful to Vincent; I've broken vows. And if he finds out, what then?

I puff out the hot, rising anxiety. Vincent doesn't know about Cal or the Facebook photo; everything is fine. Yet this morning he blocked my car in the drive with his Volvo without leaving his keys for me to move it. Was it just inadvertent parking? Or did he do it deliberately to prevent me going out?

Already at Mari's gate, I stop and stare at my feet. Can I do this again after Britt's lack of tact?

'Stop meddling, Cordelia,' she snapped yesterday. 'What do you know about having too much milk? You have no bloody idea!'

I put a hand to my breast. Too much milk, those darkest of days. Though I was only gently trying to persuade Britt to stick with breastfeeding a little longer, perhaps I was interfering. Today I'll just knock on, hand over the casserole and quickly leave. In all honesty I feel too fragile for anything else.

Decision made, I lift my head, but Britt pads down the step in her slippers.

'Cordelia!' She all but drags me into the house and tightly hugs me. 'I felt so bad all night. I'm so sorry.' She's warm and smells of sweet milk. 'I didn't realise. You know what I'm like when I'm grumpy; I open my mouth and the first thing I think comes tumbling out. Come on through. I've just put on the kettle.'

I follow her to the kitchen and crouch down to the Moses basket. Little Isak is soundly asleep and without him as a go-between, I feel nervous and vulnerable. Wishing I'd left as planned, I take the proffered drink and sit down on a chair. What should I chat about? Any baby-related questions feel out of bounds after yesterday.

'The casserole is . . . well, it's just something warm for your dinner. And do let me know if there's anything you need from the supermarket—' I begin, but Britt interrupts from the couch.

'Maybe it would be better to talk about it?'

'Sorry?'

'Mariana says you never talk about him, but in my experience, it's better to let it out.'

Too stunned to speak, I simply gape. Oh my God, she's talking about Luke.

Her expression benign, she continues to speak, expounding the benefits of saying his name, acknowledging his 'short life' and his 'part in the family'.

Staring at my coffee, I swallow the urge to shout. No, not just shout, but yell hysterically and scream: '*What do I know about having too much milk? My son was dead, but the breast milk didn't dry up for days. Don't you dare lecture me; you know nothing about losing a child.*'

Like it was only hours ago, the sheer hell slaps back. That compulsive need to go through each and every step of what happened. Playing the mental film again and again. The overwhelming, debilitating feelings of loss, grief and guilt. The inability to sleep or to function. The numbness soon followed by delusions – the fullness of my breasts, the weight of my aching arms; hearing Lukie's shuffle, his cry. The certainty that I was going mad.

And Vincent's gaze which slowly turned from love, support and understanding to something else.

Pulling away bit by bit. And taking Abbey with him.

51

Calvin

Cal rubs his face. The day is not going well. Though he was first on the shift and did all the checks on the BMW, an emergency erupted while he was getting changed, so he had no choice but to drive this old Kia. Then he had a series of call-outs which should have been dealt with by local primary care – GPs or even pharmacists. He had some sympathy for the old lady who'd clearly been terrified about the pain in her new hip, but the university students who basically had sore throats really pissed him off. Seems they thought a 999 call for three of them was good value for NHS resources.

Catching his moody reflection in the mirror, he sighs. Getting out for fresh air and stretching his legs will help. He reaches for the door handle but the radio pipes up. A Red 2 call, response time eighteen minutes, but he isn't far away so he should do it in less. Grateful for the surge of energy, he acknowledges the instructions, drags on his seat belt, fires up the siren and pulls out.

The front door of the house is ajar so Cal strides in with his kit. 'Hello?' he calls. 'Ambulance service. Where are you?'

'In here.' A woman's shrill voice in reply. 'We're in here. In the lounge.'

A smartly dressed older lady is sitting on the carpet, a man's head cradled in her lap. Her face clearly traumatised, she speaks quickly, her breathless words tumbling out.

'He mentioned feeling nauseous and sweaty this morning, but said he'd soon shake it off. I couldn't have stopped him if I'd tried; he had work to do. Then he came home for his lunch even though I didn't expect him. Came in here for a sit-down. The next thing I knew, he was calling, saying he had chest pain. Then I heard a thump and he was writhing on the floor. It was dreadful. So then I—'

Kneeling down, Cal quickly assesses the situation. The man's skin is pale, his pupils dilated. Unresponsive too: little pulse and barely breathing. He immediately calls for urgent back-up.

'How long has he been unconscious?' he asks.

'Unconscious?' As though finally registering it, the woman clamps a hand over her mouth. 'Oh my word, I don't know. He was awake when I dialled emergency services a few minutes ago. Oh Lord, *unconscious*? What on earth does that mean?'

Asking her to step away, Cal cuts through the man's jumper to expose his chest. Quickly opening the defibrillator, he applies the electrodes and stands back to administer the shock. Nothing happens. What the hell? He checks the connections and position of the pads, then tries again. No joy; the damned thing clearly isn't working. Pushing the machine to one side, he immediately begins CPR.

Her palms on her cheeks, the woman stares as he works. Then, apparently hearing something from outside, she snaps her head to the bay window and scuttles from the room.

Though Cal focuses on pushing hard and fast, the woman's overwrought voice breezes through the open door.

'You're evil! Right from the start, I knew you were evil. This is your fault, your fault. Do you hear me?'

Then a younger female tone. 'What on earth do you mean?'

'Look for yourself. It's too, too dreadful. I can't bear to watch.'

So busy checking the patient's airways and delivering rescue breaths, Cal doesn't register another presence, so the shaky outburst makes him start.

'Oh my God. What are you doing?' Then fingers are gripping his shoulders, trying to pull him back, and a voice he'd know anywhere. 'Leave him alone. Just stop it, please, stop it. What the hell are you doing to him? For God's sake, get off!'

52

Cordelia

Words filter up from the bottom of the ocean.

'Hello? Are you back with us, love?'

Disorientated and woozy, I try to lift my head. Ouch, that hurts. Why am I curled on the floor? And with a sticky sensation on my skin? I put a hand to my cheek, then look at my fingers. Blood?

Recall rushes in. Oh God, that's right. I arrived home from Britt's to Harriet's livid face and screaming. Wholly confused, I rushed into the lounge and found Vincent being attacked. That was alarming enough, but when I realised who the assailant was, I tried to drag him off, and then ... ? Yes, I was slapped from nowhere. So sharp and forceful, I lost my footing and ...

Gentle hands help me to sit up. It's a young woman with plaits and a strong Liverpudlian accent. 'Take it slowly, love. You've been out for a few minutes.' She pads my ear and nods to the coffee table. 'There's the culprit. You have a laceration to the back of your head. Here, hold this dressing against it for a minute.'

Laceration. 'Oh.'

The woman smiles. 'I'm Sheryl, by the way. And you are?'

'Cordelia.'

'Nice name. Let's have a look at you now you're back with us.' She shines a light into my eyes. 'How are you feeling?'

It takes a few moments to adjust to what's going on around me. With Harriet looking on, two uniformed men are hefting Vincent onto a stretcher. One of them is Calvin Rafferty. I come back to Sheryl and take in her dark green shirt with epaulets, an embroidered badge and an NHS logo. Same as Cal's. Oh God, he's clearly a paramedic. What the hell had I thought when I entered the house? So overwhelmed with stress, anxiety and Harriet's hysterics, my mind just assumed the worst – that he had stormed into the vicarage and was beating up Vincent the *Christian*. Right now, he and the other medic are carrying him out, which means . . . ? Oh Lord. What's happened to him?

'That's my husband on the stretcher. What's going on?'

'He's suffered a cardiac arrest, but he's breathing and OK for now. We're taking him to hospital.' Sheryl lifts her hand. 'How many fingers?'

'Three.' Her words bounce back. A *cardiac arrest*? What on earth . . . 'I need to go to him.'

She snaps on gloves. 'Let's take a look at this cut first.'

Deftly examining my head, she asks further questions. What day and month is it? What's my address? And postcode? Any pain, nausea or need to vomit? She presses something cold against my skull. 'Can you hold this until the bleeding stops? It looks fine. Always the same with head cuts. The bark is worse than its bite.'

I try to focus. Vincent is being taken to hospital . . . I struggle to my feet. Truth be told, I do feel a little dizzy, but a *cardiac arrest*? That's horrendously alarming. 'I'm fine, really. Thank you. Can I go with my husband in the ambulance?'

Sheryl's cheeks colour. 'I know you'll be worried, but only one person can ride with a patient and I think your mother-in-law has that covered.' She glances at the door and grins. 'I'm leaving you in capable hands, though.'

I follow her smile. Oh God, Cal is still there. He pats his colleague's shoulder as she passes. 'Thanks, Sheryl. See you back at base.'

When she's gone, he crosses his arms. 'You've had a head injury; I suggest you sit down.' He follows me to the sofa and stands over me, his jaw tight. 'Talk to me, Dee. What's going on?'

I frown. 'Was it you?'

'Was it me, what?'

I peer at the bloodstained dressing. 'Who—'

His expression darkens. 'You think that?' He glances down at his uniform. 'I'm a trained first-response paramedic. You think I go around assaulting family members when they get upset?'

'No, but . . . ' What on earth *was* my reasoning? Please say I'm not returning to those days of paranoia when I had all sorts of crazy, illogical notions. Lowering my head, I breathe deeply. Harriet. What must she have thought when I tried to drag a paramedic off her son? No wonder she slapped me. 'Ah, my mother-in-law.'

Cal's eyes seem to glaze. 'I expect she was alarmed about her son. I was administering CPR.'

'I know. I'm so sorry. I realise that now. It just feels so . . . so unbelievable.'

I try to absorb it, but it doesn't feel remotely real. Vincent is so vibrant, so fit. 'What happened?'

'He'd complained about nausea this morning which developed into chest pain. He collapsed and was unconscious when I got here, but I was able to ... By the time back-up arrived, his vital signs were OK and he was breathing normally. They've taken him to the Heart Centre at the hospital, so he'll be in good hands.' He rubs his face. 'Take it easy for ten minutes, then I'll give you a lift there.'

'OK, thank you.' I puff through the shock, but sudden terror splinters out. CPR is *lifesaving* treatment; my husband's heart stopped beating ... Tears shoot to my eyes. 'Vincent ... Could it be fatal, could he die?'

Cal spreads his hands and inhales to reply, but footsteps and the sound of Abbey's voice echo through.

'Mum? Mum! Why is there a car parked outside?' Her flushed face appears at the door. 'At first I thought it was a police car, but it says ... ' The colour draining from her cheeks, she looks from Cal to me. 'Mum?' she asks. 'Where's Dad?'

53

Mariana

Her cheeks sizzling from the cold afternoon, Mari shakes her umbrella and steps into the house.

'Hello! I'm in here,' she hears.

Dressed and stirring a pan on the hob, Britt turns and flashes a smile. 'Take a pew. I hope you're hungry for ...' She makes a show of ladling green liquid into bowls, then she brings them to the table. 'Soup! Or, as the carton says, split pea broth.' She pecks Mari's lips and sits down. 'So, soup or broth – what's the difference?'

Pleased to see her so full of energy and enthusiasm, Mari inspects the glossy offering. 'Good question!' Her mum would know the answer. As well as whether to be concerned about the tiny pimples on Isak's skin and his initial weight loss. The health visitor advised not to worry about either, but it isn't quite the same as asking one's mother; they're more reliable at telling the honest truth. Though is parental advice always right, despite good intentions? Pushing that uncomfortable thought to the back of her mind, she reverts to the question.

'Maybe broth is stock with bits added in?'

Britt laughs. 'And stock is . . . ?'

'Juices from the bones.'

'How very lovely!'

They eat in silence for a while. 'How has Isak been this morning?' Mari eventually asks.

'Yeah, fine. He's upstairs.' Britt looks at her with raised eyebrows. 'And I put the nappies outside. Not as far as the bin because it was raining, but out of the house as instructed.'

'Thank you.' Mari squeezes her arm. 'It just gets a bit smelly when they're left at the door. Is he asleep?'

Britt moves to the hob and shrugs. 'No crying, so probably. More bone juice?'

'No thanks.'

Resisting the urge to jump up and dash to the nursery, Mari finishes her late lunch. Why didn't Britt bring him down in his basket? She could have chatted to him if he was awake. And if he was asleep, then she'd have known he was—

She tries to bat that particular anxiety away. Incidences of sudden death syndrome are at an all-time low and it seems disloyal to have it constantly in her thoughts. As though berating her, she clocks Dee's oven dish.

'A casserole from Dee, I take it? Did she pop round?'

Britt busies herself buttering another slice of bread. 'Yup. Not for long.'

Mari's heart falls. 'And?'

'And nothing. She brought in that, then pretty much left.'

Mari waits.

'I was just trying to help.'

She puts down her spoon. 'Help how?'

'By getting her to talk about baby Lukie.'

208

'*Lukie?*'

'Yes, that was his name, wasn't it?'

It was Cordelia's special name for her baby boy. No one else used it. 'You didn't call him that, did you?'

'Maybe. Why not? You told me it.'

'I don't recall mentioning—'

Britt lifts a shoulder. 'Well, it was either you or Vincent.'

The heat spreading, Mari sighs. It's always the same with that man, just as she's warming to him, she's given a stark reminder that he *is* a complete and utter prick. 'What else did Vincent say about it?'

Britt carries her bowl to the sink.

'Britt?'

'Oh, I don't know. Just that he always wanted a son. And that Cordelia went doolally for a while.' She turns, her face flushed. 'Well, quite a while, which is perfectly understandable, of course. But—'

'But what?'

She sidles over and takes Mari's hand. 'Well, even you must admit she's a little odd at times. Take today, for example. She pretty much bolted out, saying she needed some fresh air. And after what Vincent said . . . '

'What did Vincent say and when?'

'Oh, ages ago. But he said that he was so worried about Cordelia's mental health at one time, he was afraid to leave Abbey alone with her . . . '

Mari grits her teeth. The fucking bastard! Dee had lost her son, a baby she absolutely adored. For the first time in years she'd been content and happy and settled, then the very, very worst happened. No wonder her mental health had suffered. But not trusting her with Abbey? 'That's just wholly and utterly—'

209

'I'm just repeating what he said.' Britt folds her arms. 'Anyway, it's made me think. I don't want Cordelia just turning up on the doorstep like that.' Her jaw set, she stares. 'What's important is the safety of Isak. Even you can see the importance in that.'

54

Cordelia

As though we're in a cab, I sit next to Abbey in the back seat of the ambulance car. Only the guy at the wheel isn't a taxi driver, he's a first-response paramedic who gave lifesaving treatment to Vincent. He mentioned tending to patients when I asked about his job, but I assumed he was a nurse. So lustful, so eager and smitten, I didn't scratch beyond that surface. Or perhaps he didn't offer more information? Either way, I don't know much about this man, yet I've had more intimacy with him than my husband for many years. It makes me a bad, bad person, doesn't it?

My husband, Vincent. Oh God. It still feels unreal. If I wasn't speeding towards the Heart Centre, if it wasn't for Abbey's tight, teary face, I'd think I was in dreamland. I'm still struggling to process how a jaunty early-fifties guy-about-town can transform into the grey-faced person I glimpsed on the stretcher. Has he been ill for some time and I've been too self-absorbed to notice? No, surely not. He always had robust health, and recently he's been as active, hale and hearty as ever. Could it be from severe stress or shock?

Breathlessness spreads at that notion. Oh my God; is it *my* fault? Does he know what I've done? Has he seen or has someone told him about the Facebook photograph? The timing makes sense. Maybe the troll has posted it again and this time it has revealed my face. He's undoubtedly proud that I'm his wife, his *beautiful* wife. How shocked and dismayed would he be to see me in another man's car. A thought strikes: Oh God, maybe not just my face, but other more specific, incriminating images of me and Cal in his car? I haven't dared to look.

I take Abbey's hand and squeeze it. 'OK, love?'

Biting her lip, she doesn't reply. I don't blame her; nothing is remotely 'OK' despite Cal's calm explanation to us both that luck was in Vincent's favour. His vehicle happened to be a short distance away; treatment began within a few minutes; the outlook is fair; the hospital will do tests to find out what has happened; he's in the best place.

Although she doesn't pull away, I can detect my daughter's resistance. Like my deep love for Bill, Abbey adores Vincent. And though my father didn't die back then, it had felt like it, so God knows how terrified she must be.

I kiss her hair. 'Dad will be fine; I'm sure of it.'

'Are you?'

'Yes. And everyone will pray for him.'

She gives me a sidelong glance. 'Yeah, but will you?'

Guilt grips me by the throat. Will I pray? Can I? Is this some sort of divine retribution for *everything*? Hiding the building panic, I smile. 'Yes, of course I will.'

Nobody speaks for the rest of the journey, but as we approach the hospital complex, sound from the car radio breaks through. *Pulling up outside a green building, Cal turns.*

212

'The reception is just inside. I have another call, so I'm afraid I can't come in with you.'

'Yes, of course. Thank you so much for the lift.' Then, as realisation hits, 'And for being there, for saving Vincent's life. Thank you so much.'

God, I hope I'm not jinxing it by saying it out loud. My words sound inadequate, especially after I tried to stop him doing just that, but Abbey has climbed out, so I quickly follow.

Attempting to sound a lot braver than I feel, I slip my arm through hers. 'Come on, love. Let's see Dad.'

Once in the cool lobby, we head for the desk, but Harriet's distraught voice makes us turn.

'Darling girl. Come to Grandma.'

I watch Abbey dive into her arms. 'How's Dad? What's happening?' she asks, barely holding back her tears.

I rush to join them. 'Thank you so much for being here, Harriet. How's Vincent? What have they said?'

She blows her nose and doesn't make eye contact with me. Instead she speaks to Abbey. 'We're to wait here for news.'

Feeling the usual sizzle of exasperation, I take a deep breath. Harriet must know whether or not he's alive and his daughter is right here, for goodness' sake. 'But is he *OK*?' I ask meaningfully.

She jerks around. 'He's alive, if that's what you mean, Cordelia,' she says, almost spitting the words. 'And that's no thanks to you. Where were you this morning when he didn't feel well?'

'Upstairs, in my sitting room. I had no idea, Harriet; when we woke up he didn't mention anything to me.'

'Well, that says it all, doesn't it? You trapped that poor man fifteen years—'

'Abbey, love?' I quickly interrupt. 'Here's my purse. Go and get yourself a drink and a snack from the vending machine.'

'What on earth are you playing at?' I say once Abbey has gone. I've had to listen to this particular gripe from time to time, but in front of my daughter isn't acceptable.

Though Harriet's cheeks colour, she persists. 'You snared him by deliberately getting pregnant. He might think it was God's will, but we both know differently. And as for earlier . . .'

Reliving that stunning slap, I touch the tender lump at the back of my head. Her eyes are sharp. 'Yes, what madness was that all about, Cordelia?'

A shadow appears. Not Abbey, but a woman in a blue uniform. 'Mrs Hardy?'

'Yes,' we answer simultaneously.

'Hi, I'm Anya, one of the cardiac nurses.' She addresses me as Abbey joins us. 'Your husband is doing reasonably well, Mrs Hardy. We've put him in an induced coma to help his body recover from the trauma, but that isn't unusual after a cardiac arrest. The doctor will be on the ward soon, so he'll be happy to answer any questions you have. In the meantime . . .' She taps the chart she's holding and gestures to a door. 'Can we go through a few things, medical history and so on?'

'Yes, of course,' I reply. I glance at Abbey. I don't want to leave her out, but is it appropriate to include her?

She folds her arms. 'I'm not a kid, Mum.'

'OK. This way, please,' Anya says, setting off.

The three of us follow and we sit in a small room. Smiling at me reassuringly, Anya flips over a sheet. 'So, general lifestyle. Does Vincent get regular exercise?'

In my peripheral vision, I note Harriet's furrowed brow. 'In terms of being active, yes,' I reply. 'But he doesn't have time for any sport as such.'

'Healthy eater?'

I picture our parishioners' strange offerings and reams of home baking. His morning fry-up too. 'A mix, I suppose, but mostly, yes.'

'Does he drink alcohol?'

'Yes.'

'Roughly how many units?'

Heavens, how many? He undoubtedly loves a party and each evening he has a topped-up glass in his hand, but I've hardly been counting.

Before I can speak, Harriet cuts in. 'No more than anyone else.'

'OK.' Anya makes a note, then turns back to me. 'Does he smoke?'

I take a breath before answering. It feels disloyal to Vincent, but we are in a hospital; he's had a heart attack, for goodness' sake. 'Yes, yes, he does.'

'How much a day would you—'

Loudly pushing back her chair, Harriet stands. 'What a dreadful lie! My son has never smoked. Tobacco or otherwise.'

'I'm afraid he does, Harriet,' I reply. Then to the nurse, 'Perhaps ten cigarettes a day?'

Her face puce, my mother-in-law moves towards me. I find myself cringing, waiting for the smack. Thank God it doesn't come, but she booms in my ear. 'You'll say anything to discredit—'

But Abbey tugs at her sleeve. 'He does, Grandma.'

Improper though it is, a blister of hilarity bubbles up. I quickly suppress it and watch Harriet replace her astonished expression with a patient smile. 'I really don't think he does, darling.'

'I've seen him, Grandma. Smelled it on him too.'

Though Harriet seems to slump, Anya carries on as though the exchange hasn't happened. 'Any similar previous episodes or other health problems?'

'No,' I reply. 'He's always very well which is why today is so shocking.'

'Any family history of heart disease?'

'No, none that I know of.'

The nurse gives Abbey a friendly smile. 'I think that's everything for now. I'll take you down to see your dad.'

Me and Abbey stand, but Harriet doesn't move. She looks pale and withered. Feeling a spike of guilt for my earlier unkind thoughts, I put a hand on her shoulder. 'It's a dreadful upset for us all, but for you especially, finding him like that. Are you all right?'

Her voice quavers. 'Yes. Peter, Vincent's father.' She looks up at Anya. 'In answer to your question.'

Anya sits down again. 'OK. So, which question?'

'The family one. Peter suffered from HCM.'

'As in hypertrophic cardiomyopathy?'

'Yes.'

Totally thrown, I frown. 'Sorry, but what is . . . ?' I can't even pronounce it, let alone know what it means. 'HCM? What is that exactly?'

'It means Peter has or had a heart with an abnormally thick muscle.' Anya smiles thinly. 'It might well explain why Vincent's here today.'

'Had,' Harriet blurts. 'My husband died twenty-three years ago.' Tears splash down her cheeks. 'From a cardiac arrest.'

216

'But why would that . . . ?' I glance at poor Abbey. 'I'm sorry, I'm not following.'

Anya's eyes are kind. 'I'm afraid HCM is a genetic condition passed on through families. It doesn't necessarily follow that Vincent inherited the condition from his father, but at a fifty per cent chance, it's likely.'

Stuck for words, I just stare. Inherited condition . . . We have a daughter. Why hasn't Vincent ever said anything? Presumably because he didn't know about his father's heart problem. I look at Harriet's tear-strewn face. Yes, I can imagine her keeping it from her beloved only son in a misguided attempt to protect him.

Wondering just how much Abbey is taking in, I form my words carefully. 'So equally, Vincent might not have this . . . illness. Today could just be a terrible coincidence.'

Her head down and scrabbling in her handbag, Harriet mumbles something.

I gape, disbelieving. Did I hear correctly? 'What did you just say, Harriet?'

She pulls out a handkerchief and loudly blows her nose. 'He does, Vincent does have HCM. He collapsed at theological college and . . .' She shudders. 'He was diagnosed then.'

55

Mariana

Mari curls up her legs on Dee's sofa. Though her sister has made her attic room the cosiest in the old building, there's still a dankness in the air. In the early days she could smell it – a stink like wet socks, rotten wood *and* decaying rodent – and she regularly told Vincent to get in a builder, a rat catcher or an exorcist to do something about it. For Dee's sake she's better mannered these days – marginally at least – but still she feels bad. Her seemingly invincible brother-in-law is in a coma in the hospital she works at.

She visited him in the intensive care unit this morning. Without his usual animation, he looked like a stranger and it brought tears to her eyes to see him laid so low. But she had a quick chat with the registrar and the news isn't horrendous. Thanks to the quick work of the ambulance services, he came round after the return of spontaneous circulation, and was later given the paralytic drug as a strategy to induce hypothermia, aid brain recovery and give his heart the best chance for improvement. The plan is to stabilise the body, then assess any damage to both vital organs later.

She now glances at her sister's slim back. *Since yesterday's* shocking news, they've talked on the phone, but this is the first time they've seen each other in person. How much have the medics told her? Does she know that despite an encouraging start, an SCA outcome can range from a full recovery, to permanent brain damage or even death? Her mood certainly seems strange; instead of the pale, worried apathy she expected when she arrived, Dee was pink-faced and agitated.

Dee turns from the kettle. 'Bugger hot drinks, let's have something stronger. What do you fancy? I have red up here or we could go downstairs and raid Vincent's spirits cupboard.' She laughs a dry laugh. 'They asked me how much he drinks and I had no idea.' She snorts. 'But as the mad wife in the attic, it's hardly surprising.'

'You're not the mad wife, Dee.'

She sloshes wine into two glasses and hands one over. 'Oh, but I am. I'm mad as hell. I'm flaming livid!' She thumps down and guffaws. 'Your face! I'm glad I can still surprise my big sister.'

Mari looks at her thoughtfully. She seems extremely hyper, but apart from the furious glow, her pupils look normal. 'Well, you certainly surprised me when you started shagging the thirty-something vicar at fifteen.'

'Sixteen.'

'OK. Fifteen and three hundred and sixty-five days . . .'

It's their usual banter, but Dee is frowning. 'He knew then,' she says, apparently to herself. 'Peter was already dead when we met. Yes, he bloody well knew then.'

Mari sits up. 'OK, let's rewind. What's going on, Dee Dee? Why are you so angry?'

'OK, so . . .' She takes a shuddery breath. 'When we started dating, Vincent's dad – Peter – had already passed away and I didn't ask what had happened to him. What teenager does? The information wasn't ever offered, not even when I got pregnant with Abbey.' Her jaw tight, she shakes her head. 'I know she wasn't exactly planned, but that might still have been the time to inform me his father hadn't just died from a sudden cardiac arrest, but that he had a pre-existing heart condition, one which can be fucking inherited.'

Flinching at Dee's rare use of the expletive, Mari pictures Vincent back then: styled hair and square jaw; tall, handsome, popular and perky. In fairness, little had changed until yesterday. 'Maybe he was in denial and didn't want to face it.'

Her cheeks a bright red, Dee glares. 'Don't defend him, Mariana. Maybe he was, but as a parent you have responsibilities. What about Abbey? Did he think it was OK to wait until she collapsed playing netball or tennis and mention it to me then? And it wasn't just him who'd kept it from me; it was Harriet too. All these years I've been the irresponsible, unstable parent and those two bloody holier-than-thou *Christians* . . .' She stops speaking and points a finger. 'No, Mariana, don't say it.'

'Say what?'

'That perhaps Vincent wasn't told or didn't realise the seriousness of his father's condition, or maybe he was fit and didn't think for a moment he'd inherited it, or another weak "in denial" excuse . . .'

Mari lifts her hands in surrender. 'You're right, absolutely—'

'Because he did know. Harriet blurted it out yesterday. Peter had a condition called hypertrophic cardiomyopathy. An abnormally thick heart muscle? Anyway, I was still reeling from the shock that neither she nor Vincent had seen fit to mention a possible *hereditary illness*, when *the rest came tumbling out.*

220

Vincent had a collapse in his twenties when *his* condition was diagnosed. Yes, he was *told* he'd inherited HCM too.' She stares at the ceiling, then sighs. 'I know he's in hospital, that he must have been in dreadful pain and of course I'm very worried about him, but why didn't he ever tell me? Apparently, he was given the appropriate medication to manage it. As far as I'm aware, he's been on it ever since.'

56

Calvin

Cal yanks open the lounge curtains to let in the light. It's actually a pretty nice-looking morning out there, but he's not feeling it. He's had another text from Cristina. Should he just delete it like the rest or take a leaf out of her book and tell her he isn't interested and to stop? Is ghosting or being honest the better option? She's already caused him enough bother, but he doesn't want to be unkind; it can't be easy living away from her family, scraping a living on minimum wage and possibly losing her job. Then there's Willy; he's not a man who looks in great shape.

He flops down on the couch. Friday, a day off, so what now? Before bed he promised he'd go to the gym and pound out the irritation which is pecking his mind from all angles, but when he woke up the culpability hit him like a slap. He didn't check the RRV kit in the Kia before heading out on Tuesday. It's unforgivable. Whatever he's done or not done in his personal life, his professional one has remained unscathed until now. Yes, he inspected the original equipment in the BMW before it was stolen from under his nose; sure, a faulty defib should absolutely not have found its way into the system, but the buck sticks with him. He started CPR moments after he realised the problem, but what damage might those wasted seconds have caused?

Deciding food will improve his mood, he strides to the kitchen, opens the fridge and peers at the contents. Peppers and mushrooms that are nearly past their best and steak. A stir-fry? Or even a beef sandwich if he has a baguette left in the freezer.

He peels an onion, halves it, then dices it like a chef. When he put himself through uni, he had a stint in a gastropub kitchen. He was pretty sick of slicing veg by the time he left, but he learned a few tricks and cooking is something he actually enjoys when he has the time and inclination. But today his head is in that old, creaking house. He had no idea it was the vicarage when he arrived; he hadn't set eyes on Reverend Vincent since he was a kid, so didn't realise it was him until he heard Dee's panicked voice and felt her hands on his shoulders. The relief that flooded him when her mother-in-law intervened soon turned to alarm when Dee cracked her head against the table. Christ, what a nightmare. The old woman's distress went up a notch, blending in with the sound of the ambulance siren as it arrived. Then, as though Vincent had been faking it, he started breathing just as Sheryl rushed in.

'All's well that ends well.' Hmm, that's what his mum used to say. But has it? He usually goes in with the ambulance team and hangs around for a while to see how the patient is doing, but there was Dee to look after. He doesn't want to think about her; she heightens too many emotions in him, all the feelings he had under control for years. And there's no point indulging them, is there? She's a married woman and her husband is seriously ill in a hospital bed. That's hardly a basis for romance. Besides, he no longer has her mobile number. Cristina saw to that.

Ripping off a piece of kitchen roll, he wipes his damp eyes. He became so proficient at chopping in the pub kitchen, the fumes stopped burning them back then. Perhaps he's lost his touch. Or maybe he needs a sharper knife.

He looks at the mushrooms doubtfully. A bit too bruised? Like him these days. His lips twitch at the notion. Bloody hell, *bruised*? He needs to get a grip; he really is going soft. As though answering his debate, the doorbell rings for his veg box delivery. He opens up but gapes in confusion. Incredibly, it's the subject of his thoughts. Not onions, nor fungus, nor indeed ecchymosis, but Dee.

Surprise and pleasure are overtaken by dread. Reverend Vincent. The broken defibrillator. Oh Christ. But after a second of panic, he focuses on his visitor. She doesn't seem irate or tearful. More concerned, in fact.

'Are you OK?' she asks, peering at him. 'Sorry, have I called at a bad time?'

What? 'No ...' Then realising what she means, 'No, not at all. I was slicing onions and they always make me ...' There's no time for small talk; he needs to know. 'How's your husband?'

'Fine, thanks to you. Well, as fine as can be expected, apparently. He's still asleep. They put him in an—'

'An induced medical coma. Yeah, that's pretty standard after an SCA. So ...' Trying to work out her expression, he takes in her pale face. 'Was there anything you wanted to ask me?'

'About Vincent?'

'Yeah.'

'Not particularly.'

'Then how come ... ?' Sensing that her tears are near the surface, he changes the subject and grins. 'Got it; you've come for the promised lunch.' He looks at his watch. 'Well, brunch.' Standing back, he gestures her in. 'Perfect timing. Mushrooms or not? You decide.'

57

Cordelia

Still fuelled by the mixed emotions which propelled me here, I stare at the turning mushrooms. Harriet would stuff them in her face for sure. And as for Vincent ... Oh God. I know he's extremely ill, but I can't help my feelings of hurt and offence. He conspired with his mother about his health for years. It really is unbelievable.

Knowing Harriet couldn't possibly miss a team meeting, I went to visit him in the heart unit this morning. But it was only for appearances' sake, and I left the moment the woman bustled in.

I inwardly smile at my blistering anger and the refreshing sea change; right now I actually don't give two hoots about *appearances*. Brazenly appearing on Cal's doorstep is evidence of that. But there's Abbey, so of course I have to make an effort for her.

Wearing her uniform, she appeared in the kitchen earlier.

'Oh, so you're going in to school?'

'What does it look like?'

'You don't have to if you don't want to, love.'

'There's no point staying here. And anyway ... ' She rolled

her eyes. 'It's Latin today, remember? You were the one who didn't want me to drop it. I'll get behind if I don't attend every class.' She snatched up her violin case. 'It's my music lesson too.'

I sigh away the spike of worry. Routine, normality. Good things, surely? This morning wasn't the right moment, but I have to broach Vincent's condition with her soon. The poor girl is the real victim in this mess. She might even need counselling to help her get a handle on a possible hereditary illness. But at least Mari helped last night. After I had vented for a good ten minutes, we talked through the implications for Abbey. We concluded that waiting is the obvious answer for now. Wait and see how Vincent is when he wakes. *If* he wakes.

'You're right.'

I shake myself back to today. Cal has just spoken. 'Sorry?'

He's washing his hands at the sink. 'You're right.' He opens a green refuse sack and chucks in a pile of mushrooms. 'Definitely past their best.'

'Oh, OK.' Then, 'Did I say something?'

He lightly kisses me and laughs. 'You didn't have to. Your face said it for you.'

'Did it?' I study him for a moment. Those lips, his sandalwood smell, his lithe, muscled body and that smile . . . Though I know I'm blushing, I meet his fine eyes. The arousal, the desire and old Dee Dee are there, and it feels bloody good. 'OK,' I ask, lifting my chin. 'My face. What's it saying now?'

'Hmm, a strange mix, but I'm detecting a need for a hug?'

I slip my arms around his neck. 'Something along those lines,' I reply.

*

Replete and exhausted, I gaze at the ceiling. That felt so good. It still does. So very delicious, it's difficult not to float away into oblivion. Despite it being Lent, I'd punch the air and shout alleluia if I had the energy. But my limbs are hollow and sleep is tugging me in.

My pulse finally slowing, I drift. I've never taken any drugs, never popped tablets nor had a drag of a joint. Not even sleeping pills or antidepressants when I needed them so badly. But this is how I imagine a high would be – complete chilled-out relaxation even though I should be anxious and worried about so many things. Love is indeed a drug. Dad used to gyrate to a song about that. I snort to myself. Of all people, he'd know.

Sensing eyes on me, I open my own. Cal's propped up on his arm and he's watching me intently. He kisses my hair. 'All mended now?'

I don't want to think about either Harriet's slap or Vincent right now, but I do need to explain about my bizarre behaviour on Tuesday. 'Why did you send me that text on Sunday night?'

'Asking to see you?'

'No, the later one. It scared me and—'

'Stop. What later one? When?'

'I don't know, I deleted it, but you said I'd be sorry. It was horrible.'

'Sorry for what?'

'For being a Christian, which is why I got it so wrong when I saw you in our lounge.'

'A *Christian*?' His puzzled expression is replaced by a flash of annoyance. 'That wasn't me. It must have been someone's idea of a joke in the pub. Sorry.'

His jaw tight, he's silent for a while. Then: 'What about the text you sent me?'

I take a shuddery breath. In all honesty I want to shelve Facebook and pretend it hasn't happened. 'There was a photo of us – well, of your car – on the church Facebook page. Near the river, in that clearing in the trees? I don't know who'd do that, but it completely threw me. I'm the only admin, so I deleted it, but it was so, so ... malicious.'

'That must have been horrible. Hopefully the troll has had his fun now.'

'Yeah.' Nestling against his warm body, I close my eyes. I want to forget all the bad stuff and glide a little longer in this fantasy world.

'It was a surprise to see you at my door. A pleasurable one, but unexpected.'

A jolt of guilt hits me. 'Because my husband is unconscious in a hospital bed? Does it make me a bad person?'

'Nope.' He thrums fingers on his chest. 'Who judges these things, anyway? People do, but they shouldn't. No one else knows what goes on inside anyone else's mind. It's not for them to decide how a person should react to any given situation, or how they should feel. There are norms, but many of us don't fit in that mould, much as we'd like to at times.'

'Too true,' I reply.

Norms and moulds. Have I ever *fitted*? From Daddy's special princess to a bible basher, from sexual teenager to a young mum. But those roles were taken from me one by one until I became an empty vessel which simply existed and complied. Yet the void is slowly being filled. By anger, for sure, but what else? This man absently stroking my shoulder? A person, like me, who isn't *normal*?

'Tell me about your baby. Zachary, you said.'

'OK . . . So, he's nearly six months old and lives with his mum and grandparents in Bolton.' Silent for moments, he then clears his throat. 'He's a lovely boy. He's cute, he's chubby, he smiles when he sees me. He's learned to roll over and can sit up with help. I can see all that but I don't feel whatever it is you're supposed to feel for your own child.' He puffs out a long breath of air. 'It's like the wiring between us is missing. No connection. I realise it makes me a freak. Or perhaps just a selfish shit. But that's how it is.' He pauses for a beat. 'Sorry.'

Oh God, the poor man. From the crack in his voice, I know it was a struggle to say it, even more to be so brutally honest. 'Don't be sorry,' I reply. 'Life deals all sorts of curve balls. Mari thought she wouldn't bond with Isak and now he's here she's besotted. Back in the day Vincent tried to persuade me to abort Abbey and they're as close as any father and daughter could—'

'A man of religion did that? You're joking?'

'No.' And it wasn't just that; whether or not prompted by Harriet, Vincent's suggestion that the child wasn't his was simply devastating. 'But once she was born, he pretty much wanted her all to himself. Well, him and his mother. You've met the delightful woman, so . . . '

'That must have been tough.'

'It was, but then . . . ' My nose stings. God, why am I telling him? But I know I'll continue. 'But then I got pregnant again. A boy. Luke. I was determined that this time he'd be mine; I wouldn't let them control and undermine me.'

Reaching over, Cal passes me a tissue. 'What happened?'

'He died.' I blow my nose. 'He was ten weeks old and he died.'

'That must have been unbearable.'

'It was. For a *long, long time.*'

He doesn't ask the question, but of course he wants to know. Everyone does. For seconds I'm silent. Will I tell him? *Can* I?

Pulling the bedding with me, I hitch upright. Cal has told me about his son and his painful, innermost guilty secret. Now is the time for me to do likewise. I meet his cloudy gaze. 'A cot death, but—'

'Christ, I'm so sorry. That must have been dreadful.'

'Stop.' I hold out my hand. 'No. Don't feel sorry for me. Please. I don't deserve it. That's what we told people. But it wasn't a cot death.' My heart thrashing, I inhale. 'The truth is, I killed him.'

'What?' he asks, his tone incredulous. 'You ...'

Though I glimpse his furrowed brow, my tears are too blinding to gauge his response, his shock, his inevitable disgust.

'Yes.' My chest jerks from my sobbing; it's a struggle to get the shameful words out. 'Yes, it was me. I killed my own baby.'

58

Mariana

Mari yawns as she stands from her cramped bus seat. It has been a tough week, harder than she'd imagined. The half days have been ... Rapid, that's for sure, but also unsettling or dissatisfying; she hasn't felt useful to either her clients or Britt. But at least it's Friday now – two and a half days off with Isak and Britt before starting work proper next week.

She looks out of the grimy window. The vehicle is pulling up at her usual stop, but much as she'd like to get off here, collapse on the sofa and close her eyes, there's Dee to think of.

Despite struggling to wake up this morning, she forced herself out of bed half an hour early so she could look in on Vincent before work. Still on the ventilator, he was pretty much the same. They haven't yet reversed the induced coma, so that's fine, but on her way out of the Heart Centre she spotted Dee walking down the path. Her sister's set jaw give her a jolt; she hasn't seen it since the discovery of Bill's infidelity. Once the torrent of tears and despair had passed, Dee had the same determined look then. After her passivity for so many years, surely anger and resoluteness are good signs? But look where they got her back then – she joined a cult, not just the flaming church, but the 'sect' which is Vincent and Harriet.

Now striding towards the vicarage, Mari reprimands herself. As usual she's being unfair about her brother-in-law, but there *is* a but. In a way, she's right, isn't she?

Hoping it isn't Harriet who answers, she raps the old knocker and stands back. She tries again and is on the point of giving up when the door swings open.

'Abbey!' Mari pulls her in for a hug. 'How are you doing, gorgeous?'

Her niece shrugs, so she follows her into the kitchen. 'I thought you were at school today?'

'I was, but my music lesson was cancelled so they said I could come home early.' Her tone is sullen. 'I expected Mum to be here but she isn't. There was no reply when I tried her.'

Of course; Dee's car isn't in the driveway; Mari didn't twig before. 'Maybe she's at the hospital?'

'She isn't. I called Grandma. She's there with Dad but there's no sign of Mum.' Her cheeks pink with upset, she glances at Mari, then looks away. 'What sort of wife does that make her? Then ignoring her mobile so I can't even speak to her. Great mum, eh?'

'I'm certain it won't be deliberate, Abbey. Her mind's just probably elsewhere or she hasn't twigged it's on silent. Believe it or not, I did the same the day Isak was born.' She sits at the table. 'I'm starving. Shall we get a cuppa and some monstrous cupcake creation out of one of the tins?' She smiles. 'Remember the cat lady who dropped one in her Bilbo Baggins's litter tray?'

Abbey laughs a small laugh. 'We don't know that for sure.'

'That was a cat litter topping, mark my words!' She takes in her niece's dejected and angry body language. 'Your mum was at the hospital this morning because I bumped into her. She told me you'd gone in to school today, so that's why she won't have noticed the missed calls. Bet your bottom dollar she'll realise by three-thirty.'

'She's never here when I need her.'

Mari sighs inwardly. True, Dee isn't around right this moment, but she's pretty much been a fixture here, the 'mad woman in the attic' throughout Abbey's childhood. But of course being 'here' isn't just a physical thing.

'Your mum loves you very much. I know she doesn't always hit the mark, but she tries—'

'Yeah, too hard. I'm not a baby any more.'

'I know. You're a beautiful and smart young woman.'

Stifling another yawn, Mari fills the kettle and lines up two mugs. Adolescence can be so horrible: fighting to get away from suffocating parental concern and yet yearning for it too. And in truth, not just in one's teenage years – she knows that more than anyone. She pushes away that jarring thought, but replaces it with another. Will she be equipped for all this when Isak grows up? The challenges of parenthood have already started as he was tetchy last night. She spent the early hours trying to settle him while Britt napped between feeds. Though wonderful, having a child isn't always plain sailing, that's for sure.

The drinks finally made, she perches opposite Abbey. 'Was there anything in particular you needed your mum for today?'

'I wanted her to drive me to the hospital, of course. What else?'

'I don't know. You tell me.'

Abbey rubs the tabletop. 'The stuff about Dad's heart. I know what a hereditary condition means, I'm not stupid.' She lifts her chin, but her flickering eyes show her fear. 'It means I could have it.'

'Maybe. It's a condition that can be treated, remember. But you might not have it.'

'I know; the nurse said fifty-fifty. And I looked it up.'

'OK. How do you feel about that?'

'What do you think? Not great . . . '

Mari watches the emotions pass across her face. Frightening though the HCM is, she senses there's more. 'What else is troubling you, Abbey? What else do you want to ask your mum?'

'What do you want to ask me, Abbey?'

They both jump at the sound of Dee's voice from the door. Her expression terse, she moves to the table and crouches by her daughter's side. 'It's fine, love. I know you're confused and frustrated and frightened. Just say whatever you need to and I'll try to be honest.'

Abbey flushes deeply and hot tears gather, but she glares without blinking. 'Is it true what Grandma said? Did you get pregnant with me deliberately to make Dad marry you?'

Wondering how Dee will reply, Mari tenses. But instead of the consternation she expects, there's clear relief on her sister's pallid face. 'Yes, Abbey. I'm not proud of it, but it's true. Yes, Grandma is right; I did.'

Abbey's look is appalled. 'Why would you do that?' she splutters.

'Desperation, love, need, I suppose.' Smiling thinly, Dee puts a soft palm to her daughter's cheek. 'It was completely wrong of me, but I'm so very glad I did.'

59

Cordelia

I stare out of the ward window. The crooked fingers of a branch are tapping at the glass. Are there really buds of hopeful spring, or am I just imagining it like I imagined the movement of Luke's tiny chest all those years ago? But I can't think about that now. I mustn't picture the look on Calvin's face when I confessed the dreadful truth to him yesterday.

Biting back the emotion, I revert to Vincent's corner. He's in the process of coming out of the coma. A nurse helpfully described it as turning on a light with a dimmer rather than one with a switch. They'd already weaned him off the drugs that kept him unconscious, and this morning they removed the mechanical ventilation and breathing tube. He looks so much better now; more asleep than critically ill. And he has stirred several times, almost opening his eyes. Apparently, anyway. Harriet is one side of him, Abbey the other.

The old feelings of exclusion stir in my chest, but I mustn't be self-indulgent. Today is about Vincent's waking and, God willing, *his complete and lucid recovery.*

'I'll get us a drink. Harriet, what would you like?' I ask. 'Tea or coffee? And something to eat?'

Like a deflated space hopper, the poor woman looks as though she's actually lost weight. But it's understandable; her beloved son is dangerously ill. She'll be as concerned as I am that the vibrant man we know and admire will be fully restored.

Instead of answering the question, she thrusts a slip of paper at me. 'I wrote this while I was here, *alone*, yesterday.'

'Oh yes?'

'You need to do an announcement in the church group. People will be worried.'

'Right.' Oh Lord, Facebook. Heat hitting my cheeks, I blankly stare at her loopy handwriting and grapple for an escape plan. 'Though people prefer the personal touch, don't they? Matthew must have mentioned it during this week's morning services. I think that's a much nicer way to break bad news.'

Harriet picks a thread from her skirt. 'I told him to keep it under wraps for now.'

I frown. Yes, it does make sense of the absence of condolences, casseroles, cakes and cards, but what about the 'power of prayer' I've had forced down my throat, especially by this woman? Prayer to help me grieve my dead son; prayer to make me a better mother, wife, Christian?

'What about congregational prayers?' I ask quietly.

Heaving herself up, Harriet sidles over to me. 'He's had mine. What about you, Cordelia?' she hisses in my ear. 'Don't you know Vincent at all? The last thing he wants is people to see him as weak. He's a leader and they have to stay strong.' She prods at her instructions. 'That's why you'll do it my way. Post something online to stop the gossipmongers, but keep it low key.'

I open the note and read it. 'A bout of pneumonia?'

'Yes, that'll explain his hospital stay and need for a period of recovery.'

I shake the disbelief from my head. *If* he recovers. But Harriet seems pretty certain he will and she always gets her own way. Unable to create an excuse right now, I nod. 'OK, but I won't get the opportunity until later.' Though it goes against the grain, I place a hand on Harriet's arm and use a placatory tone. 'In the meantime, have a think about the news coming through Matthew and the rest of the team. Maybe an announcement at the family service tomorrow? I think it'll be more respectful to them and kinder to the community. Not everyone goes on—'

'Grandma! Quick!'

We spin to Abbey's urgent tone. Vincent is weakly lifting his head. Harriet thunders over and hollers to me. 'Call someone!'

A guy in scrubs is already on his way. When he reaches me, he smiles. 'Has hubby woken up?'

Sheer relief drains down my spine. Vincent is conscious, that's a start. 'Yes. Yes, it looks like it.'

The nurse checks his watch and makes his way to his patient. 'Excellent, you're with us.' He raises the headboard, puts a beaker to Vincent's lips and watches him carefully. 'Just a small sip. You're in hospital, Vincent.' Then, stepping back behind Abbey, 'Who do we have here?'

Vincent closes his eyes and doesn't speak for a moment, then he holds out his hand. 'Darling Abbey,' he croaks. With a clear effort, he rotates his head to Harriet. 'Mother.'

The nurse offers him more water and he drifts off again. After a few moments he stirs, his brow creasing. 'Where's Cordelia?' he asks. 'Where's my wife?'

A thousand different emotions fighting for prominence, I finally step forward with a smile. 'I'm here, Vincent,' I say. 'Don't worry, I'm here.'

60

Mariana

The Sunday church bells accompanying her, Mari pushes the pram around the park a second time. She's been out of the house for well over an hour, but Isak has only just stopped his intermittent whimpering, so she's giving it another lap before returning him to Britt.

'Colic,' the health visitor said dismissively yesterday. 'In my experience, more firstborn babies get it than not. You can buy drops from the chemist, but there's no guarantee they make any difference.'

The NHS website wasn't a great deal more helpful: *Colic is when a baby cries a lot but there's no obvious cause. It's a common problem that should get better on its own.*

Well, thanks for that. Just what Mari needs when she barely slept all night and her partner was sobbing as much as the baby this morning. Over the last forty-eight hours she's tried all the top tips recommended on mumsnet, from laying him on his back in a dark room to swaddling him snugly in a blanket; from gentle infant massage to a tepid soak in the bath. She wasn't keen on placing a warm water bottle on his belly, though, and as she put it to Britt, '*Would we really resort to using a dummy?*'

240

'Get the damned pacifier and medicine and take *him* with you. I need to sleep,' Britt yelled from her pillow two hours ago.

Mari peers at 'him' now. He's asleep and back to little angel. And in fairness, he wasn't that bad as she meandered through the village. She even managed a coffee in Expo Lounge. It was roomy enough for a pram and she smiled sympathetically to a couple of other jaded-looking mothers. And though she isn't happy about using either, she bought the colic drops and soother from Boots.

Of course, medicines play a vital role for many conditions, mental health ones included, but she's loath to give a tiny child anything at all. If Simeticone makes no difference, why take the risk? But Britt is pretty much at the end of her tether and she'll be home alone each day from tomorrow. Sure, Mari's going against her own principles, but keeping her partner content is the priority.

The wind whipping her cheeks, Mari makes her way past the swings towards home. Hopefully, Britt has napped; maybe she'll get half an hour herself. And developments in the Vincent camp are looking good. His recovering of consciousness is fabulous news in itself; many SCA patients never do. Though his short-term memory is apparently patchy, that isn't unusual; assessments will continue until he gets stronger, then decisions can be made for the long term.

Now at her front door, she turns to reverse the pram inside as quietly as possible. But a voice she doesn't recognise makes her jump. 'Let me help you in with that.'

A wiry young man squeezes past and lifts the other side of the buggy. He grins. 'I'm Rory, pleased to meet you.'

Another person appears at the bottom of the stairs. A girl this time, pretty with prominent teeth. 'Britt! He's here.'

'That's Lindy,' Rory says. He gestures to a boy shuffling in from the lounge: 'And that's Yusuf. Otherwise known as the Fab Four. Britt being the fourth, of course.'

Then Britt's lightly accented twang: 'Britt being the *first*, I think you mean, Rory. Come on, guys, meet my baby.'

What on ... ? Mari had left her partner with a face swollen from tears, but there's no sign of them now. Indeed, with her carefully applied make-up, she looks a picture of health and happiness. She finally finds the power of speech. 'He's only just dropped off. It might not be a good idea to wake him ... '

But Britt has already scooped Isak out. 'Told you he was beautiful, didn't I?' she says to her huddle of friends. 'Aren't I clever or what?'

Followed by the Fab Three, she heads for the kitchen. At the door she turns. 'Come on, Mariana, we're on the second bottle of fizz. If you don't hurry up, there'll be none left.'

Trying not to obsess about how much champagne Britt has already consumed, Mari sits at the table with a glass. From the expensive-looking Canon around Yusuf's neck, she presumes the youthful invasion are Britt's friends from her old art college. Her arms folded, she watches Yusuf do his stuff with the long lens; Britt do hers too – from her coquettish half-smile to the full-on grin, and all her other winning poses in between. Except today she has the accessory of a baby. She inwardly sighs; is this really a modern-day 'mother and child' picture? She supposes it is; there's no better magazine headline than a celeb with a cute kid. Even more annoyingly, Isak is complying, wide-eyed and quiet in the arms of these strangers as they each take turns for a session.

The alcohol hitting, Mari yawns. Maybe she should quietly

leave and have that nap; the Fab Four aren't likely to become a Fab Five any time soon. Not that she wants to be in the gushing, giggly group, but this is her house and Britt hasn't even formally introduced her.

As though reading her mind, Lindy throws her a laconic look. 'So what do we call you?'

'Mariana is fine.'

The girl tuts. 'No. I mean, what are you? Britt's the mummy, so what are you?'

Britt's eyes widen. 'Lindy!'

Stuck for words, Mari gapes. The girl's accent is quite plummy and she has an indifferent, confident manner that grates. She begins to shape a reply, but Rory speaks first.

'"Mariana" is cool.' He peers at her attentively. 'So how old are you, Mariana?'

Bloody hell, that's direct. And rather rude, actually.

'As old as my tongue and a little older than my teeth,' she replies.

As though she's speaking Mandarin, the Fab Four exchange glances and raised eyebrows.

Lindy leans forward. 'Well, what year were you born, Mariana?' she asks slowly, as though Mari isn't capable of working it out for herself.

Mari glares. OK, she's eight flaming years older than Britt, but that isn't a horrendous age gap and surely they know that already? Bloody hell; they're really pissing her off now. 'And that's relevant, how?'

Clearly shocked by her tone, Lindy sits back. 'Age is only a number and—'

'And you're still looking good,' Rory says encouragingly.

'Right, thanks.' *Still* looking good? How fucking old do they think she is? And that entitled tone some younger people have . . . She rises. 'Well, I'll leave you guys to celebrate the birth of my son.' She plonks her Boots purchases in Britt's lap. 'Colic drops and dummy as requested.' She nods at the chilling bottle of champagne. 'Don't forget Isak drinks what you drink. I'm going out.'

61

Cordelia

I stare at my closed laptop. There's no escaping Facebook; Harriet interrogated me four times before breakfast. On the final round, she stared long and hard.

'Why do you have to be so difficult, Cordelia? The three of us should be pulling together as a family. Doing what's best for Vincent, for the parishioners, for the diocese. Letting tittle-tattle spread is not going to do that. They need a reason for Vincent's absence. I'm at a loss to understand why you haven't posted my note yet.'

I was tempted to reply, '*Pulling together as a family? Do you even understand what that means? You and your son fed me lies by omission for bloody years. Why am I surprised that you're now lying to everyone else?*'

But I didn't; Abbey was at the table, staring at her empty eggshell.

That *conversation* with Harriet has been parked, but I will definitely have it at some point. For now I'm holding on by a thread to speak to Vincent first. It hasn't yet been possible – he's still 'waking up', intermittently regaining consciousness and saying a few words before drifting off again. No doubt an earful from his wife wouldn't be looked on too kindly by the hospital staff.

Standing from my desk, I peer through the leaded window. I pleaded a sore throat to escape church this morning. How I'd have obeyed the three-line whip in the face of questions about Vincent's whereabouts, I have no idea. I saw Harriet and Abbey leave, so I'm definitely alone, but it still feels as though someone is watching me. Which they clearly were, oh God. My initial terror at the 'dogging' message was overtaken by the trauma of Vincent's collapse and then my anger, but Harriet's sixth-sense persistence has brought the anxiety and dread back big time. My breathing is shallow and perspiration dances on my spine. Will another photograph appear? Will it reveal more? Who posted it and why?

I log into Facebook, click the church page and quickly scan the recent photos. There's nothing new, thank the Lord. Indeed, there are only four or five fresh additions to the feed. Puffing out the trapped air, I almost smile to myself. Panic over; it was a one-off malicious troll. I reach for Harriet's note, then do another take. Oh Christ; a pending post waiting for approval. Decline and quickly delete? Or will I regret not *knowing*?

My heart thrashing, I open it. The same silver car fills the screen. Same veiled number plate, same windscreen. But the visibility of the passenger has changed. Like snow, the white marker has thinned and melted, and a woman is quite visible.

Nauseous with alarm, I hang my head. It's me. Oh God, it's definitely me. Trying to rise above the dizziness, I force myself to look again. The driver's side is still obscured and I'm looking forward. *It isn't an incriminating image after all. There could be* any number of reasons why I was there. And I'm wearing my cap. Would anyone recognise me anyway?

My eyes slide to the wording. *Dogging in Didsbury continued . . . Watch this space for more!*

Oh hell, more what? More photos? More exposure? Only one thing is for sure – somebody hates me; someone wants me to suffer for my sins.

My vision suddenly narrowing, I reach for my phone, my fingers pressing the digits they know best. The call is answered after three peals as usual.

'Knutsford six two seven five.'

But it isn't my dad's eloquent voice, it's Gilly's.

62

Mariana

The icy glass burning her fingers, Mari glances around the small inn. Where to rest her weary legs? Football commentary is blaring from one room and she knows from experience that the other will resemble the lounge of an OAP home.

She inwardly guffaws. The bloody 'Fab Four' and their loaded questions. Perhaps she should join the elderly after all. Maybe she'll order half a pale ale, shuffle back to Britt's groupies and let them patronise her some more. But it's no laughing matter, actually. She's only thirty-seven! Not even bloody forty. Yet her annoyance isn't just that, is it? They made her feel sidelined, excluded, and she isn't used to that.

Selecting a stool at one side of the bar, she stares at her tumbler. What is she doing with a gin and tonic at lunchtime? And drinking alone? But she can hardly walk out without at least sipping the damned thing. The publican is already looking at her quizzically. 'Need a double?' he queried when she strode in.

'Why not,' she replied on autopilot. But on reflection why did he ask? Did she look like a teary schoolgirl who'd bolted from the playground because the other kids wouldn't let her join in?

Or just bloody bitter? And why is he still glancing her way? Oh God; perhaps she resembles an alcoholic, desperately trying to hide it from the world. Like Felicity.

'*Feeling a bit off this morning. Nothing to worry you though, darling.*'

Hearing her mum's graceful tones, she sighs deeply. Is this what Felicity did in times of stress? Did she sneak to the pub and sit in a lonely corner, steadily drowning her sorrows? In truth, Mari doesn't know. She turned down the offer to read Medicine at Cambridge to be closer to her mother and was here at university in Manchester, but she rented student digs and was too busy making up for lost time and having an excess of . . . well, everything, to fully notice what was going on.

The usual guilt hitting, she shifts position. It wasn't solely her who neglected their mother – Bill had long gone, Dee was with St Vincent, then pregnant with Abbey, and Ed had started travelling the world – but she was the eldest, the child who lived up the road and the closest emotionally. The last man standing, in fact. She visited regularly, but not nearly as often as she should have.

'*Do you think you might pop in today, darling? I could do with some company.*'

Felicity Stephens. Quiet, dignified, noble. She must have been drinking heavily for years, yet she concealed it so well, staying groomed and nicely dressed, keeping the house spotless and cooking delicious meals whenever she visited. But did Mari know really? When she hugged and kissed her, didn't she smell something *off*? She was aware later for sure, but did she suspect then? Could she have done more to help?

A notion occurs. Ed lived at home until he left school. Did he know about her alcoholism? Is that why he bolted the moment he'd finished his A levels? She pictures his devastated face at the funeral. God, yes, deep remorse for leaving their mum even though he didn't know the whole story.

But her brother did well to escape. She can't blame him for that on any level.

Felicity, Felicity. It's the name she'd chosen in the event of her own pregnancy. She straightens at that thought. Yes, she was determined that's the name *her* child would have. Considering her bonding worries, that's pretty rich. She's actually incredibly lucky: Britt is more than happy to share Isak; Mari's connection with and love for their little man is exactly what she'd hoped for. What the hell is wrong with her, having a paddy and stalking off to the pub? The company of friends to wet the baby's head is a lovely event, and a few glasses of fizz won't hurt.

'By the way, that's Gordon's.'

Mari lifts her head to the bartender.

He nods at her untouched drink. 'Sorry, I'm new at this. I should have asked which gin you wanted. Let me get you another.' He gestures to the display. 'Which do you prefer? We have—'

'Gordon's is fine.' She takes a swig. 'Maybe more ice?'

'I can get you a fresh one—'

'No, really.' She looks at the guy properly. Probably around Britt's age. Hair in a topknot and the mandatory dark stubble. She lowers her voice. 'New job tip: I don't think you're supposed to offer freebies to the paying public.'

He pulls a mock-sage face. 'You're joking? Right, thanks.' Then he grins. 'This sounds like a cheap chat-up line, but I might recognise you.'

Well, this is a surprise. So's the warm feeling in her belly. Is it *actually* a flutter of attraction to *him?*

'Do you?'

'I think you know my mum.'

Mari laughs to herself. So much for thinking he might fancy her back. She's past it at thirty-seven, after all.

'And if you are who I suspect you are, I owe you more than a replacement G and T,' he continues.

'Well, I'm intrigued now ...' Mari starts. She narrows her eyes; yup, the similarity is striking. 'You're Konnie's son. Rohan? I have your dissertation.'

'Roh. And yes, you do. To be honest, I was hugely embarrassed she pestered you to read it.' His cheeks flush. 'But hugely pleased too. It's an honour to have your input. There are so many questions I'd love to ask.'

Aware of her own blush, Mari searches for a suitably sardonic quip, but she's saved by a roar from the front room. 'I think someone's won.' Three grinning punters tumble through. 'It looks like your services are needed. Remember – no freebies!'

Enjoying the rush of pleasure, Mari returns to her drink. Pathetic though it is, it feels as though she hasn't been complimented by anyone about anything for a very long time. She delves into her handbag, pulls out a pen and writes her number on a coaster.

'Roh?'

He turns from his chore. 'Yup?'

She slips it towards him. 'Ask away, any time,' she says. 'I'd be honoured too.'

63

Calvin

Cal parks the RRV outside the Heart Centre and rubs his eyes. A half-hour break at last. He's on his own today so his thoughts have swung from self-reprimand for not going to the gym to feeling bad about little Zach, from dull anxiety about the broken defibrillator to concern about Willy. But most of all they land at Dee. He still can't shape how he feels about her stunning revelation. He's shocked and outraged, for sure, but it's mixed with another emotion he can't quite define.

He drags himself back to the mission in hand. A colleague heard that Willy's had another seizure and things aren't looking good. There's always a jolt of sadness when anyone who came through his hands dies, but the old guy's advice about family still jangles. Though Cal misses his little sister, he isn't ready to make peace with his mum. But he has a son and he's determined he *will* be part of Zachary's life. He's already made a start, minding him at the weekend for a few hours while Sadie went shopping with her mum.

Not bonding exactly, but it was heart-warming to make the little guy chortle.

He reaches for the door handle but quickly sits back and shrinks in his seat. Cristina is leaving the green building and walking this way. God, he's a coward. But at least her expression is blank, there are no obvious tears.

Once she's a smudge in the distance, he puffs out his relief and makes his way to the unit. But at the doorway he spots a familiar slim back at the reception bench. Both hoping and dreading that she'll turn around, he stares. Three days ago he held this woman in his arms. After confessing that she'd 'killed' her baby, she wept for her loss as though it was yesterday. Yet it wasn't just wretched tears of grief; it was guilt too. She sobbed out her deep, deep remorse because she was stifled at the time. She'd been forced to bury it for thirteen long years.

The anger on her behalf shoots through his veins. Blame is crippling, corrosive. He understands that more than anyone. And that bloody man didn't allow her to deal with it.

He grimaces. Yup, he knows full well what that indefinable emotion is. It's fury, a violent desire to batter Vincent Hardy's smug face.

He steps back outside. It's best not to see Dee right now. They didn't argue exactly, but part of him wanted to shake her. Yes, she smothered her baby; there's no getting away from that horrific, debilitating fact. But it was unintentional; she fell asleep while feeding him. Dreadful though it is, it happens, he's seen it for himself. Co-sleeping is particularly popular in some ethnic minority groups and sadly infant deaths occur. It's tragic, unbearable for the families. They suffer, howl and grieve; they eventually forgive themselves and move on, perhaps have another baby. But that man, her husband, decided not to let that natural process occur. He played God and deemed it a 'cot death'. Goodness knows how he managed it, but the authorities agreed.

'He did it for me,' Dee said quietly when the tears finally stopped. 'He did it out of love and a desire to protect me. The stigma of sudden death was bad enough, but nothing compared to admitting it was my fault. The church community is a small one but it can be quite . . . well, judgemental.'

She took a shuddery breath and looked at him imploringly. 'Please, please, promise you'll never say anything to anyone. No one else knows and I couldn't bear people to discover what I did.' She nodded as though reminding herself. 'Vincent understood that; he still does. He shielded me from that horror and I'll always be grateful.'

Cal blows out long and hard. That apparently holy man was judge and jury. He didn't allow Dee to acknowledge it publicly, work through the guilt and properly grieve. Instead she bottled it up inside, emotionally crippling herself. And what does '*Vincent understood that; he still does*' even mean? Well, he has a pretty good idea: it's control and domination, even a form of blackmail, which she is unable to see.

64

Cordelia

I study my husband, sitting up in his hospital bed. Only Vincent could make such an amazing recovery. Sure, he still looks pallid and drawn, but his eyes are bright and lively. Harriet has accompanied me today.

'Right, Cordelia, I'll come with you to the hospital,' she said after Abbey left for school.

'Don't you have a church meeting this morning? They'll be lost without you,' I replied, searching for a reason not to have the woman's telescopic attention in the car.

'I'm sure they'll cope just this once,' she replied.

I expected a double-barrelled assault about Facebook et al during the journey, but Harriet was relatively quiet, maybe because rumour had already spread. Though the swollen numbers at Evensong should have been a clue, I didn't twig until I was swathed in condolences and unsubtle inquisitions afterwards: *'Is it true that the rector collapsed ...' 'Taken by ambulance, I believe ...' 'I told Fred the Heart Centre could mean only one thing ...' 'Please tell me our dear leader isn't dead ...'*

Harriet didn't share the team's reaction to the news, but from the expressions of the director of worship, curate, youth leader and sexton, I guessed they weren't best pleased to have heard it from '*tittle-tattle*' rather than in person.

Her hair glued into place by extra helpings of lacquer, she's now attentively listening to her son's articulate description of his 'episode'.

'Most peculiar,' he's saying. 'A little breathless and sweaty in the morning. Then – to my astonishment – BOOM, later! Central chest pain led to my arms, my neck, my jaw. A veritable tourniquet of pressure and squeezing ...' His tone becomes teary. 'But then I felt the Lord's arms around me. Holding me, keeping me safe ...'

I glance around the ward of six beds, sure the other grey-faced patients don't need Vincent's church-loud apologue. And '*most peculiar*', '*astonishment*'. Really? When it's happened before?

The irritation rising, I take a steadying breath. Yes, I am deeply grateful to Vincent for looking after me when Luke died, for barely batting an eyelid when I finally found words to explain what had happened, for his 'cot death' intervention. And for never imparting one word of blame, even though he was Luke's parent too. But. Surely I'm entitled to feel angry about *this*. His heart condition, his omission, his medication, his lie.

'So, what have they said? What happens now?' Harriet asks, taking the very words from my mouth.

'Dreary test after test, it seems. And an alarming quantity of ...' Vincent has the good grace to look embarrassed. 'Pills. They've also mentioned an ICD.' His eyes flicker to me. 'That's an implantable defibrillator. Just an insurance policy, really, in case—'

'In case you have another sudden cardiac arrest?'

My words pop out tetchy and clipped. I long to confront him about everything, especially the impact it might have on Abbey, but I don't want to do it in front of Harriet. Nor appear like a fishwife, which is exactly how I sounded just now. Yet my hands are shaking. It seems that despite my attempts at constraint, my body is rebelling. Fresh air is the answer; I need to get out.

'Just going to the ladies . . .' I say over my shoulder as I leave.

'Mrs Hardy?'

I jerk around to the giant squashed behind the nursing station. 'Yes?'

'Sorry, I didn't mean to make you jump. I'm Alan, a specialist heart nurse, so if you have any questions . . .' He studies me for a beat. 'We're here to look after you just as much as your husband, so if you want to ask anything or just have a chat . . .'

Oh God, the fishwife. 'Right, thanks. Can I use the toilets just here or do I have to . . . ?'

In truth I want to bolt, run away and not stop. But for now a loo break will have to do.

The public washrooms give me a chance to calm down. By the time I'm back by Vincent's side, the smell of hairspray lingers but the woman herself has gone.

'The café for a well-deserved snack. She didn't have any breakfast,' he explains.

It seems my mother-in-law's appetite is returning with her son's health. But that's a cruel thought. As Harriet put it last week, we are a *family* and have to pull together, especially for Abbey's sake. Composing myself, I draw the thin curtain around the bed.

'Why didn't you tell me?' I ask quietly.

'About what?'

'Come on, Vincent, you know perfectly well. Your father's heart condition. Yours. Why keep it from me?'

'There was no need, darling! I was fine; I am now. It played such a minor role in my life that I'd virtually forgotten it myself.' He takes my hand and smiles. 'Besides, which eager suitor slips health issues into the conversation when he's in love with a beautiful young woman?'

I smile thinly; I have to ignore his reasonable platitudes, stay unflustered and have my say. 'But when I got pregnant with Abbey; surely that was—'

'Hmm, a tricky old time, wasn't it? Neither of us knew what we wanted, but look how it worked out for the best—'

'Then Luke, who was planned.'

Releasing my arm, he puts his palms together and brings them to his lips in that pious gesture I've always disliked. 'Oh, darling. You struggled with the pregnancy, the birth and then . . . Well, it was a dreadful period and you weren't yourself for a long time.'

I grit my teeth. Sure, I had a horrible cold just before Luke died, and I was debilitated with grief afterwards, but I don't remotely recognise his description of my pregnancy and the birth; I was at my happiest then. But it isn't the point of today's discussion; I must ignore his equitable, lecturing tone and stick to the point. 'You have a *hereditary* condition, Vincent. What about Abbey?'

He pats my knee. 'She's fine.'

'No, she isn't, Vincent. She's worried, as anyone would be.'

'I'll have a word and explain it. She probably hasn't added two and two together.'

'Two and two? What do you mean?'

'So far so good. Her yearly check-ups show no sign she'll be affected.'

Astonished, I sit back. 'What exactly are you saying? She's had check-ups? By a doctor?'

'Yes, a heart specialist, but I didn't say that to Abbey. Just said we were going for our annual MOT.' His lips curl in that godawful level-headed way. 'You noticed, surely?'

Attempting to retain my equanimity, I stare at the floor. *Noticed* what, for God's sake? I've been all but been excluded from my daughter's whole life. The cinema, theatre, day trips, shopping. How could I possibly have known one of those outings was to see a professional if no one told me? 'No. I didn't know. I shouldn't have to *notice* things about my only child. I should have been informed.'

Vincent dips his head. 'You weren't in a mentally strong place, were you, Cordelia? We didn't want to add to the load.' He gives his winning smile. 'And there was nothing you needed to know about anyway. So far so good; we're keeping an eye on it.'

We? Fucking *we*? As though she's been listening, the 'we' takes her cue, sashaying through with a carrier bag full of goodies. She begins to drag them out, but the curtain parts and Alan appears, carrying a kidney-shaped container. He sidesteps Harriet's bulk and lines several vials on Vincent's tray. 'Sorry to interrupt, ladies. Pill time.'

'What are these for?' Harriet asks.

'In layman's terms we have calcium channel blockers, blood thinners and a heart rhythm drug.' He taps the final container. 'And of course beta blockers, the same as before.' He eyeballs his patient. 'No skipping them again, Vincent. Ever.'

'What? *Skipping* them?' Coming out of my malaise, the words burst from my mouth. 'You weren't taking your prescribed medicine? With a *heart condition*? Why on earth would you do that?'

'I did take it, of course I did. It would be foolish not to.'

Alan's eyebrows are raised meaningfully.

'Vincent?' his mother asks.

For once in solidarity, we both glare.

His cheeks colour, but he wafts a dismissive hand. 'Perhaps I've been occasionally forgetful ... '

'Well, no more *forgetful*, Vincent. For whatever reason.' Alan moves away, then looks back. 'Never. Understand?'

Winded from my clashing emotions, I watch Harriet return to her swag. 'I'll leave you two to it,' I mutter.

Outside the ward door, I stop to steady my racing pulse. When I look up, Alan steps around the nursing station.

'Everything OK?'

'Not really.' I meet his grey gaze. 'But yes, I'm fine. Thank you.'

'Angry, worried, confused?'

I smile wryly. 'Something like that.'

'That's all perfectly normal; heart problems don't just affect the patient.' He eyes me for a moment. 'It happens all the time, I'm afraid. God knows why, but even the most intelligent and rational people stop taking their meds. No one likes fatigue, drowsiness, lethargy.'

'I guess ... ' Of all people, my busy-bee husband would hate all these things. But Alan is still peering at me keenly.

'And men are the biggest culprits. Loss of their manhood; fear of impotence. Erectile disfunction is a common side effect of some drugs, and that's a pretty tough one to take.'

65

Mariana

Taking a deep breath, Mari clears her own troubles from her mind before calling the next client. 'Troubles' is too huge a word, anyway. It's more minor irritations and pique.

Britt, of course.

After the pub interlude on Sunday, Mari reprimanded herself, got a grip and went home with a fixed smile, determined to be friendly with the Fab Four. Why was her skin suddenly so thin? She could dish it out as much as anyone. Look at poor Vincent over the years, and in fairness he always took it on the chin – age and ageist quips included. Sure, she didn't want the gap between her and Britt to be a *thing* worthy of comment and speculation, but it wasn't life-threatening. Not like folk in poor Vincent's condition.

She doodles on her pad. The news about her brother-in-law continues to be positive, so that's great. No getting rid of him so easily! But neither the flaming Fab Three. She entered her house – her own bloody house – with a champagne peace offering and found the lounge in disarray. The cabinet had been emptied of her DVD collection, crisp packets and beer bottles were strewn willy-nilly, and instead of the seat pads being where they belong – on the bloody sofa – they were lining the floor, sprayed with crumbs.

A soft play area, she thought. They'd only needed the coloured plastic balls.

Reminding herself of her promise to be chilled, she went in search of them upstairs. Why she was surprised to find them all in *her* bed, she had no idea. Fortunately asleep and not naked or cavorting, but how much had they drunk in the space of an hour? In charge of a baby, too? She rushed to the nursery to check on Isak and he was sleeping soundly, thank God, but when she turned, Britt was standing at the door, her hair messy and her arms folded.

'See who's worried now,' she said. Then, 'You were rude.'

'*I* was rude?'

'Yes, they were just being friendly.'

'So it's OK to say "*What* are you?" "How old are you?" and "*Still* looking good" to someone you've only just met?'

'That's just Lindy, and Rory was giving you a compliment.' She shrugged. 'Anyway, you'd better get used to it. I've invited them to stay for a few days.'

'You must be joking. Have you seen the state of my home?'

'Our home.'

Britt's right, of course. The house is as much hers as Mari's. Like little Isak, it belongs to them both. Before Mari could apologise, Britt's eyes welled with tears. 'It's only fair, Mariana. Isak has colic and you'll be at work. You'll barely remember we exist.'

Mari now yawns. As if. As if she'll forget Britt and Isak even for a moment of her day. But the thought of working long hours, then returning home to three alcohol-quaffing twenty-something 'adults' – and the resulting chaos – is exhausting. And yet . . .

She stands and looks in the mirror. If her baby had lived . . . She starts again. If she hadn't made a decision to abort, her baby would be twenty right now. She never asked if it was a boy or a girl, but would he or she have looked like this? Dark, striking eyebrows and designer-tousled short locks – and maybe one or two frown lines? God, how she wishes she could get past this particular regret, but despite her best efforts she can't.

Leaning in closer, she plucks out a rogue grey hair. She smiles despite herself. Bloody hell; maybe she really is getting past it.

66

Calvin

At seven o'clock Cal found himself diving into his house, washing pots, fluffing cushions and slotting a couple of framed photographs in a drawer. He even changed the bedding, just in case. But the plan was to talk. That's what Dee's text had said:

Are you home today? Can we talk?

He'd been at work when the message arrived, calming a pregnant mum who was bleeding quite badly at only twenty-four weeks. Though he didn't finish until six, and the Tuesday shift never ended on time, he eventually replied:

I'll be home for half past six if that's any good?

She came back with:

Message me when you're back and I'll see if I can slip away.

He duly sent the text, but it's now eight-thirty and there's no sign of Dee. Flopping down on the settee, he groans at his own stupid disappointment. Married women have always been a no-no until now. Who wants the grief? Yet he went into this knowing Dee was just that. '*Why?*' is the question. Did he honestly want to punish her for his crushing insignificance a lifetime ago? Maybe at first. But she'd turned from that posh, dismissive girl to someone sweet and vulnerable. Like an abused dog, she was barely able to make eye contact that first day and it appealed to his annoying need to help and make a difference ...

He sighs heavily. That's all very well when done professionally and at arm's length, but he's gone way over those boundaries with her. Not just physically, but deep inside where it'll really hurt if he isn't careful.

Dragging his mind to dinner, he heads to the kitchen, but stops at a tapping noise. Is that a knock or just wishful thinking? His ears tuned for more, he strides to the door and opens it. The cool breeze hits his cheeks, but there's nobody to be seen. Daft kids, probably. He begins to turn back but stills at a rustling noise and peers into the darkness.

'Hello? Who's there?'

A figure wobbles unsteadily from behind the fir tree. 'Only me.'

His heart sinking, he sighs. 'Cristina,' he says. 'What are you doing here?'

67

Mariana

Mari takes a deep breath at her door. Day three of the invasion. Truth be told, she's pretty sick of this mix of irritation and apprehension. On the bus home she reminded herself – yet again – that she's fortunate. But a reality check prodded – what do the books say about having a tiny, helpless baby in one's life? Not just the tomes, but herself with clients who are struggling. Yup; if there are cracks in a relationship, a child and the incessant demands of new parenthood can exacerbate them.

She lets herself in and heads to the sound of singing from the kitchen. One of the *cracks* is rifling through a cupboard. Lindy. She turns. 'Oh, hi there. We seem to have run out of olive oil. Fresh pasta and parmesan too.'

Bloody hell, a 'we'. Still, if they are in it together, the Fab Three can source their own bloody food. Mari puts down her bag. 'There's plenty of dried pasta. And the last time I looked, a couple of inches of oil left. Feel free to nip to the Co-op in the village to buy a replacement, though.' She glances at the Hovis bin. 'We look low on bread. Milk too, I expect. Why don't you make a list and pop out?'

266

'Pancakes for breakfast, stir-fry for lunch,' Lindy replies, clearly preferring to explain the shortage, rather than do anything about it.

'Great.'

'We thought Italian for dinner. Always tastes better with a slug of oil added. Pure virgin, of course.'

Mari sighs inwardly. The chit-chat is heart-warming, but Lindy is looking meaningfully at her handbag. Like some teenager's mum, she rifles through her purse. Damn. An assortment of copper and only twenty-pound notes. She hands one over. 'Bring back the change,' she hears herself saying.

As though smelling money, the rest of the gang load in. Mari takes Isak from Yusuf.

'How's he been today?' she asks Britt. With pink cheeks and pink lipstick, she looks particularly vibrant and pretty, like the girl she first met.

'Screaming most of the day,' Lindy answers for her. She rolls her eyes. 'One thing's for sure, none of us want babies any time soon. He's cute when he's asleep, but other than that he's a bit of a mare.'

Mari kisses his soft little cheek. 'Well, a baby isn't just for Christmas, Lindy.' With a windy smile, Isak stretches his fingers. 'And he isn't crying now.' She clocks Lindy's glance at Britt, the rise of her eyebrows. 'I'll be in the lounge having a cuddle with this one. Italian will be delicious for dinner, thank you. In the meantime, a cup of tea when you're ready.'

No change from the twenty appeared, but in fairness the spaghetti tastes good. To soften her general grumpiness, Mari holds out her glass. 'Go on, I'll have a small top-up.'

The conversation has pretty much flowed without any input from her, but as he pours the ruby wine in her glass, Rory gives her the full glare of his amber-eyed attention.

'So, what do you do job-wise, Mariana?'

She feels herself prickle. Hasn't Britt given her friends even the basics? Other than her bloody age, of course. Still, it's a conversation opener and she's on best behaviour.

'I'm a clinical psychologist. I'm mainly hospital-based and I meet with clients to identify problems. You know – emotional, mental, behavioural ...'

But Rory is looking at his phone. Bloody rude again! Or maybe she's just boring. At least it reminds her about the text from Roh – something about questions and finishing his shift early if she fancies a chat over a drink. The thought gives her a small fillip of satisfaction: maybe she and her expertise aren't that dull after all.

Rory comes back to her. 'Sorry, saw the word "Kanye", and had to find out if it was true. So ...' He cocks his head. 'I guess you must be an LOL.'

Laugh out loud? Well, she used to before she met this bloody lot. She throws back her drink. 'Sorry, not following.'

He peers through his retro black frames. 'LOL. Late-onset lesbian. Britt says you used to sleep with guys before you met her.'

The room falling silent, all eyes turn to her. Sloshing more wine in her glass, Mari breathes through her annoyance. She has actually come across this acronym before. Not that middle-aged woman deciding to ditch their husbands and go the sapphic route after their children are grown is a 'phenomenon'

268

as some internet threads seem to imply. And she can see where this conversation is going. Perhaps she should just frame her birth certificate, hang it above the hearth and have done with it. As for labels – mental health, sexuality, gender or otherwise – she hates them. Indeed, she's written several papers on the very subject.

'Yes, I did have delicious sex with a penis or two, Rory, and I haven't closed that door,' she replies. She nudges him playfully. 'I don't suppose you fancy a quick go with an older woman? We could just bob upstairs . . .'

From the gaping looks around the table, she knows she's gone too far. Sure, Rory asked a deeply personal question, but two wrongs never did make a right. Relenting, she smiles. 'Don't worry, I'm only joking.' She nods to his mobile. 'So, what on earth has Kanye done this time?'

Striding up Clothorn Road, Mari heads for the village. Halfway through dinner she escaped from the chatter, sat on the loo and sent Roh a text to say she'd pop in to the Old Cock for the drink he offered. But she's later than planned because she still felt bad about her inappropriate quip to Rory and wanted to ingratiate herself a little more.

As she enters the pub, she laughs at her own neediness. Bloody hell; whatever happened to the old Mari? Roh immediately appears and motions to the back room. 'The table in the corner is ours. You grab it and I'll get us a drink. Gin and tonic?'

'Sounds perfect.'

'It's a bit noisy to discuss a thesis in depth,' he says when he returns. 'A general chit-chat about life instead?'

'Sounds perfect,' she repeats. 'You go first. Tell me about yourself.'

He smiles his attractive smile. 'Me? Nah. You, Dr Mariana Stephens, are far more interesting . . .'

68

Cordelia

Not used to driving in the dark, I try to concentrate on the road ahead. A torn and tattered punchbag seems the most fitting description of how I feel right now. Which blow to focus on? I've been so badly wounded by Vincent, I don't know which one hurts the most – his shocking failure to tell me about his heart condition and medication; the astonishing discovery that he's been taking our child for specialist check-ups for years; his suggestion that I was a deranged lunatic even before Luke's death – or perhaps his point-blank refusal to have another baby afterwards?

But that particular cruelty has stung for many years.

Pulling out another tissue, I wipe my eyes. I have to stop crying; it's affecting my visibility and I don't want to crash the car. Would anyone care if I did? Harriet doesn't bother to temper her hostility and Abbey barely says a word. I had to beg her to sit down to talk through Vincent's revelation.

'Can I have a word, love?'

'I need to do my homework.'

'It's important and it will take five minutes. It's not more bad news, I promise. In fact, quite—'

'I don't have five minutes, Mum. I need to finish my maths, then I'm watching *Pretty Little Liars*.'

'Abbey, please.'

Perhaps my tears threatened then because Abbey finally groaned and thumped down on her bed. 'So, what's so important?'

'Dad's heart condition, and how it might affect you.'

'Oh, that. I know; he sent me a message. Can you go now? I'm busy.'

Part of me wanted to grab her shoulders and demand answers. What had Vincent said? When, exactly, had she gone to the doctor over the years? What had she thought an 'MOT' was for? And it wasn't just that. Had Vincent been honest with her? Did he tell Abbey that they'd only know for sure if she had the HCM gene by going through genetic testing? That one could have the gene and not the condition, which usually develops later in life?

Then there was the old self-pity. *'Don't you love me at all, Abbey? If it was me in that hospital bed, would you even care?'* Or maybe: *'Don't I matter more than fucking* Pretty Little Liars?'

But I didn't say anything. As usual I clenched it all in, tears included, until twenty minutes ago. Why seeing Cal with another woman has knocked me so badly, I can't say; he isn't mine, after all. But when I finally escaped from the vicarage and drove towards Whalley Range, a nugget of hope burned in my chest. I could be honest with Cal; I'd talk to him, feel safe in his arms, replace my angst with ...

Lovemaking. Love. Who the hell was I kidding? His girl-friend, presumably, was on his doorstep as I passed. They appeared to be talking, perhaps even arguing, her gesticulating and him holding out his palms. Then, clearly crying, she reached

272

out her arms. His expression softening, he accepted her embrace, stepped back and let her in.

A lover's tiff with a happy ending. That's what it looked like.

I squint through the windscreen. The Cheshire sky is so black, I don't know where I'm going and nor does the satnav. But Mari once mentioned a new bypass, so I hope for the best and continue to drive. Going home would involve Harriet's sceptical questioning: *'Hmm. You're back early, Cordelia. You specifically said you'd be late.'*

I groan. I said I was meeting a 'friend' called Samantha Brownley. That's how bad it is; I have no pals, so I had to invent one.

Peering at the road signs, I finally get my bearings and follow the cat's eyes along the tree-lined country road until Knutsford town centre appears. I drove here once after Luke died, parked near the cottage and watched it for hours, but I didn't move from the car. Today I step out. My heart almost bursting, I pause at the gate. Why am I here? What will I say? But before doubt consumes me completely, I open the latch, stride forward and rap at the door.

Viola answers it. If I wasn't so anxious, I'd laugh at the astonishment and alarm on my half-sister's face.

'Is Dad in?' Without waiting for a reply, I brush through to the humid front room.

Clearly waking from a nap, an old man is in the armchair. Almost gasping with shock, I watch him struggle to his feet. What has happened to the tanned and handsome father I remember? The one freeze-framed in my mind?

'Cordelia! My darling girl.' His voice is the same, and though sparkling with tears, so are his brilliant blue eyes. He envelops me in a warm embrace. 'Darling, darling Dee Dee. How lovely to see you. I knew you'd come one day.'

I now know exactly why I'm here and what I must say. 'I'm sorry,' I mumble into his soft jumper.

The graphic images flash in: my mother's aghast expression and her pleas that I put down the knife; my dad shrinking away, defending his face and his chest with his arms. And me, slashing indiscriminately at whatever I can reach.

'I'm so sorry for hurting you, Dad.'

'Darling, it was no more than I deserved.'

'I'm deeply ashamed.'

'And so am I. Ashamed and sorry for hurting my girl so badly.'

Gently tugging up his sleeve, I peer at my teenage devastation which patterns his forearm. 'Oh God.'

'The scarred hero.' He cocks an eyebrow. 'An excuse for some inventive tales. Rather good ones, though I say so myself.'

I bend to kiss the thin silver lines. 'I'm so, so—'

'What on earth is going on?'

We both jolt to the sound of Gilly's haughty voice. Smartly attired and attractive, her face is a picture of sheer horror as she takes in the scene. But instead of addressing me, she snaps around to her daughter, still hovering with huge eyes. 'Did you let her in?'

'Well, I opened the door if that's what you mean.'

'And let . . . ' Apparently stuck for a description, she jabs a finger towards me. 'And let *her* in?'

'I didn't exactly have a choice.' She glances at Bill. 'Besides, she's Dad's—'

'What? His cruel and unloving daughter? The one who broke his heart.'

Viola shrugs. 'And the half-sister I've been curious to—'

274

'Viola! That's wholly—'

'Be quiet, both of you!' Bill's bellow cuts Gilly short. 'The telephone is ringing.' He steps to his side table, picks up the handset and listens for a while. 'Excellent, excellent,' he comments several times. Then finally, 'You'll never guess who's here.' Emotion splashed on his features, he hands the phone over to me.

Wondering who the heck it might be, I take it. 'Hello?'

'Dee Dee?' My brother's astonished voice.

'Ed! Is that actually you?'

'Yup, sure is. Bloody hell, am I dreaming or are you really at Dad's?'

'I know,' I reply, both grinning and weeping. 'Crazy, isn't it!'

69

Calvin

Cal stares at the bedroom ceiling. Thank God he isn't working today; his head hurts and so does his heart. The first is self-inflicted as he drank a shedload of whisky before sleep. The second – well, that's a mix. Why the hell did he get mixed up with Dee in the first place? Did he truly think he could toy with her without getting involved?

But last night was bad luck. Clearly drunk, Cristina demanded to come into the house. When he said it wasn't a good time, her face fell and she sobbed. Hadn't he heard? Willy had died.

He would have called her a taxi, but on hearing that he felt compelled to let her in. Before closing the door, he looked into the black night and spotted a red car turning onto the main road. Was it Dee's? He didn't know for sure, but after finally dropping Cristina at her flat, he sent her several texts.

You didn't make it tonight.

Hope everything's OK.

Call if you need me.

He debated whether to explain about Cristina's unexpected visit and Willy's death, but he still felt rotten about Cristina's inebriated attempts to kiss him and his kind-but-firm rebuff. Besides, was the Polo even Dee's?

By midnight he knew, though. No reply; no bloody reply! What must the scene have looked like to Dee? Then his mood dipped and his mind refused to stop the onslaught: Zachary, his mum, his piss-head bastard father, his past, his lie. He had to anaesthetise it and the inevitable night terror, so he turned to the whisky, finally drifting off with the tumbler in his hand.

Fed up of brooding, Cal allows *The Lark Ascending* to wash over him as he drives. He's drunk several pints of water, had a long shower and eaten a healthy breakfast. Head sorted. Now he's seeing what he can do about his heart.

Before leaving home he sent a couple of texts to Dee. Both went unanswered, so instead of feeling frustrated and annoyingly powerless, he set out in his car and steered by the vicarage. The Polo was in the large driveway, but so were a couple of other cars. When he came back for another loop, the three had become two.

He parks up on a side street and tries again:

I'm in the area. Nice day. Fancy a drive or a stroll?

To his surprise, Dee immediately answers:

Don't trouble yourself. Sure you have better things to do.

Disappointing, but a start:

I already have troubled myself. I'm pretty much outside your house.

Then, when she doesn't reply:

I could knock on if you like . . . :)

That brings a response:

Not funny.

Then come and talk to me.

No reply.

Last night wasn't what you thought.

As he waits for a comment, a notion occurs. The Facebook photo; a daytime walk is hardly going to work. Not near here anyway.

I'm going to pick up some bagels for lunch, then go home. They're from Barbakan Deli in Chorlton. You haven't lived until you've tasted one. Join me?

70

Cordelia

Last night wasn't what you thought.

Relieved and reassured by those simple words, I brush my hair in the mirror. Defying my attempt not to feel excited, my eyes are bright, my cheeks pink.

Last night I returned home to Harriet's folded arms. 'How is your new friend? Samantha, I think you said. Vincent hasn't heard of her either.'

Thank goodness I didn't go to Cal's place after all. Wondering how to reply, I found myself laughing. 'Bang to rights, Harriet. We'll make a Miss Marple of you yet.'

That threw the flaming woman. The look on her face was most definitely worth a mention to Mari. I would gladly have kept the mystery up all week, but I noticed Abbey's shadow just beyond the door, so I called her in.

'Is that you, Abbey? Guess what I did tonight, love.'

A cloud passed through her eyes.

'Nothing to worry about. In fact, it's something I should have done a long time ago. And I have good news too.' I took her hand. 'Let's go upstairs and I'll tell you.'

It hadn't taken long for Gilly to show me out of the cottage on the grounds that too much excitement wasn't good for Bill, but it was nice to share the story with Abbey and make her laugh, especially the spat between Viola and her mother for allowing me over the threshold. Even better, I relayed the news about Ed. Though he wouldn't be pinned down to an actual date, he's already on his way home, hopping from country to country and excited to see his new baby nephew. And, of course, to 'hang out' with his 'favourite niece'.

My father's forgiveness; soon seeing my gorgeous, funny brother and . . . I quickly compose a one-word text:

Ok.

Nodding at my reflection, I smile. Things are, surely, looking up.

Even before I've tried the bell, the door opens and Cal pulls me into the hallway. Then he pins me against the wall and kisses me so deeply that every nerve of my body feels charged, almost too tender to touch. But as he tugs at my leggings, his fingers, his urgent lips and his tongue seem to know where to caress, press and plunder.

We tumble into the lounge and shed our clothes, then I'm soon straddling him on the rug, bearing down on his penis, already in heaven. I peak far too soon, but can't help myself. As my moan escapes, Cal joins me, groaning loudly with pleasure.

Both stunned and breathing heavily, we rest in each other's

arms for some time. I eventually stir. 'I still feel light-headed and tingly, as though *that's* still working its way through my body.'

'Like after-burn,' he replies, softly kissing me.

'And that is?'

'The calories you burn after a high-intensity workout.'

I chuckle. 'High-intensity sounds about right.' But Cal is looking at me so intently, almost sadly. 'What's wrong?' I ask.

'I love you. That's what's wrong. I'd like to keep you here for ever.'

Though I've no idea what, I inhale to say something, but he gets to his feet. 'You came to talk, remember?'

Snug in Cal's robe, I lick the butter from my fingers and curl up my legs on the sofa. He's right; the bagels are tasty, and there were so many things I wanted to work through after Vincent's tumultuous revelations, but my mind is too addled right now. Besides, I don't want real life to invade this fantasy. Because make-believe it is.

'I love you. That's what's wrong.'

Such beautiful, glowing words. But they're insubstantial, impractical, unsustainable, too.

I meet Cal's inquisitive gaze. 'I went to see my dad last night. Probably pretty standard for most people, but I hated him immensely for a long time.' I sniff at the image of his delighted face. 'Probably because I loved him too much before that. You know, Daddy's-darling type of thing.'

'I can imagine.' Something in Cal's tone makes me glance at him again, but he kisses my forehead. 'Go on.'

'When I was fourteen, he got one of his uni students pregnant. Gillian. Gilly. She wasn't the type to keep it low key. Instead she turned up at our house one Sunday and barged past my mum at the door. We were eating our family dinner and she just came out with it. She was pregnant with Bill's child and she was keeping it. I suppose we kids thought it was a joke until we looked at our parents. Dad's face was puce with embarrassment and guilt; Mum's was bone white with anger.'

'What happened then?'

'She calmly told Gilly to leave and to take Dad with her. I wasn't sure which parent I hated more that day or afterwards.' I snort lightly. 'So it's divine retribution, probably.'

'What is?'

'Abbey. She's as contemptuous of me as I was of my mum. Serves me right for being so ...' Spoiled? Judgemental? Ungrateful? Selfish? None of them are nice.

Cal clears his throat. 'Emotions are complicated at the best of times, especially parent–child relationships. My own situation is case in—' He abruptly stops speaking.

'Your own situation?'

'We're here to talk about you, not self-absorbed me.'

'You're not going to let that drop, are you?'

He grins. 'Nope.'

'Seriously, though ...'

'Well, I haven't exactly proved myself on the father front so far.'

Pulling away from his shoulder, I sit upright. 'What was going on with Zach's mum last night?'

'That wasn't Sadie. It was Cristina.'

Goosebumps stab my skin. *Cristina?* 'Who's she?'

'She was a carer on a call-out a couple of weeks ago and she turned up rambling and drunk, wanting to be let in. The old bloke she looked after had died, so I couldn't turn her away.'

Surprised at the swell of jealousy, I swallow. 'What happened then?'

'Nothing,' he replies.

'Really?'

He looks at me straight. 'Yes, really.'

'Glad to hear it.' Though I return to my nest, my pulse thumps in my ears. Was it my imagination or was there a tiny flicker of guilt in his eyes?

71

Mariana

Mari scoops up her handbag and stops at the hall mirror before leaving for work. She ruffles her hair and smiles. Yup, she looks pretty damned good today. Or maybe it's because the Fab Three have finally left and she doesn't have to examine herself through their eyes any more. And, thank God, the house is back to tidy, ordered and quiet. Silence, beautiful silence, how she loves it.

As though her thoughts have jinxed it, a bleat of unhappiness echoes down from above. Isak, of course. Does she have time to dart up and give Britt some moral support? She glances at the staircase, almost jumping from her skin when she sees a figure in the shadows at the top. She blows out the fright – it isn't her mother but her partner who comes into the light, folds her arms and glares accusingly. She'd clearly hoped Rory and Co. would stay for ever but Mari apparently 'frightened them off'.

Feeling a tad guilty for being so elated at their departure, Mari inhales to say something positive, but Britt gets there first. 'You have no idea what it's like,' she hurls down. 'I'm the one who had to give birth, now I'm expected to stay at home all day and feed him.'

'Come on, Britt. You don't have to stay inside all day,' she replies. 'And you're right, I don't, but I can imagine.'

'And that's meant to make me feel better?' She flounces away. 'Whatever; it's fine,' she shoots over her shoulder. 'Go to your patients or clients or *people* or whatever you like to call them. We know they're more important than us.'

Contemplating the phrase 'heavy heart', Mari waves goodbye to Amancia and climbs in her car. Hers does feel leaden right now. God knows, she deals with tragically damaged people day in and day out. They all leave food for thought, but Seamus's case lingers, especially the horrendous self-reproach. Though hardly surprising with a house fire and a dead boy, his self-blame is so overwhelming that he's contemplated suicide several times. Inundated with constant flashbacks, he needs the flagellation to stop.

Then there's his other layer of jumbled angst. When Amancia went to brew up, he leaned forward and whispered, 'I've never asked her but . . . ' He glanced at the kitchen door. 'Even to this day I don't know if he was my . . . my biological son.'

Lifting her hand to thank the driver behind, Mari pulls onto the motorway and contemplates *biological*. In the end it didn't matter for her. Does having a child affect her work-wise, though? Is it more constructive to have gut-wrenching empathy from personal experience? Most people understand the unceasing 'what if's, replaying the hours, minutes and seconds before the worst happens, or words said in anger and regretted moments later, but feeling responsible for death is something different. Final, irrevocable, irreversible death. How else can anyone really know what it *feels* like to let a loved one die?

She blows out her hot breath. Professional objectivity is the key. One doesn't need to live each patient's trauma, just stand temporarily in their shoes.

Her thoughts shift to Isak. She still feels rotten for leaving Britt but she had clients to see and they have needs too. Distressing though it is, a grumbling tot isn't a life-or-death situation.

'*You have no idea what it's like.*'

'*You're right, I don't, but I can imagine.*'

Can she *imagine*, though? How would things have worked out if she'd managed by some miracle to get pregnant? The notion brings her back to Konnie's son. Attentive and amiable, he asked as many questions as he answered in the pub, and none of them revolved around her age or blasted late-onset lesbianism. Watching his broad smile, she found her mind wandering. Did he know his mum had impregnated Britt, so to speak? That she'd attempted but failed to inseminate Mari in the most ungainly of ways? Why it made her feel a touch uncomfortable, she can't say, but the thought of another meeting to discuss her dissertation feedback makes her check her reflection again.

Feeling rotten for being chipper, she glances at the dashboard clock. She's the monster who scared off the Fab Three. A detour home to relieve Britt for her lunch hour seems only fair.

72

Cordelia

Inhaling Harriet's usual metallic aroma, I tap the steering wheel. We've been stuck at these traffic lights for five long minutes.

'You seem ...' she starts.

Oh God, what now? I glance over to her sharp eyes but she turns to the passenger window.

Right; so she's using the half-hung interrogation technique which I rushed to complete after Luke's death – generally an 'I'm fine. Really, I am', when I most certainly wasn't. I had swung from being the happiest mum in the world, to barely existing. I'd lost my beautiful baby, a tiny precious life had been snuffed out; I was constantly walking through every moment of that horrific night, still feeling the surge of breast milk on waking and forgetting for a glorious moment that Lukie was dead, for ever dead.

Focusing on the traffic, I will those dreadful memories away. They'll never leave, I know that, but it's as though they are padded with soft wadding these days – sort of muffled but protected too. I don't want to forget the pain completely; that'd be a betrayal of my son.

'Contented.'

I look at Harriet in surprise. *Contented?* Is that what I am? At the heart of all this stress and uncertainty, can I really be that? Am I entitled to be when I'm betraying, deceiving, cuckolding my husband? I wait for the spasm of guilt, but a jolt of lightness, a fillip of pleasure comes instead: '*I love you. That's what's wrong.*' Maybe it was just words, a glib comment expressed in the moment, but despite the blip of worry about the woman Cristina, I *felt* they were true and genuinely said. Of course, there's Mari's constancy, but I haven't felt loved by anyone else for a very long time.

I drag myself back to Harriet's comment. 'I think relief is more the word. Vincent seems so incredibly well. I know he has the fluid retention, but there's no discernible brain damage.' I smile. 'That's pretty much a miracle, isn't it?'

Sniffing, she nods. 'Yes. Yes, it is.'

Her eyes are moist, so I squeeze her hand. Whatever faults this woman has, she adores her son. And she, more than anyone, will ensure he never misses or stops his medication again.

I relayed the cardiac nurse's 'loss of manhood' comments to Mari, but she just laughed.

'Don't tell me you're worried about Vincent playing away with his purple-perm parishioners?' Then, more seriously, 'People fail to take their prescribed meds all the time for hundreds of reasons, Dee. It's denial mostly. Then there's side effects, money, feeling better. Men in particular want to be energetic and fit; they stop taking the pills and they're well until they're not. Look how many people are told to stop drinking or smoking and don't because they feel fine or they think they're invincible, then WHAM. Sadly, human beings seem programmed to do things to hurt themselves.' She paused for a while. 'God knows why, but we do.'

Am I hurting myself with Cal? God, I truly don't know. Vincent is happy to tell the world about his beautiful, talented wife who he'd 'be lost without', but he hasn't declared his love since I was a teenager. Is that why another man's 'I love you' is so thrilling?

73

Mariana

Mari throws her keys on the hall table.

'Hello. Britt? Anyone home?'

A shuffling sound comes from the lounge, so she pops her head into the dark room. The curtains are drawn, but if Britt's napping, how come she's sitting upright?

She squints. 'Matthew?'

He puts a finger to his lips. 'Isak's only just dropped off,' he whispers. 'I'll pop the basket on the floor and follow you out.'

'Is Britt OK?' she asks when he emerges. 'Is she asleep?'

'No, not asleep.' He smiles. 'At least I hope not.'

'Oh, right. So she's . . . ?'

'The shops, I imagine. She just needed a couple of hours off, so she called me.'

Well, this is embarrassing. 'That's so nice of you. Thank you. Are you sure you have the time?'

'Listening and lending a hand is part of the job.' He blushes. 'And the quiet time for sermon ideas came in handy.'

She wants to check on Isak, but a little polite chit-chat seems appropriate in the circumstances. Curate-cum-babysitter. And what does '*listening and lending a hand*' mean?

'That's good. So how's it going? Standing in Vincent's shoes must be a tough gig.'

He flushes even more. 'It's pretty full on and yes, he's a hard act to follow, but it sounds as though the prayers are working, so I'm sure it won't be for long.'

Mari's lips twitch. Yup, prayers, intensive care and a shedload of drugs. 'It sounds as though you have a lot on your plate. Shall I let you go?'

He looks doubtful. 'That would be good but . . . Aren't you at work today?'

'It's fine. You get off.'

'If you're sure. I'll just get my . . .'

Once Matthew has left with his man bag, Mari opens the drapes, kneels down and peers at her soundly sleeping son. Then she notices the feeding bottle on the sofa arm. Goodness, Britt went to the lengths of expressing her milk after all; she must have been desperate. She sits back and frowns. Really? *Really?* Striding to the kitchen, she opens and closes a few cupboard doors. Nothing's there; maybe her suspicions are misplaced. Yet she still finds herself opening the bin lid and rummaging around.

Hearing the scrape of a key, Mari jerks awake. She must have dozed off for a few minutes. Turmoil always did make her sleepy. Tired when she shouldn't be, like now, when she should be at work.

She looks down at her hand. Akin to a grenade, she's gripping the scrunched box of baby milk. Is she still angry? No, more weary than anything. Sighing, she stands, but laughter beyond the door makes her pause before stepping out.

Looking bright and rosy, Britt is taking off her coat. So is

Simon the organist. Bloody hell, don't these church guys have jobs? Or maybe when the leader is away . . .

'Mariana! It's you.' Quickly covering her surprise, Britt holds out her arms. 'What are you doing here? We've been out for some fresh air and a mooch.'

A glass of wine too, by the smell of her breath. Mari manages not to say so, but her face clearly gives her away, as Simon stops divesting himself of his jacket.

'Actually, I'd better get off,' he says to Britt. 'I'll grab that coffee another time.'

'Do stay,' Mari finds herself saying.

'Yes, you must.'

But clearly Simon's no fool. 'Thanks, but I've got a piano lesson to prepare for. I completely forgot about it.'

'He doesn't,' Britt snaps the moment he's gone. 'He doesn't have a lesson. You frightened him away.' She glares at Mari. 'Is this how it's going to be? You scaring off all my friends?'

'I'm not *scaring* them off—'

'Yes, you are.' Her eyes well. 'I have no relatives here, so my friends are my family. How would you feel if I was unpleasant to Cordelia?'

Mari inhales deeply. Britt has been more than off with Dee, but she does have a point. This is her home, she's entitled to have whoever she wants to visit or stay. But, but . . . why hide it or arrange it behind her back? And why does she always do this tearful pre-emptive strike when Mari has opinions and feelings too?

'Sorry. I didn't mean to frighten Simon off, but . . . ' She opens her fist. 'Formula milk. Why didn't you tell me?'

'Oh, right, so you're *spying* on me now? Turning up when

I least expect it, then going through the dustbin? Well, that's just lovely.'

She's right, yet the 'but's are still there in heaps. 'I came home as a nice surprise because you were sad this morning and I'm certainly not spying, but I'm Isak's parent too. We agreed breast was best for at least six months.'

Britt's chin juts out. 'I didn't *tell* you because I knew you'd be like this. And anyway, *we* didn't agree, *you* dictated.'

Mari frowns. That isn't how she remembers it. But she needs to calm down. An occasional breast substitute to give Britt a break is actually a good idea. 'OK, sorry. Look, I'd better get back to . . .' Noticing the carrier bags, she pauses. One has collapsed, revealing a large tin of powdered formula milk.

Britt's eyes follow hers. 'Don't bother arguing, I've decided.'

'Decided what?'

'I'm stopping the breastfeeding.' More tears gloss her eyes. 'You have no idea what it's like. They hurt when they're full; they get hot and hard. Then they bloody leak.' She wipes her nose with her sleeve. 'But it isn't just that. You escape to work every morning—'

'To earn money for us both.'

'Then I have to abide by your rules: I have to be here twenty-four seven; I'm not allowed to drive; I'm not allowed to have fun; I'm not allowed to drink; I'm not allowed to go out—'

'That isn't true. Of course you can go out and have fun, but you've had a baby, Britt.' An image of Astrid swims before her eyes. 'Responsibility comes with him.'

'What? Giving my baby tried and tested formula milk is *irresponsible*?'

'No. No, it isn't at all, but . . .'

Isn't Isak *their* baby? Shouldn't these decisions be joint? And

Britt is twenty-nine. It isn't as though she's a teenager missing the local bloody disco. She chose to have a child; she *volunteered* for it, she planted those baby seeds in Mari's head; if she hadn't been completely sure, she should have said so. But Mari can't voice any of these urgent thoughts; they're too close to the truth.

She tries for another angle. 'I understand it's hard and that new mums feel like milking machines, tied to their babies, but you had a Caesarean, so you aren't allowed to drive yet anyway. How about a little longer before giving up completely?'

'I knew you'd say that.' Her hair bouncing, Britt moves away. 'Sorry, Mariana; my boobs, my body. I'll do what I like.'

74

Cordelia

Feeling a little bad for using a shortcut across the grass, I catch my breath at the Heart Centre entrance. It feels as though this is my patch for taking stock and preparing myself for all eventualities in my head – from irrevocable heart scarring to brain damage, from permanent disability to sudden death. But the curve balls still come thick and fast – hereditary coronary problems, medication, or lack of it, and side effects. Yet in fairness, things are looking good at the moment. Vincent is buoyant, as only he can be, and his condition is under control. Today's plan is to focus on that and not allow the invasive worm thoughts to take over.

The stroll from the car park obviously too demanding, Harriet asked to be dropped off, but I censure myself before I go in: my mother-in-law isn't all bad; she loves her son and will go to the ends of the earth for him; that is, surely, something to admire.

I head for the stairs, but my name is called from behind me. A clearly teary Harriet is squashed in a chair.

'Harriet! I thought you'd have gone ahead.'

'I did. The cardiac nurse wants a word.'

'Oh, right. With me or us both?'

Ignoring my question, Harriet sways to the lift, steps in and covers her eyes.

Oh God, another curve ball. 'What's happened?'

'Tell him he must have it, Cordelia. You must persuade him.'

'Have what, Harriet?'

The doors hiss open and people load in, splitting us either side of the space. When we reach our floor, I ask again. 'What's going on, Harriet?'

'The implant. He's—'

Her response is cut off by the nurse. 'Morning, Cordelia, can I have a word?' Alan looks at Harriet. 'Five minutes, Mrs Hardy, and we'll be with you and your son.'

Once in the side room, Alan gestures to a seat and sits opposite. 'Don't worry, there hasn't been a deterioration in Vincent's condition . . . ' The tension eases from my shoulders, but he continues to speak. 'However, as your mother-in-law knows, the consultant saw him yesterday to talk about the next steps.' He studies me and smiles thinly. 'I take it you didn't know about this?'

I shake my head. It's pretty humiliating not to be in the loop, but I can only blame myself. Yesterday I was in another man's arms, feasting on a declaration of love like a silly teenager.

Alan's grey gaze is sympathetic. 'Not to worry. It was pretty standard advice after a sudden cardiac arrest.' He leans back. 'As you know, because of Vincent's condition he's prone to abnormal heart rhythms, the very problem which caused the SCA. He'll still need medication, but the consultant strongly recommends an implanted defibrillator, what we call an ICD.' He demonstrates with his own chest. 'It's a straightforward operation where a matchbox-sized device is placed under the skin and it monitors the heart. If the rhythms become irregular, it can pace it or shock it. An ICD can be a lifesaver. We describe it to patients as their very own paramedic . . . '

'*Very own paramedic*'. Inwardly flinching, I wait. I knew from Mari that something along these lines was likely. And didn't Vincent mention it? I steady myself for the thwack.

'After the consultant gave Vincent the basics, I had a more detailed counselling session with him to help him decide.' Alan looks at his large hands. 'It's important that patients know what they are letting themselves in for. As I say, the implant is a lifesaver, not a hindrance but, similar to a paramedic, it will do its job and shock when needed, and it's literally that, a shock. People have said it's like a sudden jolt or a thump to the chest. Others have described it as like being shot or brutally kicked. Some patients feel nothing because they black out. Constantly waiting for this to happen can cause anxiety and depression; many fear it just as much as their heart problems. Others are in denial and simply don't think they need it.' He pauses. 'Vincent agreed to consider it overnight.'

'And?' I ask, though Alan's raised eyebrows say it all.

'He doesn't want it. He's quite adamant.'

Stuck for words, I stare at a wall calendar. The page for March shows semi-naked men and women with medical implements carefully placed to cover their modesty. For charity, I guess. Is this pleasant and considerate nurse on one of the months? I come back to today's challenge.

Alan speaks again. 'When your mother-in-law heard the news, she was considerably agitated. We had to ask her to calm down or leave the ward. Understandably, she wants your husband to have the ICD, but it's his decision at the end of the day. I'm sure it's one you'd like to talk through with him yourself . . . '

'Of course.' I stand. 'So what happens if he doesn't have the implant?'

'He goes home, recuperates and takes his medication each and every day. He might never have another SCA, but on the other hand, he might. An ambulance got to him quickly the last time; if it happens again, he might not be so lucky.'

75

Mariana

Mari yawns. She's staring at the same paragraph she's been typing for what feels like an hour. Every time she tries to focus, Britt's declaration blisters back. '*My boobs, my body.*' And the extra two words which were left unspoken, but are most certainly there: '*My baby.*'

She returned late to the clinic this afternoon. Sanjay had stepped in for the first client and the second had fortuitously postponed his appointment. Since then her mood has oscillated from incomprehension to exasperation to anger. Doesn't Britt want what's best for Isak? He's only a few weeks old, for goodness' sake.

She stares at the empty client chair. What might she dispassionately say to a patient in her own position? Would she hint that perhaps Britt's gold-tinged expectations of motherhood haven't matched the reality and that she should be given a little leeway? Would she suggest standing in Britt's shoes and asking how she'd feel in the same situation? And what if she was with a man who went to work and left her to fend on her own, a husband with opinions of how they should bring up their baby?

And yet . . . Whether a spouse or partner, aren't all co-parents entitled to have a say? She doesn't dominate or direct as Britt suggests. Indeed, it seems quite the reverse.

Out of control. Yes, that's how she feels.

Her mobile vibrates, sure to be Britt. Should she reply with honesty or a grovelling apology? But when she peers at the screen, the text is from Dee:

I'm here in the ward with Vincent. Any chance of you popping over at some point?

Grateful for the distraction, Mari checks the time and messages back:

Sure, I can come now. See you in ten.

Still in the land of Britt, Mari doesn't speculate why Dee has asked for her, but when she reaches the ward, Harriet's sitting outside. Her fleshy face seems to have sunk into itself. Bloody hell. What has happened?

'Hello? Harriet?' Mari touches her shoulder. 'Harriet. Are you OK?'

'No. No, I'm far from it.' Standing, she turns to the glass, so Mari looks too. His arms folded and expression truculent, Vincent is sitting up in bed, Dee on the chair beside him.

Laughter squeezes through Mari's alarm. Vincent isn't dead, thank the Lord! Then another thought: perhaps she's more fond of him than she realises. God, what an upside-down day.

Still smiling with relief, she approaches his corner. 'Vinny! You're looking a lot better than the last time I saw you.'

300

He reaches out for her hand. 'Thank goodness, a voice of reason amongst all the doubters.'

Mari chuckles. 'Bloody hell, it must be bad if we're on the same side.' She looks from him to Dee. 'So what's going on?'

Though her sister sighs, her irritation is clear. 'The consultant has recommended he has a *lifesaving* implanted defibrillator. Vincent doesn't want one.'

'Or *need* one,' he adds.

She grabs a spare chair. 'OK,' she says slowly. She studies her brother-in-law. Pursed lips, set jaw: denial. 'Why don't you need one?'

He rolls his eyes. 'Don't bother, Mariana. I've already had the counselling from the horse's mouth.' His cheeks colouring, he snorts. 'And from what I've been told, an angry mule's hoof is a pretty apt description.'

'Description of what, Vincent?' Dee asks.

He tuts. 'The shock from the defibrillator, Cordelia.'

'Which, surely can't be worse than—'

'A wholly unnecessary procedure.'

Mari leans forward. Ah, so it's denial masking fear. 'I'm no expert, Vincent, but—'

'No, you're not, Mariana, so you have nothing to add.'

'I'm not an expert in heart conditions, no, but I am one in other ways that might help.'

'Oh, so now I need a quack.'

'Not at all, but you've already gone through a horrendously frightening incident.' She smiles sympathetically. 'It's tough for anyone to discover they're not invincible, and people naturally have fears and anxieties, even post-traumatic stress after a cardiac arrest. But counselling and CBT are widely available to see you

301

through it. At the end of the day you want to be here for your family, your friends, your congregation—'

'Enough, Mariana. Now you're scaremongering. I haven't felt a dicky-bird for the last twenty-five years. I don't want or need surgery; I'm perfectly well and I'd like to go home.' He turns to Dee and looks at her strangely. 'This is my decision and I'm expecting your complete support, Cordelia.' For moments he doesn't break eye contact with her. 'Cordelia? Yes?'

Willing her to disagree, Mari watches her sister. But she simply nods, then finally speaks.

'Yes, Vincent. Yes, you have it.'

76

Calvin

Cal faces the punchbag. Raising his hands, he positions them the way he was taught, way back when, to protect his face, then he throws two punches in quick succession before performing a squat. He returns to standing and continues the jab-cross-squat sequence for a minute.

Before the football academy took over his life, he went to junior boxing club. They were happy times he usually has to push from his mind, but these days other thoughts dominate.

His emotions aren't all bad. Many of them are good, bloody brilliant, in fact. He spent the whole day with Zachary yesterday. Playing, feeding, chatting. Building tall towers with plastic bricks, reading books with quacks and moos and baas. Making his boy laugh. Cuddling and receiving adorable wet kisses. Magical moments he never imagined. Feelings of love that he never thought he'd have. A miracle, a pure unadulterated gift.

Sadie broached the subject of reconciling again. Though he turned her down kindly, he wanted to say: *'I'm not in love with you; I don't spend far too much of my day thinking about you, desiring you, worrying about you; I don't want to live with you day in and day out; I don't want to keep you safe in my arms and wake up beside you.'*

Dee Dee. Cordelia. He's never wanted to possess someone before now. Or perhaps he's possessed himself. He, who rarely uses his mobile for anything other than basic communication, is having whole conversations with her by text. Because he can't telephone her. Because he can't see her when he likes. Because she's married to someone else!

Returning to his stance, he strikes the bag at an angle, then continues fast and powerfully for a time.

Who, exactly, is he hitting? The irony of saving Vincent Hardy's life is not lost on him. Yet that's his job, it's what he signed up for; whatever the situation, he has to do that. Even rapists, murderers or violent criminals are given the same lifesaving care as every other human being on the planet. That's simply the way it is, so he'll have to make do by pummelling the holy Reverend this way.

77

Mariana

Mari packs up her briefcase. Poor Dee, poor her. Though she has to get a grip about the latter. She has nothing to complain about; Britt has simply decided, as she's entitled to, to give up breastfeeding. Yet, is there more to her general dissatisfaction? Since moving in, Britt has done exactly what Britt wants to do. From curtain choice to holidays, to nights out, to sex, everything has been on her terms. Sure, Mari has been the sap who has allowed it, but maybe now is the time to put her foot down and say no. Or kick back a little. Or at least say, *'Let's discuss, let's compromise. Please?'*

She mouths goodbye to the receptionist and checks her mobile as she walks. She texted Britt to say she'd be late home, but there's still no reply. It's hardly reasonable of her to take umbrage: Mari missed her first afternoon appointment because of Britt's disappearing act and it was only fair to return Sanjay's favour. Because that's what most people do: they take, but they give back.

'Mariana! I hear congratulations are in order!'

Mari looks up. Hurtling down the corridor and appearing as windswept as ever, it's Konnie.

'Oh, hi ...' It takes a moment to adjust. 'Congratulations for ... ?'

Clearly breathless, Konnie pats her chest. 'Britt's baby.' She puts a hand on Mari's arm. 'Yours too, of course.' She looks at her watch. 'Oh Lord. We must grab a coffee and catch up properly soon, but right now I'm late.' She backs away. 'I meant to call you when Rohan mentioned the happy news, but there's never any time. Call me! Coffee soon!'

Feeling disorientated from the usual Konnie blast, Mari watches her petite frame until it disappears. God, yes, she must call Rohan back about their dissertation chat. She will, she really will, but as his mother said, there's never any time. Not when a demanding – and undoubtedly pissed-off partner – is waiting at home.

Noting that a replacement umbrella is long overdue, Mari leaves it outside on the doorstep. If spring is on its way, she hasn't noticed it. There's a distinct chill in the air and in this flaming house.

Taking a steadying breath, she ambles towards the kitchen. The closed door doesn't feel like a good sign and her heart is actually racing. Bloody hell, Mari! How on earth has the strident professional turned into this lump of jelly? It's time to push back and assert herself.

She presses down the handle. What the ... ? The room smells aromatic and the lighting is dim ... It takes a moment to adjust. No bright LEDs, but candles tonight.

'Perfect timing,' Britt says from behind her. 'Please take a seat. Dinner will be served shortly.'

Winded by surprise and pleasure, Mari absorbs the lovely scene: her mum's best crockery, cutlery and napkin rings;

crystal flutes for fizz, glasses for both white and red. Wondering what they're celebrating, she spins around. 'This is wonderful, thank you.'

Britt pours the champagne and clinks glasses. 'You and I haven't had a chance to celebrate the birth of our little boy, have we? He's upstairs, asleep. I checked up on him just now.' Leaning forward, she places her moist lips on Mari's, then slips in her tongue, cold and icy and tasting of wine. She pulls back and smiles. 'Food first, and then ...'

Her back turned away, she busies herself for a few moments at the hob. Beneath her apron, she's wearing the skimpy denim shorts she wore the day they first met. Eventually returning to the table, she positions a bowl on Mari's coaster. 'Cauliflower, broccoli and stilton, just as you like it. Help yourself to bread.'

Mari's delight is suddenly pierced by a jangle of alarm. Could Britt have postnatal depression? A post-partum disorder would certainly explain her mood swings. But she sits down opposite with her own dish of soup, blows on her spoon and greedily slurps.

'See?' she says after a moment. 'Mummy happy, baby happy; that's what they say.' Showing those neat, perfect teeth, she laughs. 'Or is it the other way around?' She strokes Mari's leg with her toes beneath the table. 'And if I'm happy, so is my Mariana.'

78

Cordelia

It's Friday already. There's so much to worry about, it's as though my stuffed mind has simply puked out the excess and is limiting itself to what it needs to consume hour by hour. Or maybe Mari's counselling from long ago is automatically kicking in: don't constantly project by imagining what terrors the future might hold; don't examine the flawed past when there's nothing you can do to change it; carry on day to day in bite-sized chunks; focus on what makes you happy, however tiny it might be.

What makes me *happy* at this moment is Cal. His warm body is cupping mine from behind. Do I feel guilty? I'm not sure any more, and why is that? I'm betraying a loyal and loving man who's in hospital. But perhaps I'm shelving my accountability for that very reason. He's coming home soon to recuperate, and though I'm not sure what that will involve, escape opportunities will be negligible.

I glance at my watch. Should I go to the supermarket en route for home and buy a few groceries to satisfy Harriet? Or will she still be giving me the silent treatment? Well, not entirely *silent*;

her loud bashing and banging of pots, doors and cupboards makes up for her lack of speech.

In fairness, she has my sympathy this time. Vincent is being unreasonably stubborn. But what can I do? He's a *compos mentis* grown man. Surgery is the sensible option, but I have no sway, certainly no more than Harriet herself. I want to say this to her, but Abbey might hear. I discussed it with Mari and we agreed it was best not to mention Vincent's decision to her yet, but persuade him to reconsider once he's back on his feet.

I now slither round to face Cal. 'What are you thinking about?' I ask.

'That I want you to stay in this bed for ever.'

It's on the tip of my tongue to say I'd love that too, but the *accountability* hits like a ten-ton truck. I'm married with a child; I belong to someone else; though secondary to a vicar, a vicar's wife is a vocation too; I have responsibilities to Vincent and the parish. I can't offer Cal anything, not even a declaration of love.

I put my lips to his. But right now I can give him this.

Still tingling and limp, but anxious too, I check the time at the traffic lights. Three o'clock. The additional lovemaking has extended my time out of the house and I haven't had a chance to stop at Asda, but so long as I'm back before Abbey, everything will be fine. Won't it? Surely Harriet will still be preoccupied by Vincent, rather than somehow *knowing* and sniffing out my guilt like a hound.

When I pull onto the vicarage driveway, my pulse has finally slowed, so I spend a moment or two admiring my pots of purple winter pansies either side of the porch. But just as my shoulders relax, the front door fires open and Harriet waddles out in her slippers. Oh God, this woman really is telepathic. Tensing, I climb out and prepare myself for the swipe of divine justice for my sins.

Her lips are in a pout of disapproval. 'Is everything OK?' I ask.

'You have a visitor,' she replies. 'And I want to make it quite clear he's not staying here.'

'A visitor? Me?'

Confused, I glance beyond her shoulder. A man resembling something between a vagrant and a rock star lifts his hand in greeting. I find myself laughing, or even crying. I haven't seen my brother in person since Abbey's tenth birthday, but he looks handsome and wild, and reassuringly laid-back.

79

Mariana

Mari stuffs in the last of the bedding and programmes the washer. Despite a challenging day at work, she's infused with energy. Wondering what to tackle next, she absently listens to the water pump into the machine. Oh bugger, she should have waited for the towels. Britt is having an early bath, but her soaks generally take the best part of an hour, so that's OK. She'll go up in a while and top up her glass of wine.

She and Britt had such a lovely time last night that she made the effort to come home mid-afternoon. And it is Friday, after all. The upside was Britt's delighted face, the down was the thick layer of dust and bitty carpets, highlighted by the last of the daylight. So, once she'd had the pleasure of feeding and playing with Isak, she vacuumed, dusted and prepared a light dinner.

A clean house; how she loves it! She chuckles to herself. Who'd have thought she'd completely morph into her mother? Her eyes catch the Prosecco bottle. Mostly, at least. She likes alcohol as much as anyone, but the alarm bell is always there – drinking from habit is the start, a glass of something to relax of an evening, then moving on to daytime boozing, that tempting old devil who'll take the edge off loneliness, heartbreak, unhappiness, grief; all the things her mum so gracefully hid. At least until the horrific end.

Replacing that dreadful image with Britt's joyous beam, she listens out for Isak. He's still grumbly with his colic, but on the recommendation of a colleague she bought a brightly coloured helium balloon from Zo and Co, the card shop in the village and attached it to his ankle. After staring at it for a while, he worked out it moved when he did. Or at least she thought so from his smile.

'It's not a smile; it's wind,' Britt said. Her eyebrows were raised in that 'I'm his mum, I should know' type of way, but that's fair enough; she does have the day-to-day care of Isak and she's right about happiness. Like osmosis it has spread, and though Mari feels a jolt of guilt each time she makes up the formula milk, it's lovely to feed Isak herself, to watch his heart-melting gaze and search for Britt's features. His fine hair is already a strawberry blonde and though his eye colour might change, she has no doubt they'll be Britt's cornflower blue.

Not dark-haired and brown-eyed like her baby might have been, but that's fine too. She has the child she so desperately wanted; everything has come good.

The rap of the knocker brings her back from her thoughts. Wondering who it is at this late hour, she looks at her watch, but of course it's earlier than she thought. Everything has been hitched up by Britt for their 'early, long night'.

She opens up, but it takes a moment or two to adjust. Bloody hell! Her gorgeous, scruffy brother is on her doorstep, Dee Dee at his side.

He rubs his hands. 'While I do miss the English weather, it's a bit nippy just to stand out here all evening . . . '

She closes her gaping mouth. Of course she knew he was due at some point, but she didn't even attempt to pin him down with a date.

'Ed!' Reaching her arms around his chest, she pulls him in for a hug. He seems even taller, skinnier too. 'Don't you ever eat?' she asks, leaning back to take in his neat features. 'God, it's so nice to see you. Come in and meet Isak. I'll get us a drink. I'm sure we have a bottle of—'

'This?' Dee lifts a magnum of champagne. Her eyes shiny, her cheeks pink, she looks like a teenager. She nods to the lounge. 'You two go in and I'll grab the glasses.'

Ed in the middle, the three siblings sit on the sofa, drinking fizz and taking turns to cuddle Isak. Despite the intermission of several years, the chatter doesn't stop, mostly Dee and Mari bombarding Ed with questions: his current job, his latest home, the scar above his lip, his love life.

'Bloody hell, it's like the grand inquisition—'

'Which you are deflecting with panache,' Mari replies.

He's doing what Ed does best. Not answering the question by changing the subject. 'Come on though, Mari,' he's now saying, gesticulating to Dee. 'Something's going on. Look at her. Her husband's safely tucked away in hospital and she's positively glowing.'

Ed's actually right, but poor Dee is deeply flushing. Mari elbows him. 'In a hospital bed after a *life-threatening* cardiac arrest—'

'Oh, whatever; I like to see my sisters happy.' He ruffles Mari's hair. 'And you. Who'd have thought my misopaedic big sis would be a doting mother.'

'Well, thanks for that . . .'

'You always said you'd prefer a car.'

'Did I?'

Dee leans forward. 'No, that was instead of getting married, wasn't it? A Golf in exchange for the cost of a wedding.'

'Well, you've kept your word on that score so far, Mari.' Ed lifts his eyebrows. 'And as for Dee's nuptials . . . Didn't Dad turn up uninvited and try to land one on Vincent again?'

Watching Dee's face, Mari tenses. 'Ed!'

But her sister is laughing. 'Don't worry, Mari, Ed's turn for major ribbing will come very soon. Maybe we'll start in Year Four. He cried for the *whole* of assembly when he heard Miss Myers was leaving. I had to disown him . . .' She takes a quick breath. 'Besides, it's OK to talk about Dad. I went to see him.'

'What?' Mari sits up. 'Honestly? You didn't tell me.'

'Sorry, I meant to, but so much else has been—'

'Interesting.' Ed looks at Mari with mock wide-eyes. 'So perhaps Dee Dee keeps secrets after all.'

Ed and his usual wooden spoon. Mari ignores him. 'So, what happened with Dad, Dee?'

'Viola let me in but the witch wasn't best pleased. Then to add insult to the poor woman's injury, Ed called while I was there, so I was soon evicted.' Her eyes glisten. 'But it was so nice to see him.'

Ed abruptly stands and throws back his drink. 'Going some-where?' Mari asks.

'I'm not; we are. Let's get a taxi and go now.'

'To . . . ?'

'Dad's, of course. Come on, girls, all for one and one for all.'

'I'm up for it,' Dee says. She looks down at Isak, asleep in her arms. 'This little chap might be better staying at home, though.'

Mari shakes herself. Oh God, Britt! For the last hour she's completely forgotten about the bath and wine. Ed hasn't even met her yet. Surely she's heard the commotion downstairs? 'Me too, but . . . ' She gently takes her son from Dee. 'I'd better go up and smooth things over first . . . '

Already feeling bad, Mari creeps up the stairs and puts Isak in his cot. Then she peeps in the bathroom. Still steamy but empty. Taking a breath at the door, she steps into the bedroom. Her hair in a turban, Britt's turning the pages of a magazine. She doesn't make eye contact but looks meaningfully at her empty glass.

'Sorry, Ed and Dee turned up.'

Britt continues to flick. 'So I gathered.'

'Do you want to come down and say hi?'

The blue flash is contemptuous. 'Like this? In my dressing gown? Hardly.'

Sighing inwardly, Mari studies her partner's surly expression. Sure, her 'early night' plan has gone awry, but Mari hasn't seen Ed since she visited him in Singapore three years ago, and she doesn't want to miss out on this astonishing family reunion.

Feeling a ridiculous pull between Britt and her siblings, she finds herself gabbling. 'Ed has suggested we pop over to Dad's for a while. Isak's already asleep in his cot and of course I'll be back later. Thing is, Dee wants to come too, which is nothing short of a miracle, and it's so nice for the three of us to be together. I know tonight isn't ideal but we can reconvene tomorrow, can't we?'

Throwing the publication aside, Britt finally lifts her head.

'Sure,' she says, shrugging. 'Whatever.'

*

315

Leaving the empty champagne bottle behind, the three of them tumble out of the Uber and stare at their father's pretty cottage.

Ed nervously laughs. 'Are we really doing this without . . . ' He burps. 'Without an appointment?'

'It was your blinking idea,' Mari replies. 'Besides, I need a wee.' She glances at Dee. 'What do you say, Dee Dee?'

She sets her jaw like she did as a girl. 'I'm all for it,' she says, but still gives Mari a little shove to go first.

'Right. Here goes.' Aware of her siblings sniggering behind her, Mari strides up the path and raps the knocker.

Gilly has clearly heard their arrival as the door immediately opens. She blocks the threshold, her hand-on-hip stance showing she has no intention of moving. 'Your father is already upstairs and in his pyjamas, I'm afraid.'

'No problem,' Mari replies, pushing past. 'We'll go up and cover our innocent eyes.'

Dee and Ed timidly follow her into the front room. She glances at the door to the stairs. Does she have the guts to go up in the face of Gilly's furious disapproval? But she's saved from deciding as the portal swings open and her father appears in his paisley dressing gown. Wearing an all-in-one furry affair with a hood like a rabbit, Viola soon follows.

'Thought I heard a hullabaloo . . . ' Moving over a little unsteadily, Bill tries to hug all his children at once. 'What a delightful surprise. Come in, come in. Let me get you all a drink . . . '

Everyone seems to speak at once, but Gilly's shriek above the clamour stops them short. 'I'm sorry, but as you can see there isn't enough room in here.' She gesticulates around the too-hot parlour. 'Health and safety. It's as simple as that. I have to ask you all to leave.'

For a beat there's a pause, then Bill lifts his arms theatrically. 'Then we shall go to the pub!'

Gilly veritably harrumphs. 'Really, Bill? Dressed like that?'

The defiance falling from his face, he looks down at his attire, but Dee slips her arm through his. 'Onward, Father. You look very elegant, like a particularly sophisticated Sherlock Holmes.'

'Why, thank you, darling. Does someone have cash?'

'Yup, I do.' Ed grins. 'Do you think they'll accept Seychellois rupees?'

Giddy with laughter, they slip from the house, but at the gate they turn to the sound of another squawk. 'Stop!' This time it's Viola. Still wearing her outfit, she trots towards them. 'Wait for me! I'm coming too.'

80

Cordelia

I half-listen to Abbey and Ed chat. Despite my thumping head, I smile. I had such a laugh last night, the hangover is worth it. We were already half-cut when we arrived at Dad's cottage and sheepishly followed our leader into battle. Mari was always the boss, guiding me and Ed into trouble more often than not. But it was always pee-inducing fun, and yesterday was no exception.

Ed interrupts my musing. 'So do you think I'll meet the elusive Britt today?'

Wearing shorts, he raises a knee to scratch behind it. As ever, his long limbs take up the whole of the sofa. I had to lift his huge feet to squeeze into the corner. When I invited Abbey to sit in between us, she looked faintly disgusted at the sight of her uncle's hairy legs and sensibly opted for the armchair. He's addressing her now. 'Come on, Abs, spill the beans about Britt; your mum's far too polite. What's she honestly like?'

Abbey scrunches her face. 'She's really fun but—'

'But Mari's completely under the thumb?' Ed guffaws. 'I knew it! The way she scuttled upstairs to ask for permission to go out. *Still, it bloody serves her right for being so bossy with us growing* up. Did you know, when I was about five, she cut my hair as "practice" before tackling her own . . . '

I zone out. Ed and Abbey got on brilliantly the last time they met, so it's no surprise they still do, but it's lovely to see her hang on to his every word and actually chuckle. He has that knack of treating her like a mini adult; not going too far, but talking to her on the same level. Of course, I don't know for sure, but I imagine Cal would be the same. I only saw him briefly interact with his young colleague on the day of Vincent's collapse, but I sensed a great deal of respect. Until breakfast, I'd clean forgotten he and Ed were in the same class at Grasmere Road. The thought makes my belly flutter; when appropriate, I'll slip Cal into the conversation. It'll be so nice to mention his name! I haven't yet had a chance; Abbey has been chilling with us all morning, which is really, really lovely.

'She's actually OK, isn't she, Dee?'

'Mum!' Rolling her eyes, Abbey tuts. 'She's always doing this. Disappearing into space and not listening . . . '

Feeling myself flush, I come back to the conversation. 'Sorry, love? What was that?'

'Ed was asking you a question, Mum.'

'Sorry, I'm hungover.' I laugh. 'I think only one ear is working.'

'Have you taken painkillers?'

'Yeah, I'm sure they'll kick in soon.' I haven't; I still have an irrational fear of them. But I have drunk water, gallons of the stuff. 'So, what did I miss?'

'Viola,' Ed says. 'She's actually OK, isn't she?'

I picture my rabbit half-sister. 'Bunny girl. Yes, she is. I positively like her, in fact.'

*

319

As ever when washing-up is on the horizon, Abbey disappears after lunch, leaving me and Ed alone. He pushes his dessert bowl away. 'British food is truly dreadful,' he says, yawning. 'Something crumble, I'd say. No idea about the filling. Unless this was my first gooseberry experience ...'

'I see you finished it, though,' I chuckle. 'You all but licked up the last of the custard.'

'Hangover cure.'

'That old chestnut. Good job I didn't bake it; I might have been offended.'

'Another parishioner offering?'

'Yup. I could do with Vincent staying in hospital a little longer. I haven't had to lift a culinary finger for yonks.'

Ed lowers his voice. 'How are you feeling about him coming home after a couple of weeks' freedom?'

Widening my eyes meaningfully, I look to the window. Her batwings swinging with the effort, Harriet is scrubbing Vincent's car. 'Not exactly freedom.'

That's a thought. Will Vincent be allowed to drive? Is he really going to come home and carry on life as usual? Knowing him, probably. After being quiet for a few days, Harriet seems to have caught his positivity. Managing to work around Ed as though he's invisible, she's spruced up the whole house and I feel a little shamefaced after my inward accusations of her sloth.

Ed guffaws. 'Got to give her credit, she's one indomitable woman.'

'That's actually very true.' I put a hand on his arm. 'Once Vincent's back, though——'

'Don't worry, I'll move on to Mari's.' He lifts his eyebrows. 'If I'm allowed ...'

320

'Yeah.' I know Ed is hoping I'll dish some dirt about Britt, but I'm chomping at the bit to mention Cal. Abbey is upstairs and Harriet's outside, so now is as good a time as any. Hoping my zeal doesn't show, I take a quick breath.

'I bumped into someone who was in your form at Grasmere Road the other day.'

Ed smiles. 'Please tell me it was Emily Lanigan. I used to write her notes saying that I loved her before running off.'

'Did they work?'

With a faux smug look, he points to his face. 'What do you think?'

I chuckle. 'So that's a no, then.' Then after a beat, 'No, this was a guy. Cal Rafferty? Remember him?'

'Calvin Rafferty?'

'Yeah.'

'My year?'

I nod.

'Can't be.' Ed deeply frowns. 'I think you must have caught the wrong name.'

'Doh, I must have.' Anxiety tingling, I quickly change the subject. 'So, going back to Britt—'

'Because it's an unusual name and one I won't easily forget.'

The prickling turns to sweat. 'Why not?'

'Don't you remember the dreadful shock?' Narrowing his eyes, he pauses. 'Ah, that's right. I was in Year Five. You'd have gone to high school by then, but still. It was horrible, everyone was crying, including Mr Warren when he broke the news to our class.'

My throat feels gritty. 'What news?' I manage. 'What was it?'

'Do you really not remember?' Ed stares. 'That Calvin Rafferty was dead.'

81

Calvin

Feeling Ali's gaze, Cal looks up from his mobile. 'What?'

'Looking at your phone every two minutes, faraway frowns, pretty upbeat mood . . .'

Aware of his flush, Cal slips the phone into his top pocket. 'Upbeat mood, eh? When am I not?'

'How long have you got?' Pulling down the mirror flap, Ali slicks back his hair. 'So, adding two and two together, my guess is you're in love.'

'Shows you're crap at maths.'

'Is it Cristina?'

'What?'

'The object of your affections?'

'Fuck, no.'

Ali looks apologetic. 'I still feel bad about letting on where you lived the other day.'

'No worries, it's sorted.'

'But there is a woman.' Ali grins. 'Come on man, share the deets.'

Cal laughs and shakes his head. After a full-on day, he went to bed early last night and listened to Delius until he was sufficiently tired to give sleep a go. On the cusp, his phone buzzed. He considered leaving it, but when he briefly looked, he saw the text was from Dee. Not just a message, but something approaching sexting. A surprise, but a very pleasurable one, so he hitched up the mattress and responded in kind, each exchange getting more explicit until her final one:

Bit drunk. Need sleep. Love you. Night, night.

The texts are still on his phone and though all are rousing, it's the last one he's studied the most.

Love you.

Could Dee Dee Stephens truly love a guy like him? Despite the complications, the lies and the mess, could they have a future?

82

Cordelia

'Are you OK, Dee?' Mari asks again over the hum of chatter between Ed and Britt.

'Yeah, sure. I've still got a slight hangover.'

Mari tilts her head. 'A good night, though? Us all seeing Dad together.'

'Yes, absolutely. I loved it. We must do it again before Ed goes back.'

'Even with the bunny?'

'God, yes. Who'd have thought she'd be so funny.' Aware of Abbey's frown, I lean across the table and try for a light-hearted tone. 'You and Viola are only a few years apart, so you must come with us next time, love. Maybe we should all don onesies!'

My daughter gives me the usual appalled look, but I'm too agitated to care. Despite the delicious food and conversation drifting around me, I want to vomit.

My mind has been revving since lunchtime. Who the hell is the man I've slept with several times? What do I really know about him? Nothing, except that he isn't who he said he was. How have I been so foolish? Right from the start he hid things from me: his upstairs bedroom, his girlfriend, his son. Then his shouting me out of the house, the 'Christian' text. And what about the woman I saw on his doorstep? How on earth would a carer have known where he lived? And those faltering eyes when I asked him what had happened. Yes, he was lying about that too.

'Mum. Mum!' I jerk up to Abbey's scowl. 'Britt asked you to pass the parmesan cheese.'

'Sorry. Miles away.' I pass her the grater and plate. 'It's a lovely meal, Britt, thank you for having us.'

She shrugs. 'Thank Mariana, not me. She did the cooking.'

'Well, it's delicious and the table looks fab. I love eating by candlelight ...'

Britt has been surly since we arrived. She and Abbey make a good flaming team. I attempt another tack. 'Is Isak sleeping through yet? He looked so sweet when I peeped in. Chubby and cherubic like a Renaissance painting. And his hair's becoming a lovely shade of—'

'He's not fat, Cordelia. He's stayed on the same centile since birth, which is how it should be.'

I clear my throat. 'Sorry, Britt, chubby's the wrong word. I'm away with the fairies today. Too much booze and too little sleep last night.'

'I wouldn't worry.' She sweeps a contemptuous glance at Mari. 'You weren't the only one.'

Ed tops up his wine. 'My fault. I'm the bad influence.' Seemingly oblivious to the tension, he turns to Britt and carries on his questions from earlier. 'So, your dad's English, your mum is Swedish. They finally settled in Stockholm but you prefer the UK.' He lifts his hands. 'Rainy Manchester? Why, oh, why? Apart from my big sister being here, of course. I loved it in

Stockholm.' He squints. 'I was there in 2010, I think. Worked on the boats for the best part of a year. Couldn't get enough of the banks to the archipelago and Lake Mälaren.'

'My parents' house looks onto the lake. Familiarity can breed contempt.' Britt holds out her flute and Ed obliges with the fizz, pouring it like an expert. When he's finished, she smiles sweetly. 'I could ask the same question. Why, oh, why choose anywhere but *your* home town, Ed?'

'Touché! Well, I had a father who was thrown out of the house because he was a serial adulterer and as for my mother, she *accidentally* . . .'

He throws back his drink and glances at Mari. Almost imperceptibly, she shakes her head and takes his hand. 'He only does it to make me and Dee Dee love him all the more when he comes back.'

Staring at my plate, I inhale deeply. It's always like this when Ed comes home. Uplifting one minute, unbearably emotional the next. Anticipating another *'Are you OK?'* from Mari, I stand and force a smile. 'Too true, Ed. We miss you, so not so long next time, please. I'm off for a pee, so I'll look in on my gorgeous nephew. See you in a minute.'

Resisting the need to sob, I sit in the wicker chair next to Isak's cot. It's too dark to see him, but I know he's breathing. When did my ears become so finely tuned? Before or after my boy's death?

Luke, baby Lukie. I cover my face. How was I so naive? I shared the details of his smothering and so much more with a complete stranger. So excited, misguided and smitten, I barely batted an eyelid when Vincent had a life-threatening episode; instead I indulged in an adulterous affair. I have a steady husband, a good solid marriage, but someone is posting evidence on Facebook which could destroy it. I must have been deranged to be so blatant. The photograph, the bloody photograph. Who took it? Who knew?

My heart thrashing, I picture my own face staring back through the windscreen. Why reveal mine and not Cal's? Why keep the driver's side hidden, same as the number plate? I squeeze my mind back to that day in the woods. He went to check if we were near the river. He left me alone in the car and ... Of course. He took the snap. *He* is the troll. What did he say about it? *'Hopefully the troll has had his fun now.'*

Oh God, my instincts were right, weren't they? When I texted Calvin – or whatever the bloody man is called – and told him I never wanted to see him again, I was absolutely spot on. But I gave in to ...

I press my eyes shut. *Lead us not into temptation, but deliver us from evil.*

Evil ... Realisation grips my throat. What actually happened that first day we met? One moment I saw a flash of headlights, the next I was on the ground. But when I looked for a car, there was only one there. His. Calvin's. That man's.

83

Palm Sunday

Cordelia

When I enter the ward and glance at the polished gent reading a newspaper in the chair, it takes a moment to register that he is my husband. It must be the chinos and Pringle jumper; I'm so used to him reclined and wearing pyjamas, it's a shock to see him looking like the Vincent of old.

Abbey rushes forward and gives him a hug. 'Dad! I'm so pleased you're finally coming home. The house has been so quiet without you.'

He picks her up and twirls her around. Goodness, should he be doing things like that? It has always been his and Abbey's 'thing' but she's almost my height now, surely too big? Or am I just jealous, not only about their closeness, but my lack of it with anyone myself? Is that why I flung myself at the first guy who showed interest? Put myself in danger? Because apart from all my other florid thoughts, 'Cal' assumed a dead boy's name. That's not only menacing; it's unlawful too.

'Guess what? Auntie Mari is driving us home.' I return to my daughter's shiny eyes. 'Grandma decided not to come because

328

she's your "welcome party", as she put it. Uncle Ed's there too ...'
She laughs. 'I think Grandma was worried he'd steal something
if she wasn't keeping an eye on him.'

'Abbey!'

'It's a joke, Mum. You know it's a joke, don't you, Dad?'

He kisses both her cheeks. 'I do and I've missed them. Right,
I'll say my goodbyes.'

Holding himself tall, he steps over to the other men in the
ward, shaking hands and having a few words as though he was
a visiting priest rather than a departing patient.

'It was a joke, Mum. It was Ed who said it.'

'I know, love,' I absently reply.

Ed's hoping to move into Mari's for a few days before visiting
friends, but I want him to stay at the vicarage. The old three-
against-one is already bringing me out in a sweat; it'd be so nice
to have someone on my side. Only days ago I thought I no longer
needed it. It was as though I'd risen from the ashes; I felt strong,
capable and confident, but now I'm back at square one, less than
that, if I'm honest. Only I can't be *honest* to anyone about Cal.

Picking up Vincent's holdall, I follow him to the nursing station where he does the same again, greeting and thanking the
staff for their 'dedication, care and attention'.

I inwardly nod. Though the nurses aren't laying down their
cloaks and palm-tree branches, their genuine smiles reflect my
husband's charisma. I'm lucky to be part of his team; I must
accept and recognise my blessings, knuckle down and be the
compliant, perfect woman he wants. No more rebellion or defiance, no more needling his mother.

It's time to resume my duties as a benign vicar's wife.

*

Harriet fusses over Vincent all morning and early afternoon, so it's difficult to get a look in, but when she goes for a nap, I take a deep breath and tap on the lounge door. His legs on the footstool and surrounded by cushions, my husband is sleeping too. Thrown off balance, I picture him lying prone on the floor. I genuinely thought 'Calvin' was attacking him that day. Intuition again; what a fool to ignore it.

Opening his eyes, he holds out an arm. 'Hello, darling.'

Like the days when I worshipped the ground he walked on, I settle down on the worn carpet beside him. 'Nice to be home on Palm Sunday of all days?' I smile. 'A *triumphant* return, even though in a car rather than by donkey . . . '

His voice cracks. 'Yes, it is, but . . . ' He abruptly covers his face and it takes moments to twig he isn't praying but sobbing.

My own eyes stinging, I hold his shaking chest. Eventually pulling away, I pass him a box of tissues. 'That's probably done you good. You've had a dreadful ordeal and you've been incredibly brave.'

He clutches my hand then, so tightly it hurts. 'You have to help me, Cordelia. You're the only one who can.'

Alarm dries my threatening tears. 'Yes, of course I will, but how?'

'Precisely what you just said. You have to help me be courageous. I can't show my weakness to anyone else. You understand that, don't you? Mother, Abbey, the rectory team, the congregation, the community. They all rely on me to be strong. Do you see?'

'Yes, but I thought—'

What did I think? That he was all-confident and fearless and indestructible? Yes, yes, I did.

'I'm a wreck, Cordelia. That's the honest truth.' He squeezes the bridge of his nose. 'I know some things will get better with time, but right now ... I can barely stay awake more than an hour and when I am, I have no energy. Then there's ...' Lifting his trouser leg, he exposes his swollen ankle. 'Fluid retention, urine problems and dreadful constipation.'

Moved by his bleak candour, I rub his shoulder. 'Everything will be fine. And those things aren't surprising; you haven't moved properly for several days. We'll make the recommended light exercise our joint mission, a short walk every day, then increase—'

'Even apart from the damned drugs, there's lifestyle changes, things that are part of me and my job. Socialising, smoking, drinking, eating.' His voice emerges thin and teary. 'So perhaps it's a good thing when I sleep, because what's the point of living a life without pleasures?'

Rocking back on my heels, I gaze at a man I barely recognise. 'Look, I know that's how you feel right now, but you have to stay focused for Abbey. Yes, you'll stop smoking, but the other things you'll still have in moderation. And you'll do it for her, won't you? And Harriet.'

'And you too, darling.'

'Good. You're allowed to feel down, Vincent. Life has changed, it's a huge shock.' My lips twitch. 'Perhaps you're not quite as indefatigable as you'd thought.'

He sniffs and smiles too. 'Perhaps not.'

I take a quick breath. 'Which is why I'd like you to think about having the ICD fitted. Not today or tomorrow, but when you get your head around it. Yes?'

'Perhaps in a few days ...'

'And Mari could help with counselling or—'

'Really, Cordelia?' he asks, raising his eyebrows and looking more like his old self.

Relief spreading, I chuckle. 'Or she can recommend someone. But for now you hang in there, take it easy and rest. None of us want to see you dead. Agreed?'

'Agreed.' He holds his palm to my cheek for several moments. 'Thank you, darling; despite everything, I knew deep down you were strong.'

84

Mariana

Mari yawns and rolls over. Monday morning and Britt's blue gaze is accusing already. Can she be bothered with another argument? Not that they actually rowed last night; Britt's silence said it all.

OK, she let Britt down over their date night; the Stephens clan invaded their home on Saturday afternoon and evening, only reluctantly leaving at midnight. But ... Is it really acceptable to be so unfriendly? No, more than that. Other than chatting to Abbey about the superficial reality-show gossip, she was bloody rude to them all. '*Why, oh, why choose anywhere but* your *home town, Ed?*' Loaded with sarcasm. Maybe Ed had it coming with his usual cross-examination, but he was charming and genuinely interested; he wasn't asking questions to make any sort of judgement.

She sighs. Is she calling the pot black? Wasn't she equally unpleasant to Britt's friends when they were the same? Are she and Britt actually Venus and Mars? The thought stabs her heart. Oh God, are they simply incompatible?

A grumble from the nursery filters through the open door. She kisses Britt's cheek, then pulls back the duvet. 'I'll bring him in so you guys can have a cuddle while I make up the milk.'

Britt catches her hand. 'Can't you stay at home with us today?' Her eyes have now turned to deep pools of sweetness. 'Please? Pretty please? I hardly saw you all weekend.'

Mari sits on the bed. 'I'd love to be here with you and Isak day in and day out, but I have to go to work. My diary is chock-a-block with appointments.'

'It doesn't feel that way.'

'What doesn't?'

'Wanting to be here with us.'

As though the incompatibility thoughts have escaped, Mari feels her cheeks colouring. 'That isn't true for a moment, but I have to do my job, Britt. I have clients to see, not to mention money to earn. It's just a time issue, but let's plan for a holiday. Maybe you could have a gander on the internet or even nip into the village and pick up some brochures from the travel agent. Where do you fancy? The world is your oyster!' She turns to the whimpering. 'I think someone's hungry.'

Despite Isak's upset, Britt doesn't reply. She examines her fingernails. 'If it's a *time issue*, how come you had enough to help Cordelia with Vincent yesterday?'

'It only took an hour and it meant Dee and Abbey could each hold one of his arms ...'

Why did she offer? Mari thinks back to Saturday night. Dee looked close to tears all evening. Something's going on that she isn't telling them about. Over the past few weeks, and particularly on Friday, she seemed on a high. It was so lovely to witness, especially the reconnection with Bill. Their ease with each other brought back the old days when Mari had been acutely jealous of their closeness. She glanced at Ed and he nodded as though reading her very thoughts. But they'd had their mum, their beautiful Felicity. Ed still misses her deeply, she knows that.

Why has her sister's mood changed so dramatically since then? Like their mum, she's proficient at putting on a mask, but during the meal her anxiety leaked out in shadows. It has to be Vincent; he's refused to have the implant; it must be worrying.

Though she can't pinpoint why, it felt important to be there and take the happy family photograph. She comes back to Britt. 'Vincent's coming home is a big thing all around. Maybe later you could pop in to the vicarage to say hi and take Isak. He'll love that.' She squeezes her hand. 'Holiday ideas and bringing a smile to Vinny's face. Sounds a good plan, doesn't it?'

Slipping back down the bed, Britt tuts. 'Whatever. Just get the baby and stop controlling my life.'

85

Calvin

Unsure why he's driving this route rather than Kingsway, Cal heads for home. He does know, though. He's on Parrs Wood Road, where he first saw Dee Dee. Not on the first of January, but weeks before that. After years without a glimpse, there she was, running along the pavement like a gazelle. Even with the cap, he immediately recognised her, the girl who hadn't known he existed. Or perhaps the girl who knew he did, but had no interest in a 'rough' boy from a council house.

Has a germ of that teenage hatred remained in his heart? And how does he feel after seeing her with *him* yesterday?

He spotted Dee and her red-headed daughter enter the Heart Centre. Remembering the man was due out, he turned around the RRV and parked up. It took a while, but they finally emerged, then Mari Stephens zoomed in, climbed out of her SUV and gave all three of them hugs. Though he hadn't seen her for years, she looked pretty much the same as he recalled; still short-haired and alternative somehow, despite the mix of leather jacket and joggers. His arms around Dee and their daughter, the invalid posed for a photograph. They all embraced again, then climbed into Mari's car.

Christ knows why he tortured himself by watching the joyous scene. Dee hasn't messaged since their Friday-night sexting. Yet it is understandable; she has a sick husband to think of right now. He wants that man to recover, and soon. A wife would only leave a fit and healthy spouse, right?

Finally at his house, he parks up and groans. He's in cloud cuckoo land thinking things like that, isn't he? But Zachary is staying overnight tomorrow, so things aren't all bad.

Dragging his bags of heavy shopping, he hops up the steps and opens his front door. Yes, on balance he's in a good place. He'd feel a whole lot better if a text of reassurance arrived from Dee, but he has a gorgeous son. Not knowing what Zach likes best, he bought a range of provisions from jars of baby food to breadsticks to bananas. Also a couple of play cars – an ambulance and a RRV with stripes, but of course.

With a grin, he takes out the toys and puts them on the counter. 'Press here', a sticker says, so he obliges, the flashing lights and different siren sounds making him chuckle. When the doorbell interrupts, he looks at his watch. Could it be Dee? At seven-thirty, it's feasible.

The plastic vehicle beneath his arm, he strides to the door, but the blur beyond the glass is dark and shorter than Dee. Oh hell, it's Cristina. So much for his '*It's sorted*'. Preparing another kind-but-firm rebuff, he takes a breath and turns the latch, but surprise makes him gawp and words just fall out.

'Bloody hell, Mum, what are you doing here?'

86

Mariana

Not in the mood to pander to Britt, Mari goes straight to the kitchen when she arrives home. There's nothing in the oven for dinner, so she sets to work with the veg, glad of the breathing space to let her thoughts roam. She planned to use what was left from last night, but Britt appears to have eaten it for her lunch. Or perhaps she's thrown it out.

Rotating her shoulders, she sighs. She feels achy all over. Heavy limbs, thudding head, tight jaw. But it has been one of those days when everyone from Sanjay to the clients to the psychiatrist on call wanted a piece of her. She didn't even get around to returning Ed's message about staying here for a few days. She needs to ask Britt if it's OK with her, but either way they have to say yes. Dee can't be expected to have their brother lounging about at the vicarage with Vincent recuperating, and despite the new-found allegiance with Viola, Gilly wouldn't let him doss at the cottage in a million years. And she can hardly send Ed to a hotel; he's her brother, for God's sake.

Almost thinking 'because blood is thicker than water', she

pulls herself short. Blood ties don't matter, they really do not; she loves Britt; she loves Isak. Right now she simply has to tread a fine line between old family and new.

Savouring the mushroom smell, she pours her creamy sauce over the broccoli florets and chicken chunks. It's actually a simple recipe of her mother's and probably not the healthiest of meals, but a satisfying and tasty quick fix. The thought of Felicity brings her back to Ed's expression the other night; he clearly needs to talk about her; nothing has changed even after all these years; he's still desperate to know everything.

'*Feel rather low tonight. Are you there, Mari?*'

Pushing her mum's thin voice away, she walks to the stairs. 'Britt?' she calls from the bottom. 'Dinner's ready in twenty. Are you coming down?'

Sighing at the lack of a reply, she drags her leaden legs upwards. 'Britt? Where are you?'

'I'm in here.'

Mari pushes at the nursery door and takes in little Isak, napping on Britt's lap. Exasperation flips to sympathy; the poor little mite must have been unsettled for her to have nursed him to sleep. Feeling rotten for misjudging her, she crouches to kiss his downy hair.

'Beautiful,' she says quietly. 'Dinner's in twenty minutes. Shall I put him in the cot?'

Britt shakes her head. 'We're waiting for the taxi.'

'What? A taxi to where?'

A sixth sense nagging, Mari turns. Two cabin-sized suitcases are lined up by the wardrobe.

'The airport. We're going to Sweden. I went to the travel agent like you said.'

339

'Sorry? What?' She stares. Is this a joke? No, Britt's jaw is set. 'To Sweden? How long are you going for?'

She shrugs. 'A week, maybe two.'

'And you were going to tell me this, when?'

'I'm telling you now. Besides, I'm an adult, aren't I? I'm not under lock and key. I'm free to come and go as I please?'

Trying to process what's happening, Mari puffs out her hot breath. 'Yes, of course you are. But I'm your partner. We're supposed to communicate and agree—'

'Like you telling me when you'll be late home? Or jollying off to your father's without even thinking I might want to join you? Or letting your brother stay without asking me first?' Her glare is triumphant. 'Yes, Ed called today asking when would be a good time to turn up.'

Stuck for words, Mari swallows. It's all very true. 'What about Isak?'

'I'm taking him too.'

'Yes, of course.' Tears shoot to her eyes. Two whole weeks without seeing him? Babies change so quickly at this age. She gropes for an excuse. 'But what about a passport for him?'

Britt smiles thinly. 'My parents live in another country. God, Mari, you really do think I'm dumb, don't you?'

'No, not at all.' Things are going too fast; Mari needs them to slow down so she can think. 'OK. Let me drive you to the airport.'

Britt picks up her mobile and peers at it. 'The Uber is four minutes away. Bring the cases down, will you?' At the door she turns. 'Oh, come on, Mariana, don't look so tragic. My father hasn't seen Isak yet.' She smiles with those pearly white teeth. 'And Ed can eat whatever you've prepared, so it won't go to waste. It's his fault – all that chat about Stockholm, holidays and family.' She leans forward for a peck. 'Don't worry. I'll be back.'

87

Maundy Thursday

Cordelia

I steer in to the Tesco car park and park at the very far side. Maundy Thursday is an apt description of my week, never mind my day. I've been more or less attached to Vincent's side, doing my best to chivvy him along and uplift his emotional state despite feeling so low myself.

Taking a shuddery breath, I pull my mobile from my handbag. Though I've tried to avoid using it, I've felt winded with panic when checking for messages from Abbey or Mari. I don't want to hear from the Calvin person; I want him to vanish for ever. But that isn't happening, as texts still intermittently appear:

Everything OK?

Not heard from you for a while. Would be good to hear you're fine.

Hello? Just worried, that's all.

I glance around and wait for an elderly shopper to load his bags in his boot. My fingers trembling, I turn the phone on and wait for it to load. Oh hell, another message from *him*. Taking a sharp breath, I quickly open it.

What's wrong? Just tell me. I'll keep on trying until you do.

I cover my face. Even Vincent has commented on my lack of mobile use. The weather, the news, church WhatsApp group chats, the internet; I didn't realise how much I'd routinely used it. Each time he asks me to check a parish date or a football score, I feign forgetfulness and use my laptop instead.

Blocking the man seems a sensible plan, but then I won't be forewarned if he turns up at the vicarage. Because that's what he once threatened, didn't he?

I could knock on . . .

Then there's:

I'll keep on trying until you do.

Is this some kind of stalking?

I puff out my agitation. I assumed silence would be the best way to indicate that I'm no longer interested, but clearly not. I need to do or say something more definitive to make him stop.

I start to type:

I know you're not Calvin Rafferty. Please keep away.

Will that do it? Or:

Calvin Rafferty is dead. Don't contact me again.

Or:

I don't know who you really are, but I'll call the police if you come anywhere near me.

Though would I? '*Officer, please help me. A man I had sex with isn't who he said he was . . .*' As if.

Tears sting my eyes. It isn't just that though, is it? It's sheer disappointment too. With him I felt more than an object, a trophy-wife-cum-skivvy. I was no longer invisible. He made me feel cared for, valued and loved. He said the words '*I love you*' and I believed him. Absolutely believed him. We had perfect sex.

He was my fantasy, my escape. I didn't realise quite how much I needed it until this week. Harriet has appointed herself nursemaid, dolling out pills to Vincent at regular intervals and watching him swallow with a beady eye, but my allocated role is more that of a Victorian companion, not doing much but silently being there. In all honesty, it's bloody claustrophobic. It isn't Vincent's fault, but every story or witticism, each word of wisdom or prayer of gratitude sets my teeth on edge, not only because I've heard them a million times before, but because it's an act for Harriet and Abbey and the other ton of well-wishers who find their way to our door.

I tap my forehead on the steering wheel. I'm being deeply unkind; if I find the 'happy act' exhausting, God only knows how Vincent manages it. In private, he's still very depressed.

Like an ageing actor, he seems to shrivel the moment he's off stage.

I groan. And I'm his dresser, his loyal-for-ever dresser. Like the play, it's my job to keep my master's life together.

Lucky me.

I go back to my phone. That's the trouble with freedom; a taste of it and one is done for. Bloody Cal or Calvin Rafferty or whatever his name really is. He made me feel special, but it was all a fucking lie. I punch out a message and press 'send'.

88

Calvin

'I take it that the love affair is off?' Ali says.

'Sorry?'

'You're back to a moody frown.' He points to Cal's mobile on the table between them. 'No woolgathering or checking your phone every two minutes ...'

Cal lifts his head from his coffee. It's April the first and today they've rung the changes at McDonald's by sitting inside. 'Sorry, loads going on.'

'Like?'

Sipping his drink, Cal thinks about the answer. 'Some good, some bad, some confusing.'

'OK, let's start with the good.'

'What's this? "Dear Coleen"?'

'And Coleen is ... ?'

'An ex-singing agony aunt.'

Ali laughs. 'Yup, that's me. And I'm your mate. Come on, what's good in your life?'

'My little boy.' Before Ali can reply, Cal quickly speaks again. 'I know – you didn't know I had a kid. He lives with his mum.'

He inwardly groans. His own mother didn't know either until last week. The toy was the first thing she noticed when they talked on his doorstep.

'What's this?' she asked.

'An ambulance,' he replied, still thrown by her shocking presence.

Her face melted. 'Oh, son, you're a father, aren't you?'

Ali takes a bite of his second Big Mac. 'Nice one. I take it the bad and the confusing are one and the same, namely the elusive love of your life?'

The 'confusing' was actually the visit from his mum. She wants him to see his dad. '*He needs you,*' she said.

'Then why doesn't he contact me himself?'

'He doesn't know what he wants, or what he needs. But if you can't do it for him, please do it for me,' she replied.

Ali is right too. He's bewildered about his love life. Out of the blue Sadie told him that she's started seeing a new guy. It's good news, of course – that particular responsibility has been lifted from his shoulders – but after her repeated attempts to get back with him, his ego has definitely taken a blow. And how does he feel about another man around his son? Yet on reflection it has made him all the more determined to play a vital part in Zach's life, make sure there's no doubt who his real dad is.

As for Dee ... Sure, she must have her hands full with the Reverend at the moment, but surely a simple text wouldn't be too much effort. Her last words were 'love you', weren't they? How has she swung from that to complete silence? In truth, he feels empty, dismayed. Her presence gave his day-to-day life colour; it's now back to shades of grey.

Stretching, he looks at his watch. Time to get behind the

wheel and help those in real need. 'Right, a quick piss, then we're off.' He pushes his untouched fries across to Ali. 'See if you can polish those off before I'm back.'

Save for his phone, the table has been cleared by the time he returns. Ali gestures to it with a grin. 'Sounds like your love life is back on track, mate. Do you want to check it before we move on?'

Cal scoops up his mobile and peers at the screen. At last! A message from Dee.

His heart stupidly thrashing, he opens it up:

Calvin Rafferty is dead. He has been for the past twenty-four years. You are a fucking liar. Don't ever contact me again.

'Bloody hell, mate, you look as though you've seen a ghost.' The words sounds like a faraway train. Then Ali's hand is touching his shoulder. 'Hey, Joel, are you OK?'

89

Mariana

Though she spent all day at her work desk, Mari finds herself at another in her study at home. For the first time in months there's space to pull out the office chair and sit down. She's missing both Britt and Isak enormously, but is endeavouring to be positive about their holiday by keeping busy and tackling areas which would cause a Britt frown. Why the baby paraphernalia has crept from Isak's nursery into here, she doesn't know, but she's been able to clear it from every surface of the room and put it in a semblance of order. She's slotted the unopened packets of vests and rompers in Isak's wardrobe and a whole ton of nappies under the stairs. She's also made a pile of potential returns, though it's probably too late. She didn't mind Britt's baby-buying spree – she was excited too – but no newborn needs three snow suits and several hats; the seasons change and they already look far too small.

Ed has replaced Britt's absence in terms of noise and mess, and it's great to catch up on a backlog of chores, but Mari's bed feels empty. Though her mum has been a silent presence in the room once or twice, each time she reaches out for her partner in the night, the cold sheets remind her that she – and their gorgeous boy – are gone. But it's only for two weeks and Britt has been constantly in touch, complaining how dull it is at her parents' place and sending selfies of her and Isak with a hundred sad emojis or love hearts. Her affection has been uplifting and pleasing, like they're back to the days of new love.

She glances at the heap of Britt's maternity clothes. She'll put some in the wash basket and carefully fold the rest. Where to stash them? Most of them are designer labels and hardly worn; it seems a shame to throw them out. She and Britt are different shapes and have different taste, but one day she might go back to Konnie and her sperm bank. Siblings are a good thing. Though will she? Will she go through that hope and disappointment when she knows deep down it won't work, that she's cursed from a decision she made at seventeen?

She drags her thoughts back to household admin. Partly laziness and part lack of time, her utility and credit card bills are paid by direct debit. She's tempted to let house and car insurance auto-renew for the same reasons, but Martin the Money Saving Expert keeps reprimanding her in his weekly newsletter, so she feels compelled to at least open the renewal emails and glance at the figures.

As expected, the cost of contents cover has increased from last year, but can she be bothered working out how much everything is worth, then inputting the data into a comparison site? No, life's too short to quibble about an extra ninety quid. Deciding to sort it now, she opens online banking and brings up her current account. Perplexed, she stares at the screen. Sure, she's had lots of outgoings and standing orders, but can the balance be right? She scans the latest statement. Flights, foreign money exchange; Selfridges, Boots; taxis, takeaways. Perhaps they're expected, but there are several cash debits in the last ten days. Feeling the heat spread, she scrolls down further. There was an intermission immediately after Isak's birth, but before that there were two-hundred-quid withdrawals at least once a week.

Folding her arms, she sits back. Bloody hell, what does this mean? Does Britt see her as a cash cow, or is it the sort of 'stay-at-home wife' expense she should expect? No, surely not. And she gave Britt her debit card; she trusted her to be fair. The cost of the flight is extortionate, far more than they paid for both of them in the past. Did she make any attempt to find the cheapest? Her eyes catch the pile of maternity clothes. Expensive; designer. A few even have the shop labels attached.

Too frustrated to sit still, she pads down the stairs. Ed is sprawled on the lounge sofa with a huge glass of red. 'Pour me one of those, will you?' she asks.

'Are you OK? You look . . . cross.'

She snorts. 'If you lived with a woman and supported her, how would you feel if she just took the fucking piss with your money?'

Ed eyes her. 'Tricky one. If we were married or a couple, she'd be within her rights to consider what was mine was hers too.' He lifts his eyebrows. 'Especially if she was at home and raising our baby. That's a job too, right?'

'Yes, absolutely, but suppose the spending was way over the top?'

'Guess it depends on whether there were discussions and boundaries set . . .'

Mari flops down and sighs. Nope, there were no conversations or limits; in truth, the whole relationship was and still is any price for a baby. 'Yup, you're right.'

351

He nudges her and grins. 'But I'd still be pretty hacked off if I was slogging away at work and she was partying day and night.'

She takes a mouthful of wine. 'By all accounts they don't party in Stockholm.'

'Oh, they do.' He guffaws and passes her his mobile. 'I'd say Britt's having more than just a party. Take a look at her Instagram account.'

90

Good Friday

Cordelia

An echo of our wedding day, I slot my arm through Vincent's as we stroll down the aisle from our pew near the sanctuary. Harriet and Abbey follow like bridesmaids and all eyes are on us. Visitors galore have popped into the vicarage since his return home, but he hasn't attended a church service before now. I suspect he didn't fancy listening to a sermon other than his own, but today is the remembrance of Jesus Christ's death, so a family appearance at the afternoon service was deemed appropriate.

His discharge on Palm Sunday and the ensuing celebrations weren't lost on me, but I don't expect my husband to die by crucifixion or otherwise today. In fact, he's definitely improving, his napping much less and our daily strolls a touch longer. 'We'll manage the Mersey river by next week,' he said this morning.

His comment made me uncomfortably hot and is still fresh

in my mind. That walk on the riverbank with 'Cal', kissing and fumbling and wanting more. Was that really me? Yes, I know it was; the same lustful person I was as a teenager. One who was finally satisfied. But God only knows why I did something so open, so reckless and foolish.

Picturing the man, I push away the flash of what I thought was love. Am I terrified or disappointed or hurt? Angry or sad? All of them, I suppose. And he hasn't replied to my text defending himself; there isn't a wild mistake about the name that can be explained; he's guilty as charged.

Chatter and aromas breaking through, I shake myself back. To celebrate Vincent's recovery, Harriet and the squad have arranged a tea party in the kids' play area – with crumpets rather than cake out of respect for Good Friday fasting. Personally I've always considered them a treat, but food is subjective, like religion, it seems; far from abstaining for forty days and nights, Harriet has been making up for lost time since her son came home.

I reprimand myself. I have to stop these mean thoughts. Vincent and his mother are my lot, my penance. I stepped over the family threshold and look where it got me.

Putting on my best smile, I amble around the room, talking to both churchgoers and the team, toeing the party line about how fabulously well Vincent is doing after his 'scare'. Finally needing a breather, I turn for the toilets, but shock strikes me like a slap, pinning my feet to the ground.

Holding a teacup and moving towards me, it's the man who calls himself Calvin Rafferty.

Panic blocks my senses.

'Can we talk, please?' he asks.

Somehow I manage to find my voice. 'What are you doing here?' I whisper. 'You shouldn't be here. You need to leave.'

'Come and see me and I'll explain.'

Anger pierces the fugue. 'Explain that you've pretended to be someone else?' I hiss. 'I don't think so.'

'I haven't . . . ' He frowns. 'I'm not going until we've spoken or arranged something. Your choice.'

Sweat crawls down my spine. And my mother-in-law is striding over. With her usual church charm, she grasps his hand warmly. 'I know you, young man, don't I?' She studies him for a beat. 'You look so familiar. Let me place you . . . '

My heart clatters with alarm, but Cal seems to slip into professional mode. 'Glad to see your son so well, Mrs Hardy. He's certainly looking much better than the last time I saw him.'

Harriet smacks her mouth. 'Of course. Oh, my word. Goodness. My son's saviour! I must call Vincent over, he's wanted to personally—' she begins, but I quickly interrupt. If I know her at all, she'll nominate the man for a sainthood by the end of the day.

'No, Harriet. Low key, remember? Vincent won't appreciate the fuss in front of everybody.'

'Yes, yes.' Her eyes watery, she clutches Cal's arm. 'Another time, in private. Please do come and see us at the vicarage so we can say thank you properly.'

'I will, thank you.'

'Excellent, Vincent will be thrilled. Perhaps you could jot down your number and give it to Cordelia.'

As Harriet drifts away, Cal turns back to me. His jaw is set, the tension showing in his cheeks. 'I will turn up if I have to. There's important stuff I need to explain.'

'Right.' I swallow. It's difficult to swim above my sheer agitation. Where can we meet? Certainly not at his place and I'll never risk travelling or sitting in his car ever again. 'Clothorn Road in an hour. It's off Wilmslow Road, number—'

'I know where it is. I'll see you then.'

91

Joel

Joel opens the gate and hops up the step of the Edwardian house. He isn't at all sure about this, but he has to do something for his mental health. And his heart. He thought he'd be fine hidden among the church congregation, but his stomach somersaulted when Dee walked to her seat with Vincent. Why the hell is she wasting her life on him? The man doesn't make her remotely happy; the desolation was clear in her face.

He glances at the curtains through the handsome front window. Colourful and bright, they're not what he would expect from Mari Stephens. She always appeared cool and indifferent as a teenager, the sort of girl you'd need guts to approach. But he knows this is her house; the whole Stephens family lived here back then. Many a time he walked past, torn between a desire to peep through the bay to catch a glimpse of Dee and throwing a brick at it.

He lifts the knocker, lets it drop and waits. He sat on a bench in the graveyard to pass the hour, but as he was leaving Harriet collared him for his mobile number, so he's a couple of minutes late. Is Dee already here? Will she even appear?

He's on the point of giving up when a man with tousled blond locks opens up. 'Yeah?'

'Is Dee in?'

'Nooo.' Then, 'Are you expecting her to be here?'

Another voice from behind him: 'Who is it, Ed?'

Joel blows out his agitated breath. Bloody hell, this is Ed Stephens. The transatlantic accent, the hair. He'd never have guessed.

As though trying to place him, Ed frowns. 'A bloke,' he says over his shoulder. 'He says he's come to see Dee.'

'Really?' Then a laugh. 'So let the poor bugger in!'

Inwardly groaning, Joel strides into the hallway. Brother and sister both stare, their mouths open expectantly. This is not going well. He clears his throat. 'Dee ... Cordelia asked me to meet her here.'

The sound of footsteps makes them turn. Pink-cheeked and pelting through the front door, Dee almost collides with him.

'Sorry, Mari, I ran to explain but ...' She glances his way. ' ... he beat me to it.' Though panting, she chuckles nervously. 'It's nothing to worry about. He's the guy who ... He's Vincent's paramedic. I just wanted a word with him. You know, in private?'

Mari's eyebrows are raised and Ed is clearly stifling a snigger.

Dee scowls at them. 'Not funny, guys.' She gestures to the front room. 'Is it OK if we ...'

Mari takes a breath, but Ed beats her to it. 'Go for it,' he says with a grin. 'Knock yourselves out *in private*.'

Once the door has clicked to, they hover in the lofty lounge in stark silence. Her colour even more heightened, Dee eventually glances over.

'I'm here like you asked.' She folds her arms. 'Well, go on. What did you want to say?'

He sighs and perches on the armchair. 'Aren't you going to sit? There's a lot to explain.'

'I don't want explanations; I don't want to know; I want you to get out of my life, *whoever* you are.'

'That was spur of the moment, when we first met. I've no idea why I said it. It was stupid. But once I'd told the fib—'

'Fib? A bloody *fib*? Just like you took the photograph of me, I suppose. Oh dear, a silly mistake. But once you'd posted it to humiliate me, you just couldn't help tormenting me a little more, I suppose?'

'I'm not following . . .'

'You were *him*, the troll, weren't you?'

It takes him a moment to adjust his tortured thoughts. Ah, the Facebook image. He spreads his hands. 'No, I have no idea—'

'And I'm meant to believe it? I'm meant to believe anything that comes out of your mouth?' Her eyes are bright with anger. 'Just me, just my face, gradually revealed. Why was that, I wonder? Why not you or your—'

'I don't know. But that's not why—'

'We were . . . intimate . . . you and me. I don't just mean sex. I told you things I've never told anybody else, ever. To a man who . . .' She seems to grope for words. 'Who stole someone else's identity.'

His pulse thudding in his ears, Joel looks at the carpet. 'It's just a name, a stupid mistake in the moment.'

'It isn't just a name, though, is it? It's a dead child's! Pretending to be someone else isn't acceptable or normal on any level, but a poor parent's beloved—'

'Cal was my brother.'

She stops pacing and stares. 'How do I know that's not another lie? Like that woman Cristina?'

'You don't, but—'

Though he tries to drag in some air, his heart is battering his chest, his shirt stuck to his back. Can he explain, confess? Can he tell the story from the start without howling with grief, remorse and deep, ugly guilt? No, now isn't the time; he isn't ready; he might never be.

'But what?' she demands.

He shakes his head; he has to get away.

Dee follows him out. 'And what about New Year's Day?'

'What about it?'

Her eyes narrow. 'How did you know I'd be there?'

'That doesn't matter. What matters is that I'm trying to—'

She roughly wipes her nose. 'Just leave. Don't ever come near me again.'

Blood pounding his temples, he hops down the step, then finds himself turning.

'You haven't listened; you haven't listened for a fucking moment! What *matters* is that I came here to tell you about my brother and how he died.' His anger abruptly spent, he takes a shuddery breath and meets her eyes. 'I came to confess that I killed him.'

92

Holy Saturday

Mariana

Stony-faced, Mari tosses her mobile to one side. Another lovey-dovey text from Britt – and a picture of her pulling a sad face to boot. No Isak in it this time. No doubt he's with her mum and dad in Stockholm while she's 'bored to tears' partying on a yacht or dressed more like Abbey and gadding about with a bunch of friends on one of the stunning islands.

Did she truly think Mari wouldn't find out? Well, yes, probably. Britt knows she and Dee don't have Instagram accounts or bother much with social media in general. And besides, she's clearly relying on Mariana continuing to be a blind bloody dolt, a malleable fool, just like she's been for the last eighteen months.

Bloody Britt. So very good at getting her own way, batting her eyelashes and flashing that smile when needed. So polished at sleight of hand, like when she pulled out that huge 'let's have a baby' carrot.

Mari has no idea how to deal with it. To stop Ed from eavesdropping on Dee's conversation with the attractive stranger yesterday, she dragged him away to the kitchen.

'What should I do about Britt?'

At thirty-three, he's nearer Britt's age than she is, and she wanted an honest opinion.

'In what respect?'

'The photos, the fibbing, of course . . .'

'Has she lied?'

'I suppose not. OK, omissions rather than actual lies.'

He shrugged. 'You're the psychologist . . .' he started, then he sighed. 'Maybe see it from her point of view. I'd hate anyone to pin me down.'

'But not everyone is quite as commitment-phobic as you are, Ed. She has a small baby; she made a pledge, if you like, and has a responsibility—'

'Who says she's not being responsible with Isak?'

'OK, then to me.'

'Has she ever been unfaithful?'

'No.'

'Does she text you several times a day?'

'Yes.'

'If you were on holiday and were invited to a party, would you go and drink the place dry?'

'Possibly.'

'Well, there's your answer.'

She was still trying to get to the nub of what her real worries were when shouting from the hallway interrupted them. Ed's amused expression fell. 'Bloody hell, did you hear that? Shall I go and intervene?'

But the door slammed and Dee entered the kitchen. 'Don't ask,' she said, white as a sheet. 'I need to get back to Vincent.'

Now stepping to the mirror, Mari fluffs her hair. She will get to the bottom of whatever that was all about, but at present she has another mission. It isn't everyone's idea of a Saturday-afternoon outing, but she finally finished reading Roh's dissertation this morning and phoned him to talk it through.

'I know it's a big ask, but is there any chance of doing this in person so I can make notes?' he asked. 'You're very welcome here, or I can come to yours . . .'

She wipes off the plum lipstick and applies a brighter shade. Quite honestly, she needs to get out of the house. She promised Ed her car, but she'll catch the bus to Rusholme, give Roh her feedback, then she and Ed can partake in a few beers and a curry afterwards. It isn't a patch on Britt's partying, but she'll make sure Ed takes a photo and posts it.

Rohan's top room is pretty damned nice for a student's. Taking the whole roof space, it's decked out in replica furniture, including a bureau and leather Chesterfield chairs. Or perhaps they're actually pristine antiques. Most interesting. Though he is studying for a PhD, so he's older than an undergraduate . . . Not that there was a shortage of those when she climbed the two sets of elegant stairs.

The session has been heart-warming. Roh is so respectful and flattering about her work – and incredibly easy on the eye when he smiles, which seems to be all the time – plus he's bright and absolutely knows his stuff, which is hardly surprising with a medical degree. She inwardly smirks. Why didn't he pursue that route like his mum? He could have 'inseminated' her instead of scatty Konnie. And if he'd offered a personal donation, it would have been rude to say no!

She's only having a little joke to herself, but it still makes her chuckle. Bad Mari, like the old days. After they finished their intense discussion and debate, Roh rewarded her with chilled beer from a mini fridge in the corner. The first bottle quenched her thirst, the second is going straight to her head, perfect timing for her curry.

She glances at her watch, surprised at the time. Goodness, the last few hours have flown. Finishing the last of her drink, she inhales to take her leave, but a surge of loud music interrupts.

'Someone's birthday. Danita's, maybe.' Roh rakes back his glossy hair. 'You should stay and party. Fish and chips for this one, I think. I owe you big time for today, but you could call it part-payment.' He stands. 'Keep your stuff in here. No one comes in.'

Leave her Mulberry handbag as well as her laptop? Mari listens to the bass beat. Why the hell not? 'Thanks, I will.'

She follows his tall frame until he points to a door. 'The kitchen. I'm not sure when the food's arriving, but drinks are in there, dancing's in the basement.' He smiles. 'Help yourself to both. See you later.'

The high-ceilinged room is already heaving with lively young people. Remembering her last *oldist* experience with the Fab Three, a swift exit and a Jalfrezi seems more sensible after all, but as Mari turns, she almost collides with Konnie.

'Mariana, darling! Rohan said you were coming by. We're both so grateful.'

Though it's only half-past nine, she's unsteady on her

feet and her voice is slurred. Dr Konnie a boozer? Bloody hell, who knew?

She clutches Mari's arm. 'I haven't forgotten our chat and of course now isn't the time, but if we get things wrong, we need to know.' She picks up a glass, sloshes in red wine and thrusts it at her. 'Feedback. That's how we all learn. Well, case in point with you and my beautiful boy today . . .'

Pulling Mari with her, she scans the hallway until she sees Rohan. She blows him a theatrical kiss, then continues to prattle, apparently oblivious to her son's throat-slitting and gun-to-the-temple shenanigans behind her. After a few minutes she tuts. 'Why children don't believe parents can see through the backs of their heads, I'll never know,' she says, before drifting away.

Catching the tang of vinegar, Mari throws back her drink and hunts for sustenance. An overweight girl with a freckly face is guzzling down chips, so Mari joins her, ignoring her look of astonishment as she shares her greasy cone. Then she moves on to more alcohol and random hugs, finally finding herself being tugged down to the basement.

Once on the dance floor, she studies her captor. This young woman is sharp-featured with an equally sharp smile. 'I know who you are. Roh said,' she shouts above the thumping rap.

Without waiting for a reply, she drags Mari into a smooch, then plants a firm kiss on her lips. More surprised than offended, she pulls away, but the girl simply grins. 'You are an icon, do you know that? A psychology legend.' She holds out her palm. 'Do you fancy? Takes the edge off if you're shy.'

Mari looks at the tab on offer. She's Mariana Stephens; of

course she's not *shy*. And yet over the last eighteen months she's lost sight of that person, her confidence and self-worth. But it isn't all bad; she's apparently an icon *and* a legend! If she'd taken up the offer from Cambridge, she'd be that every day, but the praise still feels bloody brilliant. Plus she's at a student party and some twenty-year-old is trying to pull her. Should she suggest a selfie so she can stick it on Instagram with the hashtag #NotTheOnlyOneHavingFun?

Without thinking about it too deeply, she takes the proffered pill and swallows it.

'Twenty minutes and you'll be rolling,' sharp girl says with a grin. 'In the meantime, let's get another beer.'

'Sure. I just need the loo.'

Having shaken her keeper off, Mari glides from room to room, drinking and gabbing to anyone about anything. God, she feels good; she'd forgotten this effortless energy, inner strength and peace. An arm around her shoulder makes her turn.

'How's it going?' Roh asks.

'Good.' The inspiration sudden, she pauses for a moment. 'Oh God, that's a great idea.'

'What is?'

'Another angle for your dissertation.'

'OK . . .' He's smiling; though when does he not? 'Shall we go up?'

Grabbing a bottle on the way, she follows him to the attic, but when he closes the door, he softly pushes her against it. Oh no; embarrassing. He clearly thought 'another angle' was a euphemism . . . She chuckles to herself; it's actually quite funny. She considers how to explain but his mouth is already on hers, then his hand's up her skirt, tugging at her knickers.

366

A crossroads, she thinks. One sign says 'consent', the other 'rape'. One says 'betrayal', the other 'revenge'. But her body has already decided for her; consumed with sudden lust, she hungrily kisses him back and unbuckles his belt with knowing fingers.

93

Cordelia

His head on my chest and his breathing regular, I absently stroke my husband's hair from his brow. He's finally asleep, I hope.

It feels oddly intimate; save for hugs, we haven't been this physically close for years. Replaced by comforting rubs on the upper arm or kisses on my cheeks, our sex life stopped after Luke died. Full intercourse, at least. Vincent feigned respect for my 'fragile mental health' – otherwise known as grief – but of course the real reason was babies. He didn't trust me not to get pregnant again; he thought me incapable of rearing a child.

It was fair enough, really; I'd snuffed the life out of one of our children and was barely there for the other.

He cried again tonight, tears streaking his pallid face before he slept. That was weird too, his meekness particularly. Right now I'm the dominant spouse, full of wise words and advice about the implantable defibrillator device.

'I'm endeavouring to be brave, Cordelia, I truly am, but I've read that I'll be bruised and aching for some time,' he keened like an infant. 'They say it causes shortness of breath and darts of pain. That you can't even sleep on your left side.' Then later, 'It'll be like an alien, a foreign body inside me. It gets cold in winter, and overheats in the sun. You can't even use an induction hob, for goodness' sake!'

Nodding quietly, I listened to his list of worries and fears. They sounded petty and puerile compared to the risk of another cardiac arrest and possible death, but I'm not him; I'm not this terrified shadow of a person. I feel genuine pity, but determination too.

'It's understandable, love, but you're dwelling on all the negatives.' Then, when he tried to interrupt, 'If you had another cardiac arrest, would you want CPR again?'

'Yes, of course.'

'If you were on life support, would you want me to ensure the doctors did everything humanly possible to bring you back to us?'

'You know I would.'

'No "Do Not Resuscitate" in bold red felt-tip pen at the end of your bed?'

That brought a small smile. 'Correct.'

'That answers all your doubts. Look, Vincent, it's a clever and wonderful device, there to be your personal lifesaver. Tomorrow we'll call the consultant and tell him you've decided to have it fitted. OK? Decision made. Now go to sleep.'

Who'd have thought there'd be this role reversal one day? He's always been the strong one; I've thanked God for it many a time. Especially during that night, the early hours of that dreadful, dreadful morning. Though he had tears in his eyes, he was there for me, he understood my guilt and terror: *It wasn't your fault. It was a tragic, tragic accident. We'll say Luke died in his cot. That he simply never woke up. Understand? Trust me, Cordelia, people will be kinder; it will be better for you this way.*

I peer at his restful face. Can I extract myself without disturbing him? He's heavy on my ribcage, the slight discomfort from New Year's Day still there. Or is that just a bitter-sweet memory? The bruise, the heartache, *him*. I don't want to think about 'Cal' but I have done so almost constantly since I saw him at Mari's. Did he really kill his brother? The notion is incredible; I'm struggling to believe it. But he stole the boy's name; he lied to me for weeks; the man I loved doesn't exist.

God, *loved*. Did I love him?

Thinking that sleep will never come, I close my eyes and immediately trip into darkness. I'm running, my bare soles slapping the pavement. No one and nothing else is there, no houses, no people, no trees. Aware that the road is dangerous, I don't cross, but as I pace past the bus shelter, something catches my attention. I snap back to look. It's a pram, a lone buggy, and to my horror it's rolling into the path of an accelerating vehicle. I have no choice; I have to cross right now. My body taut, I plunge forward and—

The crushing impact jerks me to consciousness. Blowing out my trapped breath, I sit up and look around. I'm in my bed at the vicarage and my husband has moved back to his own pillow. It wasn't real, thank God. Putting a hand to my breast, I feel my thrashing heartbeat through the brushed cotton. Yes, the rib is still tender.

I quietly lie back. A nightmare, simply a bad dream. Yet the image of the car still burns behind my eyelids. Silver paintwork, bright headlights, a clear windscreen.

And 'Calvin Rafferty's' tight, angry face right behind it.

94

Mariana

Mari pulls down the mirror flap. Though it's well past midnight, the lights through the 'Curry Mile' seem unduly bright.

'Are you sure you're not over the limit?' she asks, squinting at her brother behind the wheel.

'No idea.' Ed shrugs. 'You demanded the instant lift. "Right now, Edmund," I think were your precise words.'

Just wanting to get home, she hunkers down and zones out of Ed's chatter. The evening has been too, too surreal; she can't even remember parts of it. Was Konnie really at a student party, her bleary face invading Mari's personal space and talking on fast-forward speed? Maybe she was high; everyone else was. She guffaws to herself; one good thing about being a psychologist – nothing and no one surprises her. Ever.

She inwardly groans; least of all herself.

Ed's still jabbering and she wishes he'd stop. She'd usually tell him to, but it's good of him to turn out so late and so promptly.

'Say again?' she mutters as he bumps her SUV up the kerb outside the house.

'Dee's lover . . .'

'Her *lover*?' Mari rolls out of the car. 'We don't know that.'

He laughs as he follows her with the keys. 'Oh, but we do. It's been bugging me; I'm sure I know him from somewhere.'

She stands back to let him open the door. 'The suspense is killing me. Go on, then.'

'Not there yet, but it'll come.' He glances at her, then does another take. 'You're high! Thought you were supposed to be drunk.'

'Both. Neither. I need water.' She heads to the lounge. 'Please. I'll meet you on the sofa.'

Moments later he's back with a pint glass and a bag of crisps. He settles himself in the armchair. 'Go on then, what happened?'

'Nothing. What do you mean?'

'You left at five with your laptop and a studious expression; you flag me down at two a.m. without a handbag and well, dare I say it? A touch of gurning.'

'A party. It turned into a rave,' she replies, closing her eyes.

Ed's words finally land. 'Oh God, my Mac.' She pats the cushion around her. No Mulberry either. Just her mobile still glued to her hand.

Her palms beseeching, she leans to her brother. 'Dearest Ed. Tomorrow can you do me a favour?'

'Depends . . .'

'Go back to Rusholme and recover my stuff.'

'And where, precisely, will I find it?'

'Top bedroom; the attic.'

'And why can't you make the trip yourself?'

She throws back her head and laughs. This is Ed, for God's sake, they've always 'fessed up'. Mostly, anyway. 'My PhD student – so to speak – pinned me against a door and snogged my face off.'

'And it would have been rude to say no?'

'Something like that.'

'So, what happened then?'

'It was all a bit wham, bam, then he got an urgent call from his mate downstairs. His girlfriend was on her way up.' She blows out her cheeks. 'I expect I brushed shoulders with her on the stairs. A close call and thank goodness no actual—'

'Coitus interruptus?' He motions a pregnant belly with his hands. 'That might've been a tricky one to explain to Britt.'

'I wish.'

'And that means?'

It has been on her mind in some guise or other for bloody years; she might as well just say it out loud. 'I had an abortion when I was seventeen.'

'Wow. I didn't know that.'

And though she knows it's irrational and she has no clinical evidence whatsoever: 'I think it made me infertile.'

'What?' He sits up. 'You've paid thousands of pounds for artificial insemination and—'

'Well, it hasn't worked, has it?'

He gazes for a while. 'You *think* ...'

'I know, but ...' Her throat clogs and tears burn her eyes. As illogical as it is, can she spit out her deepest fear that her *failure* is divine justice or punishment?

But Ed climbs from his chair and pulls her into a hug. 'I'm guessing you're basing this theory on something highly technical like ...' He smirks. 'Like the number of magpies you saw on a given day. So in truth there's every possibility you can and will have a baby?'

'I had my chance and I blew it. I know it's never going to happen.' She puts a palm to her chest. 'In here.'

'More like here.' He taps his temple. 'You are crackers – you know that, don't you? Bloody Mystic Meg, like our ma.'

They fall silent for minutes, but Ed eventually sighs. 'Come on, Mariana. I'm thirty-three and a big boy. Don't you think it's time to tell me what really happened with Mum?'

95

Easter Sunday

Cordelia

I gaze at the lawn through the kitchen window. Dappled by April sunshine, Vincent is sitting on the bench, sipping a mug of tea. It was his old spot for a nifty fag when his mother's back was turned, particularly by moonlight. Has he given them up? God, I hope so. Even more importantly, is he taking his meds? Yes, Harriet's on that particular mission, so surely he will be.

Before breakfast she charged up to me with an unsettling expression, but instead of the expected broadside, she dragged me into her arms.

'Thank you for talking him round,' she said. 'I know we don't always see eye to eye, but we are on the same page about Vincent.' She squeezed my hand. 'And that's what counts – family. We are and always will be that.'

My mobile rings so I pull it from my pocket. It's Mari, my real *family*. 'Hi, Mari, how's things?'

'Yeah, fine. Just a quick one. I have a thumping head.'

I smile. 'Don't tell me, Ed's a bad influence.'

'Yeah, something like that.'

She does sound pretty groggy. 'So how can I help?'

'Look, I won't pretend we didn't hear part of your conversation with the guy who came round on Friday, particularly what he said as he left, but I think you should get in touch with him.'

'What?' I shake the disbelief from my head. This morning I sat through the Easter service with clenched buttocks, worried I'd turn around and spot his glowering, tight face. 'Why on earth would I do that?'

'Me and Ed got the impression he means something to you.'

The rush of emotion cracks my voice. 'He gave me a false name, Mari. He told me a string of lies. And what he said about his brother—'

'Well, it's up to you. But if you want to talk it through with me, you know I'm here. Bye for now; I'm going back to bed.'

As though it might give answers, I stare at my phone. What does she mean? And why didn't she just *say* it as usual?

Reverting to the window, I endeavour to walk through my conversation with 'Cal'. My mind is so sluggish it's difficult to recall, but he tried to say something. He was like an over-pumped tyre, buckled with the need to let it out. But I talked over him, didn't I? I let my anger and disappointment dominate the whole exchange. And when I accused him of being the Facebook troll, he seemed genuinely puzzled.

I zoom in on the garden, the sun-marbled scene. Chatting and eating an ice lolly, Abbey has joined Vincent on the bench, and Harriet hasn't yet returned from church. Did Cal post the snap? Now is a good time to find out.

*

My fingers refusing to behave and my laptop too slow, I finally load Facebook. Over the last few days I've masked this particular trauma with layers of other emotions – dread, worry and concern about Vincent, then the clash of feelings about 'Calvin' – but the anxiety is now back in full force, battering and whipping my chest. Is the culprit still posting the picture? Does it show more through the windscreen? And suppose it names me? God, I feel faint, but I do need to know.

My eyes sweep the plethora of fresh activity, mainly heart-warming messages to me and Vincent from well-wishers. They rest on a pending post for approval. It's a photograph, *the* photograph.

Barely breathing, I lean forward and squint at the image. Yes, there I am on the right, wearing the running cap and staring through the windscreen. And as for the left side ... Oh God, it's no longer obscured; his head turned towards me, the driver is there.

Relief seeps out in a smile. The photographer isn't Cal; what-ever else has happened, he hasn't done this.

'God, you're so, so pathetic.'

I snap around to the voice at the door. 'Oh, hi! I didn't hear you come in.'

Abbey gestures to the screen, her mouth in a sneer. 'Yeah, you were too intent on gazing at your boyfriend.'

'Sorry?' I close the laptop lid. 'I was just updating the church—'

'Turns you on, does it? Having a peep?' She laughs derisively. 'I couldn't decide whether you were just plain stupid or whether it excited you to see it.'

'I don't know what—'

'Facebook settings, Mum. You only had to ask.'

Like acid, comprehension is slow but blistering. 'It was you? You kept posting the photograph?' My throat constricted, my words emerge in a whisper. 'You went to all this trouble? The gradual reveal? The taunting. The ... the wording. Why? Why would you do that?'

'Why?' Though Abbey guffaws, it's laced with hysteria. 'Because I hate you! Because you're a bitch who's shagging some random man behind my dad's back.'

Gobsmacked, I gape. This is Abbey, my own flesh and blood. I understood that someone, somewhere, wished me ill, but my own daughter? Yet what does she really know? I was in a stranger's car, that's all. 'It's not what you think, Abbey. We were just having a chat—'

'Don't fucking lie!' Angry tears wreck her face. 'Don't you think I could have taken more if I'd wanted to? Have you any idea how humiliating it was? I was with my friends. "Hey, Abbey, is that your mum in that car?" one says. Then another's pulling out his mobile to take a pic. "No, let me. I'll take it," I say. Pocketing his to make sure I was the only one with evidence of *that*? Can you imagine how disgusting it was to see my own mother snogging like she was twelve years old? And the rest.' She points a trembling finger. 'You brought it on yourself; you deserved to be punished.'

Struggling to process the clamour in my mind, I stare at the floor. What was Abbey doing in the woods and with whom? Why didn't she say something rather than take this spiteful approach? My God, how much does my own child despise me?

Yet part of me understands it too; I was there myself at fourteen, lunging at Dad with that carving knife. And though he was cowering and protecting himself with his arms, I didn't stop slashing until Mum physically held me back. '*Stop, Dee. Just stop. He's not worth it, love. You're only hurting yourself.*'

Then there's another thought: Abbey didn't tell Vincent. Even before he was ill, for whatever reason, she hasn't told him.

'You haven't mentioned anything to Dad ...'

Roughly wiping her face, Abbey lifts her chin. 'Not yet. But that doesn't mean I—'

'Mean what, Abbey?'

Both jumping, we turn to the doorway. Harriet is filling it, her cheeks red from the exertion of running up the stairs.

She catches her breath. 'Mean what, Abbey? I could hear you shouting from downstairs. I won't have it.' She rotates from mother to truculent daughter. 'Do I have to remind you both that our patient has been very ill and is *recuperating*. That means resting, not listening to arguments.' She looks to the heavens. 'It's Easter Sunday too – have some respect.'

She finally eyeballs me. 'I don't know what you've done to upset my grandchild, but I suggest you take a long walk to clear your head.'

96

Mariana

Ed puts his head around the bedroom door. 'I know it's a Sunday but it's three o'clock in the afternoon. This is getting ridiculous. You know that, don't you? I've brought you another cuppa. You need to sit up.'

Mari groans and pushes her face into the pillow. She hasn't felt this shit for a long, long time. Physically, emotionally, spiritually. Right now she wishes she believed in something other than magpies to give her guidance. Why not God? That's a superstition just as much as not putting new shoes on the table, picking up a pin or making a silent wish when cutting a birthday cake. All the old wives' tales her mum planted and nurtured. Obeying those myths didn't save Felicity though, did they? They didn't stop her buying pills from various outlets and a litre of whisky to end her own life.

'*Please answer your phone, Mariana.*'

She finally admitted it to Ed last night: their mother's death wasn't the more palatable version she'd related to him and Dee at the time. It wasn't an accidental overdose of painkillers, an understandable and tragic confusion about how many Felicity had already taken because she was 'a touch the worse for wear'.

'Unintentional paracetamol poisoning,' she firmly told them at the time. 'It happens more often than people think.'

Yes, she came clean with Ed, but what she didn't tell him was the carnage she'd witnessed. The usually pristine bedroom – this bedroom – was wrecked and perfumed by vomit and booze. Same with their mother – her unrecognisable face was yellow and patchworked by splatters of her own insides. What had finally killed her? Liver or kidney failure? Pancreatitis or lactic acidosis? Or maybe alcohol poisoning from downing the whisky, not her usual tipple of wine.

Or perhaps simply the failure of the last man standing.

How long was Mari there before calling it in? Scrubbing the carpet and wiping the woodwork, hand-bathing her dead mother with a soft sponge like a baby, gently pulling clots of spew from her hair. Changing her nightie and sheets. Opening the window until the breeze blew the stench away. All the things Felicity had managed herself until that final, fatal explosion.

Of course, Mari didn't fool the pathologist; she hadn't intended to. She just wanted to protect her younger siblings from the horror and inevitable guilt of a suicide. Her father and herself, too. She needed to alter the mental picture, replace that husk of a body with her beautiful mum, the one who'd hidden her unhappiness and alcoholism so well.

From everyone but her. She knew; Mari knew. And not just that . . .

She now comes back to her brother, still hovering, still there. He batters a pillow and climbs on beside her. 'You're on a downer, that's all.' Then after a moment, 'It's fine, Mari. I'd guessed about Mum, so it's no biggie. I just wanted to know for sure.'

Mari looks at her hands: they're trembling. Not from last

night's booze or dope, but the vision of her mother, now sitting in broad daylight at the end of the bed.

'*Why didn't you save me, Mari?*'

Ed's comment finally landing, she blinks Felicity away and turns to him. 'Why did you need to know?'

'A ticked box, I guess.' Smiling ruefully, he shrugs. 'Either way, I still feel guilty for leaving.'

'You knew she was drinking heavily?'

'Yeah, at times. But it wasn't just that.' He rakes unsteady fingers through his hair. 'She wasn't nice with it – you know, a mean drunk. She didn't make me feel very good about myself.'

Mari waits for more.

'A failure, lazy; a disappointment, a druggie. I couldn't wait to get the hell out.' He pinches his nose. 'When she said goodbye at the airport, she was our sober, loving mum, but I barely gave her a second glance. That was the last time I saw her.'

97

Joel

Joel parks the car and glances around. It's not exactly a traditional place for a stroll, but it's still pretty. The blossom has carpeted the grass in pink and the sun, although thin, is trying for a smile. He rotates to his boy in the back. 'Ready for a walk?'

Zachary smiles. He's a 'smiley baby' as Sadie puts it, but each and every one still makes Joel catch his breath. Despite everything there's this, the gift of a child; he's incredibly lucky to *feel* it.

He pulls the buggy from the boot. Getting used to it now, he opens it smoothly first time. Scooping his solid little son from his seat, he kisses his cheek and tastes cocoa.

'How come your mummy gives you chocolate?'

But it's Easter Sunday, of course, the day of all days to have a first taste. Even though their childhood garden was small, he and Calvin would search behind bushes and bins and pots, hoping for treasure. They always found it.

Squinting ahead, he shakes off the memory. Since their mother's visit, Cal has been in his thoughts almost constantly. Not that he ever went away; he was always there in his nightmares.

With a sigh, he comes back to the mission at hand.

Dee texted an hour or so ago:

Do you have ten minutes to spare this afternoon?

He was shocked to receive any communication at all after Friday, and though part of him was pleased, he sat back and ruminated. Dee shouted him down; she didn't allow him to say what he desperately needed to. And yet he understood too; she felt hurt and betrayed; she let emotion take over. And if feelings were there, well ... it gave him a flicker of *something*. Was it hope?

But he glanced down at Zach, sleeping soundly in his arms, and replied:

Sorry, I can't. I have my son with me today.

She messaged back:

**Understand completely. I'm spending time
with mine too.**

It took him all of thirty seconds to change his mind:

Zach's asleep now, but I'll be there as soon as I can.

He now scans the paths as he walks. Once, when he and Dee were warm and sweaty and tangled, she'd mentioned a memorial bench for her Luke. '*Silly,*' she'd said, '*but I'm constantly afraid of it being stolen, damaged or defaced. It's only a bench, after all.*'

He felt a sob of his own grief blister up that day, but he couldn't bring himself to be honest about Calvin. Can he do it today? But he doesn't know why Dee has messaged. Texts have no tone, no sensations. Like his existence before her. Empty and grey, but a whole lot less painful.

Spotting her fair hair rippling in the breeze, he pushes the pram towards her, Zachary in front like a shield. 'Dee?'

Clearly miles away, she starts at the sound. 'Oh, hi.'

'Are you OK?'

'Yes.' Her cheeks stained pink, she hitches herself up the bench. 'Thank you for coming.' She gently takes Zach's foot. 'Hello, you gorgeous boy. I like your shoes. Very smart. My mum always said you could tell a lot about a man by his footwear and teeth.'

'Mainly gums for now, I'm afraid.'

Feeling stupidly shy, he sits down. Though this is a cemetery and not a bus stop, there's a strong sense of déjà vu. They know each other so much better now, and yet not at all.

'It was good of you to come.' Dee turns and finally makes eye contact. 'My sister told me I should talk to you.'

Well, there's a surprise; he hardly clothed himself in glory, yelling and storming from Mari's house. 'How come?'

'I don't know. She called earlier but she sounded pretty rough. A hangover, I expect, with Ed being home ...' Then straightening her shoulders, 'Maybe because I didn't let you speak on Friday. You wanted to tell me something but I ranted over you and didn't listen.' She smiles faintly. 'Even though I know how frustrating that feels, I did exactly the same.' She puts her trembling fingers to her lips. 'And I now know the Facebook troll wasn't you.'

Her voice is strained; she's clearly holding back tears by a thread.

'My daughter,' she says. 'It was her. She saw us in the woods and was angry, disgusted. It's a shock and I'm still processing it, but I don't blame her. I'd be appalled too.'

'God, sorry. That's bad. Poor kid.'

Watching Zachary drift into sleep, they fall silent. She eventually speaks. 'What's your real name?'

Joel takes a sharp breath. She's the only person he's ever lied to about it. In that moment at the pub, he was deeply pissed off: she didn't even vaguely remember him. Though he was in the year below her at primary, they were in the same athletics team, representing the school at tournaments together. He even sat next to her on the coach and made pitiful attempts to chat her up.

Or was it just pique? On some level did he offer Calvin's name to be the favourite son just for once? The youngest with the cherubic face, the one who'd pull that innocent 'It wasn't me' expression when they were up to no good? He hadn't minded taking the blame for something or nothing, but the one time it *was* his fault the outcome was devastating.

He clears his throat. 'Joel. Joel Rafferty.'

As though deciding whether the name fits, Dee studies him intently. 'And what happened, Joel?' she asks. 'Why did you kill your brother?'

98

Mariana

In a final attempt to lure her out of the sack, Ed walked into the village and returned with a ridiculously huge Easter egg. It worked; sentiment made Mari throw her legs from the warm mattress and drag them into an old pair of torn jeans. She hasn't gone far, though, not in terms of either distance or recrimination. Self-reproach is sitting on her shoulder today; she's simply changed tack.

She rocks her head on the arm of the sofa. Britt, her Britt. Only circumstances stopped her being unfaithful last night. And even then – what exactly is cheating? How far does one go to qualify? A lustful thought or a kiss? Allowing a guy to slide his fingers into her briefs? Feeling desire bolt through her body like electricity? Or does one have to do the actual dirty deed? Well, she knows where she's always stood: lip to lip. Because the kiss is the key; once that taboo has been broken, the rest just follows.

She pictures Britt's peachy face. She mentioned infidelity in the early days of their lust. They were at a church event and she was on form with her usual tactility and hugs, eye contact and silky smiles. Was Mari jealous then? So in love with her and the rosy image of them as a family, it wasn't a conscious thought, but perhaps Britt recognised it before she did.

'I know I'm a flirt,' she said, her blue gaze almost sad. 'But that's it, just friendliness. Loyalty is important. Zero tolerance, you know? Not even a kiss, not ever. OK?'

Mari took a breath to reply, but she continued to speak. 'It's important for people to like me, really like me, you know? Mum and Dad don't.'

'Of course they do! How could they not? Parents just have a weird way of showing it. I'm sure they love you deeply.'

'But like and love aren't the same things, are they? You *love* because you're supposed to; you like because you want to.'

Now pulling out her mobile, Mari looks again at today's missive. An adorable snap of Britt's parents with Isak. Such an innocent, pure and beautiful picture. Guilt thumps her chest again. Last night. Oh God.

His spider legs draped over the armchair, Ed lifts his head from the book he's reading. 'Stop beating yourself up and open the damned chocolate,' he says.

It brings a small smile to Mari's face. She lobs it over. 'You bought it for yourself, didn't you?'

'Might have done. Worked, though, didn't it? Always knew how to get you round.'

'Pesky squirt.'

'Not heard that one for a few years.' He lifts his eyebrows. 'Did I hear you talking to Dee earlier?'

She returns the raised brow. 'You know you did.'

'Why were you so cagey? Apart from your crashing and hangover, not to mention humiliation, embarrassment, lack of handbag and laptop—'

'Oh, hilarious.'

'Why didn't you just tell her I'd remembered who he was and made the connection?'

Staring at him blankly, Mari pictures the scene. Like painting a story on canvas, each and every tragic tale she's told appears in technicolour behind her eyes before fading – she hopes – to soft pastel.

'It wasn't my place,' she replies.

Pastel means she's made a difference; she's helped her clients remove some of the sting from the harsh, agonising vividness of their memories.

She shakes herself back to her brother. 'That egg looks a lot smaller out of the box. Throw me a piece, will you?'

He chucks over half. 'Even-stevens. Or should I say Stephens.'

'Ta.' Mari chews the chocolate thoughtfully. Despite her confession to Ed last night, *her* personal tapestry is still painful and bright.

99

Cordelia

The sun has disappeared, leaving a sharp, tingling wind. Pulling the blanket from the hood of the buggy, I tuck it around the sleeping baby. My boy wasn't allowed to grow this big. The thought brings on the usual burn of sadness behind my eyes, but I'm no longer covetous, thank God. Isak's birth was a huge relief in that respect; replaced with vicarious joy, the envy has gone. It's an enormous alleviation as that sin was so wearing: births, baptisms, the family service, parties and even school events. So I'd bow out and hide away in the attic rather than face my own abhorrent resentment.

An absent mother; no wonder Abbey hates me. Before leaving the house I went to find her. No words can make up for the disgust and trauma I've caused my only child, but I wanted to say something. After searching high and low, I found her hunched at Vincent's study desk, of all places. Quickly closing the drawer, she turned, her expression sullen.

'Don't,' she'd said. 'Just leave me alone.'

Was she looking for cigarettes? I considered warning her against that route, especially with heart problems in the family, but I simply said, 'You are the last person in the world I want to hurt but I have. I'm so sorry.'

I now glance at the man by my side. I have horribly wounded Abbey and understand why she loathes me right now, but I don't regret my time with Joel. With him I felt free. And now he's here in the flesh, I know I'll forgive whatever he's done. He regrets it, for sure, the agony is etched on his face.

He hasn't spoken since stating his name, nor has he answered my question. Instead, raw emotion and uncertainty have flashed through his eyes. 'Joel?' I prompt.

'It's getting cold. Maybe I should . . . ' He looks at his sleeping boy. 'Maybe this isn't a good idea.'

Hitching closer, I rest my head on his shoulder. 'Just tell me.'

'OK.' He takes a deep, shuddery breath. 'I don't even remember whose idea it was, but I was taller, so I went to the kitchen and found the candles.' He glances at me. 'Mum was on nights, so . . . '

I wait for him to say more. When he doesn't, I ask, 'How old were you?'

'Ten, almost eleven. For one month of the year me and Cal were the same age.'

'So you were the year below me at school?'

He snorts. 'Yup.'

Wondering about his light derision, I quieten again.

'So, yeah, it was all about the lure of a candle. And matches, of course. It was fun. Lighting the wick and blowing it out, again and again.' He swallows. 'Like on a birthday cake, except these were baptismal candles. You know the sort?'

'Yes, of course.'

His expression terse, he falls silent again. He was ten years of age; whatever happened, he was only a child, so it's forgivable, surely?

'Playing with matches, like millions of other kids,' I say quietly.

'Maybe.' He gazes at me, his face hollow. 'But the alcohol was solely my idea. A last-minute snatch from the same high kitchen cupboard. A bottle of Tia Maria, half full. We didn't even like the coffee taste.' As though breathless, he puffs out. 'But it made all the difference between life and death. If we hadn't been drunk; if we hadn't been almost unconscious; if my mind hadn't been fuddled when I stumbled down the stairs.'

His voice is strangled. 'Smoke. Thick, black, choking smoke . . .' He covers his eyes with trembling hands. 'But I left Cal behind. By the time I'd realised and tried to run back, the bloke next door wouldn't let me. Then everything seemed to happen at once. My senses suddenly engaged. The taste of ash and alcohol; the stench of fumes; an orange glow in the roof, grey clouds billowing out. The discordant peals of the fire engines and ambulance. My dad's howls and yelling. Firefighters everywhere. Looks of horror from the neighbours, paramedics and police. Then finally a body on a stretcher.'

He lets out a sob. 'So small, too small. I never saw his face again. They'd covered it with a sheet.'

100

Joel

Feeling a spasm of sadness, Joel waves Zach and Sadie goodbye, opens his car door and wedges the oven dish in the passenger footwell.

What a difference time makes. Erica hugs him these days. Gives him a home-cooked casserole or scones or a fruit loaf and says, 'Thanks for having Zachary. How he loves to see you. Remember to take care of yourself, lovey.'

Every time. Does he look so dreadful? Do his culpability and rage emit from his whole being, even after all these years? Or maybe he just looks knackered, exhausted by night terrors and dreams. He doesn't know which are worse, the petrifying nightmares or comforting visions. In the former he's there in full action, classic PTSD mode, ripping away the strong arms of his neighbour, belting back into the burning house, howling and sobbing as the stench fills his nostrils and flames burn his eyes. *'Where are you, Cal? Get out! Get out! Get out right now!'*

But the latter, oh God. In those he's still eight, nine or ten years of age, at home round the table, eating pizza and chortling with Cal. Or he's an adult and answers the doorbell to find a grinning, grown Calvin on his front step. So very real, he takes his brother in his arms, laughing and weeping.

'*I thought you were dead! Where have you been? Never leave again.*'

'*I won't, mate, I promise.*'

Then, like this morning, waking up with a smile before realisation stabs him: Calvin is dead; he'll always be dead. But oh, how wonderful it was to see him.

He now watches the pylons pass by. Against all expectations, today has been a good one. He collected his beautiful son, little knowing that hours later he'd introduce him to the woman he loves, then be spitting out his guilt and confessing to her. He'd wanted to do it for so long, but was fearful of her horror and condemnation. Instead he received sympathy, understanding and affection. She was so sweet with Zachary, too. And this last is important. He doesn't know how, but he wants them both in his future.

A good day, yes. A very good day. Yet the anger is still there, burning his chest. Though weeks have passed, he can't get over the sheer unfairness of his mum's request. How dare she turn up on his doorstep and ask him to forgive his bastard of a father?

'He'd just lost his son,' she said, as though there wasn't another standing a foot away from her. 'He didn't mean it. He was distraught. He was grieving. He wasn't of sound mind, if you like. And now he's—'

But Joel cut her off. He didn't want to hear any more excuses, nor a lecture about the will of God and the power of forgiveness. Instead he politely declined and asked her to leave.

It was hard not to yell at the injustice of it all. Where was his dad when the fire started? Not in their house, that's for sure.

And why hadn't he replaced the smoke detector battery, despite nagging from his mum? And what about *her*? Why was she still defending him, taking his side, even now? That shit was happy to turn to his ten-year-old, devastated child, look him in the eye and say, '*You did this, Joel. It should have been you. The wrong son died.*'

Focusing on the road, he swallows back the bitter bile. They moved from Burnage to a different area of Manchester, but from the ages of ten to eighteen, he had no option but to live with that man. He never apologised for words said in the moment; he didn't lift any of the blame from his living son's shoulders. And though Joel was there day in and day out, he looked straight through him as though he didn't exist. When he finally escaped for university, he vowed he'd do the same. From that moment onwards, his father was dead.

Nothing his mum says will ever change that.

101

Easter Monday

Mariana

Mari rings the doorbell, then steps back to inspect the handsome facade of the period property. Though she was here on Saturday, she was wearing her teacher's hat and hadn't absorbed this cluster of huge houses, a surprising oasis amid the hustle and bustle of the curry mile.

It's pretty fabulous accommodation for students, though now she looks properly, the original building has been divided into two. Frowning, she tries to remember the layout from the party. She can't recall a great deal, only the bad bits come to the fore of her mind: snogging her fertility doctor's son, unbuckling his belt and ... Oh God, she canoodled with an electric-eyed girl too, didn't she? But the young woman kissed her rather than the other way around, so that's OK. Isn't it?

Noticing the 'lovers' door knocker, she takes another shuddery breath. Britt and Isak are due back on Wednesday and Mari has promised to be at the airport despite it being slam in the middle of a busy working day. She feels pretty nauseous at the thought.

Will her face immediately give her away? Will Britt take one look, her eyes huge and hurt, and say, '*You've betrayed me, Mariana. How could you*'? And yet, and yet . . . How much does Mari really care? Isn't she getting weary of Britt's narcissistic behaviour? Bloody hell; *narcissistic*. Where did that come from? But in truth, it fits the bill . . .

She glances at her watch. Ten-thirty. Surely someone will be up? But it is a bank holiday – Easter Monday, indeed. She doesn't want to add to her embarrassment by hammering at the door and shouting, '*Give me back my bloody laptop!*' And her beloved Mulberry. She paid a stupid amount of money for it on the tenth anniversary of her mum's death. She'd always wanted one, so it felt like she was buying it for her.

'Mariana. Over here!'

Wrapped in a robe, Konnie has appeared in the porch of the adjoining property, which makes sense of Roh's Tardis loft. 'I'm guessing the whole house is yours?' Mari asks. 'Sorry. You go first. You were saying something . . . '

Konnie eyes her rather knowingly. 'You've come for your laptop and handbag. One minute, they're in my study.'

'Thanks.'

She disappears, reappears and hands them over. 'There we are. Safe and sound.'

'Right, thanks very much. I'll get off then.'

Relieved the promised invitation 'for a coffee' won't be forthcoming right now, Mari steps away, but as though realising her lack of manners, Konnie springs forward.

'Not at all. It's you who needs thanking for all your help with Roh and his dissertation.' She doesn't quite meet Mari's gaze. 'I hope you enjoyed the party. I suspect I was a little the worse for wear and I do apologise if I spoke out of turn. Though one doesn't like to mention the word *money*, I realise it's a factor, so I do understand—'

Abruptly she turns and looks up the stairs. Wearing boxer shorts and a grin, a somewhat young and muscular man has appeared on the landing. 'Two minutes, darling,' she calls. She comes back with bright eyes and flushed cheeks. 'Lovely to see you, Mariana. We really must catch up over that coffee.'

102

Cordelia

I dry the last of the morning's pots and slot the mugs on a shelf. Harriet doesn't like large cups – she deems they're for 'workmen', whatever that encompasses.

Of course, I make a show of using one whenever I brew up, another tiny act of defiance. I used a blue-and-white stripy one earlier at breakfast, but I doubt Harriet noticed as she was infused with energy about her trip to Morecambe. She and other members of the congregation are now on their way to see the statue of Eric and imbibe a cream tea at a hotel on the promenade.

In fairness, it was nice to see the excitement in her eyes; Harriet regularly organises similar outings on bank holidays and it serves a charitable purpose as the elderly and the lonely get out of their houses, even if they are bossed around mercilessly. And some people need that *direction*, like Vincent and his medication.

I glance at the pill boxes on the worktop. Today I'm Harriet's dispensing deputy. How will I fare at persuading my husband to take them? Vincent's vigour seems to double as each day passes. Even better, he's getting used to the idea of an ICD. All-around good news, but it's important he doesn't become over-confident;

I have to remind him he isn't invincible. At dinner he covered his food in a ridiculous amount of salt, and later I caught him sneaking a brandy on top of a few glasses of wine.

The kitchen clock mutely ticks. The house feels silent without Harriet's busy presence. Bereft almost; who'd have thought? Vincent came down first thing to wish her goodbye but Abbey hasn't appeared. It's completely understandable; she's avoided me since our brief exchange of words in the study yesterday. How we'll resolve it, I have no idea. Whatever my indiscretions, I'm still her mum and love her dearly; all I can do is try my best to show it.

Like synchronicity, her angry voice splits the quietness. 'You promised and you can't just stop me now.'

My ears prick. What's going on? Abbey sometimes argues with Harriet, but never her dad.

His response is too low to hear, so I tiptoe to the hall.

'You've known about it for ages; you can't do this. It isn't bloody fair!'

What on earth . . . ? Abbey is all but screaming at Vincent in the lounge. Inching forward, I peer through the gap in the door.

'I did, yes. But . . . ' Vincent is tapping his pressed palms to his mouth. 'I've changed my mind. People gossip.'

Abbey's face is deep pink, her expression livid. 'Gossip about what?'

He wafts his hand. 'Teachers and young girls.'

'What's that supposed to mean?' Her hand on her hip, Abbey glares at him. Though she's wearing the usual crop top and short skirt, a bulky rucksack is hanging from her shoulder.

Her overnight bag? I push through the entrance. 'Where are you going, Abbey?'

Her look is dismissive. 'The music trip, of course.'

400

'What music trip? I didn't know—'

'Yes, you did,' she snaps back. 'Perhaps you've been too *busy* doing other things to remember.'

As though I'm not there, Vincent clears his throat and speaks evenly to Abbey. 'I did say yes, but I've had second thoughts. He's a grown man and you're only just fifteen.'

'What's that got to do with anything? Believe it or not, Dad, not all guys are paedos. He's a *teacher* and we're there to play music. It's a string quartet retreat. It's what proper musicians do. Four of us are going with him, for God's sake. They'll be here any minute to collect me.'

Vincent wipes a bead of sweat from his forehead. 'The answer is still no, Abbey.'

'You can't do this! It's the one thing I've been looking forward to for ages. I can't believe you're being so unfair . . .' Her eyes narrowing, she pauses. 'Well, it's not just down to you, is it?' She turns to me. 'You decide, Mum. Am I allowed to go? Or do I have to stay at home, bored to tears, with nothing to do other than spend time on *Facebook*?'

Frozen, I stare. I'm being blackmailed by my own daughter, aren't I? Heavens, what should I do? I scrabble for a solution but words fall out. 'So long as you promise to keep regularly in touch and stay safe. I need you to text me all the details of where you're staying and with whom. Mobile numbers of everyone too, including your teacher's.'

His voice reasonable, Vincent shakes his head as though I haven't spoken. 'No, no, Abbey. We're still celebrating Easter. As you know, Jesus remained on Earth for forty days after his resurrection, and during that time he appeared to believers, healed the sick and spread the word of God.'

401

'Dad, you knew the date when you agreed!'

He gives me the look I know so well. 'So I don't think Mum has thought this through properly, and when she does—'

'Well, it's tough. She's already said yes.' Abbey lifts her chin. 'You'll be fine, Dad. It'll be a good opportunity to catch up on your magazines.'

His features infused with ruddy colour, he stands. I flinch at the sudden movement, but also from his livid expression, which I've only seen once before.

Abbey pulls me into a hug. 'I will stay safe and send all the info, Mum. Thank you. Really. You won't regret this, I promise.' She points to the bay window. 'Look, there's Khushi and Holly. Got to go.'

Winded from shock and the speed of the turnaround, I don't move for a beat. Then I dart out, catching my girl at the open front door. Holding her by her shoulders, I look at her steadily.

'You are strong, beautiful, talented and clever, Abbey. Have a wonderful time but always remember this: never do anything you're not one hundred per cent sure about. Be brave under pressure, whatever it might be. Have the courage to voice any doubts. Call me if you need me. Even if you just feel strange or uncomfortable. Any time and anywhere and I'll come for you. But live life to the full, love, it goes quicker than you think.' I hand over a thick coat and kiss her cheek. 'Take this; the weather might turn. Have fun, keep in touch and stay safe. OK?'

Lifting her hand in acknowledgement, Abbey runs to the minibus and jumps in. I remain on the step, the breeze cooling my cheeks as I watch them depart. Moments later Vincent pushes past me.

'Where are you going?' I ask him.

'For some much-needed fresh air.'

'Wait. I'll come with you.'

His face is closed, his cheeks clenched. I know he's furious, but he doesn't raise his voice. 'I'm fine, thank you, Cordelia. We'll talk about this when I'm back.'

My whole being shaky, I return to the kitchen and sit down at the table. Have I acted responsibly? In truth, I don't know. Vincent has kept me out of this particular loop, but he clearly consented to the outing before changing his mind. He must have vetted it and cleared it with the school; he must have paid for the cost of food, travel and accommodation. But he decided against it at ridiculously short notice. Has he truly heard unsettling gossip about Mr Williams?

My mobile beeps, so I quickly scoop it up and open the text from Abbey. It's the address of a cottage in the Lakes, the contact information of her friends and the teacher. And then a few words:

Thanks for trusting me. I promise to stay safe. I will call if I need you. And I'm sorry x

I blow out my trapped breath. Good grief, what a rushed nightmare, not to mention Abbey's veiled threat. But am I just a little proud of my daughter? For standing up so fearlessly to Vincent's reasonable platitudes. For thinking so quickly on her feet. For bearing more than a little resemblance to her feisty Auntie Mariana. And yes, for her similarity to the smart and confident girl I used to be. She's been true to her word too. An encouraging start.

My thoughts rest on the old Dee Dee; if only I could find her here in this house. Joel knows her, though. Before leaving the cemetery yesterday, he kissed me softly.

'You are wasting your life there. Come and live with me. Pack your bags and leave. Abbey knows, so what is there to stop you?'

I so wanted to say, 'Yes, please. *Take me with you now and don't let me look back.*'

But my loyalty to Vincent runs deep. He helped me survive the direst of times; he put his own hard-earned reputation in peril by fabricating the truth about Luke's death; he faithfully promised he'd protect me and he's kept to his word. And besides, he's still recovering from his illness; I just have to hold on until he's had the implant, then decide about the future. Frustrating though it is, my husband is my priority for now.

Shaking myself down, I glance at my watch. It's nearly noon; if he isn't home by twelve-thirty, I'll drive out in the car to save him the walk back. In the meantime, I'll make him a light lunch and set out his medicine, one in each vial like Nurse Harriet.

In the spirit of Easter, I pull out three eggcups painted in bright colours by Abbey long ago. God, I hope she'll be safe. As though answering my prayers, her name appears on my phone. I open the message to three simple words: **Love you Mum**, with a pink heart emoji. I smile through my threatening tears. I've seen a million messages like this addressed to her daddy, but *this* one is for me.

Sniffing away the surge of hope, I revert to my chore, lining up the meds and popping out a pill from each of the first two packets. I move on to the third. Same as with the others, Harriet has written the layman's term – or perhaps the 'idiot's guide for Cordelia' – on the packaging, in this instance 'beta blockers'. I put one on my palm, but instead of dropping it into the beaker,

I bring it closer to my face. This tablet is marked with a P and a tiny number underneath.

Confused, I frown. I've seen these before, but ... but Harriet has written 'beta blockers' quite clearly on the packet. I blink and look again in disbelief. Am I sure? Completely, but I'll check nonetheless. A chair clattering behind me, I run to the hallway and take the stairs two at a time. Belting to the bathroom, I slide open the cabinet and scan the contents. Trying to still my thrashing heart, I take a deep breath and slowly look again. The tub isn't apparent, so I pull out toothpaste, razors, shaving foam and plasters, discarding them to the floor until only the empty shelves stare back.

It can't be true, can it? Oh God, am I *imagining* it? No, absolutely no, that 'P' is something I'll never, ever forget. I have to get Mari; Mariana will know what to do. My fingers fumbling, I grapple with my phone and call her.

'Hi Dee Dee! What's up?'

Stunned from the bombshell, I search for my voice.

'Dee? Are you there? You OK?'

'No.' A whisper emerges. 'Can you come here?'

'Sure, we're just about to eat a late breakfast but I could after—'

'No. I need you right now.'

103

Mariana

Ed looks up from his reading. 'You're going out again?' Then after a moment, 'What's up?'

'I don't know. Dee just called.'

He pulls his legs off the sofa and grins. 'If you'd told me how exciting it was here, I'd have come home sooner. I'll just grab my trainers.'

Mari doesn't know why, but instinct says she should go alone. 'Girls' stuff. Anyway, you promised to cook . . .'

He shows her his book jacket. 'Who says I don't keep vows? Jamie says it'll only take thirty minutes.'

'Hmm, been there, done it. Give yourself an hour, minimum.'

Though it only takes ten minutes to walk, Mari jumps in the car. She hasn't heard Dee sound quite like that since she called early one morning and whispered, 'Luke's dead.'

When she arrives at the vicarage, the front door is open, Dee immediately visible, hunkered halfway up the stairs. She squeezes in next to her. 'What's happened, Dee? Where's Vincent?'

Her eyes huge and startled, Dee turns. 'Out. A walk.' She holds out her trembling palm. 'What's this?'

Mari looks at the white pill. The hallway a little dim, she holds it up to the light. 'It's Propranolol.' Surprised at her sister's clear alarm, she studies her. 'They're Vincent's beta blockers, I assume.'

'Not P for paracetamol?'

'No, why?'

Dee puffs out several breaths, then finally inhales. 'And the side effects of taking beta blockers are?'

'Various. But I guess fatigue is the most common.'

'So taking them for the first time could make you sleep deeply and have difficulty waking up.'

'Yes. Why are you asking, Dee? Has Abbey taken some? Have you?'

Her voice cracking, Dee nods. 'I took two.'

'Really? I'm sure you'll be . . . '

But heavy tears are splashing her hands.

'What's going on? I don't—'

'I took two. Thirteen years ago I took two of those from the bathroom cabinet. He said they were paracetamol.'

Perplexed, Mari gazes. Thirteen years ago; only one thing happened then. 'OK, but why are you thinking about those dark days now? You were devastated, of course. You couldn't eat, slow down, stay still. Perhaps Vincent thought they'd help you to sleep, have a night of rest—'

The sudden yell makes her start. '*Before* Luke died, Mariana! That night!' Quietening again, Dee stares with hollow eyes. 'I had a dreadful cold and a sore throat, so I took them before bed. Paracetamol was allowed, right? You could still breastfeed.

407

I checked. I wasn't going to do anything reckless to harm my boy. Not in a million years.'

'I know that. Everyone knows that, Dee. Look, there's no way Propranolol caused the cot death. It couldn't have absorbed into your breast milk that fast. It was just a coincidence; it wasn't your fault.'

Dee roughly wipes her nose with her sleeve. 'You're right, it wasn't my fault.' She almost spits her angry words. 'All these years I've blamed myself for Luke's death and that man has let me.'

Still trying to work out her sister's logic, Mari rubs her back. 'No one's to blame. Sudden infant death happens even now, despite the research and reams of advice. It's dreadfully, horribly tragic, but no one is to blame. Not you, not Vincent. No one.'

Dee looks at her full on and takes a gulp of air. 'It wasn't a cot death, Mari. I accidentally smothered Luke while I slept. I took two of those from the paracetamol pot and gave him a last feed . . . ' She covers her mouth. 'I intended to put him in his crib, but I fell asleep, a deep sleep. When I jolted awake in the early hours, he was still in my arms, pinned against my chest. I begged and pleaded with God, but I already knew he'd gone.'

'Dear God. I'm so sorry, Dee . . . ' The shock is stunning, but there's more, Mari knows. Insects crawl on her skin. 'What happened then?'

'Vincent hadn't yet come to bed so I yelled for him and told him what had happened.' As though picturing the scene, Dee squeezes her lids shut. 'His face transformed into this unrecognisable person. He was so livid I thought he'd hit me. Then I hysterically explained about my sore throat and the pills falling helplessly asleep . . . ' Her eyes snap open. 'Guess what.

He was back to reasonable, loving and sympathetic then. Said it was an accident and not my fault, but that others might not perceive it that way. He was repeating what I'd already said to myself – that I'd killed my baby. I had *killed* him. So then he promised to protect me and sort everything out; I wasn't to worry; no one would know what had really happened. From that moment on it was a tragic cot death and I was never, ever, to tell anyone otherwise.'

Mari stares at her white-knuckled fists. She wants to say something to comfort her sister, but anger is preventing her from speech. Dee unknowingly took Vincent's beta blockers, prescribed years ago. The very same medication he took for a heart condition he hadn't seen fit to mention to his young wife. That fucking bastard had hidden the Propranolol in plain sight.

As though reading her mind, Dee nods. 'There were some in the bathroom recently. In a pot, a plastic pot with a childproof lid? I looked just now, but they've gone.'

Mari's jaw is so clenched, it hurts. 'A paracetamol tub with Propranolol inside.'

'Yes. I've never taken anything, not since that day. Period pain, toothache, sleeping problems, whatever; I've just put up with it. Vincent knows that. But Abbey had a headache a while back, so I took a couple through to her bedroom. It turned out she had her own supply in her drawer, so I put them back.'

Fury sparks through Mari's body. The evil, evil bastard. It'll probably make no difference, but she wants to find the damned things, even if only to challenge him to his face.

'If he hasn't thrown them out, where will they be?'

'His study, where he keeps his private stuff. No one else goes in there.'

'Right.' Mari stands. 'Come on, let's ...' The crunch of gravel echoes in. 'Fuck. Is that him?'

White-faced, Dee nods.

'OK. Keep him occupied down here. I'm going to have a look.'

Turning the porcelain knob, Mari pushes open the study door. The smell of *old* hits her first, followed by a hard impression of claustrophobic clutter. The room is lined with bookcases and shelves chock-a-block with tomes, folders and papers, many yellowing or curling at the edges. Antique gilt-edged bibles and an arc of prayer books are piled on the threadbare carpet, making the state-of-the-art printer look as though it's been transported from a future century.

A metal rail to one side displays a variety of cassocks and embroidered robes, and a display of ornate crosses are affixed to the wall. There's none of the cheap trash adorning the hallway downstairs; Vincent has clearly kept the best to himself. But one thing's for sure: this office belongs to a man who can't throw anything out.

She steps to the oak bureau beneath the window. Its red top is covered in paperwork, and various cups are stuck to the leather, evidence that not even Harriet comes in here. Inhaling the stench of stale tobacco, she slides onto the padded chair and studies the drawers. Four down each side and one in the middle. It doesn't have a handle but a hole to lock it. His hiding place, surely?

Hardly daring to breathe, she peeps into containers full of paperclips, pencils and pens. Where would he keep the key? If the beta blockers are anything to go by, he'll leave it in plain sight. She looks at the rows of higgledy-piggledy books, greetings cards and trinkets on the bookcase. A clumsy clay pot catches her eye. Surrounded by love hearts, 'Daddy' is painted on the front. Her stomach turns. Where the hell was 'Daddy' on that fateful night? He must have known Dee was unwell. Why didn't he go to bed, find Dee Dee asleep and put Luke in his cot?

Several keys are inside, but only one with the same clover pattern as the desk. Three leaves for luck. And he has been a lucky bastard, for far, far too long. Carefully, she inserts it and pulls open the drawer.

She pauses to listen. Why is it so eerily quiet? What are Dee and Vincent doing down there?

Her hands shaking, she weaves her fingers through the contents like a TV police search. Bills, insurance, receipts. Letters headed with the Diocese crest. Half-used packets of cigarettes further back. Two whisky flasks and a plethora of mint packets from Polo to Extra Strong. No tubs of pills, though. Even a hoarder like Vincent must have seen the sense of throwing them out once his heart condition was exposed.

Disappointed, she sits back. Where else can she hunt? But time is ticking; the man himself is downstairs. She pushes the drawer shut but an item blocks it, so she slips in her arm and feels around. Something is stuck to the underside of the tabletop . . . She tugs it out and briefly inspects a large Manilla pouch. Fully aware that she's going beyond the remit of her hunt, she opens the clasp, taps the other end and a magazine slithers out. Porn; how depressingly predictable. But goosebumps spread as she stares at the cover. Bloody hell, it isn't just the usual top-shelf titillation, but speciality filth – not so explicit that one can point the paedophilic finger, but the next best thing.

She suddenly stills. Oh God, a noise, the creak of a stair, then footsteps on the landing. All fingers and thumbs, she tries to shove the publication back, but the pages snag and a second envelope slides out and drops to the floor. Though she crouches and scrambles to put everything in, the sound of heavy breathing behind her is unmistakable. Almost peeing with alarm, she forces herself to look up and see who it is.

'Cordelia! What the hell, creeping up on me like that.' Her eyes slide to her sister's hand. 'What are you doing with that?'

Her face almost white, Dee looks down at the kitchen carver she's holding. 'I've decided. I'm going to kill him.'

'What? Don't be ridiculous. Of course you're not.'

'Oh, but I am. I'm going to stab him through the heart. He's going to watch the blade slide in and feel the pain, my pain for all these years.' Her eyes are opaque and her jaw is set. 'I've decided, Mari. I've been his concubine, his skivvy; his nurse; his prisoner; his fucking speech-writer.' She hits her chest. 'And I've lived with the guilt of killing my baby every day, every hour, every minute. He doesn't deserve to breathe a moment longer.'

Mari swallows. Bloody hell, the determined Dee Dee of old. That dreadful, dark secret has been bubbling inside without an outlet for thirteen long years; she must take the knife from her before she explodes.

'Look, I can see why you'd want to do that, but this isn't the way.' She cautiously reaches for the handle, but Dee tugs it away. 'OK, let's take a minute.' She puffs through the shock of this unexpected development. Dee's panting isn't from running or worry or grief, it's from sheer burning fury. 'So what happened downstairs? I didn't hear a thing.'

'He came into the kitchen and I showed him the pill, but he

lifted his hand and said, "Don't," before I'd even opened my mouth. Like this.' She raises a straight palm to demonstrate. '"Don't, Cordelia. I'm not very well." Silencing me, stifling me, ruling me, same as always. He thinks nothing will change. He thinks I don't have the guts to stop it, to stop him. He's wrong.'

'Yes, he is, and you'll show him that, but not like this. You have Abbey, me and Ed. Dad and even Viola. We don't want you to be locked up for the rest of your life for doing something stupid. There's your friend Joel, too.'

Tears seep from her eyes. 'I have to. For Luke, I have to.'

'Luke has gone, Dee Dee, a long time ago. You have to live your life, finally *live* it, not get imprisoned again. You've been crippled by guilt; don't sentence yourself to more. Take the high moral ground.'

Willing the words to break through her sister's resolute stance, she tries again. 'Look, Dee, Vincent's not worth it. You'd only be hurting yourself.'

Her shoulders abruptly slumping, Dee covers her face. 'Mum said something like that once.'

Mari eases the blade from her hand. 'Did she?'

'About Dad.'

'Oh, right . . .'

'It's not something I'm proud of. I'm ashamed of it, in fact. One of the reasons I didn't get in touch with him for so long.'

'And did her advice help?'

'Yes, yes, it did.' Dee frowns at the envelope. 'What's that?' She turns to the open drawer. 'What have you found, Mari?'

'Nothing much.' Mari inches away with the weapon; she doesn't want her sister goaded again. 'Where's Vincent now?'

'He went out to the garden to sit on his bloody bench.' Dee

413

snorts faintly. 'He looked pretty green but I locked the door behind him.' She goes back to Mari's find. 'Just show me what's in there. Whatever it is, I don't care.'

'No biggie, just a dodgy magazine. Usual men's stuff.' Mari moves to the door. 'Come on, I'll show you in a minute. We'd better go down and check on Vincent.'

104

Cordelia

Loathing tight in my chest, I stare at the vicar through the kitchen window. The breeze blowing his hair, he's still sitting on the bench, holding his mobile and gazing into the distance. What's he thinking about? His dead boy? His remorse? I doubt it; he'll be using his reasonable voice to himself: justifying, manipulating, considering how he can spin this particular episode. My mental health, probably: *'Darling Cordelia, you've always been a little fragile, haven't you? Isak will have unsettled the balance; you're imagining things that never happened; you're just a touch overwrought.'*

My fingers flexing, I glance at the knife block. Mari is right, frustratingly right. Though I want him to suffer, though I yearn to inflict it by my own hand and watch his agony, I'll lose a future that's just on the turn to something good: more openness and honesty with Abbey; my friendship with Viola and reconciliation with Dad. Joel. I would only be hurting myself. And apart from all that, I have no proof. It's my word against Vincent's, my fragrant, untouchable, disingenuous and clever husband who made me complicit in covering up Luke's death.

Mari's voice breaks through. 'So what now, Dee? He doesn't

look well at all. Tempting though it is, I don't suppose we can leave him out there for ever.'

'He's got his phone.' I snap around to my sister. 'He can fucking well use it to call me, to apologise, to beg for forgiveness. He's a shit, Mari. No, he's more than a shit. He's—'

Mari lifts her palms. 'I know, Dee, I know. You don't have to tell me. I'm completely with you; I'm furious too.' She tugs me to a chair. 'But we have to be realistic – as much as it galls me, we have to let this go and focus on your life going forward.'

'I know.' I gesture to the buff pouch, still clutched to Mari's chest. 'Show me.'

'Look, you don't need to . . .'

'For God's sake, Mari.' I grab it and tip out a magazine and another envelope, which I open. 'More of his "records for posterity".' I spread out the photographs of church events. 'He's always taking them. You know, for when they make the film of his heroic fucking life.'

'Looks like he's printed these himself.'

'Probably. Wouldn't do to unnecessarily waste Diocese money.'

'Why has he got this photo of Isak?'

I glance at the snap Mari's holding. 'That isn't Isak, it's him as a baby. There are more in Harriet's bedroom. Perfect son, perfect baby, as you'd expect.'

Mari frowns. 'No, it is Isak. It's definitely Isak. He's wearing the bunny romper. The one Viola gave him.'

'Britt brought him round before she went to Sweden; it was probably then.' Wondering about Mari's deep frown, I watch her rifle through the other images. 'What's wrong?'

But my tense-faced sister doesn't reply. Instead, she scrapes back her chair and darts from the room.

105

Mariana

Her spine icy, Mari runs up the stairs. The rabbit outfit. The only time she's seen Isak wear it is in an identical photograph Britt sent her last week. How come Vincent has a copy? How come he's printed it and several more of her son? And what about all those young women posing for his lens, a smiley, blonde female in particular. One with cornflower-blue eyes and pearly white teeth.

Her heart thrashes with agitation. Britt took the unopened romper to Sweden. That and the other pictures were taken there; the same ones Britt sent to her with love-heart emojis: at a bar, aboard a boat and on the beach. Wearing a winning smile and an inappropriate bloody outfit. Why would she share them with Vincent? Is there a perfectly innocent explanation or has that man been hiding in plain fucking sight?

Inhaling deeply at Harriet's door, she strides in and snatches up the framed portrait on her dresser. She stares for a beat, then stumbles back on the bed. What the hell? There's no mistaking the similarity: the images of baby Vincent and Isak are virtually identical.

Her throat dry, she tries to focus, to think. Konnie's surprise to hear Britt had had a baby, her comments about feedback and finance. Vincent wanting a fucking boy ... In hindsight it's so bloody, blindingly obvious: Britt didn't go to the fertility clinic as they'd agreed. She didn't need to; she had her own personal sperm donor.

She bends double and gasps. Mari Stephens, the great observer; the strong woman who is nobody's fool ... She didn't know. How was she so utterly, utterly heedless? Britt's extra flirtation whenever Vincent was around; his 'our' Britt and comments about 'family'; his bizarre presence at the hospital for Isak's birth.

Britt, her *loyal* Britt. Why the hell did she do it? Surely not love? Was it to save money, win the first-baby goal or just to please Vincent? Whichever it is, Mari has been played by them both. Made to fall in love, not only with Britt, but with her beautiful son.

'Mari! Quickly!'

The sharp sound of her sister's voice breaks the horror. Still holding the 'twin' photographs, she hurries down the stairs.

Dee gestures through the window. 'He put his hand to his chest, and then ... What do we do, Mari?' Though her fists are clenched, she sighs. 'I'd like to leave him to rot, but I suppose for Abbey's sake we should do something. You know what to do, recovery position, airways, whatever. You go to him whilst I call emergency services.'

Mari squints through the glass. Vincent is bent forward, his head on his knees. 'No.' She snatches Dee's mobile. 'No.'

'What?'

'We're not calling an ambulance.'

'What? Why not?'

Mari lifts the baby portraits. 'Because of these. Look. Isak

418

and Vincent. Virtually fucking identical.' She drags Dee to the table. 'And these. They were *hidden* in his desk. Sellotaped to the top of a locked drawer. Not just photos of Isak and Britt, but these young women too. Some of them look around the same age as you when you first met him. Faces from his *feminist* youth choir, maybe?'

Her skin pasty, Dee stares. 'So what are you saying . . . ?'

Mari prods the image of Britt. 'This woman is supposed to be the love of my life. Why would your husband have pictures of her and her son, who just happens to look astonishingly like him, in his secret stash? Printed off his shiny new printer for extra thumbing, no doubt.' She knows she's taking her anger out on Dee, but she can't help herself right now. 'And look at this filth,' she says, lifting the magazine. 'It's women posing as half-naked, adolescent girls . . .'

As she slams it down, a page falls open and a pink Post-it floats out.

'So what are you suggesting we do?' Dee frowns. 'What about the things you said earlier? My future? Guilt? The high moral ground?'

'I know, but . . .' Trying not to squeeze too tightly, she holds her sister's shoulders. 'You were right; we have to stop him. Apart from letting you take the full blame for Luke's death, apart from controlling you and keeping you here like a servant, undermining your mental health, moving his fat, ugly mother in and doing everything to keep you estranged from your own child . . . Apart from all that, he's been fucking Britt and in all likelihood grooming these girls; he's been *unfaithful* to you and probably many times.'

She glances at the crucifix on the wall. 'It's divine intervention,

Dee. He stopped taking his beta blockers because they made him impotent, because he couldn't get it up and satisfy his desires. *He* made the choice to put his own life on the line for a shag.' She releases her hold and speaks more gently. 'We just do nothing, Dee Dee. No one will ever know except us. Yes?'

Willing her to agree, Mari waits for her sister to speak, but she's staring at the pink Post-it note. Her expression hardening, she shows it to Mari.

You disgust me, Dad is written in Abbey's spidery scrawl.

'Oh God, poor child.' She looks at Dee fixedly. 'So, we don't call for medical help. We let nature take its course. OK?'

'Yes.' Dee slowly nods. 'Yes. We let that man die.'

106

Joel

Unsettling sensations of déjà vu spreading, Joel pulls his responder satchel from the boot and walks up the path. He isn't sure how he feels about this call-out. Almost at the end of his shift a text came through from an unknown number. He was tempted to ignore it, but at the lights he had a peep.

Hello, we haven't been introduced, at least not formally ...

An unusual start to a message. But as soon as he read the next part, he twigged.

You've met my mother and she passed on your number.

Expecting a challenge about Dee, he tensed, but it went on to say that Vincent had returned from a walk sweaty, breathless and with a dull pain in his chest, and should he be worried. His local doctor's surgery was closed on a bank holiday and he didn't want to make a fuss by dialling emergency services. Could Joel possibly pop by the vicarage? He had a gift and wanted to personally express his deep thanks anyway.

Joel rotates his tight shoulders. His discomfort isn't only the unofficial nature of his business. He didn't realise who the patient was until Dee appeared the last time, and more importantly, the man was unconscious. How will he feel about looking the smiling vicar in the eye? The same one who had the *eye* for his mum, both before and after Cal's death, but chose not to catch his imploring gaze, the obvious agony of a desperately unhappy child.

When he reaches the door, Dee steps out and pulls it behind her. She swallows. 'What are you doing here?'

'Vincent sent me a text.' He frowns. 'I assumed you'd know about it. He had chest pains and was worried.'

Her voice thin and breathy, she doesn't meet his gaze. 'Oh, I see.'

'Are you OK?'

'Yes, but—'

The door jerks open and Mari Stephens appears. Her cheeks are deep pink and her eyes bright. 'Dee and I were just on our way out, actually, so . . . '

'OK, I'll be quick. Where is he?'

Not budging from his path, Mari folds her arms but Dee tugs her back and gestures towards the rear of the house. 'He's sitting outside.'

Wondering about their odd behaviour, he steps in. 'This way?'

Biting her lip, Dee nods.

Followed by Mari, he makes his way to the kitchen and squints at the garden through the window. There's a bench but . . . 'He's on the ground.' He strides to the back door and tries the handle. 'It's locked. Do you have the key?'

Mari pulls out a chair and sits. 'You love my sister, don't you?'

It takes him a moment to adjust. 'What? Yes, yes, I do, but right now we need to focus on the patient. Where is the key?'

She shrugs.

Perplexed, he stares. 'Can you ask Dee? I need to get to him immediately.'

She lifts a photograph of a blonde woman. 'Do you know who this is?' She doesn't wait for a reply. 'She's Britt, my partner, my lover, my soulmate.' She holds up another. 'And this is our son. Or so I thought, but it turns out he's my brother-in-law's child; Abbey's half-brother.'

'OK.' He isn't sure what she's saying, but now isn't the moment. Keeping his tone even, he nods to the glass. 'We can talk about it later. It's vital I get to the—'

'No, we can't. We need to discuss it now.' She stares with blazing eyes. 'It turns out the *patient* is the father of my son. Vincent, Dee's husband Vincent, has been fucking Britt behind both our backs.'

'OK . . . ' The penny is beginning to drop.

She snorts derisively. 'The heart meds had made him impotent so he had to go off them to get his dick up. I think that was pretty much the reason for your last call to this abode. He'd stopped taking the beta blockers and boom.'

Joel grimly nods. The man is a complete and utter shit, but that's nothing new. Right now it's off point; his duty is to care for the ill. 'We're wasting valuable time. Will you please open up? Is there access to the garden from the front?'

Folding her arms, Mari peers at him carefully. 'Do you know about Luke? The fake story about the cot death?' Before he can answer, she continues to speak, her tone dogged. 'I see you do.

Well, it was bad enough not allowing Cordelia to face what had happened and properly grieve rather than hiding away in this bloody prison, but did you know why she slept so deeply that night? No, you don't. None of us did until today.' She takes an angry breath. 'Vincent was on Propranolol, but rather than reveal his heart condition to his pretty young wife, he stashed the drugs in a paracetamol tub and kept them in the bathroom cabinet. She took two that dreadful night. When Vincent realised what had happened, he was fast on his feet: he persuaded Dee that a sudden infant death would be a more palatable story for her; but of course he wanted her to lie, not for her well-being as he claimed, but for himself, to save his own selfish, sanctimonious skin.' She glares, steely-eyed. 'He's already had a second chance. A man like that doesn't deserve another.'

Blood pounds Joel's temples. The bastard; he pretty much crucified Dee by letting her take the blame, the whole devastating blame. But . . . But two wrongs don't make a right. He didn't save Cal when he should have; listening to searing Adagio for Strings at his funeral, he made a promise. He followed it through with the pledge to his profession: act with honesty and integrity in the patient's best interest; conserve life, alleviate suffering and promote health, whoever they are.

Inhaling deeply, he focuses. Right, he needs to find a way to the garden from outside. He strides to the hallway, but Mari's words make him stop.

'Calvin's death wasn't your fault, Joel.'

He turns. 'Sorry?'

'Calvin's death wasn't your fault,' she repeats.

'How can you possibly know about—'

'He came home at nine as promised, looked into your bedroom

424

and found you both asleep. He picked up the Tia Maria bottle so your mum wouldn't know, snuffed out the wick and went back to his card game up the road.'

Joel stares, disbelieving. '*He?* Who's he?'

'Seamus Rafferty. Your father and my client.'

His pulse thunders in his ears. Has Dee said something to her sister? But how does she know about *him*? 'What wick?' he asks.

'A baptism candle, I believe.'

Joel struggles to swallow. The fucking, fucking candle he coveted. Calvin had already been given one at his christening but Reverend Vincent turned up with another. Any excuse to ingratiate himself with his mum.

Mari's words echo back: '*snuffed out the wick*'. 'So . . . My dad came home and blew it out?'

'Seamus is my patient so I shouldn't be telling you any of this, but . . .' Her expression apologetic, she rubs his arm. 'He thought he had, but he'd been drinking heavily . . . I know this must be difficult to suddenly take in and I'm so very sorry to land it on you like this, but you of all people will understand what it feels like to live a lifetime of self-hatred and guilt.' She looks over his shoulder. 'Free my sister. Please. Just this once ignore the need to rescue your little brother. Save her instead.'

His mind sticky with shock, he looks up to Dee, crouched on the staircase. Vital time has already passed; can he do nothing, make no attempt to assess Vincent's condition or resuscitate if needed? *Free her*. He loves this woman; can he do it for her?

He peers at her intently. 'If I do nothing to help Vincent, can you live with it?' He lifts his arms. 'Especially . . . well, with the guilt—'

'Yes, she can live with it,' Mari interrupts, answering for her.

425

Her eyes seem to lose focus, then she blinks. 'Guilt is overrated.' She takes both their hands. 'We're survivors, we are strong. Together we can do this, can't we? Can't we, Dee Dee?'

'No.' Dee jerks to her feet. '*I* have to do this.'

'Dee?' Mari scrambles after her. 'What are you doing, Dee?'

Snatching a kitchen knife from the block, she spins around and points it at her sister. 'Don't stop me. Really, Mariana, do you hear?'

White-faced, Mari stares at the glinting metal. 'Please, Dee Dee . . .'

'No, Mari. I have to do this.'

107

Cordelia

Hoping I'm not already too late, I stride over the cool grass towards the figure on the ground. The last time I saw my husband in this state, he was lying flat on his back, his jumper in shreds around him. Today he's looking smart in a designer shirt and creased slacks, but he's curled to one side like a baby in the womb. The irony isn't lost on me.

Searching for life, I crouch down beside him and I'm rewarded by the flicker of his eyes.

'Vincent? Can you hear me?'

A wheezing noise comes from his drooping mouth. Then, 'Chest pain. Pressure. Help . . .'

I kneel like I've knelt in his presence for twenty years. 'I thought we could pray for the forgiveness of your sins.'

A small frown mars his forehead at the word 'sins'. Denial indeed. Or simple egotism, narcissism, a complete belief that he can prevail? Or perhaps certainty that he can manipulate and control me even now.

I channel my sheer rage into unflustered words. 'Well, there's lust, of course. Giving in to temptation, satisfying your disgusting carnal needs.' I calmly smile. 'So much so that you did this to yourself. Perhaps the Old Testament is right after all: "*For the wages of sin is death*." Romans 6:23, if you remember, Vincent.'

He tries to mumble, but I raise a straight palm. 'Don't,' I say. 'Don't speak. I haven't finished.'

I continue my reasonable, lecturing tone. 'But for me it's your sin of pride which will take you to hell. Through your vanity and conceit, you made me your possession, your prisoner, your trophy wife; you manipulated the truth about Luke's death because you couldn't bear for anyone to know you were less than manly, potent, invincible, a god. But even before that . . . did you ever work it out? If you hadn't hidden your condition and your medication in the first place, I wouldn't have taken the beta blockers and fallen asleep. I wouldn't have smothered our beautiful boy.'

He marginally lifts his head but his fringe falls forward, revealing the grey roots for his troubles.

'I loved you so much, Vincent. So blinded with adoration, I would have done anything you asked – even lain on the ground and let you walk over me wearing spiked shoes.' I laugh mirthlessly. 'Oh, yes, I actually did. But . . . ' I breathe back the threatening tears. 'But the one thing I asked for after Luke's death you denied me. Another baby. A chance to redeem myself.' I put a hand to my breast. 'New life on which to bestow this trapped, desperate love.'

Searching for his soul, I will even a flicker of remorse to appear in his eyes, but he simply looks back and mutters again. 'Help. Call help.'

My jaw set with resolve, I finally show him the sharp blade. '"Life for life, eye for eye, tooth for tooth, *wound for wound* . . ." You punished me so cruelly, Vincent. Now it's your turn. I'm

428

going to push this deep into your heart and watch you suffer like I suffered for thirteen years.'

He flinches away. Disbelieving, I stare at his crumpled face. Finally a tear, not for Luke nor for me, but for his weak, flawed and pathetic self.

'Stop, Dee. Just stop. He's not worth it, love. You're only hurting yourself.'

The anger draining from me, I abandon the knife and nod in acknowledgement.

'You're not worth it, Vincent,' I say.

And with that I inhale hopeful spring air, turn the other cheek and walk away.

The Manchester Crematorium

I feel rather than hear Dee dab her cheeks. The small movement makes me turn from my quiet contemplation. Some people would call it prayers, I suppose.

'All right?' I whisper and take her hand.

Red-eyed, she nods and smiles a sad smile. Like me, she's thinking of another casket. Luke, her boy, lost for all the wrong reasons.

The priest's devotions waft over me as always. How do I feel about today's coffin? A little bereft, if I'm honest. God knows why. A bad man who never acknowledged his wickedness to the one who suffered the most. Or perhaps in the final moments he did. Who knows?

For me the real casket is Mum's. However much my siblings cried, their grief wasn't comparable to mine. Nor was their love. Dee had married Vincent and Ed had disappeared on his travels. I was the last man standing.

Good old reliable Mariana. I once read that the name meant 'bitter'.

I glance again at my sister. 'Can you live with it?' Joel asked her at the vicarage. I thought it unfair, it made the decision all Dee's, so I had to intervene, make it for her. I knew she could cope with letting nature take its course because I had for over fourteen years. But I lied when I said guilt was overrated. That's why Felicity visits and asks her usual question.

I glance at Dee's handsome lover. How does he feel about this particular coffin? Seamus Rafferty lies in it. A man who hid the terrible truth; a dad who let a ten-year-old child carry his guilt, the whole guilt; one who never acknowledged it to him, or apologised. Was his suicide those unspoken words? Will that help Joel forgive him?

If I was in his shoes, I wouldn't. Some sins are too hurtful to forgive. Ever.

Like Britt-Marie Nilsson's deep betrayal and deceit, but particularly by keeping Isak from me by remaining in Sweden. But I have to live with that loss; I have to be strong and walk forward with my chin held high. I've had plenty of practice and I won't be alone; my mum, my adviser, my protector and ultimately my penance, will appear in the night, sit quietly on my bed and whisper: '*Why didn't you save me, Mari?*'

Dee leans to my ear. 'Have you got another tissue? I'm embarrassing myself, but they just won't stop. I don't even know why . . .'

It's trauma, of course. All those tears she was forbidden to weep for Luke, all that anger and grief and frustration which was silenced by Vincent's lifted palm. Will she cry for him when he's in his coffin, despite all the wrong he's done? Like I cried for Felicity?

'*Why didn't you save me, Mari?*'

Instead of replying to her question, I always will Mum away. But if I did, what would I honestly say? '*You stopped being the beautiful, serene woman who concealed your drink problem and sadness; you became a burden, a liability, an embarrassment; you were pitiful, demanding, claustrophobic. And ending it all was what you wanted when you drank that whisky and took those pills.*'

Wasn't it? Wasn't that what she wanted? Then why did she call me first and put that abhorrent burden on my shoulders? After I'd let her live vicariously through me:

'Work hard, keep focused, you can do it, Mari. Don't get distracted by boys and parties; there'll be plenty of time for that when you get to Cambridge, because you will! You're so talented, so brilliant, Mari.'

Then later, *'Darling, you did it! All that work paid off. You'll be going to Trinity College in the autumn. Think of the future. You're young; it'll soon be forgotten. Don't make the mistakes I made . . .'*

The *mistake* being my baby. Yet I didn't go to Cambridge after all. I turned it down to be near Felicity and took the disappointment on the chin: I'd still be escaping the suffocation of her and our home; I'd stay in digs and finally live; experience the life I'd been missing. But that's when Felicity changed, when she started constantly calling and texting and demanding, including that last explosive night.

It just wasn't fair; it was simply unfair. There had already been too much sacrifice. So I ignored her snivelling threats; I stayed at the party, drank, smoked and danced until the early hours. Yet even then she was still alive when I finally arrived at Clothorn Road. Unconscious, but breathing. Holding on to dear life by the bitten tips of her fingers. So I waited and watched until she expired.

Yes, I was the *bitter* last man standing and I let my mother die.

Closing my eyes, I block out her lily-clad casket. The phantom of conscience ebbs and flows, but it never leaves me completely. I made a choice; I have to live with it. Does it make me a better psychologist? I hope so. But as a person? Well, I've made a decision not to let it define me, to let this physician heal herself. Roh

432

has been in touch asking if I fancy hooking up again. I haven't yet replied, but perhaps I should. Go for a personal – and pleasurable – sperm donation ...

Dee also made a choice when she stood over Vincent. I have no idea what she said as we watched through the window, but she returned with the knife and asked her lover to go to him. 'You'll regret it if you don't. Go and do your duty,' she said.

As we waited for the ambulance I looked, properly looked at Joel for the first time and I shockingly saw Vincent Hardy in his face. Seamus Rafferty's suspicions that Joel wasn't his biological son were part of the tangled web of his anger and guilt. He had no idea who had cuckolded him, but the 'supportive' young vicar was mentioned more than once. Had the man been sowing his vile seeds and getting away with it even as a curate?

I sigh deeply. I don't know. Was I simply imagining my cuckolder's green gaze? Possibly; probably. He's been superimposed on my own psyche since they carried the *breathing* man out of the vicarage on a stretcher. Still, it's just a question of time. After a period on life support, his ventilator has been shut down and the feeding tube removed. Dee made the final decision, told the medics of his firm 'end of life' wishes.

With a glint in her eyes, she said her farewell: 'Goodbye, Vincent. You were right; deep down I am strong.'

Good old Vinny. That's a funeral I will look forward to: the nailed-down confirmation that the bastard is dead.

Acknowledgements

Much love and thanks to:

My gorgeous daughters, Elizabeth, Charlotte and Emily.

My delightful friends from school, university and work, the Didsbury runners, bookclub-without-a-book and cake date ladies, my prosecco pals, the GNO faithful and brilliant book-cake baker, Belinda. Never forgetting the excellent cuisine and company of the Taylors, Molloys and Mahers.

My talented writer buddies, particularly my fabulous and fun friends Sam, Libby and Carolyn.

My exemplary early readers Kate Johnson and Peter Barnes.

My supportive local bookshop, E J Morten Booksellers of Didsbury.

The fantastic Piatkus team, especially my intuitive editor Anna Boatman.

The wonderful book bloggers, in particular those who so generously and enthusiastically stepped up to travel with Dee, Mari and Cal on The Sinner blog tour.

Last, but not least, the reading public! Thank you so much for buying my novels, investing hours of your time reading them and posting such heartwarming reviews.